FOR ALL WHO BURN FROM
STRIKING BIGOTRY'S MATCH

The Powder Room

A Novel

Gregory Montoya

ISBN: 0692824693
ISBN 13: 9780692824696

Contents

The Blast

I heard hinges creak behind the bar. My light didn't spot a thing.

"SFPD! Show yourself!" I shouted, whipping out my piece.

"Chief Ferrus. That you, Faeth?" the chief said. His helmet surfaced like a sub from behind the bar. Two more firefighters followed.

"What the hell?" I holstered my SIG.

"Trap door to the basement. Whole block's connected by underground corridors." Ferrus tilted his helmet back with his thumb. "But we kept the fire contained to Bambi's. Gas leak blew."

"Why call Homicide over a gas leak?"

The fire crew had swamped Bambi's Lounge. I bent down to roll up my trousers to keep 'em outta the muck.

He pointed with his chin toward the hall. "Everybody heard the alarm and got out before the blast—everybody except the victim in the ladies' room. And she's holding a gun."

I dropped my cuffs. "Gun, huh? I spoke to the barflies outside. None of 'em smelled smoke or gas till after the explosion. So what tripped the alarm? And what kept the vic inside?"

"Asked myself the same things. That's why I called. By the way, I spotted the edge of a cell phone under your victim's thigh. Don't want ya to miss it."

"You shoulda been a cop, Ferrus."

"Faint at the sight of blood."

"Takes more than a bleed to rattle old-timers like us," I said, shaking my head.

"Who you callin' an old-timer? Say, where's Barbara Jean?"

Proper old Ferrus could never bring himself to call Detective Reeves by her initials: BJ.

"Late as usual. Takes her time tartin' up."

"She's one tall looker."

"About six feet of stacked brick," I said.

"We'll be checking the neighboring buildings if ya need us," Ferrus said.

I nodded and glanced at my watch—one o'clock.

"Dammit," I said out loud. Did I forget to top off Al's cat dish? Hell, fur pig won't starve before I get home, I told myself. Then I lit the scorched hallway in the back toward the powder room and the body.

At the shattered restroom door, I gagged on the stench. Flashes of smoldering bodies burst across my brain. My feet froze.

"Smells like barbecue, don't it, Lo?"

I heard BJ's Texas twang as she barged in the front door.

"Got a victim in there. Point for me." She'd called the presence of a body. Wadded up the vic into a score in our contest for clues.

I flinched, but her icy crack yanked me back to North Beach from Nam. No detective other than BJ got away with calling me Lo. I put my light on her.

"Yeah, I told you when I called that Ferrus found a body in the powder room. Shouldn't count. And show a little respect for the dead."

"But I declared it, didn't I?" she said, combing her thick black bangs with her manicured nails. "One to nothin'." BJ stuffed her nose with cotton.

I lit the former Texas Ranger's way with my flashlight. Her leather jacket ended at the waist of her tight gray slacks. She wore short black boots, and a 35 mm Leica hung from her shoulder just below a wide red belt. Ricky, my gay half brother, would've liked her outfit, I thought, sorry I'd chased him away.

"Don't know why you doll up to dig around a potential murder scene."

"Respect for the dead," BJ quipped.

I snorted, then packed my nose with tissue before turning back to the door. No use bitching about her cold-blooded jibes. I did once, but she'd put me in my place. Said a woman's tears translate as weakness in the world of homicide investigations, adding that if she had testes, chinks in her armor would add up to sensitive. Yeah. She'd made her point.

BJ stepped next to me in the queen-sized restroom, turned her head toward me, and sniffed my cheek. "You been drinkin'?"

I jerked back. "Shot of tequila. Couldn't sleep." The fifteen years since Ricky disappeared had balled up into nightmares about what had happened to him. He'd left in 1994 because I couldn't accept that he was gay. By the time I'd wised up enough not to care, his trail had gone cold.

"Again? You'd sleep better if you had yourself a little company once in a while." BJ knocked her shoulder into mine. "Know what I mean, Lo?"

"That's Detective Faeth to you," I said, but now she'd sloshed up Madge's face. I'd married her a couple of years after Ricky disappeared. Five years later she'd left this graying, balding grump. I couldn't blame her. She'd gotten fed up with me off at the job all the time. And she'd found out I had a brother. Looked straight into my tired brown eyes and griped at me to find Ricky. I shoulda listened.

"I could call you Detective Lawrence Oliver Faeth. But Lo's faster." BJ covered her mouth in a fake attempt to stop a giggle.

I poked my light into her hazel eyes and stole a line from Robin Williams: "If you weren't a girl, I'd rip your lips off and paste them to your eyes so you could watch what you say."

"Go on, take your best shot, dahlin'. But you ought to let Lupe fix you up. Or do you still have the hots for her, feeling safe from those fires 'cause she's married to your amigo?"

My face tingled. I should have never taken her to Frank and Lupe's place, Mac's Bar and Grill. The closest thing I could call a hangout. BJ'd noticed my temperature rise in front of Lupe.

"Fix me up? I wouldn't waste anybody's time. And can that 'hots for Lupe' crap. She's my pal's wife, for god's sake."

"Coward. The least a partner can do is pry you outta your shell." BJ rocked her head in time with her twang.

"Shell?" I growled. "Al's plenty of company and in a pinch, there's *Star Trek* reruns." My light landed on the charred corpse. "A woman," I said to change the subject. The explosion had twisted her to the floor. I prayed death had been quick.

"Nailed the vic's gender, did ya? What gave it up? The dress or that she's in the little girl's room?"

"Suppose that squares us in your cheap-ass points department," I said over the suck of my heels against the muddy floor.

I focused my light on the corpse's hand and its nickel-plated revolver. "She's got a pistol," I announced for a point ahead, then saw the cell partially covered by her thigh. I slid that bit of information up my points sleeve.

"Pistol?" BJ asked.

"Suspicious, huh?" I said, but BJ stepped back.

"Just because she's in a dress doesn't mean she's a she. This is San Francisco, remember?" Then BJ's voice sank. "Or do shims make Detective Faeth a little squirrelly?"

"Shims?" I said, bracing for another dig. Despite keeping a lid on my revulsion toward homos, she'd seen through me. Needled me every chance she got.

"You know, dahlin'. He-shes. Boys that dress like girls."

"Don't start. I'm not in the mood," I said to block Ricky's drag-queen sashay from my baggy eyes. "Call it a hunch, BJ. This is North Beach. Not the gay Castro. And like you said, she's in a dress and in the ladies' room."

I focused on the course of the blast. Debris had ricocheted off walls, splintered the powder room door, and fractured the roof. A streetlight's scrawny ray poked through the ceiling.

"We've stepped into the center of the blast," BJ said, stealing what I was about to say. She slipped her digital recorder out of her pocket and described the scene.

"Looks like ground zero to me too," I said, unable to better my own conclusion.

BJ coughed into her fist and flicked off the recorder. "All right, Mr. Self-Reliant, ready for me to capture the moment?" She slid the camera from her shoulder. "Still life with cop and corpse."

“Leave me out of it.” I stepped out of her way and into a puddle. “Shit.” Braced against a buckled stall, I poured ink out of my loafer.

“Smile, Lo.” Using her cell phone, she snapped a picture of me draining my shoe.

I flipped her off, but she’d turned to the victim.

“Get a picture of that gun,” I said.

With each click of the Leica, she got a pic, and I got a flash of her steps around the corpse. The bursts of light left me with afterimages of twisted pipes and shattered toilet bowls. BJ crouched next to the body and picked up the glob that had been the victim’s plastic purse. “Found her purse for my point up.”

“Hey, get your gloves on, will ya?” Though the fire had likely melted away any prints, I guessed BJ snubbed protocol to remind me that I didn’t intimidate her. I liked that about her.

“Prints wouldn’t have survived on this lump,” BJ said, waving the purse at me with her naked fingers.

I nodded. “Without prints or ID, Forensics will have to use DNA or dental records to identify the poor gal.”

“Pretty sure the ‘poor gal’ is a she, huh?” BJ plunked the purse into an evidence bag. Stuffed it into her jacket pocket.

I raised my voice. “Oh, that’s right. She’s alone. She must be a he. Real women hit the head in twos, right?”

She glanced at me twice before looking back at the vic. I’d expected an eye roll. Had my crack hit a nerve?

The “Dixie” jingle of BJ’s cell phone interrupted us. As she stood up from the remains, her face glowed in her phone’s backlit display.

“Gimme a sec.” Without another word, she tiptoed around the rubble and disappeared into the hall.

I’d never seen her take a private call. “What the hell, BJ? It’s almost two in the morning. Somebody fix you up?” I barked after her.

Silence.

♦ ♦ ♦

"Hell's bells, there's no sign of Rosie," BJ whispered into her phone to Dr. Marilee Crusher, grande dame of the secret women's order, Once-a-Dick-Always-a-Dick or what members affectionately called O'DAD. She slogged farther away from the ladies' room. Rosie-the-Riveter posters identified powder rooms with O'DAD's exclusive Wi-Fi hot spots. The thought of the sisterhood hijacking the World War II icon usually tickled her. But not tonight.

"Rosie musta been destroyed by the fire," she said. The hot spot, plus the vic's gun, knocked the body in the powder room from the column of accident victim into the latest tally of her target's prey.

"You didn't know. Have you called in the CSI team?"

BJ caught a hint of dread in Marilee's tone. Mild compared to her own.

"Not yet. Being busy and dumb luck is all that's stopped me from calling 'em in." BJ strained to steady her voice, gripped by her failure to stop the murders.

She pushed her fingers through her hair. Her eyes darted about the blackened lounge but registered nothing. If news of the killings got out, O'DAD, the FBI's off-the-grid asset in the war on terror, risked exposure.

"At least we'll avoid them. The three of us will come in through the basement to remove the cable and retrieve our hardware as soon as the fire department leaves. Your partner must be gone before we arrive. Otherwise...well, you know." Marilee's voice slid into a sigh.

BJ understood Marilee's sag. If she couldn't extricate Lo before they arrived, his sanity would be trounced by an O'DAD gaslight scheme. A sacrifice she and Marilee wished to avoid. But it was Marilee's "three of us" that frosted her. She knew that included the killer and her enforcer.

"Gettin' Detective Faeth outta here will be like prying a hen off her eggs." She heard her voice climb and peered over her shoulder for signs of Lo. All that followed her was an ashen breeze.

"Are your loyalties confused?"

"I can't believe you asked me that." Her reply sharpened by her envy of Marilee's bond with the other orphan, the killer. BJ had discovered that Marilee and her target's mother were like sisters. Mom killed herself in

1982. More than once, BJ had endured Marilee's dismissing her surrogate daughter's homicidal bitterness as harmless. And now Marilee had the gall to question *her*.

BJ pounded her hip.

"I apologize. I'm upset," Marilee said. "A gas explosion just took a life, and now it threatens to expose us. On top of that, unless you remove your partner before we arrive, we'll have to destroy his credibility. I couldn't blame you if you're conflicted."

"I don't care that it's Faeth. But neither one of us likes turning anybody into O'DAD's rodeo clown," BJ said to deflect her grief.

"Do what you can to remove him before we arrive, hon. You've got until the firefighters leave. Then we have to come in."

"Will do." BJ spoke crisply and then tapped off her O'DAD cell. She had little time to bounce Lo out of Bambi's. She considered faking fatigue. Maybe she'd nitpick to ignite his combustible impatience. She could stop challenging him to wrap up sooner than later.

After taking in a sooty breath, she exhaled through her nose. Such improvised efforts would be out of character and not be missed by the wily Lo. But BJ knew that Lo's contact with Marilee's team would force her to ignite a gaslight against him. And if the killer decided the old hound caught O'DAD's scent, it would be his life that was at risk.

She tromped back toward the powder room.

A Cheap Logic

I cocked my ear toward BJ's footsteps. Her silhouette came through the doorway.

What's up, BJ?"

She came up next to me and shook her head. "Nothin'."

I fell on a cheap logic. Maybe if I kept my nose out of her personal business, she'd stay out of mine.

BJ added, "I called Dr. Sandoval. Told him to bring his team down here to rule out a homicide. Why don't you go home, get some rest. I'll wait for him."

"Rule out? Clues are pointing to murder." I pinched my face but blew her off. "Bet he liked hearing his phone ring at two in the morning." I knew my CSI pal could be counted on to offer a few choice curses. But BJ's eyes wandered. She didn't seem to have heard me. I snapped my fingers at the tip of her nose. "I said, I'll bet he—"

BJ swatted my hand. "Yep. What does *como chingan* mean?"

"Thought you were from Texas. You should know," I said, snorting.

She turned away as if still distracted. Her call must've been bad news.

"You okay?" I asked.

"I said I'm fine. Didn't I?"

"Okay, okay." I gloved up and squatted next to the pistol.

BJ stepped behind me. "You're probably right, Lo."

"Huh? About what?"

"Our vic. Likely a lady." Her voice sounded weak.

I glared and watched her misty breath float through the streetlight's shaft of light. Challenging each other strengthened our findings. I wadded up a page from her book of banter and tossed it at her: "There's no barbed wire around the Castro. We shouldn't jump to conclusions. Remember?"

"I'm sure the autopsy will prove you're right."

Her backing down annoyed me. And it was tied to her phone call. But, hell, after two years as my partner, she was entitled to one off night. Still, when I reached for the vic's revolver, her grip proved as strong as my irritation with BJ.

"Leave it for Forensics, Lo."

Her call had sapped her. But she'd made it none of my business.

"No way." I grimaced and about broke a sweat before the fused knuckles cracked loose. I stuck my pencil deep enough into the barrel to hit the bottom of an empty cartridge. She had shot. Lit the gas.

"Make yourself useful and look into the chambers," I said. "She pulled the trigger at least once. See if another round's been fired." I stood, handed her the snub-nose, and lit the cylinder with my light.

"Nope. Nothing but lead staring back. I'll bag it, then let's call it a night. I'm tuckered out." BJ dropped the piece into an evidence bag and handed back my pencil.

"We're not done here," I said and almost spouted off about her phone call, but the cuffs of my pants had sucked up water, and wet kissed my socks. I shook my right foot, then my left.

"Nice two-step," BJ said, then lifted the bagged gun. "This pistol make you think the blast's more than an accident?"

Thankful for at least a weak challenge, I choked the grumble out of my voice.

"Not only that, none of the barflies smelled smoke or gas until after the explosion. The alarm evacuated the place before the blast or fire."

"Sure enough like the reliability of liquored-up witnesses."

"Do I hafta add it up for ya? Our vic didn't make it out 'cause she was cornered. A damned false alarm cleared out the witnesses so the killer or killers could do her. But there was a gas leak." I jabbed my finger at the body. "She blew herself up trying to shoot her way out."

BJ planted her fists on her hips. The evidence bag slapped against her. "Then where's the killer's body? Whoever stopped her from escaping would've been served up on the same spit."

I lowered my voice to the tone of a frustrated parent. “Maybe the perp smelled the gas. Jammed the door. Left her to choke to death. Split with everybody else.”

A swirl of soot caked my throat. Coughing, I bent over and grabbed my knees.

BJ patted my back. The warmth of her hand seemed to melt through my corduroy sport coat. Made me think of Madge. But Madge’s smile broke into clips of my mother and stepfather’s Harley splattering into the grill of a Peterbilt. Followed by me, suitcases in hand, moving back home to raise my eleven-year-old brother. I shook my head to scatter my lost family’s faces.

BJ patted me faster between my shoulder blades. “This is an old building. Probably contains asbestos. Let’s get you out of here and come back once we know it’s safe.”

I straightened up and shoved my face into BJ’s. “That’s the third time you tried to get me outta here since your phone call. What happened?”

She rocked back on her heels.

“Sorry. Family problem. Nothing I can’t handle as soon as we’re done. So let’s hurry it up.” She knelt next to the body, her back to me. “She’s alone in here, sneaks a smoke, and tosses a match into the waste bin. Accidentally starts a fire. Panics, wants to call 911, but is overcome by smoke and grabs her pistol instead of her phone. Gas leak hits the flames.”

BJ’s voice rang confident. But she was wrong.

“No phone grips like a pistol. And this is San Francisco, not Texas. Civilians here don’t pack unless they’re up to no good or scared.” I swung my light to the pink edge of the cell phone under the vic’s thigh. “Besides, she already had her phone out. There.”

“How do you know it’s hers? Somebody else coulda dropped it.”

“For Christ’s sake, she’s laying on it. Even Ferrus knew it’s hers. He’s not even a cop.”

“Ferrus saw it?” BJ’s voice pitched high.

“Ferrus told me about it. What’s the big deal?”

"Don't make me no never mind."

"Here, hold this." I thrust my light toward her.

She yanked it away. "Phone couldn't've survived the blast."

"Sounds like you'd be disappointed if it did." On the long shot that BJ was wrong and the damned mobile's screen had a secret to tell, I knelt down, clamped its edges between my thumb and forefinger, and slowly pulled it free.

BJ stood up with me, and I tapped the screen to ignite the backlight, expecting to see 911. "What the hell, 6323?" I said.

BJ tucked the flashlight under her arm and grabbed at the phone.

I jerked it back. "Where're your gloves?"

BJ glared at me and finally snapped them on. She took the phone and peered at the display. "Number's incomplete. No leads here."

"Dammit, BJ, a family problem's one thing, but dumbing down is another. Why don't you look for the rest of the number? Snoop around the damned thing's memory, SIM card, or whatever nerds call it."

"I'll bag it. We'll leave it to Forensics."

Had the soot fouled up BJ's brain? "Do me a favor," I said. "Go find the real BJ, and tell her to get in here, will ya?"

BJ raised her chin, stretching her neck before bagging the cell.

"Give it here." I wiggled my fingers until she plopped the bag into my hand. I crammed the phone into my trouser pocket.

"Doubt there's anything else in here worth looking at," BJ said. Without any more interest in the cell, she swept the flashlight around, spotlighting the scorched room.

A shattered mirror reflected back above a fractured cabinet. I glimpsed a couple of partially melted electrical gizmos behind dangling doors. Did one have an aerial? Ferrus hadn't mentioned those.

"I can forgive Ferrus for missing clues, but for Christ's sake, BJ, you passed the light right over those gadgets under that sink like they weren't there."

She shrugged. "Looks like a discarded wireless router and UPS," she said, her voice bored.

"Gimme my flashlight." I grabbed it out of her hand and aimed the light at the hardware. A limp antenna dangled from one. I had an idea of what the router did, but that was the limit of this Luddite's techno savvy. "UPS?" An image of an ugly brown van swerved through my brain.

"Uninterrupted power supply," BJ explained through a yawn.

Her nonchalance tweaked my pisstivity. "Come on, BJ, what's that stuff doing in a john?"

"You should see the junk under my sink," she said, her voice as icy as her stare.

I knew that look. I'd get no more from her. I broke off my glare and turned to the devices.

♦ ♦ ♦

BJ tracked Lo's gaze to the fingers of denuded copper poking through the ash at the bases of the router and UPS. She bit her bottom lip. Instead of dislodging him, she'd guided his nose right up O'DAD's skirt, obliging him to stay and run head-on into Marilee and two killers.

All she could do now was keep Lo's hands off the proof of what he'd seen—that router.

That You, Sandoval?

BJ jerked her head toward the sound of tromping coming from the bar area. Marilee? Her feelings for Lo bit like fangs. She brought her hands to her chest.

Chief Ferrus's helmeted head popped through the doorway. "Hey, you two, we got all the hot spots. We're heading out. Place is all yours."

"Thank ya, suh," BJ said, without a tad of relief that it wasn't Marilee. She and the killers would be close behind. BJ's head spun. Maybe with the help of her FBI handler, SFPD's resident shrink, she could cushion the crash of O'DAD's wrecking ball to Lo's career. But welling tears doused any hope of saving their partnership. It would die along with her promise to reconcile her college soul mate, Ricky, with his brother, Lo.

♦ ♦ ♦

I squatted in front of the cabinet containing the hardware. Felt Ferrus's rumbling diesels as they rattled the powder-room pipes. But when I turned to BJ to ask for her help bagging the gizmos, she stood where I'd left her.

"BJ, you haven't been right since your phone call. Wanna tell me about it?"

"Told ya. I'll deal with it," she snapped and looked away.

"All right. I'll mind my own business." I'd never seen her locked up so tight. Something terrible musta happened. I softened my voice. "Help me bag these things, will ya?" Then I heard steps. "That you, Sandoval?"

A chunky, ball-peen-headed outline with a shaggy ponytail rocked through the door behind a blue halogen glare. She wasn't my wiry friend. I stood up and stepped next to BJ to see who'd come in.

"Name's Dr. Marilee Crusher," the figure in the shadows said, her tone maternal, confident.

Who was she? And where was Sandoval? My belly curdled. "I don't know a—" but the doc stabbed her light into my pupils. I raised my hand between my eyes and her blinding beam.

"Relax, Detective. I'm a new coroner. The other team was called to a Burritt Street homicide."

"Listen, Doc," I said, trying to keep my cool, "I'm used to working a crime scene with Sandoval."

I'd heard they'd added a new coroner, and Burritt Street rang familiar, but the more I dodged the doctor's light, the more she stabbed it into my face. This rude stranger ground her heel into the same nerve BJ'd been stomping on.

Blinded by the glare, I couldn't focus on her or the two other fuzzy images appearing behind her, carrying equipment cases. One skinny one, taller than Crusher but shorter than BJ. The other stocky and shorter than the rest. I couldn't make out their faces, but their calves and feet appeared bulky. What were they wearing?

BJ squeezed my arm. "Lo, it's okay. I've met Dr. Crusher." Her Southern twang had shriveled into a whisper. Crusher kept poking her halogen into my face, and my partner sounded like she'd lost her nerve. Who was this new doc? Steamed, I jerked my arm from BJ's hand but dropped my light.

"Settle down, Detective," Crusher demanded as I knelt for my flashlight.

My light's rolling beam caught the toes of her firefighter's boots, and I glimpsed her coveralls. Compared to my soggy socks, I guessed the doc came better prepared. But Sandoval covered his hair, and being new didn't excuse shitty manners.

I stood right into her glare, causing me to step into BJ, knocking us back.

"Get that light outta my face."

"Detective...Faeth, right, hon?" the doc said, lowering her lamp.

Sure she would've been advised of my name, but I'd never met her. "I don't remember telling you my name," I snarled.

"Dispatch gave it to me. Sorry we got off on the wrong foot. Tell me, have you found anything worthwhile?" she asked, pouring honey into her voice. Her aides positioned themselves shoulder to shoulder with her.

Just as my blur started to fade, the short one shot a beam right into my pupils. "Dammit—watch it, will ya?" I said and looked away.

But I heard BJ say, "Melted purse, a gun, and a phone. That's all."

My blood pressure spiked. "What about that stuff under the sink?"

"Lo, it's been a long night. Let Dr. Crusher's team take over. If they think that junk is important, they can bag it." BJ's voice had recovered its melodious sway. "You go home. I got the gun and purse. Give me the phone, and I'll log 'em all into evidence."

"Beam me the fuck up, Scotty, I'm surrounded by aliens." It burned me that BJ snubbed the router and wanted to leave it to the doc. "Gimme the purse and gun, and I'll see that Sandoval gets them."

"Now, now, Detective," Crusher said. "We're all on the same team." Her tone sounded as sincere as a whorehouse madam's.

"Sure enough," BJ said. "Let me have the phone."

"Go ahead and take it," I said before I shoved my flashlight into my belt and grabbed BJ's wrist. Then I slapped the phone into her palm. "You and your pals wrap up. I'm outta here."

To hell with all of them. I had a plan to make sure that router got to Sandoval. I shouldered my way through the doc and her cronies. "Excuse me," I said.

Staggering through the muck, I shot my right foot out from under myself in front of the crippled sink and grabbed the counter to break my fall. I landed on my side, face-to-face with the router. Snatching the contraption, I tucked it under my muddied coat, cursed, and fled out the doorway. The cackles of Crusher's team faded behind me.

A Cruel Treat

BJ squinted toward the busted cabinet. She prayed coincidence explained the stocky but agile Lo's slide in front of O'DAD's hardware.

She watched Marilee light a path toward the dangling doors.

"Jax, time to pull the cable, UPS, and router," Marilee said.

The squat nineteen-year-old waddled over and crouched down. "The router's gone," she hollered.

BJ joined Marilee and the killer, Havana, in their slippery dashes toward Jax. They huddled behind her.

"That cop took it. I'll get him," Havana said and started to bolt, but BJ spun her around by her shoulder. Havana flailed her arms to keep on her feet.

"Finesse, remember?" BJ said, braced for a punch. Havana resented her friendship with Marilee and made no secret of it. Now she'd laid hands on her. But Havana jerked away and lurched toward the door.

"BJ is right," Marilee scolded. "O'DAD's secrecy depends on tact. And BJ has the phone. A phone we haven't confirmed is O'DAD issue. Even if it is, without that router it's useless. Right, Havana?"

"Right," Havana said, but O'DAD's IT maven glared at BJ.

BJ felt the heat of her stare but Marilee's voice had succeeded where her grab had failed. Still, BJ knew that even the maternal bond of O'DAD's grande dame held limited sway over Havana. Away from Marilee's stern eye, the killer would grant Lo no quarter. None to her either, if Havana decided she was protecting Lo.

A grim prospect snaked through BJ's soul. Despite her lack of hard evidence against the killer, if Havana turned on her, a bullet in self-defense would justify shooting her. BJ doubted Havana's goons had the cojovaries to go on "liquidating" transgender women without her.

Havana jutted her hand toward BJ. "Gimme the phone." Jax postured next to her mistress.

"Can't. Have to turn it in as evidence," BJ said, fighting to sound sensible.

Havana traded glances with Marilee and Jax. "Give it up," Havana ordered.

BJ plowed through the fault lines of her affection for Lo and forced resonance into her throat. "The fire chief saw it. He'll corroborate Lo's charge that we found a cell phone. That'll strengthen Lo's credibility. Weaken my efforts to discredit him."

Marilee's chin fell to her chest. Returning her gaze to Havana, she said, "If it is an O'DAD phone, what are the chances of it being linked to our router and exposing O'DAD?"

"Virtually zero," Havana said, sounding disappointed that she'd dismissed her cause to get Lo. "Without our proprietary feed, they can't access our website." She dodged Marilee's eyes and then puffed her chest and growled, "But they could trigger current through our router's circuitry. Become curious when a standard feed fails to produce a signal. Maybe start looking in powder rooms for one that does."

"That'll be the day," BJ said.

Marilee sighed and said, "Havana's right. We must err on the side of caution. We'll retrieve our router. But BJ will have to turn in the phone."

Jax asked, in a meek voice, "What does finn...ess mean?"

BJ and the rest turned to the teenager. Marilee stroked the youngster's cheek. "It means to be crafty, honey. We use finesse to solve problems instead of lowering ourselves to the violent level of men."

Havana whipped her blond tresses over her bony shoulders. "Finesse or not, we've got to recover that router."

"Faeth's an old fart," BJ said, feigning contempt. "He can barely manage his department cell. Doesn't have a clue what the router's for. Besides, I'll get it back."

Havana drew back her snaky lips and spoke through clenched teeth. "Before he gets it to that guy Sandoval?" She shifted her gaze between BJ's face and Marilee's. "I'm not going to bet our secrecy on cheap finesse."

BJ iced her tone. "Leave him to me."

Havana, though a forehead shorter, squared off in front of BJ. Jax stiffened a half step behind Havana.

Marilee squirmed in between, her pear-shaped torso wedging BJ and Havana apart. "That's enough. BJ will handle her partner." She poked her face nose to nose with Havana's. "Your grandmother and my mother founded O'DAD as a hedge against male aggression. They would be appalled by your...your macho belligerence."

Havana evaded Marilee's eyes but said under her breath, "You fight fire with fire."

Marilee leaned farther into Havana, forcing her to stumble back. "We are here to protect O'DAD. Not lapse into the barbarity our sisterhood protects us from."

Havana's face hardened. "Easy for you to say. Your mother didn't kill herself after catching your dad in bed with a freak."

BJ watched Marilee's body wilt under her motherly load. She had confided to BJ that she'd made painfully little progress toward succoring the embittered Havana since her mother had stuck her head in an oven and turned on the gas. Havana blamed Syklona Haez, her father's mistress and O'DAD's first transgender intruder, for her mother's death.

Marilee softened her voice. "Your father was weak. So much so that his heart stopped after your mother left us."

"He died because that fucking *thing* vanished," Havana said, tonguing her cheek.

Marilee bristled. "Don't you dare use that kind of language to me, young lady."

"Sorry." Havana stroked her nose with her index finger.

BJ studied her hateful target. Havana's father's lover had disappeared after her mother's funeral. Presumed dead, her body never surfaced. BJ figured she'd been Havana's first kill. Havana's current crop of victims sprang up after she'd completed O'DAD's national website in 2000.

Wherever Havana traveled, BJ witnessed a spike in unsolved, transgender female robbery-homicides. All occurred in vetted O'DAD powder rooms. The local cops wrote them off as random. In 2007, Havana landed in San Francisco. So did the bodies on powder-room floors.

BJ stepped away from the trio and surveyed the damage. She imagined Havana's glee over her victim's breathing gas like her mother. That the vic blew herself up must've added a cruel treat.

The Smelly Gizmo

I turned off my rumbling old Buick and jammed the gearshift into park. The rolling wreck rocked to a halt under my carport's flickering fluorescent light. My watch read 3:45 a.m. I reached for the door handle, but the router called to me. I pulled it out from under my seat and held it by opposite corners. The housing stank of scorched plastic. BJ's lack of interest in the thing and her conniving with Crusher throbbed like a hammered thumb. But this baby held secrets. An image of the victim tapping her cell arced my brain. Why'd she punch in 6323, not 911?

I set the sooty mess in my lap and heaved a breath over my fight with BJ. The partner I knew never came back from her zero dark thirty call. "Family problem," she'd said. But why not tell me? I humphed. What'd Madge used to say? That I'm "unapproachable."

I decided I shouldn't have taken the router, to call BJ. I stuck my hand into my pocket for my cell, but my belly bit back. Crusher's goddamned blinding beams had been more than rude. She didn't want me to see hers or her crew's faces, did she? Something was going on. And BJ was in on it.

Ticked off, I felt eyes on me. I yanked out my pistol and scanned the carport—empty, except for a little fog. Shit. Was I paranoid?

My brain slid back to the time after my mom and stepdad had died—before I'd caught Ricky in drag. Combat nightmares had ripped through my sleep. I'd wake up to my own screams of "they're walkin' 'em in!"

Ricky would find me sitting up, sweating. "Y-You okay?" he'd stammer from the doorway.

I'd become one irritable SOB, and Ricky sleepwalked through middle school. The sharp little twit threw in my face that when Mom and his dad had died and the hospital social worker told us to go to grief counseling, I'd made him do it alone.

What the hell, I'd thought. Counseling had helped the torn-up kid. So I dragged myself to the VA's outreach counseling center.

After months of therapy, my dreams lost their punch. I'd started sleeping better, so I skipped appointments.

My counselor warned me that I avoided "deeper issues."

"Nah, I'm cured," I'd said. But he'd argued that whatever I kept buried could worm up as "fear of intimacy and even paranoia." I glanced down at my cocked SIG. Had the fucker been right?

I caught a whiff of the smelly gizmo. Crusher's stabbing lights and that BJ would've left it made me swipe it. I shook my head and looked around my flickering carport before lowering the SIG's hammer.

Plodding up the stairs to my condo, I looked forward to a clearer head after a few hours of sleep. I opened my door, left off the glaring lights, but squeezed through to block Al in case he tried to make a run for it. Gordo wasn't around. The arrangement of my furniture hadn't changed since the movers set them down. A plus in the dark. After Madge divorced me, I'd moved here and dumped all reminders of our marriage. My fault, I'd figured. Hadn't dated since. My counselor's warning about "fear of intimacy" needled back. Thought I'd left him in the car. Fuck him. Besides, where's Al?

My fall at Bambi's had caked my side with grubby soot. Damn, I'd have to remember to put a blanket over my car seat. I hoofed it to my bathroom. Tossed my filthy clothes next to my bloated hamper.

Flipping on a light, I found Al snoring next to his empty stainless-steel bowls on the floor of my vacant dining room. Did I forget to leave him food, or did he eat it? Thinking of my tiff with BJ, it occurred to me that the little vermin gave me someone to care about without screwing it up.

I poured fresh bottled water into one bowl and packed the other with his favorite "grain-free cold-water salmon and savory chicken recipe" cat food. I scratched his ear. Woke up the gray blimp. He stretched, caught a whiff, and went to work.

Watching him gorge himself, I recalled telling the vet Al was one macho cat. That my elderly neighbor had rescued him but he attacked her other two cats. Talked me into taking him because she worried that rescue would put him down if she returned him. He was already a two-time loser when she'd tried him. I'd bragged that nothing startled him. Slept through anything. Defiant too. Ignored me when I called.

The vet had said, "Clumsy as an ox, I'll bet." When I asked how he knew, he'd told me Al couldn't hear. That an old inner ear infection had gotten to him. Said not to let him outside—that a big dog could sneak up on him.

I stroked Al's back. He lifted his butt but didn't stop eating. Being deaf didn't affect the porker's appetite.

Back in my galley kitchen, I held my breath to dodge my trash can's rot before opening the doors under the sink. I grabbed a plastic bag, stuffed the router into it, and crammed it next to the trash. Why add the funk of burned plastic?

Turning the corner of my dining area, I scolded myself for not putting in a cheap dinette set. Hell, who cared? I wasn't one for company. Even when BJ had insisted on meeting Al, I'd blown her off. Always met her downstairs if she picked me up.

After a quick shower, wrapped in my tattered robe, I turned off the lights and plopped on my couch. Switching on my console TV, my eyes drew to my brother's imitation Ming vase lamp on the end table. I'd kept it. Never thought about why until it started poking at my fears about what had happened to him. Screw it, I needed to sleep. TV could wait.

My combo answering machine and phone sat next to Ricky's lamp. I traced the phone line to the wall and unplugged it. Then I pressed off my SFPD cell. The only mobile I bothered to carry.

With the confidence of Helen Keller, I strolled into my bedroom, dumped my robe on the floor, and shut my dusty miniblinds. My box spring and mattress lay on the floor like a hippie bed. Madge had kept our bedroom set. I crawled under the covers, closed my eyes, and visualized that router's metallic guts spread out in front of Sandoval.

"He'll crack your code faster than you can say da Vinci," I mumbled.

The thump of BJ's siding with Crusher kept bouncing me out of my doze. She'd never turned on me before. I flip-flopped on the mattress and socked my pillow until the doorbell interrupted my slugfest. Who the hell? Nobody dropped in on me. Ever. A second later, the door rattled between rapid, heavy blows. A cop's knock. BJ? Had I felt her eyes in my carport?

"Lo, open up," BJ demanded.

My mood perked up, but I nixed it. She'd come for the router. Barefoot in the dark, I skipped my hand across the Mexican blanket draped over Mom's sofa on my way to my door. I'd better remember to toss it on my muddy car seat. I peeked out the spy hole. She was alone. The door shuddered before BJ's driving fist, thumping my eyebrow. I jerked back, rubbing my forehead.

BJ raised her voice, "Lo, we gotta talk. Open up."

I cracked open the chained door and spoke through the slit. The links strained against my pull. "What do you want, BJ? And keep the noise down," I said through a yawn, playing it casual. I'd be damned if I'd let her know she'd clipped my eye. I reached for the chain keeping me from her but made a fist. No, not after she'd ganged up on me with Crusher.

BJ looked down. "So that's Al."

"Shit," I said and reached down to grab him. Good thing his belly stuck before making it through. I stood up, cradling him in one arm.

"Lo, why'd you take off with that router?" BJ asked, her eyes darting between me and Al. "You didn't log it in as evidence. That's tampering."

Did she come to keep my ass out of a sling? I spread my fingers across my forehead and squeezed. Wait a minute. She'd called it evidence. At Bambi's, she'd called it junk.

"I don't know what you're talking about."

BJ shook her head and folded her arms across her chest. "I half expected this. Don't force my hand, Lo."

"Force your hand? What are you gonna do? Rat me out to Captain Rhodes? Tell him you think I split with evidence?" Al started to squirm, but no claws—not yet.

"Are you gonna hand it over or not?"

I watched her fists glance off her hips and dangle at her sides. Two years into a trusted partnership pressed my shoulder against the door. The rusty chain sagged. But then my guard shot up.

"You didn't give a shit about it at the crime scene. Why the big change now? Besides, even if I had it—and I'm not saying I do—you think I'd be dumb enough to bring it home?" I looked down. Man, I was in boxers and almost let her in.

"You're backing me into a corner, Lo."

Her tone sounded like a plea, but the threat irritated me. "Go on, tell the captain you think I took off with evidence. Go home, get some sleep. We'll talk later at the station." I slammed the door. Good thing, too. Al started to windmill, claws sprung. He hit the floor with a thump.

Through the peephole, I watched BJ strut off with her fists clenched at her sides. What if she ratted me out to the captain before I could talk her out of it? Should I have given her the fucken thing?

I decided I'd take the router with me to the station. Leave it in my trunk until I talked to her. Make nice, then log the gizmo in as evidence.

♦ ♦ ♦

BJ stewed in her car, distracted from the nighttime chill. Unless she recovered that router ASAP, Havana'd be gunning for Lo. But it was the imminent death of her commitment to Ricky that pricked her heart. Back at Berkeley, she'd bet Ricky that Lo would come to miss him. That she'd fulfill her dream to become an FBI agent and see to it that her path would someday cross Lo's. Use the edge of his grief to chip away at his pigheadedness. Get him to embrace his sibling once again. A wilted Ricky had left it to her.

She started her car and pulled away from the curb. As she rolled down Pierce Street, bittersweet memories of her and Ricky bubbled up. Being her parents' only child, their sudden deaths had quickened her bent at recognizing the orphan in others. Ricky's bowed shuffle through

UC Berkeley's Eucalyptus Grove declared the gravitational pull of his sadness. His vacant eyes evaded the gaze of others.

Despite Ricky's efforts to ignore her, she'd goaded him until he'd let her mope about campus with him. She'd learned that when Lo had caught him in drag, he'd made him promise to stay in the closet. That he isolated himself to keep people from hearing the woman inside gasp for air. A prisoner he kept to satisfy her jailer—Lo.

Though traffic was quiet at this hour, BJ stopped at a crosswalk for a tall, homely girl walking her fluffy terrier. Their eyes met. The stroller's eyes rimmed red. Sleepless. Crying? In her, BJ saw herself at UC. She'd wandered about in her baggy jeans and faded rugby shirts, trapped tall in her big bones and flat chest. She'd never drawn a second look from the fellas she desired. She stared until the girl stepped to the curb and looked back. Caught in a past life, BJ dropped her gaze and hit the gas.

BJ bisected Golden Gate Park toward Lincoln Way. The park's gardens and meadows forced a break in the crammed city. She recalled that by Ricky's senior year, she'd helped him loosen Lo's chains to free the woman inside. Behind Lo's back, his wardrobe was as attractive as that of many a self-possessed coed. Off campus, his feminine persona strutted through those Bay Area quarters safe for an emerging woman in her short dresses. To no one but BJ did Ricky reveal his flight plan: finish school, close his trust account, and escape his brother.

BJ pulled into her garage and punched the remote, closing the door behind her. She stroked the implanted contours of her firm breasts and then tweaked her nipples. Inspired by Ricky's revolt, she'd floated the idea of breast implants for herself. Ricky bristled that her beauty needed no surgeon's blade to reveal itself. She'd countered that his opposition reflected his surrender to Lo.

After college, she'd found an artistic surgeon. He'd sculpted the once-invisible girl into a head turner. She hadn't stopped at titties.

Gaslight

BJ shifted on the gray fabric seat of her blue hybrid as she turned onto Vallejo Street. She would arrive early at Central Station. Catch Captain Rhodes before Lo dragged in.

She sped past the booth of the commercial parking structure next to the precinct, staring straight ahead. She knew eagle-eyed Max Webster would be perched inside. She didn't need her squirming guilt over what she was about to do to Lo piqued by a wave and a smile from Max, Lo's buddy and hers.

Lo's bond with Max had provided oomph to her plan to chip away at Lo's backward LGBT notions. After all, Lo's friendship with the African American owner of the parking facility had plowed under his white conceit. He wasn't as hopeless as Ricky thought.

BJ turned left into the station's garage. In her haste, she hit the driveway hard. The scrape frayed her nerves. Shaking off the bounce, she now faced gutting Lo's reputation.

The institutional two-tone green of the squad room caught her attention. The dowdy dark-green paint ended halfway up the wall, followed by its mint-green cousin up to and across the dusty ceiling. She and Lo often bitched about the drab surroundings on their way out to satisfy their shared tastes for ethnic cuisine. More than once Max had shaken his head and said, "You two gringos know that Mexicans make menudo from tripe?" BJ chuckled at the memory.

She nodded greetings to the other cops as usual as she lengthened her stride toward Captain Rhodes's office. Her desk faced Lo's in front of the captain's door. Though hurrying to miss Lo, she danced her fingertips across Lo's mess of sticky notes until they reached her desk and brushed between orderly stacks of typed reports. Despite their shared affinity for breakfast burritos, she and Lo were opposites, after all. A faint smile creased winglets into the corners of her ample lips. Then she caught a whiff of Old Spice.

"Detective Reeves, where's Faeth?" she heard from behind, smelling a dash of coffee breath.

BJ spun around and met Rhodes face-to-face. "Captain." At first she dodged Rhodes's eyes but then met his gaze. "Long night at Bambi's. Probably still asleep. Can I have a word with you?"

"Certainly. Any conclusions about the blast?" An oily strand of brown hair slid from his glossy dome and bent backward on its roots at the nape of his neck. He pursed his lips and squinted as he reached behind and swept the rebel tress back atop his shiny head. It slithered back over his collar.

BJ glanced away, pretending to miss his attempt to cover his crown. "Can we talk first?"

Rhodes opened the door to his aluminum-framed glass office. His vertical blinds dangled open as an expression of his "open-door policy." BJ wished for a little privacy while toileting Lo's reputation. Might've eased her queasy belly.

BJ sat in one of Rhodes's cushy oxblood leather chairs facing his oversize and ornate desk. The portly captain shuffled across his Oriental rug and then plopped into his antique wooden desk chair. Despite his paunch, the captain only wore tailored suits. Today's Armani was no exception. Neither was his loud, paisley tie. She and Lo both found him pretentious.

A shadow cast from outside startled BJ. She turned, expecting Lo.

Her eyes met Detective March's. The young, buff, and predictable pig, raised his coffee cup in greeting. He'd been trying to jump her bones since day one. BJ snarled, glanced away, and concentrated on dialing back the thump of her pulse against her ears. She leaned back and rested her fingertips against her cheek. She'd at least look calm.

Rhodes leaned forward, causing the seat's springs to squeal. He laced his fingers together atop his green blotter. "What is it, Detective?"

"Faeth and I argued over the evidence at Bambi's. He's been edgy lately, but I thought it would pass. That's why I didn't mention it before." She couldn't stop the pain of what she was about to do from rippling her face. Hoped Rhodes would miss her betrayal. Read her ache as concern.

"Go on, Detective Reeves."

"Faeth's got to be burned out, right? What else could explain him leaving me alone at the crime scene this morning?" A cramp in her belly made her want to bolt for the bathroom. Time she couldn't waste.

Rhodes swiveled a quarter turn, giving BJ his potbellied profile. She watched him eye the plaques, photos, and other framed accolades carefully hung on his mahogany-paneled back wall. Tenting his fingers, he contemplated his accomplishments. Or so it looked like to BJ. Hot spikes tore at the base of her throat.

"Detective Faeth is a good cop. You think I need to order him to take time off?"

She needed more than the captain's nibble. A vacation would leave Lo's credibility intact. He and that router could be taken seriously. Neither could she tell Rhodes what to do. Had to make him believe his actions were his own. She saturated her voice with disappointment and shook her head. "Vacation. I don't know."

"I can't remember the last time he took one."

BJ knew Rhodes had dodged the draft during the Vietnam War and fancied himself as a great judge of character. She cast a deliberate glance at the captain's Peace Corps commendation, his alternative to military service. "Faeth's been talking a lot about Iraq and Afghanistan lately. Been real irritable. At times downright hostile toward cops who never fought for their country."

The captain followed BJ's glance to his commendation, cleared his throat, and pressed his lower lip against his upper. "That bad?"

BJ anted up. "I smelled alcohol on his breath at Bambi's. The poor boy might need more than time off."

The captain swiveled to face her. "Has he been drinking on the job?" he asked, offering her another nail for Lo's coffin.

BJ hesitated. Cleared her throat. "Don't know. Says he drinks to sleep."

"You should've come to me sooner. I'll pull him off duty and see that he gets professional help."

BJ released a silent breath. She knew the drill. Lo would have to see SFPD's psychiatrist for an assessment. Dr. Mason Tobac, her undercover handler. She'd make Tobac restore Lo's reputation once he was out of harm's way.

"I'll assign Detective March to work with you on the blast investigation," Rhodes added.

BJ shot up her palms. She didn't want him humping her leg while she tried to recover the router. "No need, sir. I'm sure that the evidence will prove that the blast was accidental. I'll go check in at Forensics. See what they got."

Rhodes pressed his fingertips onto his blotter and stood up. "Go home and get some rest, Detective."

The captain had tossed her a chance to rifle Lo's condo after he left for the station. Stretching her arms and faking a yawn to mask the burn in her throat, she said, "Think I'll do that."

She grabbed her belly outside of Rhodes's office, rushed into the women's restroom, and puked into a toilet. She heard the door swish open. "You pregnant, girl?" wisecracked Officer Lakesha Jackson.

No toilet paper. BJ snatched a seat liner and wiped her lips. She turned to Lakesha. "Nothing more than fast-food burp-back." She forced a smile.

"Got something in my desk that might help. Come on," Lakesha said.

Jackson had always reached out to her. Invited her out a few times. She'd declined. Better to keep people at a distance while undercover. BJ leaned over a sink and splashed water on her face. "I'm fine, thanks."

Outside, BJ bolted into the police garage. Her careful scan didn't turn up Lo's bloated Buick. She slammed her car door. The thud echoed throughout the garage. She'd case Lo's place, make sure he was gone, and then break in. The idea of sacking his condo held all the appeal of a roadkill brunch, but maybe she'd get lucky and find that router.

A Jack Ruby Gut Shot

I careened onto Vallejo Street, lead footed and groggy. My balding tires squealed across the asphalt. The stink of burned rubber seeped into the car, overpowering the soot smell sifting through the coarse wool blanket draped over my seat.

Cruising past Max's booth, I caught his snickering smile and waved back. Sure, he'd caught my sloppy turn. He'd know, too, if BJ beat me to the precinct. She'd stop by to bitch about me.

I'd cooled off and decided BJ had snapped out of it. Recognized the router as a clue. She'd banged on my door in the middle of the night to straighten things out, but I'd showed her my ass. Would she cover for me? Or rat me out to the captain?

Max might help me deal with BJ. See what he thought about me apologizing. Admitting that she'd pissed me off by siding with Crusher. How I might get her to a roach coach for breakfast before she spoke to Rhodes.

I squeezed my Buick into the pint-sized parking space and strolled toward Max's next door. Most of the white cops assumed that Max slept in a flophouse. Didn't know he owned the cash cow next to the station. But a good cop needs more than one set of eyes and ears. I'd made a habit of cozying up to people who mixed it up with the public.

Max's sharp mind cost me, though. Punctured my white-bread ideas about African Americans. The first time I spoke to him, I couldn't have kept up with his educated lingo if it hadn't been for my four years at San Francisco State. We'd hit it off, and he'd let me know that he'd also used the GI Bill for college. He'd been a marine in Vietnam. Made it home and gotten an MBA.

When BJ came from Texas, with no help from me, she impressed Max by striking up a conversation and asking just how many degrees he had. The first time we invited him to join us for beers, he did, after saying,

"Damn. This is the first time cops have ever invited me to do anything except keep my hands where they could see them."

Max sat in his booth on a padded stool in his pressed khaki pants and polo shirt. A dog-eared paperback, *Invisible Man,* lay on a counter between the bank's cash bag and electronic cash register. Max thumbed a wad of bills, his fingers flattened by the effort.

Wedging one foot on the curb of the booth, I knocked on the window. "Sci-fi, huh?"

Max flinched. His nimble fingers straightened the last crumpled bill as he stretched a rubber band around the loot. He slid open the window, held up the book, and ran his finger under the author's name. "That say H. G. Wells?"

"Ralph Ellison? Oh," I said, clueless.

I watched Max put the book down, then bag the money. He didn't seem to mind me seeing him lock the dough in a safe under a scuffed green floor tile.

"Max, you dress like you're about ready to tee off," I said to rib him a little.

"Where have you been? Tiger Woods gave all blacks permission to dress like Jack Nicklaus."

"Thought you were African American," I said.

"We were black, back in days of the Panthers. You're on the street. How much has changed?" Max swept his hand in front of him. "I own this. But you and BJ are the only two badges interested enough to know that." Max's eyes twinkled above his sly grin and his voice dropped low. "BJ has come and gone. The girl drove right by me. Didn't even wave, let alone drop by for a chat. Can't believe she split without her shadow. You two have a fight?"

"BJ came and went?" Jabbed by the news, I stumbled back. Had she told Captain Rhodes about the router? Taken off before she had to face me? I'd put her in the switches by keeping the damned thing. But why not talk to me first? She'd tried, but I'd slammed my door in her face.

Max folded his arms. "What's up with you two?"

Tugging on a loose thread hanging from my coat cuff, I said, "I messed up this morning. Put BJ in a bind."

Max leaned back. "What'd you do?"

Avoiding his stare, I spun around and headed toward the station. Maybe BJ told another cop where she was going. I spoke over my shoulder, "Another time. Over beers."

"I'll buy," I heard him say.

♦ ♦ ♦

BJ unfolded her leather burglar's kit as she scanned Lo's hallway. Her nimble fingers probed the lock with her skeleton keys, nudging back the tumblers. Lo had never invited her in, but—with the exception of a fat cat—she expected a lean world.

Slipping in, she shifted her eyes around Lo's drab surroundings. Didn't see Al. Lo's faded, naked walls confirmed her predictions. The only pleasant hue radiated from the faux Ming vase lamp on Lo's end table. An indigo-blue dragon slithered around the polar-white contours of the lamp. Its incongruity with the rest of Lo's anemic décor bled into a tender ache born from her days with Lo's brother. She knew the lamp had once belonged to Ricky. Grumpy had kept it. Tears welled up but couldn't blur her images of Captain Rhodes bludgeoning Lo with her lies. Reconciling Lo with Ricky buckled under the blows.

BJ clenched her teeth. Lo had thrown the first punch by taking the router. Not her. Her tears retreated.

♦ ♦ ♦

I dragged my feet into the precinct. Bugged more by my fouled-up partnership with BJ than by how to defend myself against corrupting evidence. Man, did I have things ass-backward.

BJ's desk faced mine. It was an arrangement I looked forward to. Not seeing Captain Rhodes was another pleasure, but there he stood in his fancy suit and screaming tie. I looked down and pulled at the lapels of my Kirkland sport coat.

"Faeth. In my office," he said, turning before I could shrug and ask why.

My temperature spiked, scorching off my guilt. Thanks, BJ, I thought. So much for loyalty. I shouldn't blame her. But I did.

I followed Rhodes into his glass office. His open blinds exposed us to the snooping glances from the squad room.

My boss waddled to his desk. I glared at the wall behind him, plastered with photos of himself shaking hands with VIPs and framed certificates recognizing him as an accomplished brownnose. He sat back in his squeaky old desk chair and let go a hiss. Musta been steamed that I'd held on to evidence. Brown hair combed forward from the back of his neck slid off his scalp. He whipped the greasy strands to the top of his head and patted them down. The scent of aftershave peppered the air.

My resentment at BJ smoldered. I pulled the door shut. In my head I rehearsed how I'd explain that curiosity got the best of me. Made me hold onto that router.

"Guess you spoke to BJ," I said.

The captain nodded and motioned for me to sit in one of his padded chairs. The ambitious bastard had paid out of his own pocket for these leather monstrosities. He wouldn't risk having the chief's tender rear, or even the mayor's kissable butt, park on less worthy thrones. I plopped down. No scotch or cigar for this beggar.

"Faeth, I want you to take a couple of weeks off."

I stiffened. "Wha...what?"

He pointed his hand at me like a judo chop. "Detective Faeth, you haven't been off duty in years. It's time."

What the hell? At the edge of his desk, Rhodes's gold pen and pencil leaned back on their marble base like bent goal posts. I glared between them like a gun sight.

"I got a homicide to solve."

♦ ♦ ♦

BJ felt the vibration of her O'DAD cell. Havana's picture glared back.

"What is it?...I'm searching his place now....No, I don't need your help." BJ caught herself. Havana's offer posed advantages. If they worked together, she could keep an eye on the killer. "I'm sorry. I could use a hand. We don't have much time. How long before you get here?"

BJ heard a rap at the door while Havana's voice sneered over the phone, "Open up." Apparently she and Havana would be watching each other. On her way to the door, BJ plastered on the gracious smile of a Southern belle.

Havana strolled into Lo's condo chewing a wad of gum. A conservative blue suit hung from her skeletal frame. Jax followed in bib overalls. Havana pointed toward the short hallway and told Jax, "See if the bedroom is through there. Check it out." Jutting her chin toward the other side of the couch she said, "I'll start in the living room."

BJ felt the thick air stir as Havana breezed by. Havana locked her gaze to BJ's. "Lets get to work, then." Her stern demand floated on her Juicy Fruit breath.

"I'll finish the kitchen," BJ said, keeping an eye out for Al as she closed the door. Still hadn't spotted him. She felt the weight of her boots as she rounded the counter into Lo's tiny kitchen.

♦ ♦ ♦

Rhodes tented his fingers. "You have a fine record, and I've never had to worry about you before."

Worry about me? The chair's leather creaked under my squirming ass. This had to be BJ's idea. Her cheap effort to soften her hit by selling Rhodes crap about me needing a break. No wonder she couldn't face me. To hell with both of them. I played dumb.

"Why the worry, Captain?"

"We'll call it a vacation. But I want you to take time off. Start therapy. Get a handle on your drinking." He glanced over his shoulder at an engraved plaque praising his leadership. Looked back at me with a slight smile that suggested I should be thankful for his generosity.

BJ'd told him I'd been drinking. What else had she fed him? I slid to the edge my seat and blurted, "What's this about, sir?"

He frowned and shot back, "The Faeth I know would never abandon his partner at a crime scene."

I sprang up and slapped my hands on his desk. "Wait a damned minute. I left BJ with that doctor—Dr. Crusher. A new coroner."

"Dr. Crusher? She hasn't been in the field yet. BJ was alone when Sandoval's team arrived."

"Sandoval's team?" My knees started to give. I pivoted, leaning on one hand while the other grabbed the arm of the chair behind me. I sank into the swollen cushion and mumbled, "They were at that Burritt Street homicide."

Rhodes shot me a what-are-you-talking-about squint. "My, my, Detective, you're confusing reality with Hammett's *Maltese Falcon*."

"Shit," I mumbled and chased my retreating hairline with my fingers. Crusher had fed me a patsy pill, and on cue, I'd spit it up in front of my boss.

Crusher's high beams suddenly made sense. What better way to make me sound like a fruitcake than for me to argue she was there without being able to recognize her. I felt the blood drain from my face. I'd been set up.

"You aren't doing well, are you? Here." From his breast pocket, Rhodes tossed me a business card. The glossy white card with its cheesy extended hand logo landed at the edge of his desk in front of me. I read the private psychologist's name. Everybody knew she was his girlfriend, but he denied it.

I flicked the card back at him.

"Calm down, Detective," he said, glaring at me. "I'm trying to help."

"This is a setup," I growled.

♦ ♦ ♦

BJ didn't fear Havana but rubbing shoulders with her made her feel like she'd been pimped out to a sweaty john. And where was Al? BJ yanked open the cabinet doors under Lo's sink. She gagged on the putrid smell. Shoving aside a tequila bottle, she lifted the trash can's plastic liner and felt for the shape of the router. Nothing pushed back except cardboard and cans. Peeking into the bag, moldy pizza crust and empty gourmet cat food tins fumed back. Al eats better than Lo, she thought. All she'd found in the other cabinets were mismatched plates, rusty coffee mugs, and glasses filmy enough for a double feature.

She heard the sound of a parting zipper and looked past the counter into the living room. Watched Havana drop a stripped sofa cushion and toss its cover aside. Havana clomped over the discarded cover and reached for the next cushion.

BJ stiffened. Felt the urge to pounce on the callous Havana. Instead, she twisted around and slid to the floor with her back against the cabinets. She dragged her nails along the scuffed linoleum.

♦ ♦ ♦

Rhodes leaned back in his chair, its springs squawking under his weight. "Why would your partner and Sandoval set you up?" he asked.

The captain hadn't mentioned the router. BJ'd made light of the thing and tried to get me out of Bambi's before Crusher's crew came for it. Those broads were burying more than a murder under my reputation.

"Not Sandoval," I hissed. "Bet he got to Bambi's late?"

"Around four thirty," Rhodes said, stretching his "four" while tilting his head, as if to say I would've known if I'd been there.

"It was around two when BJ said she called him. He and his team don't take that long to get anywhere. Crusher'd split by the time Sandoval made it."

"I see." Rhodes inspected his tie before bellying up to his desk. "So it's BJ and Dr. Crusher who are orchestrating this conspiracy against you. For what purpose, might I ask?"

The more I opened my mouth, the more numb nuts thought I'd spun a bearing. The key out of psych lockdown hid in that router. I couldn't turn it in now. Until I could tie the damned thing to Bambi's victim, I was cooked. I needed to back out of the bongo bin and get that router to Sandoval on the q.t. I shook my head.

"You know what, sir? Maybe you're right. A couple of days off might do me good."

The captain took a deep breath. "What about the conspiracy, Detective Faeth? I have to be candid. You're a war veteran. It's my understanding that post traumatic stress disorder can pop up anytime to interfere with judgment. I don't think a couple of days will be enough."

My pulse kicked into passing gear, and I squeezed the chair's thick arms to keep from dropkicking baldy. This had nothing to do with Vietnam.

I watched Rhodes's eyes widen as he saw the blood drain from my knuckles. He pulled out his smartphone and stroked its screen. "Consider yourself on vacation until you've been evaluated and cleared for duty by our department psychiatrist." Rhodes brushed his phone's display faster.

Had numbskull forgotten to enter the shrink's number? His bumbling provided a needed distraction. I held back a laugh and patted my trusty notebook in my shirt pocket. My numbers were penciled in.

After a mumbled "Crap," Rhodes glanced at me, then flipped through his Rolodex. "Doctor...Dr. Tobac. Here he is." He grabbed his landline and punched in the number.

♦ ♦ ♦

Jax popped out of Lo's bedroom. "Nothin' much in there. Bed's on the floor. I'll check out his bathroom," she said, stepping in. "Ugh. His hamper is stuffed, and there's stinky clothes on the floor."

"Glove up," Havana said. "The man's a pig."

"Phew. Covered cat box in the tub," Jax said, followed by a cat's hiss. "Ow!" she yelped.

BJ stifled a chuckle. Sounded like Jax found Al, and he got piece of her. She saw Al pad out of the bathroom as fast as his tonnage allowed. Hooking into the dining room, his hind legs slid out from under him, but he kept kicking. Righted, he loped to his empty bowls, sniffed, spotted BJ, and then galloped into Lo's bedroom.

Jax limped out of the bathroom, rubbing her bloody ankle. "That sucker flopped outta the tub into my leg and raked my ankle to get going."

"Make sure you wash up, dahlin'," BJ said, shaking her head. She glanced at Havana, who rolled her eyes and said, "Back to work."

BJ drove herself to Lo's hall closet. Patting along the top shelf, her hand skipped a stack of magazines and landed on a bulging shoulder holster. Her fingertips told her she'd discovered Lo's old .45 automatic. She recalled Ricky's story of how Lo had mailed the Colt home a piece at a time from Vietnam. He'd told Ricky it had saved his life more than once. She brought her hand down. Caught in the spiral of her own secrets, she studied her fingers. Her grip on her pledge to Ricky—gone.

"Find something?" Havana's voice cracked from across the living room.

BJ snapped out of her reverie. "Nothing but junk."

She feared that rifling his house was a long shot. Lo likely stashed the router somewhere else or kept it with him until he could get it to Sandoval. Marilee covered the crime lab in the event Sandoval turned up with the device. If Sandoval got his hands on it, the risk to O'DAD's secrecy would bounce Sandoval to the top of Havana's hit list.

BJ had to intercept Lo before he passed the router to Sandoval. But how would she make him listen to her after she'd torched his career?

♦ ♦ ♦

The captain twirled his fat pen as he spoke into the phone. "I'm fine, Dr. Tobac. Thank you. How is your lovely wife, Natalie? What?...The sole survivor of a multicar collision?"

Man, oh man. I'd learned about survivor's guilt at the VA. The poor lady would never forget the ones who hadn't made it. Sympathy ratcheted down the strain in my gut.

"I'm sorry about your wife." Rhodes stroked his forehead with his fingertips. "Ah, I have a serious matter to discuss. I would like you to evaluate one of my detectives."

Rhodes's chicken-shit change of subject blistered my butt. My knuckles bled again to keep me from lunging at him. Then I heard him say, "Detective Faeth abandoned his partner this morning."

I grabbed the edge of his desk. "I didn't abandon BJ."

Rhodes curled his hand over the receiver and said through stretched lips, "Settle down, Faeth." Without taking his eyes off me, he continued speaking with the shrink.

Furious, I listened to Rhodes tell the doctor that I thought there was a conspiracy against me. Watched him scribble notes. Then he said, "The doctor wants me to ask you some preliminary questions."

I stroked my mouth. "Do I have a choice?"

"Not if you want to get back on duty. Now, have you had any recent head injuries?"

"No," I sneered. Rhodes jotted down my answer.

"Do you take medication for any reason?" He held his pen in the air.

"Hell, no." I squirmed, struggling to stay cool.

Like a pleading parent, Rhodes raised his voice and said, "Detective, the doctor just wants to know if you've been ill or injured recently."

"Not until now."

Rhodes glanced away, then returned my glare and scribbled another note.

He hung up and told me that the shrink wanted me to have a complete physical before he saw me. "He wants to rule out a medical cause for your distress."

"You mean like a Jack Ruby gut shot?"

Holding his pen between his fingers like a cigarette, Rhodes pushed up against the arms of his chair, adjusted his ass, and sat back down. "As of now, you're suspended with pay. As far as anyone else is concerned, you're on vacation."

"Vacation. Uh-huh." I knew the pissant thought he was being generous, but he was more concerned about how one of his cops nuttin' up would reflect on him than he was about me.

"One more thing," he said, extending his palm. "Hand over your shield and piece."

"Disarm the loose cannon, right?" I snarled. I pulled out my badge, then yanked my pistol from its holster. Feeling naked without them, I hesitated.

Rhodes waved his fingers. "For your own good. Until you're right again."

I'd leave bruises if I touched him. I plopped the gun and badge on the edge of his desk.

He stretched across his desk, but the top of his belly caught its edge. Rhodes flopped like a seal, grunting, but he grabbed my shield and pistol. Glaring at me, he shoved my badge and gun into his desk drawer. I glanced down at his rug to keep from laughing.

In a gloomy voice, he said, "Faeth, until you're cleared for duty, I don't want you to have any contact with Crusher, BJ, Sandoval, or anyone else in the department without my permission. I'm confiscating your department cell too." He patted a spot on his desk.

"Come on, Captain. You know nobody memorizes numbers anymore. You're robbing me of my phone book," I said, straining the sarcasm out of my tone. He hadn't a clue that this Luddite backed up his numbers on paper. I tossed the cell onto his desk.

"I'm counting on it. Otherwise, your career could be in serious jeopardy." He picked up his phone and scheduled my physical for tomorrow morning at "eight o'clock sharp."

I couldn't stomach looking at chrome dome any longer. I bolted, slamming his door behind me.

"Don't slam the door," Rhodes hollered.

I brushed past gawking cops and sped outside.

♦ ♦ ♦

"Our router's not here," Havana announced from Lo's living room, her arms folded across her meager breasts.

Jax stood in Lo's bathroom doorway and nodded in agreement. She peeled off her surgical gloves.

"Guess we'll just have to wait for fatso to come home, surprise him, and get him to hand it over to us ladies," Havana said, saccharine sweet.

BJ knew about Havana's deadly surprises. She wasn't about to let Havana add Lo to her sham robbery-homicide list.

"I know the ol' boy. He won't have it with him. He's got it hid somewhere. Nobody's gonna find it without him." BJ struggled to distill the challenge out of her tone. Mask her defense of Lo. "Let me take a run at him. Alone."

Havana glared at BJ. "Thought you tanked his career?"

"Deep-sixed it," BJ said without a flinch.

"Your leverage is spent." Havana glanced at Jax and then back to BJ. "We'll wait here. You mosey along and let us get our router back," Havana said mockingly.

BJ whipped out her phone. "I distinctly remember the good Dr. Crusher instructing y'all to let me deal with the recalcitrant Detective Faeth. Let's call. See if she's changed her mind."

Havana irritably conceded. "Don't bother. We'll leave him alone. For now."

BJ had shoved Havana out of the way for the moment. She put away her phone and skulked out of Lo's condo behind the pair. She split off from them without a word.

By the time she slid into her hybrid, she'd tumbled back into the tangle of how to conjure up a private meet with Lo. Convince him she'd gotten him suspended for his own good. Persuade him to hand over the router.

BJ poked along San Francisco's clogged streets. As she waited at a red light, the thought seeped in that Lo had stolen her chance to reconcile him with Ricky. The ooze hardened into a mean, ironic path out of her fix. Leave him to Havana. After all, the hate that poisoned Lo's love for Ricky also fed Havana's homicidal appetite. Lo had made his bed years ago. Let him lie in it with Havana.

BJ's conscience skidded into her pledge to Lo's brother. Her body shuddered. Ricky hungered for acceptance, not vengeance. The light turned green. She stomped on the gas, as if to power out of her spiteful dive. With her nose up, the glimmer of a plan to save Lo broke the horizon. BJ steered toward home and her laptop.

♦ ♦ ♦

Sitting in my driver's seat, BJ's double cross ripped through my intestines like a loose spool of razor wire. I tried to focus on the router. That damned thing gave me a shot back at her.

I aimed my key at the ignition, but my head spun. Suspicions about BJ's flaky attitude after her strange phone call at Bambi's clipped my pisstivity. Crusher'd called her. But hadn't she tried to push me out of there before Crusher arrived? Came to my condo and warned me I'd backed her into a corner? She'd tried to protect me.

Oh, fuck. I'd gotten too attached to her. She didn't give a shit about me. I jammed the key into the ignition. Creeping out of the precinct garage, my Buick's tired springs creaked as the front wheels dipped from the driveway into the street. I steered toward my Cow Hollow condo, my eyes peeled for one of our vanishing pay phones. Never missed not having a personal cell—until now.

I found a public phone on Lombard Street, parked, and pulled out my address book. The phone's blue cutaway housing hadn't protected the face of the black phone from some asshole's sticky soda spray. Thankful for the dry receiver, I plugged in my coins and through the tacky gunk punched in the number of Sandoval's lab. With the phone wedged between my shoulder and ear, I wiped my fingertip with the used napkin I had in my pocket. "Dr. Sandoval, please."

"Who is calling?" the police cadet asked dutifully.

"Captain Rhodes, Central Station," I hollered over the downshifted burp of a big rig. The truck's cloud of diesel exhaust wrapped around me. Not my day. While I gagged, the cadet said, "Sir, he's not in. Can I take a message?"

"No, thanks. I'll call back." I pounded Sandoval's cell number into the gummy keys. The ring rolled into his voice mail. Damn. I couldn't leave a message. What if Rhodes checked Sandoval's department cell? The captain could review our SFPD cell logs, but he'd need a subpoena for our home phones.

I dialed Sandoval's home number. His answering machine kicked on. This time I left a message to contact me at my home. I explained that Rhodes suspended me. Took my police cell and restricted me from contact with anyone in the department without his approval.

Where was Sandoval? Without thinking, I ran my sticky fingers across my forehead, gumming up my already piss-poor mood. I paged him, entered my landline number, and sped toward home.

A Crack in the Cement

I rolled into my carport. Exhaustion had sapped my temper. Still, jagged pieces of a puzzle pricked my drowsy head. A suspicious blast with a lone dead shooter. A router I wasn't supposed to see. Crusher's phony CSI team. Worst of all, BJ's shank in my back. And her blade had cut me out of a helluva lot more than a homicide investigation. That vic's murder hid something bigger.

I moped to my trunk for the router. Shit, I'd paged Sandoval. Left my home number. I snatched the router, charged to my condo, but opened the door slowly. Didn't see Al.

Lifting my eyes from the floor, I saw that my sofa's cushions were stripped, the covers tossed on the rug. A burst of adrenaline shot my hand to my empty holster. Frozen, I listened for the rustle of an intruder. Only the faint whine of the refrigerator motor drifted into my ears.

Tiptoeing to my closet, I scanned the place. BJ had tossed my pad. Better not have let Al escape. My lean closet didn't appear trashed, and she'd left my Colt. I grabbed the .45 and drove a slug into the breech. With my old friend locked and loaded, my pulse slowed. With its muzzle in the air, I squirmed out of my police shoulder holster and into the .45's. Al poked his head around the corner from my bedroom, then loped over to his empty cat dish. "Anh," he said, glancing between me and the bowl.

I peered past the dining room into my kitchen, then right into my bedroom. The place was quiet except for the fridge's hum and Al's bitching. My search turned up nothing missing, though my drawers had been rifled. BJ had come for the router. She'd pissed on my career and then tossed my pad. But the door was locked when I got home. She'd picked the lock and locked up when she'd left. How considerate. I stomped to the front door, hooked the chain, and did an about-face. Time to check my answering machine.

The steady light said no Sandoval. Where'd he go? I thought about calling Rhodes, but I couldn't prove that BJ tossed my condo. If I told him she'd been searching for a router neither one of us told him about, he'd drive me to the loony bin himself.

After feeding Al, I zipped up my cushions and flopped onto the couch. BJ's shiv twisted inside like a hot poker. Had she used the past two years to set me up as her patsy? Or was I just handy? I squeezed my head to pinch out an answer. As if it mattered. Either way, she'd fucked me. Why was clammed up in that stinking router. And the only person I knew who could spring its secrets hadn't called back.

I found my remote, punched on my TV, and channel surfed until I caught a *Star Trek* rerun. "Come on, Sandoval, call," I mumbled. My muscles started to sag. I fell back and nodded off.

The doorbell pinged through the Borg's collective drone, "Resistance is futile." BJ? I punched mute.

"Lo, I heard the TV," BJ called.

Slipping off my loafers, I crept to the door. Squinting out the spy hole, I fish-eyed Judas.

BJ rocked on her heels. "I don't blame you for getting up on your hind legs, but you forced my hand."

Oh, right. Like she's the victim. I kept my mouth shut.

She kept glancing over her shoulder. Her hands balled into fists. Did I see fear? Was that what I saw at the crime scene? When Crusher arrived, BJ seemed to shrink in front of her. I shook my head to snap out of it. My feelings for her cracked my balls.

I watched her cock her fist toward the door. She hesitated. Would she pick my lock again? Instead, she slipped on latex gloves and fished an envelope out of her jacket's inside pocket. She tapped the peephole with her finger. I jerked back, peeved for doing so.

"Pay attention," she growled. "Next time I won't be able to talk 'em outta bushwhackin' ya at home. Read this."

My temp spiked. She expected me to believe that she'd saved me from an ambush? I strained to keep from yanking open the door and shouting, Go fuck yourself. Or else, Get in here.

BJ slipped the blank envelope under the door and stomped off.

I picked up the letter by its edges. Despite myself, her crap that she'd saved me from an attack stirred up my feelings for her. Made me want to believe that I'd read fear in her. I clucked my tongue. Told myself to quit finding excuses.

I pulled a pair of gloves of my own from my hall closet. After snapping them on, I shook her envelope next to my ear. No powdery plop.

"Right," I said out loud. BJ didn't need anthrax to snuff my career. Fucken 9/11 had kicked up everybody's paranoia, not just mine. I walked over to my lumpy couch and flopped down next to the router. I landed on the remote, cutting short the blast of a Borg cube.

"Fine." I turned on Ricky's lamp and held the white envelope to the light. Seeing no telltale shadows, I pulled my switchblade, slit open the envelope, and removed her typed, unsigned note.

Like a tired fluorescent light flickering on, it occurred to me that I had never seen BJ's handwriting. She always voice-recorded her notes at a crime scene and typed them later. She used a facsimile stamp for her signature. She was hiding something. Just like I'd ignored my brother's feminine tastes, I'd let my feelings blind me to BJ's suspicious habits.

I read the letter out loud so I could hear over the brawl between my suspicions and excuses for her. "Lo, you're a good cop. I am too. So you'd better appreciate the limb I'm straddling here. I'm undercover, tracking a serial killer and her lackeys who shield themselves behind a national security asset. Your theft of that router jeopardizes my mission to stop her without exposing that asset. It also puts you in her crosshairs.

"And don't go trying to use this letter against me. Anybody could have written it, including a paranoid cop desperate to save his career."

She didn't have to throw that in my face. But national security? Undercover—a mole? Not for SFPD—I would've known. The pulse of SFPD's grapevine pounded through the veins of us old-timers. FBI? CIA?

Who else would be protecting intel sources? NSA? Protecting her cover could explain why she didn't leave handwriting samples.

I pounded my knee. What the hell was I thinking? She's trying to get me to drop my guard. I read on, muttering out loud, "My promise to retrieve that router pronto was the only thing that got the killer out of your condo today. Because she can strike at any time, keep your eyes open for a gaunt, five-foot-nine, snaky-lipped blonde named Havana Vives. She's got frigid blue eyes and disguises herself with wigs. She's also partial to Juicy Fruit gum."

What about that bowling pin who called herself Dr. Crusher? What's her piece in the puzzle? She led that crew, for Christ's sake. BJ thinks I'm gonna believe this shit? I started to wad up her note, but hunger for clues kept me reading.

"She recently picked up an enforcer. A stubby, no-neck, bowlegged nineteen-year-old who calls herself Jax. No trace of her given name. She sports a butch haircut, and I've never seen her in anything but jeans or bib overalls. You ran into them at Bambi's.

"Don't believe me? I followed Havana here two years ago. Check out the spike in the transgender-female homicide rate over the same period."

She talking about shims? I gagged on a shot of Ricky in drag. Did Havana get him? No way. But how would I know? I'd deserted him. If BJ's not lying, I should help her. Her note suddenly felt like a debt-due notice on Ricky.

"I had to orchestrate your suspension to keep my mission, me, and your meddling butt safe. You keep that router, I lose my undercover cred. That happens, and we're both targets. And keep Sandoval out of this. There is nothing to be found inside that router. If he gets it, all you've done is put his name atop the killer's hit list.

"Return it now. This can all fall behind us as a bump in my operation, and I'll see that you get your badge back. You fought for this country. Do your part to protect this intel asset."

Warning flares burst about my brain. "Slick," I blurted, trying to spit out her hooks. Ricky's fate also fattened her bait. But my memory of BJ's losing her nerve in front of Crusher bled into her anxious glances over her shoulder at my door. The chance that she was telling the truth took the torque out of my testes. Hell, she'd given me descriptions of the perps.

I felt Al thump against the couch. Front paws plucked at the seat while rear claws raked its side, trying to boost his dangling ass. Ears back, he finally made it. I waved him over, but he flopped onto his back, righted himself, then licked his crotch. Damn, I wished my choices were that easy.

♦ ♦ ♦

BJ lengthened her stride along Cow Hollow's crowded sidewalks. She knew Lo had been at his door. She'd watched him bolt into his condo, heard his *Star Trek*. She couldn't blame him for playing possum—for his silent fuck-off. But she'd also counted on his being coiled up, keen to strike back. She'd given him a list of places and times where he could find her.

A crack in the cement caught her heel. She tripped. Had she also stumbled by giving Lo a peek behind her mask?

♦ ♦ ♦

My brain bugged me to shred BJ's typed con. But my suspicions kept slipping off my feelings for her. It didn't help that the killer she'd described targeted trannies. Drag queens like my brother, right? I squeezed my mouth and kept reading.

"Don't use your phone. You can bet it's tapped. Until you give me the router, hide." My neck hairs popped up. Hide, hell. I wasn't gonna lay down. I read on. "I figure I've got until tomorrow to get the router back before I lose control of the situation. The next page lists times and places for us to meet. Tonight's best. Bring it."

My suspicions flared and burned away my brother's ghost. BJ wanted the router back before Sandoval saw it. Never said what the murder hid. National security, right. BJ could be a dirty cop involved in torching upside-down buildings in an insurance scam. A boon in this age of foreclosures. It'd explain how she paid for her pad over in the Sunset District. Me nosing around the death of an innocent bystander could pry the lid off the scheme. Or maybe she's not a killer but found out life's cheap to her cronies. I give her the router and she speed-dials Rhodes. Tells him I've harassed her and gets skid-lid to pop my career like a nasty zit.

My brain hit a snag. If it was an insurance scam, why the hubbub over the router? The Crusherteers had gone to great lengths to recover the damned thing. And BJ said that Havana broad would kill to get it back.

My heart pounded in BJ's direction. Trust her, fork over the device. Keep Sandoval outta the crosshairs, and get back my badge. But BJ's blade gouged back. Hand her my only trump card? That router held the key to clearing my name. I couldn't bank on her, but I could on my pal Sandoval. She'd left me no choice.

I pulled an evidence bag out of my pocket and stuffed in BJ's envelope. I'd pass it to Sandoval but keep the note. Maybe I'd get lucky and he'd find a print. See if she was who she said she was and if anybody else's prints popped up. Have him check out Bambi's mortgage too. See if the owner was upside down. And on the outside chance she'd told even part of the truth, I'd have him check out tranny homicide rates and warn him about Havana and Jax.

I yanked off my rubber gloves. Time to break down and buy an untraceable cell. If Sandoval called before I got it, I'd tell him my landline might be tapped. That I'd call him back on a burner.

Hunger and exhaustion took control of my immediate future. Partial to my belly, I headed to the fridge for leftover pizza. Before opening the door, curiosity got the best of me. I skimmed BJ's list of meeting places. At midnight tonight, she'd be at Benny's, an all-night East Bay eatery across the Bay Bridge. I'd go for the pleasure of poking my finger into her chest. Demand answers. I folded the pages into one narrow strip. The paper's odd touch felt familiar. But hunger had the better of me. I stuffed her note into my wallet.

Flipping open the pizza box freed the rotten smell of homegrown penicillin. The stink killed my appetite. I slammed the fridge door and wandered back into my living room, where I sprawled on the couch next to an unconscious Al. My eyelids slammed shut. My thoughts scattered, and I passed out.

♦ ♦ ♦

BJ rounded the corner to see Havana and Jax leaning against her car. She ran head-on into Havana's serrated tongue.

"Don't see our router. You had your run at him," Havana said, studying her outstretched nails. "A swing and a miss with your search, and since your begging didn't pay off, strike two." Havana glanced at Jax. "One more strike, and we're up." Jax raised her chin at BJ and folded her arms across the bib of her overalls.

BJ didn't need a reminder about their brittle patience or that out of her or Marilee's sight, the two weren't above pouncing on Lo. She'd mimic Havana's narrow assumptions to make her believe she wielded the same spite.

"O ye of little faith," BJ said, slapping the air between them like they were old sorority sisters. BJ enjoyed watching her adversaries' eyelids flutter in confusion when she failed to match their hostility.

"Meaning?" Havana asked, straightening her back. Jax pumped her tennies in place.

BJ cast glances over her shoulders, signaling to wait for a bevy of pedestrians to stroll by. She huddled with her foes and lowered her voice. "He's buried our router. The ol' coot demanded an explanation for why I got him suspended before he dug it up. I fed him a good one."

Havana tilted her head. "How could you get him to trust you again?"

BJ swished back a step, flipped the back of her hair, and then slid her hand down her thigh like she was rolling down her stockings. "It don't take much of a coo from a Texas belle to convince a lonely ol' boy that he couldn't expect her to risk her little ol' fanny to save his. Sakes alive, he knows he corrupted evidence." To toss the carnivorous Havana a little meat, she added with a whip of her tongue, "He's old but still has a pecker, don't he?"

Havana snorted. "They're never too old not to think with their dicks, are they?" She leaned back on BJ's fender. Jax simmered down as well and leaned against the parking meter. After a glance at the pulsing red display, she deposited a quarter.

BJ winked at her. "Thank ya, sugar."

"What'd you tell him?" Havana asked, her voice frosty.

"I know his low opinion of women. So I reminded him of how we ladies stick together. That my girlfriend Dr. Crusher was just itchin' to get into the field. So certain she'd dazzle the forensics chief with her initiative, she and her assistants showed up ahead of Sandoval without authorization. But when he took off with that router, he put everybody in a stew. Dr. Crusher had to hightail it outta there to keep her job. Left me to cook up a fib to cover everybody's behinds, including his."

"Your 'fib' took a dump on his career," Havana said. "I wouldn't buy it."

"I told him I softened up his AWOL to the captain by explaining he was overworked. Did him a favor."

"And keeping quiet about our router—how'd you explain that?"

BJ didn't falter. "That was the best part, dahlin'. I said I didn't say anything about it to buy him time to get it to me and me to get it into evidence before the captain found out."

"How do you know he hasn't already turned it over to that Dr. Sandoval?"

"You know Marilee is on the lookout for that." BJ didn't bluff on that one.

Havana pushed off of BJ's hybrid. "When's he giving it back, then?"

Jax cocked her ear toward BJ.

Weary of the charade, BJ gulped down her scorn for the two and gave her voice a little extra Southern lilt. "Faeth's going to call me tonight for a meetin'. I'll snuggle next to him with a playful thigh-to-thigh nudge, and after my soft breath pats his ear, he'll be beggin' me to take it."

"We'll see," Havana said, twirling her hair behind her ear. Then she locked her gaze with BJ's. "Won't we?"

Jagged Memories

My .45's grip poked my rib cage, gouging me out of my sleep.

"Anh," Al said, sitting on his haunches across from me on the coffee table.

"Yeah, yeah, I'll feed ya in a minute," I said, massaging my side. Dull light peeped through my miniblinds—sundown. My condo's chill reminded me BJ'd pissed in my Wheaties.

And Sandoval? I wondered and rubbed my eyes. The phone hadn't rung. Sandoval could prove BJ's story. That thought T-boned another. He could also show she'd fucked me.

My gut rattled. Shook loose the idea of Mac's Bar and Grill. Its tiny kitchen hardly qualified the place as a grill, but Frank cooked up a mean burger. That, some suds, and an eyeful of his sexy wife, Lupe, were the boosts I needed before staking out Benny's. Gettin' the jump on BJ.

After I'd shut Al up with a pile of "grain-free, pasture-raised chicken and turkey," I dragged my olive-drab rucksack from the floor of my closet, stuffed the router in, and slung the pack's strap over my shoulder. The hike past the yuppie eateries on Union Street to Frank's place would do me good. Maybe stumble into a store to pick up a burner phone.

I'd met former buck sergeant Frank Padilla at the VA. Frank came to do volunteer work. He'd told 'em that he didn't need counseling. That he just wanted to give back to the grunts who'd done the real fighting. He'd said that he was rear echelon in Vietnam and only been shot at once or twice. The crafty counselors, combat vets themselves, knew nobody had been safe in Vietnam. So they said, "Sure," and the next thing Frank knew, he was volunteering in my rap group, upchucking memories that wrung the sweat out of him.

I'd kidded him, "What kind of Chicano wears a guayabera shirt every day, then names his place Mac's?"

"Pancho's Pisto Palace on Union Street? No curb appeal," he'd shot back.

"What's *pisto*?" I'd asked, throwing up my hands.

"Booze," he'd said with a chuckle. He'd been trying to teach me Mexican slang ever since.

I strolled into light-deprived Mac's and eased up to the bar, letting my eyes adjust. The long carved wooden bar hooked left into the wall near the entrance. The wall's glass liquor shelves reflected the tiny white Christmas lights dripping down in front of the racks of glasses above. I didn't see Frank, so I leaned over to take in his wife pulling an ale tap.

"Hi, Lupe. Frank around?"

Lupe's forty-plus years had been easy on her. Still slim, she wore a wide, black belt to accent the slopes of her hips. The fabric of her peacock-blue miniskirt wrapped tightly around her firm rump. Her flowing black hair, streaked with gray, spilled over her bare shoulders. I found those steaks defiantly hot. So much so I forgot all about asking where to score a phone.

Turning from the tap, Lupe's full lips parted into a warm smile. "Faeth, where you been? Long time, no see." Her barrio tongue clipped the space between her words in an accent every bit as tasty as BJ's.

"Fighting crime. Making San Francisco safe. Can't you tell?" I slid back onto a barstool, self-conscious about sucking in too much eye candy.

"I feel the love," she said as she tossed down a coaster and planted a pint in front of a leering yuppie in a business suit. "Frank's cooking. You want your usual cerveza, jalapeño-burger, and fries?"

"Yeah. Make it a Dos Equis. Thanks."

I strolled over to their jukebox and punched in "Susie-Q," "Fortunate Son," and in a nod to my beat, "I Left My Heart in San Francisco." Drifting into an empty red Naugahyde booth, I slid the router next to me, firm against my leg. I hoped Frank would come out of the kitchen to join me. Lupe strutted over to the kitchen window at the end of the bar. The gap under the mahogany counter's drawbridge provided a perfect view of her booty as she bent over to speak to Frank.

"Francisco. Your amigo Faeth is here," she hollered.

"He want his usual?" I heard Frank's husky voice from the kitchen.

"*Claro*, of course," Lupe answered.

"After this, the kitchen is closed," I heard Frank say.

Grinning, Lupe swayed over from behind the bar with my beer. "Burger and fries coming up. And don't be such a stranger, *mijo*."

Mijo radiated warm, like fire to a chilly man. It's what Mexican American parents called their sons. But if you were lucky, Lupe called you *mijo* because she liked you.

"It's been too long, hasn't it? As soon as I clean up this town, I'll be planted here so often you'll have to pry me out," I said.

Lupe folded her arms over her perky breasts. "What you need is a good woman planted at your side. When are you gonna let me introduce you to one of my girlfriends?"

"Too old for that," I said. Wasn't going to risk disappointing her by failing her friend.

Lupe batted the air with her slender fingers and headed back to the bar. I ate up the sway of her hips until my thoughts slid into my ex-wife.

Madge had been beautiful to me. But her digging around to get me to "open up" about my dead parents hadn't stopped with them. She'd asked me why I'd hid being in Vietnam. Shocked, I'd said, "How'd you know?" Madge replied that she'd guessed because she couldn't see me dodging the draft. Then she ran into my old high school girlfriend at Macy's. Admiring the same purse, they'd chatted until they figured out they knew me. My ex asked about my brother. When Madge got home she bawled me out for not telling her about Ricky. Ragged on me to "be a real detective and find him." Instead, I went to Father Harlan, my old priest. Told him my wife was cracking the whip to find Ricky. Confessed that I worried about him. Wanted to find him. He'd asked to see me and Madge together but said, "Ricky must renounce his attraction to men before he can be found again." To that, Madge said, "Screw Harlan. Find your brother." Caught in the switches, I dived into work.

When I'd told Frank Madge had found out I'd been to Nam, he said he couldn't keep any secrets from Lupe either. We'd agreed: women's intuition—unbelievable.

Frank brought over my burger and fries in a paper-lined red plastic basket. He stuffed his chef's apron into the corner of the booth and scooted in, holding a Corona.

"How's it going?"

"All right," I said, trying to sound convincing.

Frank sipped his beer and stroked his long mustache. "Seen Les lately?"

"Not in a while." Les was another member of our rap group. He and Frank were amazed that counseling mumbo jumbo worked. I'd kinda known since it helped Ricky after Mom and his dad died.

I recalled the VA sessions where I'd talked about raising my little brother. Before I'd caught him in drag. I had doubts about being a father.

"Faeth. Faeth," Frank said, louder the second time. "You all right?"

Frank hadn't missed my silence. Group therapy had taught us to recognize ache's grip on the tongue. I'd never told anybody that Ricky had turned gay. Only that he'd disappeared.

I swallowed hard and ducked behind a petty wish to fatten up Frank. "Just tired." I pointed to my fries. "Have some." Guys my age as slim as Frank bugged me.

Frank raised his hands like I'd held him up. "No. That gringo food will kill you. Besides, I had *chicharrones* earlier."

"Uh-huh," I said, nodding. "Pork rinds, those will clear your arteries."

Frank arched his back, laughing. "So, what's been happening?"

I forced my thoughts away from Ricky and toward that mysterious router snug against my leg. But without Sandoval, I couldn't figure it out. I crammed confidence into my voice. "You know, Frank, I'm feeling behind the twenty-first-century techno-curve. Maybe it's time for me to retire."

Frank's eyes searched my face. "What are you going to do off the job and single? You'll go stir-crazy."

I chomped my burger to hide my flinch. I'd ignored my itch for a woman's touch since my divorce. Frank didn't mean to bump that scab.

"I'll think of something."

Frank waved for his wife's attention without looking away. "Lupe, bring us a couple of shots of Porfidio Barrique."

"What'd you say?" Lupe said, her voice rising in defiance. She cupped her hand behind her ear.

Frank scowled. "Bring us a couple of shots."

Lupe whipped her thick hair behind her shoulders. "I'm sorry, *cabrón*, but I don't think I heard you right."

I stretched back my lips. "Help me out here, Frank. She called you an asshole, right?"

Frank nodded to me and said, "Asshole, SOB, take your pick." He rolled his eyes and smiled at his wife. "*Por favor*, Lupita. Please, at your earliest possible convenience, bring us a couple of shots."

"That's what I thought you said, *mi amor*." She turned and reached for the tequila.

Frank and Lupe's tender banter always cramped me up with envy. It dusted my belief that the cost of a younger, pretty woman was paid in peace of mind.

Lupe sashayed over. The stride of her tapered legs threatened to reveal her taste in underwear. Damned if Frank hadn't caught me leering the first time I'd met her. He must have recognized from my wince that I'd expected a bitch slap. Instead, he'd shaken his head, chuckled, and said, "You gotta look. That's the point. Mexican women dress to impress us. Not like the gringas. Who dress to impress each other."

"Here you go, *viejos*," Lupe said.

She was right to call us old men. I felt it in the wisdom of my hots for her with her long, thick graying hair. Only a seasoned man recognized hair like that as the sexiest thing he'd ever seen.

Bending down to set shots in front of us, she'd added a saltshaker and slices of lemon. But her cleavage caught the corner of my eye like a junkyard magnet. Straining my pupils away, I focused on the tequila, tapped my shot glass, and said, "Thanks, Lupe." I glanced at Frank. "Damn, why'd you break out the expensive stuff?"

"To clear your head, amigo."

I played dumb. "What do you mean?"

"Help you decide whether or not to retire." Frank licked behind his thumb and sprinkled salt on the wet spot. Raised his glass.

After salting my knuckle, I lifted my glass. "*Salud*," I said, then slurped up the salt.

"*Salud*." Frank lapped up his salt. Together we slammed down our fluid hammers, then chomped our lemon slices.

The smooth Porfidio coated my throat and tingled throughout my chest. After a hesitant glance toward a busy Lupe, Frank picked up our empty bottles and excused himself to get us fresh brews.

Puckering my lips, I drew in a cool breath to tickle tequila's lingering sparkle. The powerful liquor popped loose a pet memory of me and my kid brother. The smart aleck had put together the initials of my first and middle names, Lawrence Oliver, and combined them with my last, Faeth. He'd giggled that he'd "tattle" about my "Lo Faeth" to Father Harlan. The twerp easily badgered me into one of our best-outta-three wrestlemania bouts.

The images relaxed me. Hell, I thought, I trust Frank. Maybe I could talk to him a little about Ricky. Get my brother off my chest. Sleep better.

Frank scooted into the booth with a couple of long necks and set mine on a Mac's coaster. I tilted the bottle toward him. "*Gracias*," I said.

"*Por nada*." He clicked my bottle with his.

After a sip, I picked up the coaster, flicked it around, and let it go spinning back on the table. My earlier BS about retiring suddenly didn't feel like such a bad idea.

"If I retire, I'll track down my brother." The idea pinched out painlessly. Musta been the liquor's lube.

Grinning, I said, "He looked up to me. Said he wanted to be a cop someday too." I slid my jaw from side to side, eating up my kid brother's eager image. But it soured like the deal we'd made after I'd caught him in drag. After days of battle, he'd promised to stay in the closet if I'd shut up about his sick urges. That silence hardened for six years. Then he split without warning.

"You know, me and Les always admired you for raising him. I remember when you told us that he disappeared. I think we were all sitting right here." Frank spread his arms over the table. "Even you couldn't find him."

"He cut all ties," I said, and strained to meet his gaze. Guilty over my lame effort to find him. I'd checked his trust account to follow his money trail. He'd closed it. Then I waited for a call that never came. The relief I'd felt when it didn't had since bellied up as shame. Now it hijacked my sleep. I licked the inside of my mouth.

Frank reached across the table and squeezed my wrist. "To me, you lost a son."

Shame seeped out of me. What kind of father rejects his kid? I slid my arm out of Frank's grasp. Speaking to the center of the table, I said, "I figured he'd pop up sometime. Let myself get lost in the job."

Frank took his beer and rocked the bottle. "He's been gone how long, now?"

"Fifteen years," I said, my chest not an ounce lighter.

"*Chingao*," Frank hissed, exposing his teeth.

"Yeah, it is fucked up," I said. Second thoughts about crackin' open Ricky's door piled into my throat.

Frank dropped his voice. "He was eleven when your parents—"

I coughed, then stammered, "Yeah…a fifth grader."

Frank raised his hand without shifting his eyes from my face. "Lupe, more shots."

He must have felt the heat of Lupe's glare. He passed her a weak smile and said, "*Por favor, mi amor.*"

Looking back at me, he said, "You never talk about your parents."

Thankfully he'd changed the subject. "How about those shots first?" I said.

Lupe brought us refills on a perfectly balanced tray that defied her delicious sway. I inhaled through my mouth to taste her scent as she set my glass in front of me. After another swig greased my tongue, I said, "They met in January of fifty-two."

"I remember your mom's name, Hannah, but not your father's."

"Oliver Faeth." I recalled my mom saying how Oliver became my middle name. "My dad hated being called Ollie. Gave me his father's name. But Mom insisted on Oliver as my middle name." I clipped a chuckle. "Couldn't they figure my initials would be chopped down Lo?"

Frank cracked up. "I know better than to call you that."

Lightened by the joke, I went on. "Dad was twenty-three and Mom was eighteen. Youngsters, huh?"

Frank smiled. "People grew up faster in those days."

"She was a clerk in the front office at the Richmond Ford plant. My dad limped in, leaning on a cane, to drop off a job application. He'd caught a bullet in Korea. Tore up his thigh. Ford hired him."

My mother's warm face slipped between us to interrupt. I caught my breath and went on. "Mom said he'd avoided her glances but she finally got him to talk to her. He later confessed he'd thought she was checking out the gimp. Didn't take him long to ask her to get married."

"Liked to have met them," Frank said, nodding his head.

"When the plant closed, Mom got an office job at a paint factory in South San Francisco. The only gig Dad could get was as a bank night watchman. Mom suspected because of his leg. Said they struggled to pay rent." My liquor-greased drive hit a rumble strip. But I recalled catching Mom mutter to herself after he died, "Every cent of his VA disability went toward his life insurance." At seven years old, I didn't understand why those words contorted her face.

"*Hermano*, I remember how hard it was for you to open up about your mother and stepfather. All we could get out of you about your father was that he passed on the job."

Slowed, but I couldn't stop the hemorrhage. "He lost a shootout against bank robbers. Took on a pair of Thompsons with a revolver." Then it hit me. Dad died so we wouldn't have to sweat rent. My lungs froze. My hand covered my mouth.

Through static I barely heard Frank say, "You're the son of a brave man. And he'd be proud of the father you became."

Proud? Dad gave his life for Mom and me. All I'd sacrificed was Ricky.

I strained toward the click of Lupe's heels for a lifeline away from my guilt.

She set shots and beers on the table. "These are on me. It looks like you're into serious male bonding."

Frank raised his shot glass. "To Oliver Faeth."

I raised mine with just a slight splash down my twitching fingers. Dad deserved a better son and Ricky a real brother.

Lupe put her hand on her hip. "His name's Lawrence," she said to Frank.

"I'm toasting his father, *mi amor.*"

Lupe didn't have a shot for herself but circled her fingers and raised her hand to ours. "To your *papacito*," she said and joined us with her mimed shot.

Welcoming the numbness, I said, "My turn to buy a round."

"Amigo, it's on the house." Frank glanced over at Lupe who'd made it back behind the bar. "I'll get more Porfidio."

Alone and thankful for the break, I decided to indulge my bulging bladder's pinch for relief. Holding the router tight, I clomped down the grill's rear corridor behind two twentysomething gals, a blonde and a red-head. Both in painted-on white jeans. I soaked in the rhythmic sway of their heart shaped booties. They sauntered into the powder room next to the men's room.

The only light shining in the dim hallway hooked my attention. The brass fixture illuminated a framed World War II–era Rosie-the-Riveter poster. Obviously Lupe's touch. I remembered Frank's praise for Lupe's hard work. It made him feel guilty. More than once he'd said, "Lupe lets me tend bar and cook, but that's about it. I don't even have to clean the restrooms. She takes care of all that."

Perfect timing brought me out of the men's room behind the blonde and redhead. I'd never seen two gals go in and out of a powder room so fast. I envied their confident strides and hoped their youth would leave them with few jagged memories. None with burrs like mine to prick their souls. Whew. Did I think that? Frank's tequila—good shit.

Slouching back into my booth with the router, I watched the redhead shoulder her way through a gang of customers and buttonhole Lupe. Frank served beers to a couple of young men topped with backwards Giants caps. He said to Lupe, "I'll take care of it." Lupe shook her head and said, "No, *mi amor.* I'll replace the paper towels. You take care of these folks." She nodded toward the barflies in front of her. Frank tilted another frosty glass under a tap.

Lupe strode into the ladies' room. On her way back, she shot me her broad smile. The blonde and redhead soon swished down the hall toward the powder room. Sadly, I didn't see them the rest of the evening. I didn't notice Lupe carrying paper towels either. My eyes musta been glued to her caboose.

♦ ♦ ♦

BJ paced her living room. She squinted into the face of her tambour mantel clock—only ten. She decided to leave early for her midnight rendezvous with Lo.

Stepping outside to her driveway, she gave little credence to Havana's promise to leave Lo to her. She combed her fingers through her hair and inspected her hybrid. She fingered a tracking device tucked into its wheel well. She shoulda known better than to leave her car in the driveway. What else could she expect from Havana? But more than Havana's tracker chapped her behind.

"Hell's bells," BJ whispered as she recalled trying to convince Marilee that those powder room murders were not random. That a killer lurked inside O'DAD. Marilee had chuckled and said, "A murderer among us? None of the investigating jurisdictions found a connection between those unfortunate deaths. You of all people should have more confidence in your colleagues."

BJ tilted her head into each shoulder to stretch her taut neck. She scanned her neighbor's parked cars before rolling out of her stubby driveway. All were familiar. She turned her corner and drove past a Volvo she didn't recognize. Could've sworn she made out the tops of a couple heads sunk down to the dash. Shortly before she swung right, the Volvo's headlights lit up her rearview mirror. BJ figured that Jax drove while Havana rode shotgun.

She parked in a bank lot on Irving Street and then strolled to the ATM. Out of the corner of her eye, she watched the Volvo turn and disappear around the corner. She assumed to circle the block. Hybrids dotted the traffic lanes in the Bay Area. She'd seen lots of twins of her blue sedan. Like the one near the ATM machine. BJ darted to the innocent hybrid, dropped her purse, and planted the transponder in its wheel well. She ran back to her car and shot off toward the Golden Gate Bridge.

By the time she sailed into Marin County, she snickered at the image of O'DAD's rogues realizing too late they'd trailed a decoy. Still, she'd take the circuitous route over the Richmond Bridge to Benny's in the East Bay—insurance against the duo's getting lucky and once again nosing up her fanny.

BJ left Highway 101 in Corte Madera and headed east, certain she had lost the Volvo. As she skirted the shoreline, San Francisco's city lights sparkled on the bay to her right. She reflected that she could spot the most cunning of pursuers. But she hadn't spotted Lo. Would he be at Benny's, lying low to spy on her, make sure she was alone? She cracked open her window. The crisp breeze sucked out her confidence. What if Lo ignored her note—her warning? Had already passed the router to Sandoval? That brainiac could beat the odds, dig out clues from O'DAD's router and phone. Feed 'em to that bloodhound Lo. The gas pedal pushed back against her suddenly lethargic toes as she rolled past San Quentin Prison.

A punitive horn burst from an impatient BMW startled her to surge onto the Richmond Bridge on-ramp. The Beemer's blast kicked up her fear that she might've lost all influence over the surly Lo. A dangerous proposition.

♦ ♦ ♦

Frank had strolled back to our booth clutching the Porfidio bottle over his heart like the Pledge of Allegiance. Hear, hear, I thought, then dropped my chin to my chest in a wasted effort to block a burp.

"What about your stepfather?" Frank asked as he sat.

Should I release the tourniquet? I bowed my head. "Never got to know him that well."

"*¿Porque no?*"

"I was already fifteen when Mom married him. Busy playing high school football and hanging around a church activity group." My throat cracked dry. Made me hit my beer. "Led by Father Harlan." I glanced between a cigarette burn on the table and Frank's face. "Joined the army as soon as I turned eighteen."

"I remember you talking about that priest in rap group." Frank tilted his head and furrowed his brow. "Don't recall you mentioning your stepfather's name?"

"Albert Devlin," I said. Then my mind swerved into my mother. "Mom accused me of not giving Albert a chance. Guess I shoved Harlan between us." Then I added, "Harlan never stepped between me and my mom." I looked up at Frank, shocked at my own confession. Then my cat's furry face popped into my head. Was Al short for Albert?

Frank shrugged. "You were a macho teenager. Was he good to you and your mother?"

"Yeah, he was," I said, but that truth yanked up that I'd snubbed him for the priest who helped bury my brother. Porfidio's glide hit the skids. I looked up at Frank and before he could ask anything else, I tossed out, "What about those Giants, huh?"

Frank lifted his fingers from the table without raising his wrists. He'd heard the door slam. "Sure. What about those Giants?" He took the Porfidio and filled our shot glasses.

We blew off the salt and lemon for the rest of our slammed dunks. I forgot about BJ and Benny's, and the next thing I knew, Frank brought me home in a cab. He made sure I got into my condo without letting out Al. Guess he wasn't as wasted as me.

I fed fur pig and checked my answering machine for messages. None. What the hell happened to Sandoval? That was it. I'd track him down as soon as I could pass a sobriety test. I plopped onto my couch and lapsed into a coma.

Dammit, Lo

BJ arrived at Benny's and checked the dining room and restrooms for Lo. As she peeked into the men's room, an exiting bling-bedazzled homeboy greeted her with a pearly smile. His grin collapsed against the flash of her badge and her harsh glare. He slithered away, grasping the crotch of his saggy jeans. Reminded BJ of that dick March. She guffawed. But the shrinking back of that young man's head created a vacuum that sucked out her own foolery. She'd gotten caught once with her heart exposed, but the man had slapped it to the floor. Since then, one-nighters were as far as she'd go.

She returned to her car with a cuppa joe. Considering her and Lo, she decided if it weren't for Ricky, she would've let their relationship skim the surface too. If she had, she wouldn't be here sipping weak coffee to warm up.

From her obscure corner of the parking lot, she eyed the comings and goings at Benny's. Periodically she cranked on the engine and heater to stop the clatter of her teeth. But without Lo, her temperature climbed with every tick of the clock past midnight.

BJ couldn't conjure up her partner no matter how many times she wiped the fog off her windshield. She nursed down the last of her coffee and hissed, "One o'clock and no Lo." And she had to pee.

Her plan to recover the router trickled into the toilet with her last shot of caffeine. "Dammit, Lo," she muttered as she felt her options shrink along with her bladder. Failure to retrieve the hardware this time meant strike three to Havana and Jax. At best, they would act on their own, out of range of her and Marilee. At worst, they'd accuse her of confused loyalties, of shielding Lo. Turn on her.

Her note had provided Lo with two more rendezvous. She thought about how to strengthen her bait. BJ knew Lo had shot home to raise Ricky when their parents died. Transferred his trust fund into Ricky's. Told him he didn't need it. That he had the GI Bill. Lo'd always had her back until she'd stabbed him in his. Though madder at her than a wet hen, he's also paternal.

BJ started her car but leaned forward to rest her chin on top of the steering wheel. The engine's subtle vibration massaged loose a way to fatten her lure. She fell back in her seat. Her note warned of the risks of keeping that router. She'd play up the danger to herself. The ol' coot would be suspicious of a distress call. See it as a trap. But subtlety might dilute his paranoia.

BJ shifted into reverse. Even though Lo stood her up, she could count on his fingering the pulse of the station, especially about her. Rhodes had advised her that he had confiscated Lo's department cell and prohibited him from contact with her or anyone at the department. But she knew Lo had contacts who didn't give a rat's fanny about Rhodes's ban.

She never missed a shift and personally checked in at the precinct each morning. Lo would find out if she didn't. So this morning, she wouldn't. If Lo bit that bait, he'd make her note's next meet at 11:00 a.m.

As for Havana and Jax, she'd see to it that they'd be busy explaining to Marilee why they'd tried to follow her in defiance of her orders to leave Lo to her.

BJ circled the block before pulling into her garage. She didn't see the duo's Volvo. She wondered if they'd hidden the sensible Swede or replaced it, realizing she'd spotted them. Or worse, they'd waylaid Lo. Gotten the router. She shook off a sharp chill.

She found Havana and Jax sitting on her stoop when she pulled into her driveway. She prayed that they hadn't succeeded where she'd failed. That Lo still lived.

She parked in her garage, came out through the driveway, and closed the door behind her. Before her toes hit the first step of her porch, Havana craned her neck. "I don't see our router." Jax stood and stretched her chin, mimicking Havana.

BJ cast glances up and down the block and put her finger to her lips. "Shush. It's late." She'd listened for anything glib in the killer's challenge. Had they retrieved the device?

"Well, where is it?" Havana demanded, again ruffling the calm of the Outer Sunset.

BJ threw up her arms and said, "Inside." Behind her chagrin danced relief at Havana's implied confession that they hadn't gotten to Lo.

At the door, the two pressed on either side of her as she drew her keychain from her purse. She shook her head, pushed open the door, and said, "Won'tcha come in?"

The scowling duo followed BJ into her living room and plopped in the middle of her cushy sofa. BJ languidly lowered herself into her wingback chair across from the pair to conceal her sniping fears.

She knew that without the router her leverage over Havana hung by a snot. But Havana's defiance of Marilee provided her with clout. She taunted the glowering twins. "Tonight was a test. Faeth wanted to see if I was operating alone. He kept the router hidden. Good thing I was by myself, wouldn't you say?" She enjoyed watching Havana's lips squirm. Jax's eyes darted between her and Havana.

"All I know is that you didn't come back with the router. Looks like strike three to me." Havana glanced at Jax, who endorsed her maven's call with a nod.

BJ jabbed. "By the way, what do you think Marilee will say when I tell her you tagged me with a transponder?"

A warped grin knotted up Havana's chin. "I did it to protect you. Didn't want you to face fatso alone."

BJ sneered, "If I hadn't lost you two, you woulda scared him off. If you don't stay out of it, we're going to lose that router."

"Looks to me like we already have," Havana spat.

"Let's ask Marilee what she thinks." BJ whipped out her cell.

Havana threw up her palms and said, “Don’t bother her. This is between us.”

BJ thumbed her cell. “Too late, it’s ringing.” BJ counted on Marilee to chastise Havana.

After BJ explained to a groggy Marilee that Havana had planted a tracking device in her car, Marilee insisted on speaking directly to Havana.

“She wants to talk to you,” BJ said, and handed her the O’DAD mobile.

Havana lowered her voice and strode into the hallway for her butt chewing. BJ followed and leaned against the doorway. She savored Havana’s hostile glances between her sputtering ifs, ands, and mostly buts.

BJ imagined Marilee’s tirade about O’DAD’s sisterhood and tradition of finesse. Though she might slow Havana for the moment, BJ held out little hope it would last.

Havana tramped toward BJ, holding out the cell. “She wants to know if we can all meet here later this morning. Eight thirty.” She slapped the phone into BJ’s outstretched fingers and shoved past her into the living room.

Her meeting with Lo in mind, BJ said, “Sure, the earlier the better.”

After confirming their meet with Marilee, BJ addressed the Bobbsey twins.

“Since we’re all going to meet here tomorrow, ya’ll are welcome to spend the night.” She didn’t relish the idea of killers sleeping under her roof, but at least she’d know where they were.

“We’ll be back,” Havana said. She glanced at Jax and jerked her head toward the door.

BJ followed as they marched out. Then she locked the door and fell with her back against it. Too tired to shower, she crawled into her sleigh bed in nothing but her taupe silk thong. She snuggled into her pillow and hoped that her AWOL in the morning would nudge Lo to her meet.

Three Syringes

I shot up to the thud on the floor. Al spun off my belly. Had I fed him? My rheumy eyes blinked open toward the sound. My .45's muzzle lay against the router's bulge in my rucksack. I grabbed my buzzing head. Dizzy but no ripping headache? I took stock of my tingling body and tongued my parched mouth. Thirsty but no pain yet. Damn, still tipsy.

How hard did I crash? Did Sandoval call? My answering machine's steady red light signaled empty. I yanked up the receiver and knocked over Ricky's lamp. The tough vase hit the shag carpet without a crack. I slapped the air and left it on the floor. No dial tone?

"Shit."

I'd forgotten I'd disconnected it yesterday. I plugged it in and called Sandoval. Answering machine. I slammed down the receiver, recalling it might be tapped.

I glanced at my watch. "Seven thirty. Christ." My physical's at eight. I called the clinic to reschedule. Better to postpone than show up drunk.

"Nothin' for two weeks? I'll be there," I said, desperate to get back on the job.

Dammit. No time to buy a disposable cell.

After holstering Mr. Colt, I lurched into the bathroom. Gulped down a glass of water, then washed down a couple of aspirins, hoping to soften the throb once I sobered up. After rinsing my face, I splashed on after-shave and gargled with mouthwash.

I knew I'd be late. But if Nurse Tsige was on duty, she'd cut me some slack. The Ethiopian immigrant had served as an army nurse in the first Gulf War. She'd weaseled out of me that I'd been to Nam. We became fast friends.

But if Dr. Snyder was at the clinic, my buzz would end up highlighted in my chart. He never forgave me for the ticket I gave him twenty-five years ago. The minor injuries he'd seen me for in the past had never served up a chance for him to get me back. He wouldn't miss it now.

I swung by my fridge, yanked a bottle of water from the shelf, and stuffed it into my jacket pocket. Knew I'd need it. But Frank's tequila still left bounce in my step. I wouldn't have felt half bad if not for my damned appointment.

"Anh," Al said, as he rubbed against my leg.

"No, I'm not forgetting you," I said, reaching for his can of Mother's Organic Kitty Food.

With the router in my rucksack and wearing the clothes I'd slept in, I got to the clinic late. A skinny nurse I didn't recognize sat behind the counter in the drab reception room. I strode up, but her cloudy gray eyes wouldn't budge from her computer. I cleared my throat.

"Detective Faeth. Here for my physical." I tried not to sound ignored.

She pounded the keys, then snapped, "You're late."

"Squeeze me in tomorrow. I'll come back, I promise," I said against all hope.

"Today, or in two weeks. Your call," she said, her nose glued to her screen.

"I guess I'm stayin'."

"Take a seat. You'll be called. Eventually."

I took a swig of water to cool off, then sat next to a uniformed cop with his arm in a sling. He coughed into his good fist and moved to a chair across from me. Too much aftershave?

Soon I heard the nurse say, "He was late," followed by Tsige's rhythmic tone. "It's all right, we have time to see him now."

Tsige's bright grin lit up the hallway where she stood. The flowers on her colorful scrubs seemed to glow against her caramel skin. Bracing a manila medical record against her chest, she said, "Detective Faeth, please come with me."

Nurse Ratched's glare followed me to the mouth of the corridor.

"Detective Faeth, how—" Tsige winced, stalling our stroll down the hall. She flipped her long, braided hair over her shoulders and pushed herself up on her tiptoes. She swept her nose across my collar. "All-night party, bad boy?"

Damn, I smelled like the drunk BJ told Rhodes I was. But what could he do, suspend me again?

"Yeah, I overdid it."

Tsige paged through my file as she glanced at me. "Is this a routine physical?"

"Not really." Didn't know what else to say.

"There's nothing in your record that suggests an alcohol problem."

Rhodes's spin on my suspension peeked outta the fog. "Forced vacation. Hadn't taken one in years. Hadn't had a physical either. Drank too much 'cause I don't like being told what to do. Even for my own good. Hey, who's the doc today?"

Tsige clucked her tongue, prepping me for the bad news. "I am afraid it is your old friend Dr. Snyder."

The toaster's in. But I couldn't afford the wait for the next appointment, could I?

She led me to an exam room, where I hung up my shoulder holster and rucksack, then draped my jacket over them. I rolled up my sleeve so she could take my blood pressure. She also took my temp and handed me a backless faded-blue gown.

"Take your clothes off down to your underwear, and put this on. When the doctor is finished, don't leave before you see me again."

I didn't know what she had in mind, but I dipped my chin and said, "You got it."

After I changed into the gown, I sat on the paper-lined exam table. Had my cheeks clamped against the chill or in fear of Snyder's pitiless finger?

The door swished open and in stepped Snyder in his long white coat. Flat-footed in his Birkenstock sandals, he squinted.

"It's you," he said and yanked my folder from the door rack.

Ricky had once said that the best way to destroy your enemies is to make them your friends. Hell, it's worth a shot, suggested my twinging rectum.

"Dr. Snyder, that ticket was twenty-five—"

He poked the air with his index finger to shut me up without looking up from my chart. In a tone as sincere as Dr. Crusher's, he said, "Tut-tut, detective. Water under the bridge." Then his voice rumbled deeply. "Turn around and bend over."

I watched Snyder snap on his gloves. "Is this necessary, Doc?"

He squeezed a glob of gel onto his finger. "You're over fifty. It's routine."

After a probe I swear included figure eights, Dr. Snyder inserted his stethoscope into his ears. It struck me that he'd performed a double rectal insertion. I choked off a laugh. He leaned toward my heart but jerked back.

"You are one ripe cop."

"Yeah, I went a little overboard last night." I reeked and couldn't blame Snyder.

"Just last night?" Snyder then held up a breathalyzer and pointed the tube in my face. "You know the drill. Blow." The slow climb of the digital numbers didn't strain the contempt out of his voice. "Count your blessings. You're below .08."

"Smelly but legal," I said before I could stop myself.

"Instructive," he countered.

I tried to keep the ass out of my tone. "I'm telling ya, Doc, I don't have an alcohol problem. You caught me on a rare morning."

Snyder licked the corners of his mouth like a wolf sizing up his lunch. "Let's allow the lab results to speak for themselves, shall we? Who knows what they might find. Cirrhosis, perhaps?"

Shaddap, Faeth, I repeated to myself,

After scribbling in my file, he said, "Stay here and wait for the phlebotomist to draw your blood." He left without another word.

I got dressed after the lab coat took my blood and waited for Tsige. Felt confident my results would be fine. Took some comfort in that Snyder wasn't the shrink.

Tsige swooped in, closed the door, and said in half a whisper, "Detective, roll up your sleeves." She held up three syringes but noticed my focus on the needles. She chuckled. "You will thank me for these when the alcohol wears off."

"What are they?"

Tsige flicked each syringe with one of her shiny nails as she told me their contents. "Thiamine, folic acid, and super B vitamin complex with vitamin C. Trust me, they will ease your hangover." Then she reached over to where my coat hung and tapped the top of my water bottle in the side pocket. "Do not stop taking in fluids either. Now let Tsige start with your right arm." She swabbed her target.

Eager to return to duty, I asked her if there was anything she could do to flip those lab results ASAP.

"I will push along my friends in the lab," she said as she broke the syringes into their disposal box.

I slowed down outside on the clinic steps and whipped out my wallet for BJ's note. I'd missed last night's chance to poke her chest. Today at eleven she'd be at Golden Gate Park's Conservatory of Flowers. I checked my watch: less than an hour to go. Buying a cell would have to wait.

From my trunk, I traded my sport coat for a hooded sweatshirt and mirrored wraparound shades. I had a stop to make and couldn't be recognized.

Let's Mend Fences

BJ had opened her door for O'DAD's grande dame just before eight thirty. The killers promptly followed. Marilee insisted on making breakfast and then started their meeting with, "Let's mend fences."

BJ sat on her sofa across from Marilee. She'd quietly muted her landline and her SFPD cell to avoid Rhodes. He and her fellow cops, especially Lo, had to see she not only hadn't shown up at the station but didn't answer her phones either. She counted on her absence to snag Lo.

The ladies' sewing circle dragged on. With each passing moment, the risk of Rhodes sending a cruiser to check on her ticked up. She couldn't risk being found at home. It would contradict her alibi that she'd been out following leads.

She shifted in her chair, trying to convince herself that Lo swallowed her bait. That he'd meet her at the Conservatory of Flowers. BJ shot a peek at her mantel clock over Marilee's shoulder. The squeeze of its filigreed hands now on the downside of ten. Less than an hour from her meet with Lo. She felt like a trapped fox hankering to chew off its leg.

"BJ, did Detective Faeth schedule a meeting?" Marilee asked, apparently catching BJ's glance behind her. Her voice sounded innocent enough.

"The problem is, he hasn't." BJ jabbed her finger at her SFPD cell next to her O'DAD mobile on the coffee table in front of her. "Been waitin' for his call. I would've told you." She regretted her curt reply, driven by their tedious meeting. She'd anticipated plenty of time to ditch Havana and make it to the conservatory.

"Of course, hon," Marilee said.

BJ watched Marilee's smile wilt before it reached her eyes.

"Would she?" Havana perched herself at the edge of BJ's Windsor chair. Jax, cross-legged at her feet, cocked her head. "She likes the guy," Havana said.

BJ bristled at Havana's contempt and snapped, "You two amateurs would've scared him off last night if I hadn't—"

Marilee put up her hand to cut off BJ and spoke to Havana. "If Detective Faeth had caught you two last night, it would've cost us all of BJ's influence over the man. He'll get the router to her today." She smiled at BJ. "Won't he, hon?"

BJ, stuck in her own bluff, snarled at Havana and Jax, "That's the deal." Out of the corner of her eye, she caught Marilee's glance back at the clock. Her fire toward the killers frosted with alarm. Her only influence over the two remained through Marilee. If she failed to retrieve the router today, it would plop manure on that sprig of doubt in Marilee's eyes. BJ visibly shuddered, but recovered to stand up and announce, "Pee shiver. Goin' to potty."

Marilee and the twins traded glances and BJ swore she felt their gazes follow her out of the parlor.

♦ ♦ ♦

I stashed my Buick a couple of blocks from Central Station. With my hood up, mirrored wraparounds on, I hustled toward Max's garage. See if BJ'd stopped by and coughed up a lead or two.

Max sat in his ticket booth, his eyes moving across the pages of a crumpled paperback I'd never heard of, *The Outsider.*

I rapped on the sliding window and said, "Psst, Max. Have you seen BJ?"

Max casually raised his gaze and slid open his window. Crinkling his nose, he said, "Whew, brother. Water company turn off your shower?"

Tsige might have saved me from a crushing hangover, but she was powerless over my reek. "Look, I let go a little last night. So, what about BJ?"

"Didn't see her, and you can't miss that roach-head hybrid of hers. One more antenna and it's exterminator bait. Makes me wonder what kind of kickbacks Tokyo gets from Texaco for keeping those hybrids so bug ugly."

BJ didn't show? My heart pounded up BJ's warning if she lost her cover: "We're both targets." I'd missed last night's meet. Was that enough to dot her head with a laser sight? A rattle outta Ricky's closet reminded me that she wasn't the first I'd deserted.

"I can't think about your Big Oil spin now, Max." My voice dropped, tugged by my fear for BJ's safety. "Do me a favor, call the desk sergeant. Ask if BJ's checked in."

Max squinted. I knew that look. He'd spotted rustling in the tree line. But he pulled out his phone, and I gave him the number.

"She hasn't called or come in." Max's tone bottomed out. "Yesterday, BJ drove by me, staring straight ahead like she didn't know me. Then took off without you. Today, she didn't show and you creep in here worried sick about her. And you can't even call your own station. What's up with you two? BJ all right?"

"Ahem...ah, that's what I'm going to find out. Gotta go." I spun around to split.

"That's all you got to say?" Max asked.

"Sorry." I hotfooted it toward my Buick and Golden Gate Park.

I crouched down to pet an elderly lady's shaved poodle across the street from the Conservatory of Flowers. As the old gal excitedly explained "Brigitte thinks she's human," I checked out the people entering the swanky glass structure. No BJ or anyone fitting her descriptions of Havana or Jax. I stood up, complimented the lady's spoiled pooch, and said adios. Flipping up my sweatshirt's hood and slipping on my shades, I strolled into the conservatory's humid air.

While my mirrored shades focused on the exotic plants, my eyes searched the twisting aisles for BJ and possible tails. No one appeared interested in me, and I didn't see BJ. Between my talk with Max and the traffic, I'd arrived twenty minutes late. Maybe she'd come and gone. I gulped down my disappointment with a slug of water.

Missing BJ fanned my fears for her safety. I stalled before a carnivorous red flower. My sappy ticker's next shot was point-blank. What if she's dead? I'd come here to see her in one piece as much as to get answers, hadn't I?

BJ's AWOL knotted up with Ricky's disappearance. Cramps bit my gut. If I hadn't deserted Ricky, those teeth wouldn't be as sharp. I massaged my belly.

Dammit, I shouldn't have stopped by Max's. I bolted outside to find a pay phone. Needed to hear BJ's voice.

After a drawn-out hike to find a pay phone, I paged through my address book for BJ's number. I punched in all but her final digit when my finger froze. Maybe she's okay but under suspicion, keeping her from our meet. If I called and left a message—and the killers had access to her phone—it'd rip the skin off her cover. If she didn't answer, I'd have to keep my trap shut. I pressed the number and listened to her Dixie jingle roll over into her voice mail. I decided it was time for some old-fashioned gumshoe. I'd hit her house.

She'd Take A Shot

BJ locked her keen eyes on anybody and anything that remotely smacked of a tail as she ground through traffic toward Golden Gate Park. She'd bugged out of Marilee's lunch invitation after Havana and Jax's acceptance, citing police obligations.

She'd called the mystery number logged as a missed call, and a drunk answered with a slurred "Hell-oh." A pay phone. Who else but Lo would've used one? Rhodes couldn't track it. She wished the old technophobe would buy a burner.

BJ's dashboard clock put her close to noon, nearly an hour late. If her AWOL drove Lo to Golden Gate Park and she'd missed him, once she surfaced unharmed, he'd never fall for that again. She bit her bottom lip. She'd take a shot at finding him at the conservatory.

♦ ♦ ♦

Cruising past BJ's, I watched the uniformed cop get into his black-and-white parked out front. Had he talked to her?

I circled the block to avoid the officer, doubled back, and banged on BJ's door. Not a sound. After peeking through her windows and seeing no evidence of a struggle, my foggy brain ran aground. My snooping had got me nowhere.

I glanced at my watch. Sandoval took lunch between twelve thirty and one. He could call BJ anytime. I hauled over to Hunters Point and our Forensics Division. Good thing I carried a duplicate badge. Today it would come in handy.

♦ ♦ ♦

BJ scoured the conservatory. Without Faeth, hope spun into doubt. Had he come? Why should he? If he had, what'd he make of her no-show? Had he called from that pay phone? Had to be him.

Stepping outside, BJ knelt to pet a granny's cropped poodle. She hated poodles but felt the old were unappreciated. She forced out a "Nice puppy." As they chatted, BJ scanned the vast green lawn for a chance glimpse of Lo.

"Brigitte's so spoiled, I'm afraid it goes to her head." The giddy senior laughed. "Even that gruff, swollen-faced gentleman with the one-way sunglasses was taken by her."

BJ popped up, her simmering tummy cooled. Lo? But before she could speak, Grandma leaned into her and through a sly grin whispered, "Musta been looking for you too. You the reason that poor man drank so much? Broke a few hearts in my day too. Smell a bender a mile away." Without a blink, she pointed toward JFK Drive. "Missed him by a few. But maybe you can catch him. He walked thataway, toward the panhandle."

"Thank ya, ma'am," BJ said with a wink. She sauntered off. The spring in her step furnished by Lo's attempt to meet her. That his was the mystery call.

BJ searched as far as Haight Street. Didn't find Lo. Had she squandered her last ounce of influence over him? Her stride became sluggish, and she felt her department cell's vibration. Multiple messages from Captain Rhodes. She had to check in at the station to assuage her hysterical boss. But it'd give her a chance to quiz Max. Maybe he'd seen Lo.

She slipped her hybrid into the precinct garage and beelined to Max's. She turned the corner smack-dab into his gaze.

Max slid open his window. "You all right?"

"Of course," BJ said, taken aback. Then she figured, Lo talked to him. But what'd he tell Max?

Max glanced over BJ's shoulders. "Faeth catch up with you?"

"You saw him." BJ brushed dog hair from her knee to distract Max from her thumping jugular. "Been looking for the ornery cuss."

Max's gaze never broke. "Came by this morning looking for you. Worried sick. And, why can't he call your station?"

There was no hiding trouble from Max, but she couldn't let it bleed into a target on his chest. "We're at odds over a case. Captain made him take time off to cool down. What'd Grumpy say?"

Max folded his arms across his chest. "He's as vague as you. But from where I sit, he thinks you're in danger."

Boosted by Lo's acknowledgement that she's at risk, BJ patted Max's windowsill. Would it be enough to get him to her note's last meet?

"I'm not a cop, but if there is anything I can do to help, you tell me," Max said, his voice as serious as a heart attack.

"Don't you worry, dahlin'. We'll be okay," BJ said, touched by Max's offer. But she'd lied. Until she recovered that router, nobody was okay. She stomped off toward the station.

It Don't Pass the Smell Test

I pulled next to the guard booth at the Forensics Division at Hunters Point. The sleepy-eyed rent-a-cop gave my backup shield a courtesy glance and waved me through into the parking lot. I spotted Sandoval's classic '58 Chevy and parked. With luck, he hadn't taken his lunch break.

Sneaking behind a communications van, I realized that the tequila-fired bounce in my step had fizzled out without detonating an explosion in my head. Except for a dry throat and a fuzzy brain, Nurse Tsige saved me.

My eyes filled with the naturally tanned Sandoval strolling out of the building in his cargo pants and Pendleton shirt. I watched the mustachioed PhD take a rubber band from between his teeth and tie his dark hair into a ponytail. He slid into his shiny black Impala.

"Where the hell have you been?" I hissed under my breath. The router squeaked from my rucksack. I glanced down. My grip on it had become bloodless, white. Then I remembered. I'd unplugged my phone. Sandoval couldn't reach me at home if he'd tried. My mind relaxed, as did my grip on the router. The grateful plastic creaked in relief.

Sandoval had installed seat belts in his cherry Impala. So while he buckled up, I crept over and rapped on his spotless passenger window.

Sandoval's dark eyes widened above his raised cheekbones. He scanned the lot while leaning over to the passenger door to pop up the lock. "Get in but stay down. The word is you're persona non grata. That you nutted up on BJ."

So much for Rhodes's vacation cover.

Sandoval continued. "I've been trying to reach you. Got your message that Rhodes took your cell. When I returned your page, your answering machine didn't pick up."

"I forgot that I unplugged it," I said, crawling onto the tuck-and-roll front seat while clutching the rucksack to my chest.

Sandoval rolled even his English r's. At first, his LA barrio tongue didn't square with his smarts to my gringo ears. But I got to know him. He explained his "verbal swagger" with a defiant grin. "Every time I open my mouth you're going to hear this proud Chicano from East Los Angeles." I'd watched a lot a fools trip over his tongue, only to be stunned by his IQ. He was his own man.

On my belly, it occurred to me that he was my brother's age. My respect for him snapped back, stinging Ricky's scab. He wouldn't have turned his back on his brother. I stalled.

"Come on, come on, homeboy," he said, unfreezing me. He stretched over me and shut the door. "What's in the backpack?"

"I got something to show you. Where've you been? I've been calling your house."

Sandoval twisted his ignition key, and I felt the V-8 rumble. Flipping his hand toward me as if to toss me the name, he snorted, "With Chata." He looked over his shoulder and backed up the Chevy.

Bobbing up my head I said, "Chata. Your new girlfriend?"

"Yep. Keep your head down till we get outta the parking lot," he said, shifting into drive. Then he pinched his nose. "Phew, *fuchi*." He cranked down his window. "You smell like last night's cantina."

"Tequila mind douche," I said as the cool air whipped away my smell.

"Anyway, the night before last, I had a couple of shots myself at the Dew Drop Inn. That South of Market Street bar. This fine lady hits on me. The next thing I know, my little head has talked me into driving us to a no-tell motel. Guess who pulls up behind us?"

"Chata?" I shook my head, sorry I'd asked. Streetwise Sandoval pulled wide past the guard booth. No sense in us being seen together. I squished under the dash.

"Scorched by the fire in Chata's eyes, the other babe split faster than enriched uranium. I sobered up quicker than a Mexican in a *migra* raid." He glanced at me. "You know, immigration. I've been trying to fix it with Chata ever since. Took her to lunch yesterday, dinner last night. Trying everything to convince her that I'm not the whore I really am."

Knotted up, I started to unfold from under the dash.

He waved me back down. "Wait, let's put a little distance between us and Forensics. BJ told me you got all weird at Bambi's and split. *¿Que pasó?*"

"You spoke to BJ today?" I asked, excited that she was okay.

"Nah. At the crime scene."

My heartbeat took a dive. BJ's body, splayed in a smear of blood, cracked between us. "Listen, BJ didn't report for duty today. Call her cell. See if she answers."

Sandoval dug for his smartphone, his eyes darting between me and the traffic. "You're worried about her." Then he hesitated. "There's a condition."

"What's that?"

"You can't talk to her."

My temp spiked. "Why not?"

Sandoval rolled his eyes. "Like I said, the word is that you're persona non grata. No stop signs between that and your message that Rhodes banned you from department contact. You wanna keep your job?"

Sandoval was right. Especially if I was BJ's patsy. Still, I grumbled, "Deal. Call her." I watched him cram his Bluetooth into his ear and with a voice command call, "Detective Reeves."

"*Hola,* BJ. *¿Cómo estás?* Sandoval listened, then stretched his face in my direction. Telling me he hadn't caught any distress.

My relief felt dirty. Like I'd been had. Did she skip checking in at the precinct to hook me? My cheeks started to burn.

"*¿Todo bien?*...Not really, eh?...Uh, why'd I call? I tried reaching you earlier at Central Station. They told me you hadn't reported in—You're there now." Sandoval bared his teeth and scrunched his shoulders.

"Musta called before you got there....Of course, lots of detectives follow up on leads before hitting their station. Shoulda called your cell....At Golden Gate Park, huh?...Sure, if I see Faeth, I'll tell him poodle lady said hello. He'll understand?" Sandoval shot me a crooked smile.

I nodded. BJ'd gotten to the park after me. What held her up? Maybe I should be worried.

Sandoval went on. "Oh, I called to tell you I got nothing new on Bambi's blast. You know, keep you in the loop....Sure, if I hear from him, I'll tell him to call you." He disconnected. "She knew you were listening."

"She say so, or is that your gut talking?" I asked, irritated by the tingling in my legs for lack of circulation and my confusion over BJ. "Can I get up now?" I added, desperate for relief.

Sandoval did a double take and flapped the air between us. "Get up, homeboy. Get up. And leave my gut out of this. You're the one who listens to his *panza*. Didn't take much for BJ to see through us. She knows I don't call to say I got nothin' new." His voice pitched with the obvious.

"Poodle lady, huh?" he said, his weak smile growing bigger. "You went to meet her, didn't you? So much for Rhodes's orders, eh? Come on, tell me what's up."

I tried to punch through the cobwebs. "Sandoval, I'm not sure. And yeah, I did try to meet her. Get some answers. Now I'm counting on you for some."

♦ ♦ ♦

BJ recognized Sandoval's empty update for what it was. Lo's amigo's flimsy excuse for a fishing trip. She'd bet money Lo'd been sitting there, listening. Understood she'd showed late for their meet. But he couldn't know the bind that held her back. And likely figured she'd baited him.

She damned herself for missing him. Her skin tingled with fear that he'd snub tonight's meet. Then the obvious struck her. He'd give Sandoval the router. She slapped her desk.

“Something wrong, Detective?” Rhodes said from behind. He peered down over his coffee mug.

BJ forced a smile. “No, suh. Just thought of something, that’s all.”

“What is it?” he said, sipping his java.

“Just a hunch. Tell ya if it comes to something, Captain.”

Rhodes glanced at his watch, mumbled, and waddled into his office.

She inhaled deeply and studied her partner’s desk. How could she get him to tonight’s rendezvous and to bring that miserable router?

BJ stared into her desktop and wiggled the mouse. The screen’s glow seemed to burn with images of Sandoval’s nose in that router.

♦ ♦ ♦

“Help me out here, Sandoval. What time did you get to Bambi’s?” I said.

“Around four thirty, just after BJ called and interrupted my marathon pleas to Chata for forgiveness.”

“She told me she called you at two.” Though he’d only confirmed what I already knew, I flinched at reality’s bite.

“BJ lied,” he said through a disappointed stretch of his tongue.

“Listen, you know Dr. Crusher?”

“The new coroner? I see her around.”

Sandoval would have told Rhodes if anyone else was at the crime scene, but I had to hear it for myself. “Was she or anyone else besides BJ inside Bambi’s when you and your team arrived?”

He furrowed his brow. “Uniforms were outside, but BJ was the only one inside the place. Why’d you ask about Dr. Crusher?”

“A woman calling herself Dr. Crusher led in a team while I was there. Said your crew was busy at another homicide.”

“You’re not sure it was her?”

Rubbing the back of my neck, I said, “I’m sure, but I’ve never met her and she kept blinding me with her flashlight. Kept me from getting anything but a blurry look at her.”

Sandoval stiffened his back, and I recognized the skeptical slide of his jaw from one side to the other. His objectivity often clashed with my hunches. "That your *panza* saying it's Dr. Crusher?"

Turning my whole body to face him, I raised my voice. "It's more than my gut. An imposter wouldn't have bothered blinding me. One look at the real Crusher, and I'd have to admit she wasn't at Bambi's. Yours and BJ's reports that BJ was alone at the crime scene stacked up against me insisting an imposter was there woulda guaranteed my place in a rubber room. They wouldn'ta missed that chance."

Sandoval kept his eyes on the oncoming traffic. "How do you explain her phony CSI team getting into Bambi's without being seen by anyone but you?"

"Whose side are you on? North Beach is full of interconnected basements. Crusher's team could've easily snuck in."

"Suppose that's possible," he said, his tone bored and unconvinced. Sandoval punched his Impala through a yellow light, chirping the tires.

"At least do me a favor. Can you get me a recording of Crusher's voice?"

Sandoval casually nodded. "We digitally record our reports. Shouldn't be a problem capturing hers. You remember it?"

"Yeah. Thanks." Sandoval's jury was out on Crusher until I could say, That's her voice. "What'd BJ tell you?"

Sandoval squeezed his red-and-white steering wheel. "BJ told me that you'd been drinking and that you two argued over whether the vic's death was a homicide or an accident. That you lost your temper and split." Sandoval glanced between me and the traffic. "I know you can get touchy. But you leaving her alone? I know better than that. When I quizzed her about it, all she did was throw up her hands and walk away. That didn't sit right with me either. BJ always has a read on things, especially you," he smirked.

My confidence staggered. BJ knew me, all right. My feelings for her kept finding excuses for her. Couldn't admit she was mixed up in hiding more than a murder and had made me her fall guy. I clenched my jaw, but BJ's warning that I'd put her between me and the killers socked back. I shook my head to shake it off.

Sandoval raised an eyebrow. "You okay, homeboy?"

"Yeah, yeah, I'm fine. BJ and Crusher are covering up a killing. A murder that threatens to expose something bigger."

His head jerked back. "Something bigger?"

With no more than a hunch locked up in that router, I ignored his question. "What'd BJ submit into evidence?"

"A burnt plastic purse, .38, and a cell phone."

"No UPS, right?"

"Uninterrupted power supply? No." Sandoval glared at me like he'd caught me snooping through his diary.

He looked away, and I studied his profile. He'd arrived after Crusher and her gang. I knew Crusher's crew took the UPS and cleared away any other evidence before he got there. But his hot glare? Had he found something the Crusherteers missed?

I slid the router out of the rucksack. This time I got his needled squint. "You're connecting dots, Sandoval."

Torn between his attention to the traffic and his interest in the router, he said, "Let me find a quiet place to park." Sandoval wove us toward Natoma Street and parked under the bus terminal overpass.

I stripped the plastic bag off the router and handed it to him.

Sandoval took it by its corners, his eyes fixed on the thing. "You got this from Bambi's?"

I nodded once, then added, "My prints are all over it. Probably smeared the hell out of any others."

With his eyes fixed on the device, he muttered, "BJ never mentioned it." Turning to me he said, "Where was it?"

"In a cabinet under the powder-room sink. This is making sense to you, isn't it?" The stench of urine seeped into the car as he studied the router. "Couldn't you find a nastier place to stop?"

He snorted a laugh. “Take a whiff of yourself.” He rested the router in his lap and tossed his hand toward the homeless packed into sleeping bags along the sidewalk. “Look around. Like them, we’re invisible here. Just the way polite society likes it.”

I hadn’t noticed the bums. Last night’s tequila apparently fouled up my eyesight along with my smell. “Don’t change the subject.” I poked toward the router. “Did you find hardware related to that thing?”

Sandoval’s gaze wandered off. Sliding to the edge of the seat, I growled, “Dammit, Sandoval. What is it?”

In a hollow tone, he said, “I didn’t find any hardware or Internet cables at the scene.”

I raised my voice. “Then what?”

He pointed with his chin toward my belly. “I told you, trusting your gut is your thing. My job is to dig up the evidence to support your intuition. Or not.”

Damn him. The tight ass had something but wouldn’t spill it without his tangible proof. I reached over, grabbed the router, and crammed it back into my rucksack. “You’re as useful as jock itch. I’m outta here,” I said, and gripped the door handle.

“Don’t split on me like you did BJ,” Sandoval said and snickered. “Until I get inside that router, it’s no more than any other pedestrian device.”

I sat back on the edge of his seat and glared. “Then you’ll check it out?”

Sandoval nodded. “Of course.”

His tone told me he was in my corner. I still needed to know what he held back, but confronting him hadn’t popped it loose. Sandoval knew I liked BJ and that she’d set me up. If I told him I’d go back to her for answers, would he cough up his secret?

I locked my eyes to his. “There’s something else, Sandoval. BJ came to my condo after she got me suspended.”

“What’d she have to say?”

“I was pissed, so when she knocked, I kept my mouth shut. Acted like I wasn’t home. But she’d heard my TV and banged on my door.” He didn’t need to hear I'd almost wimped out and let her in. "She slipped a note under my door before stomping off. It said I was in danger. Gave me a list of places to meet her. That's why I went to Golden Gate Park."

"You've been threatened," he said.

There was no question mark in his tone. What'd he know? "I'll meet her and trade this router for answers." I hoped that would crack him open.

Sandoval cringed. "Don't do it, homeboy. Your dead vic may not be the first."

"Whoa. Now what are you saying? No more hide-and-seek, pal." My fingers dug into his seat cushion.

He glanced at his crumpled upholstery. "A couple of years ago, a hooker was found garroted in the ladies' room of a Tenderloin bar. Her death was written off as an unsolved robbery-homicide."

Another powder-room death? BJ's note said she's tracking a serial killer. My squirrelly belly said he had more. "Give it up, Sandoval," I snarled, scratching the air between us.

"I later heard that she'd gone to Tenderloin Vice and asked for police protection. She knew them. Had popped her once or twice. She said members of a secret society were after her."

Secret society. Not a gang of arsonists torching upside-down buildings in an insurance scam. Points for BJ. But no link to national security. "What else?" I said.

"She said they wanted her dead because they'd found out she was a transgender girl and that she had evidence to expose them."

My brother's image in spiked heels sliced between us like a rusty blade. Against the sudden kink in my belly, I asked, "That hooker was a guy passing as a girl? A...transvestite?"

"No, transgender."

I blinked. "And the diff?"

"I'm no expert, but I think transvestites just dress up like the opposite sex. Transgenders are more inclined to surgically reverse their plumbing, like that Tenderloin vic," he said with about as much strain as if he'd described somebody changing the part in their hair.

That made my brother a transvestite, right? Relief swamped my belly until soured by dread. "Sandoval, does one lead to the other?"

"Don't know."

I dropped the question next to my shattered relief. But if I helped BJ stop Havana, maybe it'd be a payment toward my debt to Ricky. "That vic give up that secret society's name?"

Sandoval paused and took a breath. "I'm sure my homies at Vice noted it. I'll pull her case file."

"Why'd my router remind you of that?"

Sandoval's cheeks deflated after a weak whistle. "Vice told me they brushed her off as a paranoid crack whore and gave her the number to rehab. But she insisted she had proof and dumped a router out of her purse."

The vic had a router. I'd put BJ's name on a bullet by stealing that damned device. Father Harlan's gay bashing thumped about my head and jarred up my brother's memory. Is Ricky dead? Is that why he's barging into my dreams? Grief rooster tailed across my chest. A real man would've defended his kid brother. A real cop would back his partner.

"BJ's a mole. Penetrated a clique that kills transgener women. Her note said so," I mumbled.

Sandoval glared at me. "Keep your fists up, homeboy. I liked BJ too, but you're looking at her through your heart's lens. The only thing we know for sure is that she screwed you."

Staggering but in BJ's corner, I said, "What about your dead hooker and his router?" My voice cracked. The thought of a man cut into a woman chapped my throat.

"Let's not latch on to odd coincidences." Then his voice lowered. "I'm sorry I brought up that Tenderloin whore. BJ's threat knocked me ahead of the evidence."

Straining to loosen my vocal cords, I said, "Nice to know your ticker can rev over that digital brain of yours once in a while."

"Look. Bambi's vic didn't possess the router. She happened to die in a powder room where you found one. But if her vagina isn't original equipment, maybe there's a connection between her and that Tenderloin hooker. Maybe?"

Despite Sandoval, both our victims were murdered in powder rooms and involved routers. Plus, his hooker's murder coincided with BJ's arrival in San Francisco. Another part of BJ's note could hammer at coincidence. "See if there's a spike in homicide rates for transgender females over the past two years. Her note says they're higher," I said, then thought out loud, "Is there a difference between transgender and transsexual?"

"Transsexual is an old-school term, I think. But listen, you're missing the obvious. That note's got you making excuses for BJ. Don't be her sucker."

"She put herself in danger passing it to me," I said, ignoring his warning.

He patted the top of his steering wheel. "Let me see it."

My elbow cramped reaching for my wallet. What if the keen bastard spotted something I'd missed? Showed me I was BJ's chump?

Sandoval's chin dropped toward his chest, but his eyes never left mine. "Come on, homey. Give it to me."

I dragged out the note and put it into his palm.

Sandoval fingered the paper as he read. "Strange texture. Typed, not signed. And cryptic." He glanced at me. "Maybe murky enough to sucker you in. And that national security rap? Hard to resist, eh?"

He'd said maybe. "No obvious trip wires?" I blurted.

"No, but it don't pass the smell test." He shook his head, adding, "She tells you that if you give me the router, you'll put my name atop the killers' hit list. Can't you see she's trying to scare you away from answers? Give me back the router."

"Smell test? She described the killers, Havana Vives and Jax." In lockstep with my gut, my ticker nixed me as BJ's patsy.

"Sounds like she pulled those names from a comic book. And why not describe Crusher?"

I shook my head, convinced I'd compromised BJ. "Maybe she's saying that Crusher is no murderer. Says right there her mission is surgical. She's after those Havana and Jax broads. You're wrong about her."

In a tight voice he said, "Okay, then let me help you prove it. Don't do anything until I've reviewed the case file from that Tenderloin homicide and checked out that router."

"I should get it back to her," I said.

"No way, homeboy. Until I prove otherwise, you're BJ's mark. Hand it over."

"Okay, okay, but make it quick." Though I'd caved, I didn't intend to wait for him to prove BJ's innocence. I'd make her note's next meet, but in a tip of my hat to Sandoval, I'd go in disguise. Make sure BJ was alone before exposing myself. Not because I thought it was a setup, but because those Havana and Jax characters could be shadowing BJ too. My partner might need backup. Once certain BJ was alone, I'd reveal myself. Let her know I intended to turn over the router.

I pulled out the Baggie containing BJ's envelope and dangled it between us. "This held BJ's note. Check for hers or anybody else's prints. See if BJ Reeves is a cover name. And run those names, Havana Vives and Jax."

Sandoval clucked his tongue and said, "Without any more detail, all I got is one and a half names. You ask me, they're nothing but worms on a hook."

"Give it a shot, will ya?" I said, rocking the Baggie back and forth.

Sandoval nodded and took it. With his index finger crookedly pointed in my direction, he shook a loose fist at me. "Don't meet up with BJ until you hear from me. *¿Comprende?*"

"You've got the router. No point in meeting her without it," I said, then changed the subject. "Can whatever's in that router be connected to the missing UPS or my victim's phone?"

"UPS, no. Phone, maybe." After what I took as a thoughtful pucker, he said, "BJ knew you had the router. So why did she risk turning in the cell?"

"Chief Ferrus spotted the phone near the body. BJ couldn't risk her cred by not logging it in."

Sandoval smirked. "You splitting from the crime scene made it easier for her to lift her leg over your rep than the chief's, eh?"

I wasn't amused. "What can you learn from the router and cell?"

Sandoval shrugged. "To be honest, a router is a forwarding device. It's not intended for storage. On the surface, there's no reason for BJ's interest. Still, with all the shit splatter around this thing, it must be worth something. I'll connect it to the lab's Internet and fire it up with your victim's cell. See if they're unique. And I should be able to find stored web addresses in the phone and possibly unravel an access code or two."

From the depths of my Luddite brain emerged the dull glimmer of an idea. I looked around the interior of the Chevy as if searching for light. "Do women's bathrooms have Internet access?"

Sandoval crinkled his nose. "Who'd want to net surf in the toilet?"

My thought crystallized. "Nobody. That's the point, see? Who'd look in a powder room for a secret, uh...what do you call them?—Wi-Fi hot spot?"

Sandoval shook his head. "Your feelings for BJ have choked off the oxygen to your brain."

On a roll, I ignored his shot. "The vic was trapped."

"What?" he said, his face twisted.

I drove on. "My vic died because she knew what your vic did. About that secret society's hidden hot spots. The killers locked her in the powder room and triggered the fire alarm to scare off witnesses."

"What are you talking about, triggering the alarm?"

Braced for his skeptic's thump, I was struck instead by his fat gaze. "Yeah, the witnesses from the bar said the fire alarm went off before they ever smelled smoke or gas. Not a whiff until after the explosion. Except for the lone vic, nobody got a scratch."

Sandoval's gaze drifted. Mentioning the fire alarm, like the router, jarred something loose.

I followed a hunch and asked, "Was that Tenderloin hooker locked in a ladies' room while an alarm cleared out everybody else?"

He squeezed his lips together before he spoke. "An alarm emptied the bar just before closing time. The fire crew found her body in the ladies' room. No evidence of her being locked in, though. There was no fire."

I whacked his dashboard. "See, Sandoval? Same MO. Except this time my vic had a gun, and there was a gas leak."

Sandoval glared at my hand hovering over his dash, reached over, and popped open his glove box. He yanked out a buffing cloth.

"Sorry." I closed my hand and drew away my fist.

Sandoval wiped away my hand print, then growled, "If killers cornered your vic and used the alarm to clear the place, why weren't they caught in the blast?"

BJ busted my chops the same way. But my gut insisted I was sniffing around the right berm. "The killers musta been at the door. Smelled the gas, so sealed it shut. Let the gas do their job. The vic panicked, tried to shoot her way out. Blew herself up."

Sandoval's tone took on an irritable beat. "Bogus alarms and locked doors would alert their victims. Killers would lose the element of surprise." Sandoval ran his hands across his temples and with his thumbs flipped up his ponytail. In a flat voice he said, "We have to consider those alarms coincidental."

I chopped the air between us. "Unless the gas leak wasn't accidental."

"Now what are you talking about?" he said with a pitiful strain.

"Can't you see? The victims are trapped. While the alarm clears the bar, the gas knocks 'em out, compensating for your lost 'element of surprise.' Then Havana and Jax come in to finish 'em."

My friend rolled his eyes and said, "That's paranoid, man. You better make yourself a tinfoil beanie to deflect those galactic signals. You know what? Maybe BJ's right, and this is about you needing a time-out at Mac Adamia's farm."

"Listen, whatever shields Havana and Jax is deep underground. That's why it took a mole like BJ to penetrate it."

Sandoval shook his head. "You are trippin'." He shifted his whole body to face me. "Look, your loco theory is born out of your feelings for BJ, not your head. You gotta promise me to stay out of her way until I check out that phone and router."

"Yeah. I will." I hated lying to him.

He glanced at his watch. "We better make like babies and head out." Sandoval cranked the ignition key and fired up the throaty V-8.

I raised my palms. "Let's not chance being seen together. I'll get out here."

He let go of his gearshift, leaving it in park. "Now that's using your head, not your *panza*."

I told Sandoval I would get a disposable cell phone. Call him with the number, and stay clear of my condo. He'd try to be finished with the router tomorrow and call me with a meeting time. He promised to bring me a copy of my victim's case file, including the coroner's report, if he could get them without arousing suspicion. I reminded him to check BJ's envelope for prints and to run those stats on transgender-female homicides.

We'd meet up at Uncle Ho's bar in Chinatown. My buddy Jack, the manager, let us use the bar's exclusive loft when we needed privacy. As usual, we'd enter from the back alley, through a former opium den's hidden passage.

I almost took BJ to Uncle Ho's once. But after I'd taken her to Mac's and put up with her needling me about Lupe, I'd decided to shut up about my hideouts. I was glad I did.

As I struck out through the funk on the street, I took BJ's note from my wallet. I recalled an FBI course on homicide investigations I took years ago. The bureau trainer offered a variety of theories and gadgets employed by the FBI. I fingered the oddly textured paper. Licking my thumb and index fingers, I squeezed a corner between my wet fingertips. The pointed edge dissolved instantly. Standard-issue spy fare. The bureau and the CIA used it. A cornered spook could piss on his notes and poof, they'd be history. BJ was a mole.

BJ's note said tonight at six, she'd be at Yerba Buena Gardens in front of the Martin Luther King Jr. Memorial. I stuffed it back into my wallet. I'd call her as soon as I got my hands on a burner. Pumped, I looked forward to seeing her.

I fled Natoma's fumes, heading toward First Street and a taxi while mulling over the crime scene. But what had happened there between BJ and me boiled up with Ricky in the mix. She'd given me a hard time about our victim's sex. She'd said, "Just because she's in a dress doesn't mean she's a she." If Ricky was killed, it'd be my fault.

I hit First Street and torqued my thoughts back toward who BJ worked for. Only the FBI held jurisdiction within US borders. She had to be bureau. And what the hell did this mysterious secret society have to do with the country's security?

Joe Bagadoughnuts

I slid into the backseat of a cab and gave the goateed driver directions to my bank. Today's plan required my undercover props. Active credit cards with matching fake IDs sat in my safe-deposit box. I'd leave no spending trail for Havana or Jax to trace.

By the time Rhodes discovered the credit card activity, my name would either be cleared or it wouldn't matter. From the bank, I'd hit the nearest car-rental agency, then sneak into a mobile-phone store for an untraceable cell. My under-the-radar link to BJ and Sandoval.

The hack sped down First Street with his head halfway out the window to blow away my stench. Wind-whipped grit swirled up from the floor. I coughed and wiped my eyes. But the grainy debris didn't strip away my anticipation of seeing BJ. The similarities between Sandoval's hooker's murder and Bambi's dead vic were no coincidences. Tonight I'd meet BJ. Drag outta her what she hid. Nix Sandoval's suspicions. Make her let me in on the action.

After I stank up the bank, the cabdriver gladly left me off at a car-rental agency. I requested a compact import. Nobody who knew me would expect to see me tooling around on imported wheels.

The frowning clerk leaned on me to buy additional insurance once he caught a whiff of my cantina cologne. After initialing the forms to bloat the rate, I headed to a fly-by-night cell phone storefront over in the Mission District. I paid cash for the untraceable burner.

Outside, I pocketed myself into the doorway of a boarded-up business and called Sandoval's personal cell. Left my new number on his voice mail. I imagined the obsessive bastard as too busy digging around in that router to answer. I also called the shrink's office and left my new number. Didn't need the shrink telling Havana what time to nail me if she'd tapped my home phone.

I hesitated to dial BJ. If I couldn't promise her the router tonight, why bother? But Sandoval had heard her voice today, not me. I punched in her number.

"Who's this?" Her voice seemed to climb with anticipation.

"It's me," I said, and could hear the din of the squad room.

"'Bout time, dahlin'. Making our date at six?"

"Yeah, won't miss this one," I said, afraid she'd ask about the router.

"Bringing my present?"

Empty-handed, I couldn't lie. "Tomorrow. For sure."

BJ snorted, then said, "Hold on. Headin' outside."

Silence. Did she hang up? "You there, B—"

"Don't go blarin' names all over the airwaves, ya hear?"

"Yeah, sure. Sorry," I said, miffed at the sudden drop in my sperm count.

"You gave it to somebody else, didn't ya?"

Her heated tongue sparked a flare. "Yeah, because it wasn't his heel grinding my nuts."

"Bring it tonight." Her tone sizzled.

"Can't. Outta my hands till tomorrow," I said, then heard myself whine, "Can we still meet tonight?"

"What for?" she said, her tongue a pointed icicle.

"For you to look me in the eye and tell me I'm not your patsy," I said, scraping mettle into my tone.

After another second of dead air, BJ said, "I suppose I owe you that."

"Listen, you leaving from home or the station?" I said, planning to make myself her shadow in case Havana and Jax tailed her.

"Why?" she asked, stretching the question.

I bit. "Don't want you flying solo on the way."

"I've made it this far alone. Don't need you stumblin' me up again. Nobody can miss that boat of yours."

"Okay, okay," I said. But stung by her swipe, I mocked, "See you…you know where. And hey, I'm not driving my 'boat.'"

She hung up without another word. Left me guessing where she'd be leaving from. I'd take my shot at catching her trail at the station.

♦ ♦ ♦

BJ's relief that Lo had reached out exploded when he confirmed he'd passed the router to Sandoval. Sure he was defending himself. But at Sandoval's expense.

She paced the sidewalk and speed-dialed Marilee to see if she'd caught Sandoval with the router.

"Hi, hon. Retrieve our property?" Marilee asked without a smidgen of judgment. Her question an answer for BJ.

BJ didn't hesitate and replied, "Meetin' tomorrow. Called to tell ya."

Marilee expressed her disappointment at the delay but said she didn't blame her. Tramping back toward the station, BJ entertained no illusions beyond having bought a little time. Still, Marilee could catch Sandoval with the router. Even if the clever nerd kept it hidden, her failure to get it tomorrow, no matter how convincing her excuse, would damage Marilee's confidence in her. If Havana found out Sandoval had the router, she'd pounce.

Dammit, Lo, she thought as she entered the precinct, but then her burners flared under Marilee. Mama Bear gladly ignored Havana's orchestrated robbery-homicides. Viewed them as unrelated events. It followed that she refused to take a stand against O'DAD's exclusion of transgender women. Too controversial, she'd said. It could rip apart the sisterhood. It stuck in BJ's craw that O'DAD's grande dame hadn't allowed their murders to addle her conscience.

Back at her desk, her phony notes about Bambi's "accidental blast" grew fuzzy. Her burn over Marilee's blindness, along with her confidence, fizzled out. Not only had she not stymied the murderer, but if she failed to recover that router, she'd serve up two more targets, Lo and Sandoval. Three, counting herself.

♦ ♦ ♦

I nosed through San Francisco's thick traffic in the little import. BJ's accusation, "I've made it this far alone. Don't need you stumblin' me up again," played like a riff I couldn't get out of my head. Then the needle skipped from BJ to Ricky. He'd been the first I'd abandoned in a free-fire zone.

By the time I beat back my guilty conscience, I'd bubbled up on Haight Street. Inspired by Natoma Street's bums, the Haight's second-hand shops didn't disappoint me. I picked up a bitchin' wool overcoat and swell tattered overalls. The outfit clashed nicely with a pair of cracked patent leather shoes. I threw in a plaid shirt and a stocking cap. Then at a costume shop I copped a spray can of black hair color to cover what was left of my graying hair. A straggly matching mustache topped off what I imagined Ricky would call my ensemble.

I clomped through Golden Gate Park with a shopping bag in each hand until I found a secluded clearing. There, I changed into homeless Joe Bagadoughnuts. I strolled back through clusters of the park's homeless to test my disguise. Musta worked. More than one offered me hits of weed and cheap wine. I set off toward Central Station to shadow BJ.

Max snickered, said that my outfit suited me, and told me I'd missed BJ by minutes, "Again."

I turned to go but couldn't forget Al. "Say, Max. Do me a favor?"

"Sure."

"May not make it home for a couple of days. Need to make sure my cat is fed."

"Hardly believed it when you got him. Finally get to meet…what'd you name him?"

Max seemed unable to control his grin.

"Al. His name's Al." As if on cue, good memories of my stepfather poured out. "Short for Albert," I said.

"Albert?"

"You in or not?"

"Of course," he said through a chuckle.

I gave him my extra condo key. Then I called my neighbor who'd given me Al. She agreed to feed him while I'm gone. Max promised to top off Al's bowls before giving her the key.

I shot over to BJ's, gambling that she'd headed home. I cruised by as she sat in her driveway watching her garage door creep open. She pulled in, and I slid down to eye level with the dash and waited. I'd found her. Finally, a break. Max was right, that damned hybrid did look like a roach's head.

BJ's garage door opened up again after five. I watched her craning over her shoulder as she backed out of the narrow driveway. Not seeing anybody else in her car mopped up any lingering doubts I should've kept about her. Only the unknown whereabouts of Havana and Jax kept me from running over and knocking on her window. Despite the bumps in our last phone call, I wanted to talk to her face-to-face.

As soon as she disappeared around the corner, I fired up my rental to follow her.

A couple in a beige Volvo cut in front of me on Geary Boulevard. Their golden retriever sucked air through the rear side window. Irritated, I tapped my brakes but didn't hit my horn. I didn't need attention.

Tooling east, I realized that the Volvo lagged behind BJ and matched her every lane change. The mark of amateurs. I bet the backs of those pinheads belonged to Havana and Jax. The pair wouldn't escape BJ's sharp eyes. I jotted down their license number.

♦ ♦ ♦

BJ spotted Havana and Jax. The lame hussies still drove that Volvo. But the pair's threat to her meeting with Lo quickly doused her sparkle at their bungled tail. And Havana had defied Marilee's demand to leave Lo to her. Marilee had lost her grip on the killer.

She had to lose the Volvo, now. From the center lane, BJ fishtailed right onto a one-way, inches from the bumper of the hoopty between her and the corner. The clunker locked its brakes to keep from T-boning BJ. Homeboy mashed his horn.

In her rearview mirror, BJ watched the Volvo, trapped in the center lane, continue on Geary through the cloud of burned rubber.

♦ ♦ ♦

Dammit, lagging behind BJ a lane to her left, my frantic honking and jabs into the right lanes only tightened the ranks of the traffic. I got sucked straight past BJ's gutsy right turn.

Though certain that BJ ditched Havana and Jax, their following her meant that they suspected her—or worse, that her cover was blown.

On foot between where I'd stashed the car and Yerba Buena Gardens, I flashed my duplicate badge at a rutty-faced homeless man hunkered down in a doorway behind his bulging shopping cart. I gave him twenty bucks and told him I'd return his cart later. He grumbled until I opened my coat and introduced him to Mr. Forty-five. He wadded up the Jackson and stuffed it in his shirt pocket. I split for the gardens.

♦ ♦ ♦

BJ moseyed into Yerba Buena Gardens from Third Street, between the park's arts gallery and theater. She headed toward the Martin Luther King Jr. Memorial's waterfall. Drawing in a taste of the crisp breeze, she felt confident she'd lost the dynamic duo. Found herself looking forward to seeing Lo.

♦ ♦ ♦

I strained, pushing that cart crammed with all of the bum's possessions. Especially when steering the damned thing up the curved grade of the sidewalk bordering the park's esplanade. Bent me in half, forcing my weight against the cart's to keep moving. Its billowing trash bags dangled like ballasts and swung against even a mild turn. I'd been wrong about the homeless. They did work for a living. Sandoval was right too—I'd become invisible in my disguise. People looked right through me yet swarmed wide around me.

I glanced to my left, caught BJ tooling in toward the waterfalls in front of me. A slight smile tugged at my mouth. But my grin broke at the sight of a golden retriever entering the park from my right. That Volvo's hound strained its leash against the angular pull of a lanky ponytailed blonde on a collision course with BJ. Her bony body and her crew cut partner's stubby build fit BJ's descriptions of Havana and Jax. Shit, Jax was a kid. Hardly looked nineteen.

My ticker raced. BJ'd ditched them. How'd they find her? And why the ballsy walk in the park if they meant to spy on her? Whoa, were they hunting me? Figured where BJ landed, I'd show up? Bitches didn't know I knew what they looked like. My conscience stumbled. Shouldn't call a kid a bitch.

♦ ♦ ♦

Clouds of mist kissed BJ's cheeks as she approached the falls. She swept her eyes about the gardens in search of Lo. Didn't expect the old grunt to walk right up to her without a little recon first.

She didn't catch Lo but looked straight ahead at the strutting figures of Havana, her pooch, and her okeydoke, Jax. Her temper ignited, steaming the fall's mist. She'd shaken them. How'd the butchers find her?

The pair waved like sorority sisters and strolled to meet her.

Out in the open, they'd set out to be seen. But why? BJ's memory spun back to the morning's meeting with Marilee and the pair. Marilee had caught her furtive glances at her mantel clock, causing her to ask,

"BJ, did Detective Faeth schedule a meeting?" The fact that she asked exposed doubt. Her defensive, "I would've told you," had triggered Havana's countercharge: "Would she?"

A frigid pause gripped BJ. They aimed to sabotage her recovery of the router. Destroy Marilee's shaken confidence in her.

♦ ♦ ♦

I watched BJ stall at the sight of the killers. They'd blindsided her. Maybe it wasn't me they were after. Maybe they'd popped up to show her she couldn't shake 'em. To serve notice: Get the router or else.

Time to let BJ know she had a party date. I rolled down the grade in front of the waterfall and, towed by the cart's weight, slashed between BJ and the cutthroats. My eyes locked with BJ's, but Fido musta caught a whiff of me. He barked and lurched at me hard against his leash.

"Get away from him," Havana sneered, yanking the poor dog's choke chain. "That tramp stinks."

♦ ♦ ♦

BJ recognized Lo's puffy brown eyes and stocky build as he swooped between her and Havana. His presence comforted her—usually did. But what'd he wallow in to pick up that foul odor? She stomped toward Havana and Jax.

Haloed by spray, she threw up her hands. Demanded to know why they'd followed her.

♦ ♦ ♦

I stopped at a brimming trash can at the east end of the memorial, behind BJ and the killers. Rummaged through it. The rumble of the falls drowned their voices, but Havana leaned back from the press of BJ's face. Jax flanked Havana, her face jerking back and forth between the two. Her bulging eyes seemed to beg Havana to release her muzzle. BJ'd back off but kept going back. Each time she shoved her face deeper into Havana's. I expected flames to burst between her teeth.

Havana finally stood her ground, and they almost butted heads. Jax wedged herself in between. BJ stomped away, back toward me. Havana and Jax followed and let their dog's nose skim the ground inches from BJ's heels. BJ locked her head forward in her angry stride, but her eyes didn't leave my face until she passed. Yeah, partner, I got your back.

The stretch of BJ's legs pulled her a length ahead of the retriever. Havana released the hound. I watched the dog gallop toward BJ, catch up to her at the theater to dance circles around her. BJ crouched and petted the four-by-four stalker. She glared at Havana and Jax.

BJ stood and Jax poked her finger into her chest. BJ slapped it away. I reached for my shopping cart. A bum and his speeding cart through the middle of a catfight could give BJ the break she needed.

Before I could barge in, BJ swaggered off. Jax lurched after her, but Havana grabbed Jax's arm. They let her go.

As BJ's distance grew, so did my disappointment over our blown meet. Would she double back? Should I hang around until Havana and Jax took off? I looked around for a spot where Joe Bagadoughnuts might use his cell without being seen. I leaned into the cart and rolled away.

Reclined in the middle of a clump of shrubs, I felt the day's adrenaline drain into the soft dirt. But this boomer had no time for a break. I fumbled out the burner, turned it on, and called BJ.

"BJ, you okay?"

Her line died.

I dialed again. "Hey, it's me."

"How many times I hafta tell ya to keep the air traffic controllers guessin'?" she said before she took the edge off her voice. "I'd be better if I had my hardware. Nice seeing ya, though. Would've liked to greet ya with a peck on the cheek. Providin' I got past the smell."

I imagined her kiss but mentally kicked myself. She's my partner, dammit. "I'll get it to you tomorrow."

"What time?" Her voice smacked with urgency.

"Don't know yet," I said, not liking the delay myself after what I saw. "Hey, can't we meet now?" I'd muster the energy despite my rubbery muscles.

"Not till I figure out how those two found me."

"Makes sense," I said, unable to wring the disappointment out of my voice. "Call you tomorrow."

"The sooner the better."

The patter of paws interrupted me punching in Sandoval's number. The killers' retriever must have picked up my scent and came prancing toward my hideout. In the distance charged Havana and Jax. I bolted for my cart and spun it between me and Fido. The cart clattered and skidded back and forth as I kept the dog at bay. The fat trash bags lashed to the cart swung wildly. I kept my mouth shut. Couldn't risk them recognizing my voice.

Havana shouted, "Wussy, Wussy. Get away from him." The dog turned tail, showing his gender. He sprinted back toward her, ignorant of his mean tag. That and her sidekick's crew cut made me think they were gay. Havana snapped on Wussy's leash and towed him away.

I remembered Sandoval's hooker had said that one of the reasons their secret society wanted him dead was because they found out he was transgender. Did these two belong to a gang of lesbos with homicidal contempt for anyone with balls, whether they still hung or not?

I decided to put distance between me and the killers before calling Sandoval. I headed back toward the cart's owner. On the other side of Third Street, I reached for my phone. Rifling my pockets turned up nothing. Goddammit, musta dropped it fighting off Wussy. I wrestled the cart back to the park, but I couldn't find the burner. There had to be a public phone between me and the cart's owner.

♦ ♦ ♦

BJ inserted her Bluetooth under the pissy-yellow glow of the parking structure's energy-efficient lights. She leaned back in her driver's seat before contacting Marilee to bitch about Havana. She didn't believe an iota of Havana's cock-and-bull story that it was all a coincidence. That she and Jax just happened to come to this park to walk Wussy. "Why else be out in the open?" Havana had said.

It occurred to BJ that Havana had taken a gamble. Sure, the killer intended to torpedo her cred with Marilee. But how could the shrew miss that scaring off Lo had made her and Jax responsible for the man keeping evidence of O'DAD's existence? Had Havana's jealousy over Marilee's favor crashed her judgment?

BJ fondled her O'DAD cell. By now, Havana had called Marilee about their run-in at the park. Laid out her cockamamy excuse. But even Marilee would have to see through Havana's coincidence. Recognize it as her stab at credibility.

She reviewed her own script before calling. She'd explain to Marilee that Lo had moved up their meet from tomorrow to hand off their router. That Havana had popped up and scared him off. That her shenanigans had cost them their router's recovery.

♦ ♦ ♦

The shabby old man held out my twenty in his shaky hand as if to return a deposit. His tremor reminded me that I'd threatened him with a gun. A brutality I'd picked up to survive the war. As a cop, I reserved it for scum who deserved it. Like a wallop between the ears, I realized that the invisible old man didn't.

"No. Keep it. Thanks for lending me your cart," I said and shook his greasy hand.

After a frustrating search, I finally found a pay phone. Growing up, it seemed phone booths stood on every corner. Seldom saw any homeless. Now, the opposite was true. Felt ass-backward. I fed the dinosaur its coins.

"Sandoval," he answered.

"Faeth here," I said over the traffic.

"What number you calling from?" he said.

"Public phone. Lost my cell."

"No wonder I couldn't reach you."

"You tried calling me?" I said, making it his turn to talk. I couldn't tell him I'd tried to meet BJ. Had turned off my cell at the gardens.

"Yep. Meet me at Uncle Ho's. Noon tomorrow."

"Why not now?" I asked against the protests of my worn-out carcass.

"Not done yet. Not easy poking around this thing when you have to shove it in a drawer every time somebody strolls by."

"All right, then," I said, a little guilty about my tired relief.

♦ ♦ ♦

BJ called Marilee. The jingle of her phone ricocheted about her head like a stray bullet. Would it strike her or Havana?

"Hello, BJ," Marilee said, but a siren drowned her voice.

BJ waited for the whine to clear, but as it died at Marilee's end, it came to life at hers. She shuddered. Marilee was here. She'd tailed her. Spotted her for Havana.

Marilee's betrayal lit up her defenses. She cut the call to rob Marilee of the siren's tattling scream. Keep her thinking she didn't know. The ambulance sped by and BJ waited until the night soaked up its treacherous shriek. Any logic about why Marilee would subvert her recovery of the router skidded across the pavement behind that rig. BJ choked back squalls of accusation before calling her back. "Sorry, accidentally thumbed off. Need to tell you something."

"What is it, hon?"

BJ attempted to plumb Marilee's senseless conniving with Havana by distilling her words into a victim's rue. "Could've gotten the router tonight if not for Havana's meddling."

"Tonight?" Marilee hadn't the decency to even fake a reaction to Havana's presence.

"Faeth called me, said to meet him at Yerba Buena Gardens. Said he'd hand it over."

"You told me tomorrow."

Marilee's edge twisted into the bore of a dull pain, cautioning against any sudden moves. BJ held. "Last-minute thing. Besides, thought I'd surprise ya. But Havana showed up. Likely scared him off."

"Did you see Detective Faeth?"

"No, but I'll bet the cagey ol' coot was lyin' low until he could make sure I was alone. Couldn't miss me with Havana and Jax with all their hootin' and hollerin' how-de-dos." BJ stuck to her logical guns and lowered her voice. "Marilee, only one reason for Havana's grandstanding—"

Marilee cut in. "Grandstanding or not, you don't know if Detective Faeth made his own meeting. We must assume he's leading you on while his friend Dr. Sandoval examines our router."

"Just 'cause I didn't spot him doesn't mean he didn't show." BJ spoke over her thumping chest. Her voice as dry as the ashes of her sway over O'DAD's grande dame.

"My time for spying on Dr. Sandoval is over. I'll search his lab." Her terse reply left no room for negotiation.

"I'll help you," BJ said and started her car. Its innocent purr rubbed irritably against her mangled clout.

"No, no. I'll do it. The Forensics night-shift crew are used to seeing me, and the staff are hungry for grapevine grist about what happened between you and Detective Faeth. If you show up, the buzz will surely alert Dr. Sandoval if he's there."

Exactly what BJ intended.

"I'm leaving for the lab. We'll touch base in the morning," Marilee said and hung up.

Whatever knocked the sense outta Marilee left BJ dizzy. And Havana had ripped fate out of her grip. The sting left raw imagery of her immediate future juggled in the clumsy hands of Lo and Sandoval. She tried to convince herself that cagey Sandoval wouldn't be caught with that router. That Lo would return it tomorrow, as promised. But even if he did, would that restore Marilee's sanity? Rein in Havana?

BJ's confusion took a nauseous dive. Marilee's turn against her gouged deep, personal. She'd tried to deny that when she'd met Marilee, her mother's sweet memory cracked her heart open to the good doctor. But she did compete with Havana for Marilee's affection.

Tears flooded her hazel contacts. A dull but familiar tingling rose from within. BJ welcomed her body's numb retreat from the tombs of those she loved. Marilee prized Havana over her. So be it. Her tears dried-up. She shifted into drive and rolled into traffic.

BJ's garage door slid down behind her. Flipping the light switch to the upstairs stairwell did little to brighten her mood. She reckoned she'd end up in a cross fire between Havana, Lo, and Sandoval. That no matter who stopped a bullet, her surgical op had already bled out.

⬩ ⬩ ⬩

Hidden inside Union Square's oblong pay toilet, I rinsed the costume dye out of my hair. The water splashed black into the steel sink. I changed back into my regular clothes, doubling my fumes. I couldn't wait for a shower to scrub away the scum of the past two days.

As much as it sat sideways in my gut, I headed to my buddy Les's. See if I could crash at his Noe Valley flat. My old rap group partner, an accountant, offered to do my taxes, free. I'd always said that if he needed a ticket fixed, all he had to do was ask. He never did and I never took him my W-2. We were friends, not networkers. But now I needed a safe corner before stepping back into the ring. A new cell could wait till the a.m.

This Was a Mistake

I'd parked the rental a couple of blocks away from Les's flat for hoof time to make sure nobody followed me. I trudged up his steep stairs and pushed the bell.

Les cracked open his door. "Faeth." The pitch in his voice showed his surprise. "Come in."

I pressed my finger to my lips and whispered, "Shh. Is your girlfriend here?"

"No. Why?" Alarm flashed across his eyes behind his wire-rimmed glasses. He looked over my shoulder.

I slipped in between Les and his doorway. His interrupted sniff caught my fumes but he didn't say anything. Though alone with him in the hallway, I kept my voice low. "I'm sorry to barge in on you."

"No problem. Who's after you?"

Just like me and Max, combat had taught Les that the engine of vigilance was fear. "Honestly? Still trying to figure it out."

"You want to hunker down here?"

He'd made it easy, saving me from having to ask. "Listen, if it's any both—"

"Like I said, no problem. *Mi casa es su casa.*" Les combed his fingers through his thick salt-and-pepper hair. "But Lily has a key and could show up at any time."

Les had invited me out with him and Lily, but I'd always found an excuse not to be a third wheel. I'd never met her in person. More than once while sucking suds with Frank and Les, they'd complained how their women badgered them about me and their other bachelor friends. Madge had interrogated me as well when we were married. We figured women's nosy nature gave them an edge against us single dogs leading astray their housebroken pups.

Bad enough I was single, but given the circumstances, this was not the time to expose Lily to the threat against me. This was a mistake.

"Les, I can't put you and Lily in a bind." I started for the door.

"No. Wait. I'll tell her that the landlord is fumigating the building. I'll stay with her in Oakland." Les hesitated, then added, "Unless you need me to watch your back?"

He was no dummy, but I had to keep him at a safe distance.

"No. Nothing that dramatic. I've pissed somebody off. I just need a hiding place where I can sort it out."

The tilt of Les's head told me he had more questions, but he dropped the subject. "I'll call Lily," he said, tapping the screen of his phone.

"You're on your way here?" he said and started to pace. "Oh no, that's great."

I pointed to myself, then the door, but Les waved me back, shaking his head.

"But we can't stay here. I just remembered the place is going to be fumigated tomorrow....I know. It's my fault. I got the notice weeks ago and forgot all about it. I came home from work and found a reminder taped to my door."

Les read my lips that I was leaving. He raised his finger, signaling to wait.

"Head home and I'll meet you there. What?"

We both turned to the rumble of a car coming to a stop.

"I'm ready to go right now, honey. I'll meet you at the door....You have to pee? Of course. No problem....What do you mean, 'nervous'?"

Les pointed his finger toward the back door and threw me a key.

I bolted out and locked it. The narrow hallway began at his front door and ended at the back, splitting his flat down the middle. The corridor provided a clear eyeshot from the backdoor window to the front. Hidden by the darkness outside, I crouched on the top of the back stairs and peeked through a corner of the window. Petite Lily flung open the front door.

When Les first mentioned to me and Frank that she was Vietnamese, we weren't surprised. He'd talked about his sympathy for the Vietnamese in rap group. Though he hadn't smoked since Vietnam, he'd kept his Zippo lighter. He'd nervously flick it open and closed during group. He'd dropped it once. Our counselor picked it up and asked him if he'd share its engraving. Les read, "Napalm Sticks to Kids Too."

Instead of dashing toward the bathroom, Lily darted into Les's living room, then met him in the hallway as he came out of his bedroom. He held his gym bag and a laptop. I couldn't hear her, but I read her whack on his chest, followed by her finger in his face.

She backed him into the bedroom. After a quick search, she peeked into the bathroom and headed toward the back door. I jumped under the wooden staircase and hoped the silky-haired beauty wouldn't crawl after me.

Envy of Les and Lily's relationship clipped my fear of being caught until the backyard light flared on and I heard the lock click open. Lily's steps midway down the stairs sprinkled dirt and paint chips on my head.

"Lily. Have I ever given you a reason to distrust me?" Les asked.

Even I recognized Les's strained calm.

"Yes. You are a man," she said in her singsong accent.

I couldn't help but admire her tough wisdom but cringed as she took another step down the stairs. I held my nose to keep from sneezing.

"Believe me, honey, I'd never allow anyone to come between us," Les said. More a plea than a statement.

The shuffle of Lily's feet stopped. "You won't if you don't want to end up black and blue." Her voice rang with humor.

I heard the rustle of clothes and imagined their hot embrace. I felt like a ghetto kid with my nose pressed against a candy-store window.

Braced for a Body Count

The sunup bled through Les's thin curtains. Hours before my noon meet with Sandoval. I decided that until then, I'd wash my clothes, buy another burner, and follow up on my meager lead—that Volvo's plate numbers.

Showered and in clean clothes, I indulged my belly with a fat breakfast burrito from a roach coach parked in the Mission District. Refueled, I searched out that mobile phone storefront.

After I spoke to my neighbor, who confirmed she'd fed Al, I couldn't stop thinking that as long as Sandoval had that damned device and BJ didn't, they both stood in the crosshairs. I couldn't wait and called Sandoval. "Let's meet," I said.

"Can't. Got deadlines I let slide while I checked out that router of yours."

"Dammit, Sandoval, can't you bring it now?"

"Calm down, homeboy. I'll meet you at noon. This your new number?"

"Yeah," I said. "If you can make it sooner, I'll be at Ho's by eleven. And don't let Crusher catch you with that thing. Hear me?"

"Don't be a *vieja*. You worry like an old lady." Then he said, "See ya at noon. Gotta go."

I started to dial BJ, but without the router, I couldn't think of a good reason to bother. I wanted to call her with more than a new phone number. To tell her she could have the router right now. I felt as useful as tit implants on a nun.

My burped-back jalapeños reminded me of Rhodes's mandatory psych exam. I called the clinic. Nothing scheduled. The irritable clerk said they were waiting for the results of my physical. I started to tell him my new number, and he said, "Have it," giving me back my home number. I spat back not to call me there and made him write down my new cell number.

"Okay, all right," he said, and got nastier when I told him to repeat it back to me.

Rhodes's suspension bound up with my fear of exposure, squeezed the juice out of those peppers splashing around my belly. Exposure to what? A blindside hit from Havana on the steps of the shrink's office? Or that I'd be found too psycho for duty? Fuck the burn. I'd make myself useful and track down that Volvo.

♦ ♦ ♦

BJ's silk pajamas did little to blunt the smack of the morning chill as she sat cross-legged on her bed, sipping tea. Her fitful sleep hadn't restored her. She'd awakened at the same grim fork in the road she'd faced the night before. One side ended with Havana dangling her, Lo's, and Sandoval's heads over O'DAD's equipment. On the other side, she stood facing Marilee and her surrogate daughter, handing them the router. Not a tad closer to understanding Marilee's turn against her.

Her O'DAD cell jingled. Marilee's face glowed on the display. With no good reason for her to be calling so early unless she'd caught Sandoval with the router, BJ braced for a body count. Still, she answered as if nothing had changed.

"Mornin'."

"Hon." Marilee's voice fell somber. "The Bambi victim's phone is signed out to Dr. Sandoval."

Barely able to contain her relief that Sandoval lived, BJ said, "Jeez Louise, Marilee, that's his job."

"Of course, but I'm certain he also has our router. If he has both, O'DAD's secrecy is jeopardized."

BJ strained to keep from blurting, Conniving with Havana jeopardizes O'DAD. Instead, she bared her teeth and said, "You saw him with the router?"

"No, but Havana and Jax found your partner's car in the Forensics parking lot. They searched it thoroughly. No router. He had to have left the car there after giving the router to Dr. Sandoval. I'm sorry, hon, but you must face the fact that your Detective Faeth has led you on a wild goose chase while his friend studies our equipment."

Unable to cure Marilee's blindness toward Havana, BJ still needed to distract her from Sandoval. Smooth his handoff of the router to Lo. Get him off Havana's to-do list.

"Marilee, I've got the same bee in my bonnet. But even if Sandoval does have it, the Holy Trinity isn't complete without O'DAD's fiber-optic feed. And only we sisters know to look for Rosie to find it. No man has the range of imagination to do that. At worst, Sandoval will be bogged down cogitatin' on why a standard Wi-Fi won't liven up the thing. What do you say to breakfast? We can strategize."

"Strategize? And ignore Sandoval?"

"If you didn't find the router, he's probably returned it to Detective Faeth. I think that Faeth would've returned it to me last night but for Havana poking her beak in my business," BJ said, her breath heating up. She inhaled slowly to cool down.

"Come on, Marilee, let's go eat. I'll buy."

"It'll be on me. But after I take the morning for another pass at Dr. Sandoval. I'll meet you for lunch....How about Chinatown's Yangtze Restaurant?"

Dammit, BJ thought. At the risk of snipping Marilee's flimsy commitment, she asked, "How about eleven thirty? Beat the crowds?"

"All right. If I don't find the router, I'll have Havana keep an eye on Forensics to monitor Sandoval's movements."

"Marilee—" BJ snapped but then regained her composure. "Marilee, what if Dr. Sandoval has already returned the router to Detective Faeth? It'd be a waste of time."

"Hon, your Detective Faeth has disappeared. Dr. Sandoval is our only link to him and the whereabouts of our router." The strain in her voice crawled up. "We must track Dr. Sandoval's movements."

"What if Faeth saw me with Havana last night? Spots Havana and Jax tailing Sandoval and gives up on me? Doesn't call me?"

BJ heard Marilee heave a sigh. "Let's put those possibilities on our lunch agenda, shall we?"

"Then you'll keep Havana away from him until we discuss it?"

"I'm sorry, hon. No. Not until we locate our router."

BJ pleaded, "Marilee, you'll tell Havana just to keep an eye on him, right? To notify us if she suspects he has the router so I can zoom in after it?"

After a dreadful silence, BJ listened to Marilee's weak, "We'll play that by ear."

♦ ♦ ♦

Against Rhodes's orders, I called my buddy Roscoe over at the Tenderloin Station.

"Faeth—long time, no see. How's it hangin'?" His smoker's rattle pelted my ear.

"Low and to the left, but hey, I need a favor on the q.t."

Roscoe coughed to clear the sludge. "Sure, what's up?"

I couldn't put him in the switches by hiding my suspension, so I said, "Somebody's trying to set me up. Got suspended. Not supposed to be calling you without my captain's okay."

"I heard that shit over the grapevine. What happened? You find out your partner's a lesbo? She drop a dime on you for wisecracking about faggots?"

"Nah. No, that's not it. Tell ya about it later. But I need your help."

"Name it."

"Right now, run some plates for me?"

"Lay them numbers on me."

Roscoe traced the tags to an independent car-rental agency over in the Sunset District. BJ's neighborhood. He gave me the address, and I reminded him not to mention my call. I sped to that Volvo's lot.

Out in the Sunset, I spotted a rare parking place. I had to hike several blocks to the damn rental agency. I caught my breath, flashed my badge, and asked the sales associate about the Volvo.

"Sorry, sir, but, like, it's against the rules to give out our customers' private information, okay?" The cheerleaderesque bimbo sucked her lips up to her nose.

I slapped my badge on the counter, jabbed my finger at it, and said, "I'm investigating a murder. Withholding evidence is a crime."

She fluttered her eyelids, huffed, and punched in the Volvo's plate numbers. "It's rented to a Helen Waite." The bimbette bit her knuckles to keep from laughing.

She woulda liked me to go straight to hell and wait. Instead, she gave me the address to the Plinth Motel in the Marina District on the north side of town. A spasm screwed down my spine. The place sat near my Cow Hollow condo.

When I pressed for a credit card number and the car's scheduled return, pom-pom girl said that Waite had paid cash and that the return date was open ended. I gave her my disposable cell's number and ordered her to call me when the car showed up. I'd heard a more convincing "certainly" from Curly of The Three Stooges. I did manage to bully out of her Waite's Virginia driver's license number.

Stuck in traffic on my way to Waite's motel, images of BJ's fight with Havana and Jax stirred my fears for her life. I swatted away scenes of stubby and her skinny pal pounding splinters under BJ's fingernails. The scattered visions clotted back in the form of my brother, Ricky. His mouth twisted in screams under the swing of Jax's hammer. I squeezed my mug to wring out Ricky's, but his face twisted back.

Within blocks of the motel, the traffic light switched to green, but the twit thumbing his cell in front of me hadn't noticed. My temper cracked, mercifully erasing Ricky's ghost. I leaned hard against the import's alto-pussy horn. Not the punishment I wanted to dish out.

Scaffolding blocked the entrance to the Plinth Motel. A sign read Closed for Renovation.

Bruised by the bum's rush, I called Roscoe and asked him to run Waite's driver's license number by the Virginia DMV. Moments after his rumbly "Affirmative," he reported the number as bogus. That Volvo's empty lead left me starving for answers and disgusted that I didn't have my sit-down with BJ yesterday.

Empty-handed on Lombard Street with an hour and a half before my meet with Sandoval, I wondered how much more shrinkage my nuts could take. If it was true that Havana and Jax gunned for anyone with balls, whether they still hung or not, I supposed I should take pride in their grudge against me.

But Wait, There's More

I got to Uncle Ho's an hour early. Little light seeped into the windowless Chinatown dive. Not a soul sat at the long dogleg bar except my pal Jack, the manager. Ho's empty darkness matched what I could prove about the explosion at Bambi's. That neither my brain nor my belly connected a dot between the murders and national security darkened my mood. I counted on Sandoval to shed some light.

Jack sat at the crook of the bar at the back wall, his face aglow under the book light clipped to the top of his ancient brass cash register. He glanced up from his racing form and greeted me with a firm handshake. He hadn't seen Sandoval. I told him to keep an eye out for him.

"Loft's all yours," he said, then swept his hand toward the stairs.

I parked on a wooden chair at the big, round table. Two of its four legs teeter-tottered, knocking against the floor. Weighed down with hunches but without an ounce of proof, I massaged my temples. The press of my elbows on the cranky table quieted it down. What did Sandoval find?

The question pricked my nagging grief over Ricky, then ruptured, flooding my head with images. Seven years after a Peterbilt splattered Mom and Ricky's father into eternity, a fit, thirty-five-year-old uniformed me snuck home early to steal some study time for the detective exam. I'd expected to find my eighteen-year-old brother nose down in his books. I'd hung up my utility belt and locked up my pistol, only to be startled by a Village People blast outta Ricky's room: "It's fun to stay at the Y-M-C-A / It's fun to stay at the Y-M-C-A."

"Ricky! Dammit, Richard. Turn that shit off!" I'd shouted.

The Village People blared back, "Y-M-C-A / You'll find it at the Y-M-C-A."

I sprang toward Ricky's bedroom, clipped my knee on an end table, and hop-limped to my brother's room. I flung open his door.

"Ricky, what the fu—"

The sturdy high school senior froze with one hand in the air and a leg kicked out like a chorus girl's. His bulging pale green eyes were framed by a blond wig with thick bangs. The strap of his pink blouse slid from his shoulder. Red lipstick girdled his gaping mouth.

Reeling in disgust, I grabbed the doorjamb to stop the room from spinning. My own flesh and blood, queer? How was I going to look to other cops? My gut knotted up, cramps dropped me to my good knee. I leaned against the doorway. Glancing up at Ricky, I saw fear in his eyes. I felt my revulsion melt away in my love for my little brother.

Ricky's glossy lips trembled as his limbs drifted down to his sides. He stumbled to his boom box and twisted down the noise. After a hesitant reach, he squeezed my shoulder, but I jerked away. With his hand still above my shoulder, his voice sputtered, "Lo, I'm sorry you had to find out this way."

"Huh? Aren't you ashamed?" I spat in disbelief.

Ricky stepped back, his face hardening. "I've nothing to be ashamed of. You've got to understand, this is who I am."

Stunned, I couldn't speak. Damn, the twerp was my brother, but gay and telling me to live with it. My heart twisted in the switches. What had I done to be saddled with such a fucked-up test? Live with a drag queen, or dump him into an orphanage?

Jack's Cantonese burst loud and stalled my limp down memory lane. I peeked downstairs to see if I'd been followed. Jack had the receiver of the bar's pay phone pinched between his ear and shoulder. His voice calmed, and I watched him move his pencil down his scratch sheet, ticking off bets. The bar remained empty except for me and him.

I managed to replace visions of Ricky with Jack's bookie scribbling at the other end, but my brother's scab still throbbed. My demand that he stay in the closet caused a tense truce. He took it for six years before he disappeared. Had he survived the likes of Havana?

Back at the table, I raised my gaze to the black ceiling. I craved the simple days of murder for profit or passion and wished that my brother were straight and safe. That he'd come home. I rested my head on my forearms.

The clop of steps perked up my ears. I looked downstairs. Sandoval trailed that ropy Jack as they strolled into view along the arc of the bar. Both trotted up the stairs, Jack clutching a couple of damp beers. Sandoval carried a brown grocery bag with bread and celery tops poking up. What the hell? I'm waitin' while he shopped?

Jack placed the bottles on the table and lit a fingerprint-smudged candle lamp. Through the rapids of his Chinese accent, he said, "You two look like you been sucking lemons. I won't let anybody bug you." At the bottom of the stairs, he hooked the ragged velvet rope across the staircase entrance.

Sandoval set his bag under the table between us. I thought he'd better have brought me more than a veggie.

"Well, what've ya got?" I asked, glaring. His sweaty brow and bloodless cheeks shined in the flickering light. The fear stamped on his face trumped my craving for facts. I eased back. "What the hell happened?"

"Me and my ride just did a doughnut in the middle of Kearny Street. Barely missed getting T-boned by a bobtail truck that ripped through a red light." His voice fizzled as he stroked his thighs. "You know this town—yellow lights mean now or never, eh?"

This morning's images of a hammering Jax torturing Ricky flashed between us. Except now, Sandoval jarred under her blows. Crusher musta spied him leaving with the router. She'd ordered a hit. BJ was wrong about her. "Crusher saw you with that fucken router."

"Nobody saw me with it," Sandoval snapped. "But just in case, I hid my car blocks away and made sure I wasn't followed on foot."

"Nobody saw you with the router?" I said and leaned into him. "Then why stash your car?"

"No harm in being cautious. It was an accident, all right? But maybe you're right about Crusher showing up at Bambi's. This morning when I tried to record her voice for you, she acted suspicious."

He sucked in a long breath. "She strolled by my lab, so I switched on the digital recorder in my pocket, met her in the hall, and said, 'Dr. Crusher, you starting to make sense out of the chaos in this place?' She slid up to me without a word, smiled, and pulled the recorder from my lab coat. She tapped the record light, punched the off button, and then said, 'I saw a red glow. Waste of batteries.'" Sandoval wiggled his finger in front of my nose. "She wagged her finger in my face, turned around, and then strutted off, dragging her pointing finger behind her. Cagey, eh?"

"Yeah," I said, holding back my Told you so. That battle-ax was onto Sandoval. "Listen, Crusher ordered that rig to nail you. You got to ditch that '58 Impala of yours. Nobody else in the goddamned world drives one." I dragged out my car keys and dropped them on the table. "Take my rental. It's parked in the Portsmouth garage."

He threw up his palms and muscled his voice. "I didn't sneak in here to stir up your paranoia. Crusher hasn't seen you and me together. She's got nothing on us. You know city drivers are color-blind. Every light's green to 'em."

I slapped the table. "Christ, Sandoval, Crusher's not like you. She don't need to see us together or you with the router. Everybody knows we're pals." Glancing away, I said, "Goddammit. Because of me, you're marked. I shoulda listened to BJ."

"You're paranoid, homeboy. Relax."

Though my belly lurched otherwise, could Sandoval be right? Had my fears about Ricky's fate turned into paranoia to prove my VA counselor right?

"All right, all right," I said, sat back, and reached for something tangible. "Did you run those names from BJ's note?"

With a weak flip of his hands, he said, "Nada. Nothing on Jax, and no rap sheet popped up on your Cuban capital. No blips on social-media radar either. Did have a homeboy at the IRS check tax records, though. Found a traveling computer consultant named Havana Vives." Sandoval tilted his head. "Never late with her taxes."

Of course he had a homeboy at the IRS. And Havana, brainy. Bright enough to kill and scatter her tracks. Shaking my head, I said, "How about BJ? Is Reeves a cover name?"

"Didn't dig around her backyard yet. Got distracted by your victim's file." Sandoval set the beers out of the way, fished a folder out of his grocery bag, and plopped it in front of me. "That's your vic's autopsy report. She was a he."

I forgave Sandoval for shopping, but my fears for Ricky cramped my hand. I hesitated. "You said, 'was a he.' Present or past tense?"

"Past. Go on, check her out."

Without a choice, I tilted the folder toward me. A loose photo slid to the table. I couldn't believe the beauty staring back had been a guy. "You're kidding me, right?"

"Nope. Your vic's cojones had been surgically removed and her joystick inverted to create a vagina. Along with her artificial breasts, she inserted butt implants and bought collagen lips. She'd been dosed with estrogen to get rid of body hair and round out her face. Shaved her trachea too."

Sandoval's tone rolled without a bump. Eager for a distraction, I said, "Okay, okay. Too much detail. Who was this guy?"

"DNA ID'd your crispy critter as that congressman who skipped bail after his indictment for molesting a congressional page. They'd registered his DNA before he got away."

"How'd you find this head shot?"

"Easy. I ran her name against obits with the same DOB. He'd stolen a dead girl's birth certificate and Social Security number. I tracked her to a bunch of dating sites. Same photo on all of them. Took a screenshot of her pic."

"Unbelievable," I mumbled at the photo, then read a gal's name underneath. Had Ricky butchered his manhood? Changed his name? Static clogged my head. Sandoval was saying something. I turned to him and forced myself to speak. “Say again. What?”

“Incredible, eh?” Sandoval said. “Anyway, like I said, I didn’t find any electronics at Bambi’s. But beneath a sink, I’d found a hole the right size for an Internet cable. There were also electrical outlets nearby. Didn’t mention them yesterday because you were already trippin’.”

I latched onto his words like a rope outta of quicksand. “So, you agree that Crusher and her team could’ve cleared the cable and UPS,” I said. “Did you check for anything suspicious about the gas leak?”

“There you go again. The leak was accidental. Those false alarms at Bambi’s and where the Tenderloin hooker was killed had to be coincidental. It makes no logical sense any other way,” he said, tossing up his palms.

“All right, I know, the perps would’ve been killed in the blast too,” I said, unable to defend my biting hunches. “What else ya got?”

“I pulled the files of that Tenderloin homicide,” he said and looked away as if pursuing an afterthought. What distracted him? Before I asked, his eyes met mine and he continued.

“She complained that she’d been chased by a car. Had to dive out of its way a couple of times to keep from getting hit. Vice noted road burn on her hands and knees.”

He’d juiced up my earlier fears about that murderous rig. I popped to my feet. “That’s what just happened to you,” I said and drove on. “Not even you can call that a coincidence. That’s what distracted you right now, isn’t it?”

“I suppose caution requires that we consider it,” he said, staring up at me.

“Even your digital brain can’t ignore those coincidences. What about transgender-female murder rates? You compare them?”

He pulled out a manila envelope. “Laszlo did. Handed me these results on my way here. I didn’t have time to check ’em out.”

I liked Laszlo Singh, his reliable assistant. The Indian immigrant was as smart as he was goosey. Nobody could pronounce his first name, so Sandoval nicknamed him Laszlo, after Singh's hero, some Hungarian nerd. I sat back down and read the numbers.

"Tripled in the last two years. Most of the bodies found in powder rooms. Reported as robbery-homicides. All unsolved." Then I shoved Laszlo's report under Sandoval's nose and raised my voice. "Also hit-and-runs by stolen vehicles. Go ahead, ignore those 'coincidences.'"

"All right," Sandoval said, straightening his back. "Let's both be careful, then. If Dr. Crusher ordered a hit, what does that say about your defense of BJ?"

"What are you talking about?" I said, knocked off balance.

"If I'm digitally nearsighted, your feelings for her poke your eyes out. I told you yesterday that BJ's note didn't pass the smell test. When I pointed out that she hadn't described Dr. Crusher, you defended her. Said, 'Maybe she's saying that Crusher is no murderer.' It's Havana and Jax she's after. That I was wrong about her."

I couldn't tell him that I'd watched BJ mouth off to Havana and Jax last night. That she didn't know she was up against Crusher too. Not without a fight, distracting us from that rig that barreled down on him.

"You're right. We gotta be careful. Listen, it may be too late to keep all the heat off you, but I'm guessing that Crusher is more interested in who has the router than who's seen it. I'm taking it off your hands. Where is it?"

He glanced down at his grocery bag. I lurched under and grabbed it, banging my chin on the table. One look below the bread confirmed I again held the kill magnet. What'd he do with my rucksack? It'd been with me since Vietnam. Fucker. I rubbed my chin.

I set the bag on the floor to my right, placing me between it and Sandoval. Despite losing my rucksack, I snatched up my rental keys and jingled them in front of his nose.

"Take my damned car, will ya? Disappear till we figure out a way to let 'em know you don't have their junk anymore."

After a miffed glance at the keys, Sandoval said, "You know me and my *carrucha* are inseparable." He changed the subject. "Don't you wanna know about that router?"

The bastard was as stubborn as me. "Yeah, yeah, sure." I tossed the keys on top of the file. That battle wasn't over.

Ignoring my keys, he said, "The thing is a real puzzle. You may be disappointed."

I steeled for another dead end.

"At first glance, it looks like any pedestrian hardware."

Not in the mood to follow every brilliant step to his conclusion, I growled, "But?"

He leaned forward, forearms on the table, palms up. "Look, all a router does is provide a bridge between end points," he said, spreading his fingers as he spoke.

"Bridge" I kinda got. "End points?" I said, lost and irritated again.

"The website is one end point, and in our case, the other is your victim's phone. And the router is the bridge between them."

"Got it."

"But though your vic's phone activated the bridge, nothing shot across from the other side."

"Why not?" I spat, shaking my head.

"Dunno," he said and flicked something off the table I didn't see. "Could be a proprietary website inaccessible through a standard Internet feed. That phone has an unusual modification."

I caught the bottom line, despite his technobabble. "Let me get this straight. You couldn't reach that secret society's website, right?"

"Right."

"Then we got nothin'," I said, ready to let Rhodes keep my badge and check myself into a nursing home.

"Not exactly," Sandoval said with a leap in his voice. "I discovered an access code."

"How?" I said, afraid to get too excited.

"Too easy. The last numbers your vic punched in were—"

I blurted it out, "Six three two three. Those numbers were displayed when I found the phone."

"But wait, there's more," he said playfully, then slipped his smartphone from his cargo pants. With the weight of his arms gone, the tabled rocked and clunked on my side.

While his finger skidded around the face of his phone, he said, "I thought you were making excuses for BJ when you put the two homicides together." Then he jutted his chin toward my gut. "But as loco as you can be, sometimes that *panza* of yours nails it."

I glanced between him and his cell. "You connect a dot?"

"It's as circumstantial as you can get before chiseling it into evidentiary stone, but your vic dialed the acronym of that secret society the Tenderloin hooker said was trying to kill her."

"What is it?" I demanded.

"Check it out." He slid his phone's dial under my nose. "What's the last alpha symbol under the numeral *6*?"

I forced myself to indulge him. "*O*."

"The first under the number *3*?"

"*D*."

"The first under *2*?"

"*A*."

"And, again, the first under the number *3*?"

"*D*. So it spells ODAD?" I shrugged my shoulders.

"It stands for Once-a-Dick-Always-a-Dick. That secret society's name. Vice's interview notes show an apostrophe after the *O*. Their vic pronounced the acronym O'DAD."

"Once-a-Dick-Always-a-Dick. Sounds perfect for a gang of lesbos gunning for guys who hack off their pricks to pass as women."

"You think O'DAD is lesbian?"

I hardly heard Sandoval's question over the blare of whether my brother's penis was still attached. Over the noise, I said, "It follows, if you ask me."

Sandoval added, "Ever heard of the VIPS?"

"For Christ's sake, what's that?" I asked, thankful that his question yanked my attention away from Ricky.

"Another acronym. Vice's hooker said VIPS stood for the Vaginas in Parity Society, or Vips for short."

I gagged like I'd caught a cigarette butt in a slug a beer. "Vaginas in Parity Society?"

"Yep. Told Vice that Vips were dedicated to promoting transgender girls to the same status as women-born women. That Once-a-Dick-Always-a-Dick denied that they were girls because they'd been born men. Refused them O'DAD membership."

Ricky's image, spread-eagled under a surgeon's blade, convulsed my belly. I picked up my damp beer and rolled it across my sweaty forehead.

Sandoval looked at me, nodded, and said, "Only in America, eh?"

I dredged up my detective voice. "That vic told Vice that Vips wanted O'DAD membership?"

"That's right."

"Do Vips lose their dicks and become lesbos?" I asked, tonguing my mouth to get rid of its sour taste.

"Don't think so, homey."

"So, if O'DAD isn't a lesbian gang—"

"Begs the question, What's O'DAD got that Vips are willing to risk their lives for, eh?" Sandoval said.

BJ's national security peeked from behind his question. Still out of range of an answer, I kept quiet, put down the beer.

Sandoval looked me up and down. "Guess your *panza* is out of ideas. Anyway, I discovered a counterintuitive modification to your vic's phone."

"Counter what?" I said.

Sandoval leaned forward again. "Its range is powered down. To capture the Wi-Fi signal, you have to be within ten, fifteen feet of the router. Real retro tech. You know, like World War II–era bandwidth."

"World War II," I murmured, then flashed on that wartime Rosie-the-Riveter poster outside the powder room at Frank and Lupe's place. Frank's praise for Lupe's work ethic echoed between my ears: "Lupe lets me tend bar and cook, but that's about it. I don't even have to clean the restrooms. She takes care of all that." Did Rosie mark the spot of a hot-wired powder room at Mac's?

"So, to connect, you have to be close."

"Yep."

"Like inside a ladies' room."

Sandoval wrinkled his brow. "I suppose," he said.

"Yesterday I had to squeeze out of you that your Tenderloin vic died in a powder room. That he had a router and was targeted by a secret society."

"You keep saying 'he'? I told you she traded her pee-pee for a *panocha*....A pussy." He flapped his hands, suggesting I didn't get it.

"Once-a-Dick-Always-a-Dick, remember?" I sneered, refusing the vic his female claim. But before I could jab Sandoval with whether he'd fuck a Vips, my brother's ghost knocked me into the murderers' ranks. They killed to deny the same claim, didn't they? Under Ricky's spotlight, the decent side of my conscience belonged with the VIPS. Blistered by the glare, I ducked back under my hunches.

"You just said that my router would work in a powder room. There's got to be a reason they're hidden in ladies' rooms. And for their short range."

Sandoval rolled his eyes. "You're leaping ahead of the evidence."

My memory of the two girls sashaying into Lupe's powder room swept up on me. If the rock of their heart-shaped booties didn't mark the sway of homicidal lesbians, were they straight gals murderously protective of a secret hidden in powder rooms? I lifted my eyebrows and said, "Go on."

"That router contains a series of electronic gates."

"English, Sandoval, English," I said.

"Like I said, none of my lab's wireless equipment blew life into that router from their end. But when I punched in 6323 from your victim's modified mobile, circuits lit up like a Christmas tree. Opened up about half the router's electronic gates."

"What do you mean gates?" I asked.

Sandoval's chest rose, then fell. "Look, you know what a toggle switch does?"

"Okay, yeah. Turns something on or off, right?"

"Right, but in this case, I mean opens or closes. *¿Comprende?*"

"Yes, yes, I get it," I groaned.

"It appears that half your router's gates open and allow access in response to a proper entry code. But might require a different exit code to trip closed and terminate the connection. I discovered that when your vic's cell fired up the router but couldn't shut it down. When I simply turned off the phone, instead of the router fizzling out, the closed gates sprang open."

"So what the hell did that tell you?"

Sandoval cast a discouraged frown. "Who knows?"

"Dammit, speculate. And with something I'll understand."

He shrugged his right shoulder. "Off the top of my head? A variation of the two-man rule?"

"You mean like the two independent confirmations necessary for a nuclear launch order?" I said, impressed by his Cold War example.

Sandoval nodded. "You said to speculate, homeboy. It's a stretch, but maybe two codes are required. An entry and an exit."

I rocked back on the hind legs of my chair. Years of watching paired-up women stroll in and out of ladies' rooms paraded across my brain. They marched right into my amazement over women's intuition. Could powder rooms hold the secret to how Madge knew I'd fought in Vietnam and why Frank couldn't hide anything from Lupe? Were those answers stored in powder rooms, protected by a two-woman rule?

Like a burst from the hairy flashbulbs of my youth, it struck me and sizzled.

"That's it. High-tech souped-up women's intuition. O'DAD collects files on men, only accessible in powder rooms. Vips couldn't ask for a bigger stamp of womanhood than O'DAD membership."

Sandoval swatted the air between us. "Your generation took way too much LSD."

Sparks flew. "Chata," I snapped, kicking forward. The chair thumped the floor. "That's how Chata busted you with that bimbo."

Sandoval jerked back. "Eh?"

"O'DAD keeps files on us, including who's spoken for and by who. Gives a fast track to the O'DAD member whose old man is caught straying. What's the name of that bar where you hooked up with that babe?"

"Dew Drop Inn," he said, his mug warped as tight as his voice.

"Bet there was a Rosie-the-Riveter poster near the powder room, huh?"

Sandoval's face froze but he couldn't deny it. Recovering, he spat back, "So what? You see Rosie all over this city. Don't mean a thing."

"Bet it's a marker for an O'DAD hot spot."

"Didn't see one at Bambi's."

"Fire got it. Come on, what are the odds of Chata driving in behind you to that no-tell motel? Some other tart could've been checking you out at the bar, scheming to steal you away from the bimbo chatting you up. But first she had to know if you're spoken for. She hits the powder room and your profile. It not only tells her about Chata, but it's linked, or whatever you call it, to Chata's cell. Bet it only took one keystroke to drop a fat O'DAD dime on your whoring ass."

This time I couldn't stop shooting from my mean hip. "Your one-night stand couldn't check your status because he was a Vips. Hell, you owe O'DAD for keeping you from dipsticking a man." I shouldn't have enjoyed watching Sandoval's face go spastic. But I did. The handsome bastard got all the beauties. The only gals I attracted wanted me dead.

Sandoval took his first swig of beer, then said, "This is what I get for joining you on your speculative space walk?"

With fuel to burn, I brought the package together. "You just said that two people are required for the security of the website. One with an entry code and the other with an exit code."

"Two codes. Not two women."

"Yeah. But in other words, an intruder with only one code could enter a powder room but not exit? Like your Tenderloin hooker and my Bambi's vic."

"I'm talking about entering and exiting a website, not locking someone in a bathroom. I'm calling Rhodes, tell him to break out your straitjacket."

"Sandoval, they both died in powder rooms," I said, on a roll.

He leveled his gaze to mine and said, "You know what? Forget I said anything." Aggravation strangled his voice.

I glared. "It's more than turning a website on and off. Those entry codes are bait for Vips. O'DAD invites them in to nail 'em. Those hot spots are hidden in powder rooms, where transgender females without exit codes expose and trap themselves."

Sandoval leaned in, nose to nose with me. "Look, I'm gonna give you one more chance to listen to reason before I drive you to psycho lock-down. Maybe your vic's phone has two codes, but I'm not clever enough to unravel the second. The speculative possibilities are endless, as you delusively demonstrate. And listen to yourself. Using an exit code as an intruder alert defeats the purpose of blocking site access or catching intruders. While O'DAD's waiting for an exit code, a Vips can finish surfing their site, leave it open, and go home. For your loco scheme to work, silent alarms have to trip at entry so security can pounce while the vics are occupied surfing." Sandoval spread his arms. "Besides, not even Blackwater can hire enough muscle to patrol every powder room." Sandoval jabbed his finger at my beer. "How many of those have you had?" He retreated, his face smug.

"Blackwater changed its name," I said, as my train of hunches jack-knifed against his logical barricade. With nada concrete to punch through it, I shoved myself away from the shaky table.

Sandoval lurched for the wobbly brews. With a bottle in each hand, he looked around Ho's loft as if to make sure we were still alone. "Look, it's nonsense that the vics are lured and trapped, but I'll buy that the murders are connected and allow you the benefit of the doubt for a proprietary O'DAD website. Even that they're stashed in the occasional ladies' room."

Sandoval set the beers down and pulled an evidence bag from his breast pocket. Dangling my vic's phone between us, he said, "Tonight, let's hit the bar where that Tenderloin hooker was killed. Sneak into their powder room to test out 6323."

I didn't need my gut to tell me the height of O'DAD's alert status. My trail might be cold, but that murderous rig was hot on Sandoval's. And from what I saw last night, Havana had drawn a bead on BJ too. BJ'd get the router today. Restore her undercover chops. Take the heat off Sandoval and me. "Hell, no, Sandoval. They'll be expecting us."

Chuckling, he said, "I'll dress in drag, and you can be my date."

Was the fucker channeling my brother? I plucked the phone from his fingertips. "Christ, you just dodged a hit. Your trail is about as cold as a mouthful of jalapeños." I grabbed the car keys and tossed them in front of him. "You need to take my fucken rental and lay low."

"Like you said, they're more interested in who has it than who's seen it. Before O'DAD lost me, they had to figure I had their hardware. Planned to meet with you. That's why they tried to nail me before I lost them. Now they can't be sure I still have it. They can't kill me now."

My head agreed, but my gut wasn't so sure. "Yeah, but as soon as they spot that ride of yours, they're gonna be so far up your tailpipe you'll never shake 'em. So nix to your Tenderloin bar till things cool down, all right?" He watched me stuff the phone into my pocket.

"All right, homeboy. You got a point." Sandoval leaned back, as if propelled by his now-piercing glare. "But don't you go sneaking into a powder room without me. *¿Comprende?*"

"Sure, sure," I said, keeping my trap shut about my own plans for that phone.

He extended his hand and said, "Then gimme back your vic's cell."

"Nope. With the whereabouts of the router and the phone unknown, we've doubled our leverage. Without them, O'DAD's less likely to hit ya."

I watched him study me. "Suppose I can keep it signed out, for a while. Then what's your next move?"

I couldn't risk a fistfight by telling him my plan to return the router to BJ. "I got a lead on that Havana character's car. Tell me, what does Crusher look like?" I asked, to change the subject and get the doc's description.

Sandoval's stare faded, and he said, "She's a *gabacha*."

"White gal, huh," I said. "And?"

"Portly. Well into her sixties. The way she wears her hair trips me out. She's got a little, cherubic face, too small for her long neck and big hair. Her head looks like a fastball pitched into hay. Sound familiar?"

"All except the big hair." Then I recalled the ball-peen, shaggy pony-tailed silhouette at Bambi's. "Hair musta been tied back at the crime scene. What color?"

"Looks like it used to be dirty blonde. Mostly gray now."

"Thanks," I said. "By the way, any prints on BJ's envelope?"

"Not even BJ's." Glancing at his watch, he said, "I gotta head back to the lab."

"We better be right about O'DAD's stay of execution," I said, my voice limp with doubt.

He scooped the photo into the folder and picked it up. Stepping to the front of the table, he tucked the file under his arm and said with a smirk, "Don't worry, I'll look both ways before crossing the street. The worst thing Crusher's gonna do now is keep an eye on me. Besides, she don't know if I figured out that the rig intended to hit me or if I blew it off as an accident. I return to Forensics, it'll keep her guessing and distracted from you. Give you wiggle room to follow up on Havana's *carrucha*."

"Watch your back," I said. I didn't share his confidence as he skipped down the stairs.

I waited awhile to give him a head start. Then I lifted my weighted ass and rocked down the steps. Laid some cash on Jack and snuck out the alley exit toward the garage. I'd call BJ as soon as Sandoval and I put distance between us.

An Awful Hunch

Horn blasts and the screech of tires stopped my zigzag among the busy mah-jongg tables in Portsmouth Square. The whine of wrenching steel tore out an awful hunch: Sandoval? I charged toward the crash.

Blocked by a swarm of rubberneckers at the corner of Kearny and Washington Streets, I tiptoed to look over their heads. A bobtail truck had slammed into and wadded up Sandoval's Impala. I recognized Lee, one of the uniforms holding back the crowd.

"Lee," I hollered and caught his attention. "That's Sandoval."

"Let him through," Lee shouted, waving me toward him.

I bulled my way through until I could see the back of a graying blond head tending Sandoval. Crusher. BJ squatted next to her. He'd survived, and Crusher came to finish him off. BJ in on it?

Tightening my grip on the grocery bag, I yanked out my .45 and lurched past Lee.

"What the hell," Lee said and wrapped his arms around my waist from behind. "What's the matter with you?" he screamed in my ear. "The perp's long gone. Put that gun away."

"Dammit, let me go," I spat as we swung around, knocking over gawkers too scared to scramble for cover. Cries of "Gun! Gun!" spurted from the crowd.

"Settle down. You fly over there waving a piece, you'll scare the crap out of that doc taking care of him," Lee said, arching his back, and lifting me off the ground. I lost traction, causing my scrambling feet to skid on the pavement. Other cops sprinted toward us, weapons drawn. A young sergeant I didn't recognize hollered, "Drop 'em, Lee. Give us a shot."

Lee held me and shouted, "He's a cop. His buddy is in that wreck."

An ambulance siren cracked through my rage. I watched Crusher step back next to BJ as the paramedics muscled in. Stretching my neck, I caught Sandoval nodding his head. The tough bastard made it. He'd beaten Crusher.

BJ glanced at Crusher between glares at me. I read the slide of her jaw as, Get outta here before Crusher sees you. Was she being slick? Trying to say she wasn't in on the hit?

Surrounded by uniforms with drawn weapons, I holstered mine. Surprisingly, I hadn't spilled the groceries—dropped the router.

Raising my hands, I said, "Sorry. Sorry I lost it, but that's my pal in that mess."

Lee relaxed, and I shook off his grip. Keeping an eye on me, Lee waved away the other uniforms and said, "It's okay. He'll be all right now." The officers hesitated, then moved away, addressing the crowd, "Okay, okay, show's over."

The paramedics clamped a brace around Sandoval's neck and lifted him onto a gurney. The tough nerd jabbered on, gesturing with his good arm as they rolled him into the rig. With Sandoval out of Crusher's hands, my temp sputtered down.

"Anybody see the driver of the truck?" I asked Lee, peering into my brown bag at the fucken router. Then I lifted my gaze right into Crusher's. Behind her, BJ rolled her eyes and pounded her hips.

"Apparently uninjured. She escaped on foot."

"She." No surprise there. I wanted to shoot Crusher, leering at me from across the street, but payback would have to wait. Too many witnesses. And why the fuck hadn't BJ warned Sandoval and me? Didn't she know? Was it staged near her as a shot across her bow? Crusher leaned her head toward BJ's and mumbled something. BJ muttered back without taking her eyes off me.

"Yeah," Lee said. "Some witnesses said it was a short guy, and others said it was a woman. Those closest agreed she was butch." Then Lee pointed up toward the traffic camera. "We're counting on that to ID her."

I humphed. I knew the image would fit Jax. The little pit bull who threatened BJ at Yerba Buena Gardens.

Crusher and I traded dirty looks as she pressed her cell phone to her ear. She hadn't found O'DAD's router or phone—knew I had 'em. The reckless bitches nailed Sandoval without recovering their equipment. So much for the logic of our insurance policy. Now I'd replaced Sandoval in their crosshairs.

Caught in the switches of dodging a hit or covering Sandoval, I looked at the male paramedics and told myself he'd be safe in that ambulance. That I had time to become invisible and make it to the hospital undercover. I apologized to Lee and melted into Chinatown's crowded streets.

From a tourist trap, I bought a pair of cheap shades, baseball cap, knockoff sneakers, and a hooded sweatshirt with matching cheesy yellow striped sweatpants. Also bought a black backpack. Its first tenant, the router. I dumped the groceries.

Back at Uncle Ho's, I changed clothes in the basement's piss-fumed toilet. I'd ditch my car, but my friends Mr. Forty-five and Mrs. Switchblade would stay with me to guard the phone and router. Jack volunteered to call a cab for me and said he'd stash my street clothes.

With my tail between my legs in Ho's basement, I felt like I'd nailed that target to Sandoval's chest. I called San Francisco General Hospital from my disposable cell. If Sandoval made it, he'd be there.

Each ring snapped the knots in my belly. Each recorded prompt ahead of a human voice cracked across my skull like Chinese water torture. After an eternity in digital hell, the walls fell. The ER nurse told me Sandoval had just arrived and was stable.

I wouldn't be the only one who knew he'd survived. I had to get to him, cover him. Where's that lousy taxi?

A question burned: Did BJ know about the hit? I pounded in her number.

"Detective Reeves, who's this?" she asked officiously.

"It's me," I whispered.

"Hey, dahlin', this a new number?"

I recognized her phony glee as a public front. "Were you in on Crusher's hit?" I spat into the phone.

After she clucked her tongue, she said, "You know me better than that, girlfriend. Shame on you."

I wanted to believe her, but warning flares popped around my skull. "What the hell am I supposed to think, catching you and Crusher at the crash?"

"Hold on, dahlin', I'm in the middle of lunch. Gimme a sec." Above the strain in her voice, I heard the scrape of a chair and the rattle of plates. The sound of traffic overtook her. I missed the quiet of our extinct phone booths. Back on the line, BJ said, "Listen here. Neither one of us knew. Dr. Crusher thinks it was an accident. You and I know better."

"She ordered Sandoval's hit," I jeered.

"She saved his life. Ask him. Then think about what you're sayin'. Don't make sense to order a killin' and then turn around and save your victim."

"Oh, so it's a coincidence that you happened to be nearby?"

"Dammit, yes. Anybody see either one of us driving that rig?"

"You coulda spotted his Impala for the killer."

"From inside the Yangzte? You know it's got no windows. But hell's bells, that lowrider of his is about as subtle as the popemobile." Then BJ leaned on me. "You gonna return my things before somebody plows into you?"

"Fuck your precious gadgets. It's time to blow the lid off that homicidal sorority of yours. That's right, I know about O'DAD and their Internet cheat sheets on guys. Petty secrets not worth a drop of blood to save."

For a moment, all I heard was the bustle of traffic. Then BJ shot back in a low voice, "You listen here. I'm as sick as you are over Sandoval, but you seen any towers fall since 9/11? You think the Golden Gate is still standing because Al Qaeda or some latter-day Tim McVeigh likes strollin' the span? Not likely. You can thank our petty sorority for that. Ya hear?"

"Wha...what are you saying?"

"I have to spell it out for ya? No man denies his pecker, low-watt fanatic or not. He'll sock his good book under his pillow or shove his *Turner Diaries* between the mattresses for a peek between a lady's legs. Since 9/11, O'DAD's 'cheat sheets' have provided the intel that's kept this and other towns from being blown to high heaven."

BJ's national security point pierced my rage, but not in time to stop me from blurting, "That supposed to justify murder?"

"Pay attention. O'DAD and Dr. Crusher aren't the enemy. The sisterhood relies on finesse. Like the scheme that's got you bound up in your suspension. How many times I hafta tell ya, the killer and her flunkies are rogues?"

I started to mull over what BJ'd said, but Jack shouted from the top of the stairs, "Sir, taxi here." He knew better than to call my name, and I had no more time to make nice with BJ while Havana zeroed in on Sandoval.

"Gotta go cover Sandoval's back," I said to BJ.

"What about my things?"

"You'll have to wait," I snapped and hung up. I darted up the stairs with my cap on, hood up, in shades, and holding my backpack. Out the front door I jumped into the cab's backseat, looking like a jelly-bellied jogger. Gasping for breath, I ordered the cabbie, "SF General. And step on it."

♦ ♦ ♦

"Detective Faeth, BJ?" Marilee asked as the Yangtze Restaurant cashier counted change into her pudgy hands.

"Uh-huh," BJ answered. Her energy sapped by what Lo now knew, by her failure to recover O'DAD's equipment, and her powerlessness to stop Havana's attack on Sandoval.

As they stepped out onto the sidewalk, Marilee said, "No coincidence that we saw him at the accident. Since Dr. Sandoval didn't possess our equipment, we must assume he gave it to your partner. Is he still promising you the router?"

Marilee's words scraped like sandpaper. BJ mulled over ways to get her to muzzle Havana as they strolled up Columbus Avenue. Searched for a path to Marilee's conscience. She finally answered, "Yes, but—"

"Yes, but what?" Marilee snapped and then continued. "And did he give you any idea of what Dr. Sandoval learned from our equipment?" Her words seemed to puff out in cadence with her labored steps up the avenue's grade.

BJ gambled that underneath Marilee's irritability, her conscience gasped for air in the vacuum of Sandoval's injuries. She pounced. "No, but Detective Faeth's convinced the accident was a hit you ordered."

She watched Marilee grab her chest and stumble back against the City Lights bookstore's corner window. The glass rumbled but held.

Mohawk-coiffed and tie-dye-garbed Samaritans bolted out of the literary landmark to help.

"She's fine, she's fine," BJ said, her arms folded, locked in a mean delight seeing Marilee reel from a blow born from her blindness toward Havana.

Marilee caught her breath and assured the gaggle of do-gooders bracing her that she could stand alone. BJ stepped in and took Marilee by the arm. Thanked the Good Sams and shooed 'em away with Marilee's need for air. She and Marilee slipped into Kerouac Alley.

"That dreadful accident a murder attempt at my calling?" the doctor sputtered.

BJ whipped out her wedge. "Marilee, there were no skid marks behind that stolen rig. Faeth added that up with our missing equipment. A hit's no big reach."

Marilee's face twisted into painful eddies.

BJ thrust her blade into Marilee's tie to Havana. "You can't fault Lo's logic. You told Havana to keep an eye on Sandoval."

Marilee's face hardened. "Lo?"

Her slip of the tongue leaked her intimacy with Lo. "Detective Faeth's nickname," she said, her recovery as weak as her voice.

Marilee's chest rose. Charged with breath, she said, "BJ, you of all people can't possibly believe that I—"

BJ interrupted. "No, no, of course not. All I'm sayin' is that under the circumstances it looks like attempted murder. And for heaven's sake, you heard the witnesses descriptions of that truck driver. Fit Jax down to her prickly crew cut."

Marilee's eyelids fluttered.

BJ twisted her blade. "Can you tell me that Havana don't have it in her to sic Jax on Sandoval? How are ya gonna feel when that traffic camera IDs Jax?"

Marilee gasped. "Oh, my god. When I phoned Havana to let her know about Dr. Sandoval's accident, she didn't sound surprised."

BJ saw the blood drain from Marilee's face. "Because she already knew. Call her. Demand a come-to-Jesus meetin'. Make her fess up or prove her innocence. Tell her Jax was caught on camera."

Marilee rummaged through her purse. "I know your relationship with Havana is strained, and she can be rigidly task oriented. But this had to have been an accident, hon. Nevertheless, I'll meet with her and Jax. See if I find any evidence to support your and *Lo's* suspicions," she said, her stare lingering.

BJ felt Marilee's stress on Lo push back against her blade. She watched Marilee punch up Havana's number and listened to her voice deflate. She instructed Havana and Jax to meet her at La Rue Restaurant in Oakland, another O'DAD haunt—BJ had made it a point to learn the locations of all the Bay Area O'DAD hot spots since the Bambi explosion. Not a hint of accusation skirted off Marilee's tongue. Not a peep about the traffic camera.

BJ saw her wedge fall to the alley floor. How could Marilee miss Havana under the light of Sandoval's hit yet dismiss her over her use of Faeth's nickname? BJ's glare at Marilee flipped and penetrated her own soul. Had ducking motherhood robbed her of any accounting for Marilee's knack for finding excuses for Havana?

She stumbled back. Where had her fierce independence gotten her, except behind a badge, undercover and alone? Noble, or conveniently cut off from being a wife or mother? BJ quaked. Her naked heart pounded against a bitter question: Would she ever be as complete a woman as her mom, as Marilee?

"BJ, are you all right?" Marilee said, interrupting her call to Havana.

BJ caught her breath. "Yeah. Fine. Really, I'm okay."

"Are you sure?" Marilee kept her eyes on BJ.

"Oh yeah. Just upset over Dr. Sandoval." BJ tugged at the hem of her jacket. "Go on, don't leave Havana hanging."

Marilee squinted but then relaxed her gaze. "Your color seems to be returning." She spoke into her cell: "Havana, I'm back."

BJ forced her attention on Marilee's promise to meet with Havana and Jax. It'd take time Havana'd otherwise use to finish off Sandoval. Precious moments Lo would use to muster his friend's defense.

BJ's SFPD cell rang. Captain Rhodes's name glowed back. She'd never uploaded his pic. "Reeves here.…Affirmative, I am with Dr. Crusher.… Right now?" she asked, wrestling the strain out of her voice.

Marilee ended her call to Havana. Gave BJ a curious look.

"Rhodes is asking us to meet with him. Heard you treated Sandoval," BJ said, feeling that even bumbling Rhodes wielded more control over her fate than she did.

Marilee took BJ's arm and said, "Come on, hon. Let's go visit that captain of yours. Give him our versions of the accident."

"Thought you're gonna meet with Havana?" BJ snapped, unable to stop her sudden flare.

"She and Jax can enjoy La Rue's tasty appetizers all by themselves while they wait for me." Marilee's pleasant tone appeared to ignore BJ's sizzle.

Did Marilee's delay—and pass on her sudden flare—suggest an unconscious crack in her wall around Havana? BJ humphed and then let her wishful thinking evaporate.

"Did you say something, hon?" Marilee said.

"No, ma'am," BJ replied as they clomped toward their cars.

♦ ♦ ♦

The cab shuddered over a pothole as it swung left onto Stockton Street. I rapped against the Plexiglas divider and snarled, "Faster, faster." The bearded hack shoveled the air in front of him with his hands. "Yeah, yeah, I see the traffic," I said.

Guilt swamped my pathetic veins. If I'd let BJ have her way at Bambi's and written off the death as accidental, she'd still be my partner and Sandoval wouldn't have been hit. I fought back. Told myself I'd only done my job. That Sandoval wasn't my fault.

Happy Hour

I stopped the cab a block away from the hospital to give me recon room before funneling into its narrow corridors. I imagined the place swarming with cops checking on Sandoval. That Havana couldn't strike again until the brothers in blue thinned out. Wishful thinking?

From an isolated spot outside, I phoned again for an update on Sandoval's condition. After grinding my teeth between voice jail's brutal prompts, an ER nurse informed me he'd transferred to their ICU, intensive care unit. He'd made it, so far.

My loose plan required lurking about ICU's neighboring halls, swiping a pair of surgical gloves—they'd come in handy later—and catching a trusted member of Sandoval's team. I'd warn him that the hit-and-run was no accident. That it was a contract hit put out by a drug trafficker we'd put away for murder. Explain that was why I was on the lam and that Sandoval needed around-the-clock protection.

I trotted up the stairwell to ICU to avoid being caged in an elevator. Panting near the unit, I peeked around the corner of the pharmacy. The floor crawled with cops taking turns going in and out of Sandoval's room. Officer Lakesha Jackson glanced my way as I ducked back. Hooded, I hoped she'd take me for a jonesing doper fleeing detox on the same floor.

Moments later, Laszlo Singh left Sandoval's room and entered an elevator. I raced down the stairs to the lobby. Doubled up and gasping at the bottom of the stairwell, I peeked into the lobby.

Laszlo spoke to Lakesha by the gift shop. His head moved like a hawk's. Something was up. Her lips read, "I'll walk out with you," but Laszlo shook his head and turned back toward the elevator. She shrugged and took off toward the exit.

I hid in the stairwell and waited for Laszlo's return. He'd be back. I didn't have to wait long. He exited the same elevator and headed toward the door. Had he intended to ditch Lakesha?

I kept him in sight until I could ease up on him in the shadows of the parking structure. I dropped my hood and whispered, "Laszlo. It's me, Faeth."

Startled, he spun around, his arms shooting out for balance. "Dr. Sandoval said you'd come." Shaken, his words bobbled on his Indian tongue like a hot chili. "Told me to make sure I was alone."

Sandoval was conscious. The tightness in my chest relaxed. But what the hell did he spill to Laszlo?

"What'd he say?"

"Dr. Sandoval told me and our captain that he suspects it was not an accident. That a mafioso he helped lock up took out a contract on him. Captain Jaden posted a patrol officer to his room twenty-four seven, and only authorized medical staff are allowed contact with him. The officer already rejected one rude doctor. I also checked his room for bugs."

"Wise moves," I said. "Hey, was that booted doc female?"

"Yes. Why?"

"Can't rule out a gal as a hit man." Seemed everybody were leaps ahead of me—including Havana.

"Of course not. Dr. Sandoval told me you had been involved in that case too. That your captain fears that your name may be on that contract, so he ordered you into hiding. I am happy that you were not suspended," Laszlo added.

"Can't always trust the grapevine," I sneered.

Even banged up, my sharp pal figured the less Laszlo knew, the lower the chances of tacking a target on him too.

"How is he?"

"The doctors are guardedly optimistic about his recovery." Laszlo poked the bridge of his thick glasses back up his teardrop nose and went on. "Dr. Sandoval spoke softly into my ear. 'Watch for Faeth, and tell him that if it were not for Dr. Crusher, I would be dead.'"

"He sure?"

Laszlo stared at me. "He made it a point. Wanted you to know that without her, he would have bled out before the paramedics arrived."

I coulda shot her. Could BJ be right, that Crusher's innocent? I met Laszlo's eyes and dumbed up. "Lucky she was there, huh?"

Despite what BJ said, she still could've ordered the hit but saved Sandoval's life when she couldn't find O'DAD's equipment. Presumed he'd given me the router and phone. Needed him alive to bait me into the open. I scanned the garage.

"Somebody might see us. Let's get into the car."

"Yes, yes, of course." Laszlo popped open the locks, and we slid into his SUV. "Detective Faeth, you left your car in our parking lot. Can you believe that someone broke in? The seats are slit open, and the door panels are torn out, as if they were looking for something."

My belly soured. It didn't take a genius to add up that if the router wasn't hidden in my car, my pal had it. Leaving my car in the lot had pointed out Sandoval to Havana.

"Probably took my satellite radio and CD player."

Laszlo would never know that the radio/tape deck died long ago, and I'd let the repair shop trash it after pronouncing it dead.

He did a double take as if he didn't buy my story, but then seemed to concentrate on backing out of the parking space.

I slouched down and pulled my hood back over my head.

"I asked Dr. Sandoval many questions, but he said the less I knew, the better. Who's after you?" Laszlo's tongue pricked the middle of each word and snipped off their endings.

"Listen, we don't have all the answers yet. But he doesn't want anybody else to get hurt. For now, it's best that you don't discuss this with anyone."

Laszlo's face crumpled. "How can I? I know nothing." Then Laszlo darted his eyes between me and the road. "Dr. Sandoval said to quietly run a background check on Detective Reeves. He didn't explain why. Do you know?"

"Sure, sure, I do," I stammered, bugged that Sandoval dragged Laszlo in to check on BJ. But I understood. The fucker, hospitalized or not, was still checking on whose side BJ was on. Whatever doubts Sandoval had about BJ, my gut remained sure that she was a mole. But finding out her true identity could lead us to her handler. The more I knew, the more juice I had to muscle into BJ's op. But what the hell to tell Laszlo?

"Routine ID confirmation on everyone near us," I said, and thought, Weak man, weak. Then I added, "He'd already checked out everybody else, hadn't got around to BJ yet. What else did he say?"

"He said he would call you and that you knew better than to call him. That you never know who might be near and answer his phone."

Sandoval's security gave me range to dig up dirt on O'DAD. Sneak in and out of a powder room. Hack their website. Tell BJ I'd keep my mouth shut about O'DAD if she let me in on nailing Havana and Jax. But first I needed more cash, an ink marker, paper, tape, and a recorder.

"Let's hit an ATM."

"Of course, Detective."

After my stops, Laszlo dropped me off on Natoma Street, by the bus terminal. I'd make my first step toward a counterstrike from the sidewalks of the invisible homeless.

♦ ♦ ♦

BJ sat sucked into Rhodes's club chair. Marilee's Pollyanna chatter about Sandoval's accident and her fortunate presence nearby grated her nerves. The question of why Havana'd struck before confirming Sandoval had O'DAD's equipment kept grinding outta the mill.

"You're awfully quiet over there, Detective," Rhodes said sprightly.

BJ glanced up. "Just cogitatin' on Dr. Sandoval's miraculous luck."

"Amen," said Rhodes, who then turned to Marilee and asked if the Yangtze menu had changed.

BJ lapsed back into her thoughts. Havana had to figure that if Sandoval didn't have the router and phone, he'd passed them off to the evasive Lo.

Had she decided to kill the techno-savvy Sandoval, along with whatever he knew? His death certain to draw out Lo with their equipment? Even if Sandoval survived, a retaliatory and reckless Lo would surface to protect him. Did the cunning killer intend to flush out her loyalties too by forcing her to choose between saving Lo's fanny or protecting O'DAD? Audible knots snapped through her tummy.

Rhodes's phone rang.

"Captain Rhodes." He cupped the receiver and whispered in BJ and Marilee's direction, "It's Captain Jaden."

BJ slid to the edge of her seat to listen in on Sandoval's boss's call. "Is he all right?"

Rhodes nodded in the affirmative and flapped the air with his free hand. BJ assumed he wanted to concentrate on Captain Jaden's call. Lord forbid he do two things at once.

BJ traded glances with Marilee as she tried to cipher Rhodes's series of "Uh-huhs." But when he grinned and said, "The traffic camera captured the truck driver's image," she held no doubt whose squat form had scurried away from the wreck—Jax's.

"What's his condition?" Marilee demanded as soon as Rhodes said good-bye. Her urgency reflected the good doctor BJ admired.

"He's stable, and they believe he'll make it. But they're handling the crash as a murder attempt ordered by an organized crime figure. Someone Sandoval's dogged forensics put away." Rhodes leaned back in his squeaky chair and assumed a thoughtful pose. "Captain Jaden has ordered around-the-clock security. As he should."

BJ assumed a battered Sandoval had orchestrated Jaden's order. She felt a flutter of relief at his alert defense. Then Marilee's fingertips touched her wrist. She turned to meet the doctor's longing stare.

"Detective Reeves, imagine, it was an organized-crime hit all along. And they've captured the driver's image to prove it."

BJ fought to keep from jerking away. From tearing at what remained of her tether to O'DAD's grande dame. A thread that could be strengthened by Jax's image in flight from the wreck? Marilee needed to see that video. With Sandoval's protection in place and Havana chilled over cold appetizers at La Rue, BJ stood up and glared at Marilee. "Let's go see that video."

"I'm already late for another meeting. You go. Call me with your findings."

BJ heard her words dance off her tongue like a mother convinced of her child's innocence. Her resentment spiked but splintered against her orphan's doubt. Would her own mom have been so devoted to her?

She bolted out of Rhodes's office, wondering how long Marilee would keep Havana stalled at La Rue. When stubborn Lo would call for their meet. In the meantime, she'd confirm that Jax had driven that rig. Rub Marilee's nose in it.

BJ hastened her stride to her car.

♦ ♦ ♦

Humping my way out of Natoma Street's stench, I fingered my vic's cell through the plastic evidence bag in my pants pocket. Certain it would unlock O'DAD's treasury of dangling-dick dossiers. I could hear Sandoval bitching about my tinfoil beanie. Yet I felt that proof of my sanity was just four keystrokes away—6323. My next stop, a place to meet BJ with an O'DAD hot spot.

Bambi's had burned down, and Sandoval's Tenderloin bar might've nixed its site after that hooker's murder. That left Sandoval's watering hole. I waved down a taxi on First Street. "Dew Drop Inn, South of Market," I said.

The cabbie glanced at his watch and cheerfully said, "Just in time for happy hour."

Along our stop-and-go route, the talkative hack told me all about his plan to reduce the snarling traffic: Anyone who worked but didn't live in San Francisco had to take their cars and be out by five. Then he and the other cabbies could haul around the gawking "touri," his term for tourists, and share the streets only with locals. My occasional "uh-huhs" kept him yakking. Allowed me to attend to the more serious matter of being followed.

Interrupting the hack, I had him drop me off down the street from the Dew Drop Inn. I drew my hood over my head and ducked into the recessed entrance of an empty storefront. I dialed BJ.

"'Bout ready to give up on ya," she said. "Gimme a sec." Her tone then took a serious plunge. "No more dallyin'. You gotta return my things."

"Where are ya?" I asked.

"Stepped into a hallway here at Forensics. Been watchin' the replay of the back of Jax's head gettin' smaller and smaller as she hightails it away from Sandoval's wreck."

"Good enough to ID her?"

BJ answered after a pause. "For you and me. But the camera caught only a partial of her face."

"Shit. All right, meet me at the Dew Drop Inn, South of Market, at six p.m." By then I'd have been in and out of its powder room, pumped with enough intel to force BJ into letting me in on knocking out the killers.

"No, not there. Too confined." Her words sizzled like a lit fuse.

Her sparks told me that the inn did hide an O'DAD Wi-Fi hot spot. Perfect.

"There, or forget it," I said, not to be denied what I needed to avenge Sandoval and pay a deposit on what I owed my brother. I hung up.

♦ ♦ ♦

BJ hissed. Lo's ultimatum reeked of more than macho crap. The old hound possessed an O'DAD cell. No doubt Sandoval had discovered Havana's simpleton access code—ODAD—and given it to him. Hell's bells, he'd spouted off 6323 himself at the crime scene.

She knew his next step. March right into O'DAD's website. She stuck her head back into the video lab and said, "Gotta go. Catch you later." She had to get to the inn early. Intercept Lo before he pussyfooted into that powder room. Before Havana found out.

Dead Right

I slunk into the Dew Drop Inn and planted myself where the long bar hooked into the side wall—at the mouth of the hall leading to the powder room. Shielded behind a cappuccino machine, I dropped my hood but squeezed my baseball cap down onto my forehead. The front and rear entrances stood in clear view. Blending in easily with the happy hour alkies—nobody looked at me twice.

Angling for a trip to the empty powder room, I followed a pair of women in their business suits and tired hair toward the restrooms. Rosie the Riveter's lit-up and framed "We Can Do It!" poster next to the door told me I'd hit the jackpot. As the two entered, giggling about whether the guy who'd been buying them drinks was in fact a bank VP, I glanced into their inner sanctum. It had a stall where I could hide. Looked and sounded empty except for the pair going in. I'd sneak in as soon as they left.

No one so much as glanced at me when I doubled back to my barstool without going into the men's room. Twenty minutes dragged by before the gals strutted out. I crept down the hall and peeked into the powder room, primed with a slurred apology in case it wasn't empty. Alone inside, I latched the door. I could surf O'DAD's net locked in. But first, I wanted to cop an exit code.

I snapped on the surgical gloves I'd lifted from the hospital and wrote "Out of Order" with my ink marker on the paper I pulled from my backpack. I taped the sign to the stall door opposite the sink, then unlocked the powder-room door. I hid inside my tiny out-of-order stall, latched it closed, and crouched on the toilet seat. My digital recorder at the ready. All I needed was a pair of gals to come in and click into O'DAD's website.

The bathroom door swung open. The two voices didn't come toward my stall. I tiptoed off the lid and peered through the crack between the door and the partition. A silky-haired brunette and a shapely black girl chattered on. Jeez, I felt like a pervert.

"Are you ready to get serious?" the black girl said.

"Uh-huh. From now on, no more Fakebook horn dogs lying about themselves to peel off this babe's thong," the brunette said. "Time for O'DAD's naked truth," she added with a giggle.

I watched them fish their phones out of their purses. The brunette punched her keypad. I gently squeezed the record button on my recorder and raised it to the crack in the partition.

The black girl asked, "What did that flirt tell you his name was?"

"Schuyler Colfax, 'at Stanford.'" With two fingers from each hand she scratched out air quotation marks. "You know, like I'm supposed to be impressed. He is kinda cute, though. Let's see if he is who he says he is."

The black chick rocked her head. "Yeah, and if he is, let's find out how many other girls he's hit on this week."

I thought, Whoa, O'DAD could tell them all that? The brunette tapped her keypad. I presumed she'd entered an access code, then the guy's name. She draped her dark hair behind her ears and held up her display between her and her pal.

"Picture and name match."

"That's a bonus." Then the black girl snatched her friend's phone. "And he is at Stanford."

Her pal grabbed it back, and they both burst into laughter. "To jockey a lawn mower." Together they sang, "Lo-ser." The brunette stroked her shapely hip and followed with, "It's going to take more than a gardener to rescue me from Walmart."

What bimbos, I thought.

"Shoe size, girl. At least check out his shoe size. See if you're missing anything," the black girl said.

Her pal playfully slapped her arm. "Selma, you slut."

"Time to call Michelle," the brunette said. "I placed the transponder in her fiancé's wheel well, like you told me."

Transponder. That's how Chata had caught Sandoval. That'll teach him not to doubt my gut's radar. I jutted my ear toward the girls. I should have brought a Minicam.

Selma's fingers danced across her keypad. "Hi, Michelle. You and Mike are still engaged. Right?...Well, me and Kim just saw him leave the Dew Drop Inn with a Vips.... Of course she's a Vips. Any other woman would have checked O'DAD for Mike's status and found out that he's yours."

I about slapped my forehead but caught myself. Hell, O'DAD did keep Sandoval out of the sack with a Vips. Now, that's national security. I gulped, thankful I'd been faithful to Madge. I shook my head. Needed to focus.

Selma nodded toward Kim and went on speaking into her phone. "Kim transferred the transponder frequency to your phone....You're welcome. You'd do the same for us. Good hunting." She turned to Kim. "See, O'DAD sisters stick together. You want to check out Schuyler's family history? Maybe he has a rich cousin."

Family history? How deep did O'DAD records go? I watched Kim shake her head no, and took that as my cue to focus on their fingers. Sandoval said he'd been able to fire up the router with my vic's phone but not shut it down. I squinted for an exit code.

Kim slid her phone back into her purse, so I concentrated on Selma's long fingers. From my angle, I followed the bounce of her fingertip across her phone's keypad. Her glossy nail clicked three times from the upper right corner down across to the lower left corner, and then back two clicks along the bottom. Like a topless *Z*. Looked to me like 35789.

Better than nothing. If Sandoval was right and I couldn't shut it down, I'd be able to leave it on and walk out. But if my hunches were accurate, I'd be locked in and dead right.

The pair strolled out of the powder room. I stepped to the entrance and locked the door a split second before a push from the outside. The knob twisted back and forth. Sorry, my turn to surf. Hoped she didn't have to go bad.

♦ ♦ ♦

BJ yanked on the locked powder-room door. She'd have to hold her pee. With no sign of Lo, she dismissed a frightful twinge that he stood behind that door. She'd beat him here, hadn't she? She'd arrived almost two hours early. Ready to get the hardware and equipped with a sedative to sideline him until she knocked him off Havana's to-do list. She made her way back to the front of the inn and sidled onto an empty barstool.

Despite the male bartender, the inn's owner could still be a Havana sympathizer. She wanted a drink to slacken her nerves but needed a clear head. If the bar's owner recognized her, she could have alerted the killer.

♦ ♦ ♦

I slid my vic's cell phone from my pocket and punched it on, opting for the phone's keypad. Here at the gates, I hesitated. Suddenly unsure if O'DAD's picture of me was the evidence I wanted. My nervous thumb hovered over the 6. Maybe I'd look up Sandoval's file instead.

Fuck it. I pounded in ODAD.

♦ ♦ ♦

BJ waved over the bartender and ordered a mineral water with a slice of lime. The swoop of someone onto the stool next to her caught the corner of her eye. She turned to face Marilee, in her baggy jeans and a polar fleece jacket. Hardly the outfit of a San Francisco coroner.

"Marilee!"

Marilee swept her gaze about the bar. "I assume this is where you intend to meet Detective Faeth?"

"Why else would I be here?" BJ damned herself for her caustic slip. But Marilee knew her presence would sabotage her meet with Lo. And how'd she track her? She'd been especially watchful on her way to the inn after last night's siren had tattled on Marilee. Over her puzzled flurry, she said as a matter of fact, "You know, if Faeth sees you he's off."

"I intend to disappear right away, hon."

BJ recognized that same wilted smile she saw yesterday at the ladies' sewing circle. A symptom of Marilee's failing confidence in her. Havana hadn't missed it either and had said so. She'd shuddered but excused it as a pee shiver and left for the potty. But she'd abandoned her phones—Hell's bells, had Havana slipped a tracking device into one of 'em?

"Marilee, did you let Havana put a tracker in one of my phones?" BJ asked.

"I did."

"Which one?"

"Ours."

BJ yanked apart her O'DAD cell while Marilee continued, "It's no secret that Havana holds doubts about you. She insisted on following you, but I told her no, that I would, and prove to her you'd recover our equipment. Lay to rest her suspicions."

"But Havana and Jax showed up last night, not you." BJ felt the heat of her glare cool. Doused by her own misplaced trust in Marilee. She should've known better.

"Havana called me to confess that against my wishes she'd followed you. Said that you had seen her and recklessly dashed out of her sight in front of speeding traffic. She asked why you'd do that if you had nothing to hide." Marilee's voice took a dive. Her eyes wandered and then focused back on BJ. "I do tire of your squabbling. So I told her I'd locate you and tell her where you were so she could see for herself that you wouldn't betray us."

Marilee had been played like a cheap kazoo. BJ darted her eyes about the bar.

"Is she here?" she snapped.

"No, hon, this is between you and me. For the moment."

"Then you should leave," BJ said, bound up in what Lo might do if he saw Marilee.

"I'll be waiting in the inn's office," Marilee said and slid off her barstool.

BJ plopped the tracking chip into her mineral water. If she didn't recover the hardware this time, her juice was spent.

♦ ♦ ♦

Colorful icons glimmered on the phone's display as I scrolled down: Archives, Video, IM, E-mail, Twitter, and Tracking. The latter included GPS. Beneath a rainbow-flag icon sat an instruction box that read, "For gay sisters, steganographic subfiles are available. Encrypted secondary access codes are required and available through O'DAD. Apply online." I half expected to find the throbbing message, Current or past penis bearers need not apply.

I tapped Archives. Like a credit-card prompt, blank windows appeared with instructions. "Enter presumed name and stated age, or download image." Damn, I'd just been denied thinking camera phones gimmicky. I punched in my info and another prompt appeared: "To speed search, specify geographical parameters."

Though clumsy with the tiny keypad, I entered San Francisco. Surprised at how much Faeth the city had, I scrolled until I found my date of birth.

My selection brought up my aka, Lo, and a thumbnail photograph of me draining my shoe at Bambi's. Fucken BJ.

My pisstivity staggered under the shock of notes available from my high school girlfriend, Madge, and a few others dumb enough to date me. Madge hadn't run into my ex-girlfriend at Macy's. She'd read her notes, which told of my brother. At the end of my ex-wife's comments, she'd included my shoe size. In bold flashing letters appeared "Size 13 = red herring."

"Chicken shit," I snapped and pounded in 35789 to shut down the ballbuster. From the door, I heard the clack of metal. I blew it off as someone trying to get in. Gave her a moment to leave and crept over to crack it open. Check if the hall was clear before I snuck out. The knob wouldn't budge.

A series of rapid beeps interrupted me. Across the phone's display flashed "To terminate, enter code from sister's phone NOW."

Son of a bitch. I needed codes from two different phones. That damned Sandoval had nailed it with his two-man rule despite himself. The room's lights flickered above. Around me I heard the drone of electrical motors and the dull slide of metal. I turned to see steel slats accordion over the small bathroom window. A boiling heap gurgled up and stung the back of my throat. I glanced at the display. "Intruder protocols imminent."

I tried dialing out. "Access denied," flashed back. I dialed 911 on my disposable. No signal. Jammed?

Fire alarms burst into my ears. The display read "Sister-pair failure. You have thirty seconds to safely interrupt O'DAD security protocol: rogue kill." An audio countdown commenced: "Thirty, twenty-nine, twenty-eight, twenty-seven, twenty-six…" Sweat pressed through my pores.

♦ ♦ ♦

Fire alarms stirred up the happy hour crowd. BJ recalled Lo's suspicions about Bambi's alarms and spotted Marilee clogged up with others at the front door. She shoved her way through the mob and grabbed her sleeve.

"Marilee, wait. Maybe I can prove Detective Faeth's suspicions about Havana."

Marilee pulled away. "How?"

"Do you smell smoke?" BJ asked.

Marilee sniffed the air. "Not yet." She glanced toward the exit. "We should go."

If Lo's belly was accurate, there was no fire. She had nothing to lose at this point. "Marilee, the alarm is a distraction."

Furrowing her brow, Marilee said, "What on earth are you talking about?"

BJ gambled on catching Havana and Jax or a couple of Havana's little Eichmanns pouncing on a Vips in the powder room. She'd nail the pair, and she and Marilee could save the victim.

"I'll show you. Come with me to the powder room."

Marilee's eyelids fluttered. "Only until we smell smoke."

BJ grabbed her sleeve. Pulled Marilee through the crowd, rushed by her fear that Lo could be behind that door.

♦ ♦ ♦

"Shit," I mumbled before launching myself at the door. I bounced off, almost dislocating my shoulder. The countdown taunted me through the throb of my shoulder. Stumbling back, I drew and slammed a round into the breech of my semiauto. I zeroed in on the doorknob until a foul smell screwed into my nose. Another change flashed across the phone's display: "Gas siphon engaged."

Bent on not being dead right about the gas, I whipped out my switchblade, dived to the bottom of the door, and started digging. If I could punch through to the other side, I could suck clean air. My lungs filled with an oily stench. The room faded to black.

♦ ♦ ♦

BJ and Marilee had threaded through the crowd. The doorknob to the ladies' room stood fast against the twist of BJ's grip. Like Lo said, Bambi's victim had been cornered. BJ shouted over the alarm, "It's locked."

"Whoever is in there has to hear the alarm. Why haven't they come out?" Marilee said.

BJ remembered that Bambi's vic had pounded in 6323, Havana's new and too-easy access code, before firing her gun. She yanked out her O'DAD cell and did the same. She shoved the cell's display under Marilee's nose. "See for yourself."

Marilee muttered, "To terminate rogue kill protocol, enter exit code from sister's phone."

"Grab your cell. Punch in your code. We gotta close that security loop." BJ prayed that the vic remained alive.

"I can't believe it, but I'll do it." Marilee fumbled for her phone and entered her code. The alarm fell silent.

That cinched it, BJ thought. Havana's simple access code lured in her vics. And, their only way out was in a body bag.

BJ twisted the knob of the freed door, hoping to catch a shocked Havana and Jax standing over a battered Vips. The door cracked open but a body blocked it. BJ's ears were greeted by the whir of ventilation fans. A whiff of gas socked her nose. Another gas leak? Like Bambi's? The dying fumes flitted around her recollection of Havana's mother's suicide. Had Havana contrived a method to gas her victims?

Glaring over her shoulder at Marilee, BJ shoved open the door as wide as possible, spouting, "You smell that? Gas."

BJ turned to the body crumpled on the floor. "My god, it is Lo." She dropped to her knees and pressed her ear to his chest. "Got a beat." She tilted back his head, brought her mouth to his. Gave him her breath.

Marilee relocked the door. "We mustn't risk exposing O'DAD to prying eyes."

BJ glanced up at a bewildered-looking Marilee. Watched her raise her phone and say, "I'll call Havana to help us."

"Don't you get it? She's responsible for this," BJ snapped. "Your love for that girl's gotcha stupefied."

Marilee dropped her arms to her sides, and her head slowly moved back and forth as she whispered, "No, there has to be another explanation." She raised her phone and her finger over the keypad.

BJ sprang to her feet, yanked at Marilee's phone, only to be met by her surprising grip. They whipped together, chest to chest. BJ spun and slammed her elbow into Marilee's temple. She collapsed onto Lo.

♦ ♦ ♦

Had somebody kissed me? The taste of fresh air began to dissolve the static from what sounded like BJ's voice. A couple of hazy images spun above me. Then one of 'em flopped onto my chest. A second later, a mouthful of ether gagged me back into the darkness.

♦ ♦ ♦

BJ shoved her chloroform pad back into its Baggie and into her pocket. Her more durable solution to sideline Lo sloshed inside a syringe. But that injection had to wait for a safe distance from the powder room.

She pulled Lo's hood over his head and then chided herself for the waste of time. Marilee would tell Havana about Lo. She hooked his arm behind her neck. With adrenaline-pumped muscles, she lifted him to his dragging feet. Lo's backpack with its precious O'DAD cargo was draped over her other shoulder. They staggered out of the powder room. One fall to her knees was all it took for a buff boozer to grab Lo's other shoulder. BJ's quick smile kept him there.

The bartender shouted from the front, "False alarm, false alarm. Come on back. Free rounds on the house." The owner of the bar must've seen her lugging out Lo. Made stark sense to restore business as usual. Keep the curious buzzed instead of asking what tripped the alarm. Likely notified SFFD the alarm went off accidentally. BJ figured the only reason Havana's minions hadn't pounced was because they'd seen her with Marilee. That cushion would lose its feathers soon. She and Lo had to get out of there.

Lo's load rocked them through the relieved throng jostling into the inn through the back entrance. Murmurs of the false alarm flittered about the thirsty crowd seeking their abandoned cocktails.

"Pardon us. Too much to drink. Excuse us," BJ gasped between lurching steps. But Lo's weight pressed lightly compared to the strain on BJ's soul. She'd smacked Marilee—hard. Sacrificed her for Lo.

She and her new BFF flopped Lo into her hybrid's backseat. When the guy asked to see her again, she gave him a fake name and SFPD's nonemergency number.

BJ couldn't let Marilee languish until someone with a bloated bladder stumbled on her. She yanked out her phone and punched 911. Reported a passed-out lady in the Dew Drop Inn's powder room, spat out the address, and hung up before dispatch asked for more. She thumbed her cell's off icon and then stared at the SFPD phone. It would be traced directly to her. "Hell's bells," she groaned. There'd be no denying she'd been with Marilee, let alone hittin' her. Marilee would come to and dismiss the powder-room evidence against Havana. Dump on Rhodes that she'd smacked her. Use that to weave a gaslight yarn into a straitjacket just like Lo's. And Havana'd be unleashed, gunning for her.

A collage of images spun, tangling up BJ's chest as she drove away. Lo's brush with death, her blow to Marilee, Marilee's collapse. Her thumping heart struck a flash of her parents' wake. Her eyes flooded before visions of herself standing breathless, staring down at Mom's bloodless face. Abandoned, alone.

Her mother's face morphed into Marilee's. And she'd killed her. BJ's belly convulsed. She gagged back the retched heap. Against the bile, she told herself Lo had faced death, not Marilee. Justice demanded she defend him. But reason bit back. A smart girl would've let Marilee call Havana. Let Havana traipse into the powder room. Watch her squirm as she tried to explain to Marilee her rogue kill protocol. Let her rip off Marilee's blinders.

Choking, BJ gasped for air like a sputtering diver cracking the ocean's surface. Marilee's blindness toward Havana had triggered her elbow. But it was her own jealousy of Havana that accelerated it into Marilee's skull.

Her spirit sank deeper. The deaths of her parents had swallowed her judgment and spat out rage. She caught her own stunned image staring back from her windshield. It mutated into Havana's enraged leer. Spikes stabbed her abdomen. BJ grabbed her tummy. Had she become Havana?

Horn blasts pounded her ears. Flashing high beams walloped her rearview mirror. The light had turned green. She hit the gas, unaware of how she'd made it to Mission Street. Guilt's bubbles burst about her boiling belly. There'd be no atoning for what she'd done. Neither would there be subtlety in Havana's vicious reply.

Out of her mangled soul spit a yearning for Havana's attack. It'd give her a shot at the killer with nine millimeters of due process—or give her a way to die trying. Neither offered the redemption she didn't deserve.

BJ honked and zipped between cars and buses. She needed to dump Lo before her showdown with Havana.

A Walk in the Park

Surrounded by night, BJ rolled away from where she'd hid Lo. She'd slipped the grumpy motel manager a couple of extra twenties for his help in depositing her knocked-out partner into bed. She'd shot him up with a sedative. Enough to pin him down until either Havana's or her own head topped a pike.

BJ gazed at the charcoal sky. Its darkness paled compared with her mood. She should've tranquilized that bull long before he barged through the door of her china shop. BJ hit the gas and shot through a yellow light.

"Shoulda-coulda-woulda," she humphed. "Too late now."

She knew she'd find Havana with Marilee. That'd be their O.K. Corral. She strained against her elbow's ache to convince herself that Marilee had been treated on scene and gone home. She punched on her police scanner to see what happened after her 911 call.

The chatter said an unconscious Dr. Crusher had been rushed into Emergency at the UCSF Medical Center. The news socked the wind out of her and billowed guilt's white flag. She fixed on offering her neck to Havana. Punishment would be swift.

BJ steered toward the hospital, plowing through dips and potholes. Her hybrid shuddered. If she rolled over for Havana, the raging bitch would turn on Lo and Sandoval for what they knew. It didn't matter that they couldn't prove a lick of it without the router and phone. She couldn't cotton to those boys paying with their lives for her failure. BJ sucked in a long breath. She'd neutralize Havana.

BJ swung around a gouge in the road. But what if Havana prevailed? What hedge could she plant in defense of Lo and Sandoval? For now, Sandoval had a guard. But Lo? He had to be unlocked from the shackles of his suspension. Free to rally with that boy in traction. Tobac held those keys. But contact with Tobac risked his bouncing her back to DC. The protocol for compromised ops. BJ's tummy pinched between Havana's rock and Tobac's hard place.

The dry ringtone of her FBI cell pummeled her eardrums. Tobac likely heard about the ruckus at the Dew Drop Inn. She ignored him. "Not till I finish this," she mumbled.

Tobac rang back. Then again and again. Since his wife's accident, the shrink had become edgy but never hysterical. His incessant rings hammered her conscience. She'd knocked out Marilee. Had she killed her? Tobac knew, didn't he? She had to find out. BJ answered tightly, "What's up?"

Tobac's voice pierced back, demanding they meet.

"Why now?" she asked, desperately plumbing for what he knew. Tobac refused to tell her. "On my way," she said, gnashing her teeth against images of Marilee gutted on a coroner's slab.

BJ aimed her hybrid toward an obscure little park in Marin County for her rendezvous with Tobac. The minor stretch north of San Francisco proved especially jagged.

A layer of fog swirled at BJ's feet as she clomped along the deserted park's manicured lawn. She turned up her collar against the misty chill. The pleasant odor of freshly cut grass wafted in the moist air. Refreshing any other time.

Spotting Tobac's lurching gait, she increased her pace. They traded nods beside a dew-pimpled picnic table. He set a gym bag on the attached bench.

The freckle-faced shrink stuffed his fists into his jeans and locked his elbows. With his shoulders pushed up to his ears, he reminded BJ of a rutting boy steeling to hit on her. She lost patience.

"Why'd you make me hightail it out here in the dark?"

She'd never heard him clear his throat before he spoke, but she couldn't tolerate the delay. "Spit it out," she demanded.

"Dr. Crusher's in a coma."

BJ buckled and plopped onto the wet bench, numb to the dew sucked up by her pants. Sputtering for air, she buried her face in her hands. The image of Marilee on her back in a hospital bed disintegrated, exposing her mother's ashen face staring out of her coffin. Tears burst through her fingers.

She felt Tobac gently squeeze her shoulder. He'd never touched her before. "What happened?" he asked.

She hadn't told him about meeting Lo at the Dew Drop Inn, but she wasn't the only female agent who briefed Tobac on O'DAD website activities. She took a shot at her ID being lost in the chaos at the inn and Havana too grief stricken to have BOLOed her on O'DAD's website. She broke through her sobs to say, "How would I know?"

Tobac's hand slipped from her shoulder. "Let me put it another way. Even before Havana announced on O'DAD's website that you helped Detective Faeth escape after he assaulted Dr. Crusher, an anonymous tip told the paramedics where to find her. Don't pretend that the Dew Drop Inn is not where you and Dr. Crusher followed Detective Faeth, the legs of O'DAD's router and phone."

The old shrink could see around corners. And Havana had blamed Lo for Marilee's coma. BJ inhaled through her nose. She'd parlay Havana's deadly protocol to keep Tobac from booting her to DC. Convince him that discovery made her the lynchpin to stop the murders.

"Detective Faeth sneaked into the powder room. Accessed O'DAD's website. He found out the hard way he needed an exit code from a second O'DAD phone."

Tobac interrupted. "Old news. Codes from separate devices foster mutually dependent security. So, what do you mean, 'the hard way'?"

"I told ya before that easy access code smelled to high heaven. A Vips nabs an O'DAD phone, hits a Rosie-the-Riveter powder room all by herself, punches in ODAD, and opens the site. Doesn't know she needs a sister's phone to get out. Exactly what Faeth did to trap himself."

"Trap?" Tobac said, shaking his head.

"The room hermetically seals and pumps in gas without that second phone's code. A false fire alarm clears the place. With everybody hightailin' it the other way, gas nails the vic, then the body's garroted and robbed. That's how Havana, or her flunkies, stage those robbery-homicides."

Tobac drew the slack out of his jaw but kept his dubious leer. "Not plausible," he said. "The time between the alarm and the arrival of the fire department is insufficient."

BJ held her ground. "Hell's bells, it is if the killers are already there. There's no shortage of hateful women. Havana could set her traps in businesses owned by accomplices."

"Then how did you get past them at the Dew Drop Inn?" Tobac countered.

Feeling like Lo must've felt when she'd challenged him, she replied, "They saw me with Marilee. Know she opposes violence. Didn't want her to catch 'em, so bled out the doors with the drunks."

BJ watched Tobac squeeze his face and mutter about Havana symbolically reenacting her mother's suicide. He raised his voice and said, "Why was Dr. Crusher struck? She must've been as appalled as you by your discovery."

"Thinks she's Mommy," BJ snapped, anger searing her grief. "Can't accept Havana's guilt. Started to call her for help to get Faeth outta there."

Tobac spiked an eyebrow. "Was Detective Faeth conscious when you found him?"

BJ hesitated. Knew Tobac had just asked which one of them had hit Marilee. But she couldn't brush Lo with that tar. "No," she said with half a breath.

Tobac folded his arms across his chest. "You struck Dr. Crusher to save Detective Faeth. Squandered an opportunity to force Havana to explain herself to Dr. Crusher. Not like you, BJ. But now's not the time for the analyst's couch. You've got packing to do. Havana's pegged you as a traitor. Said to text her with leads to your whereabouts." He glanced at the gym bag. "There is a blond wig, a baseball cap, blue contact lenses, and glasses in there, along with a change of clothes. Our photographer is waiting for you at the safe house. You need new ID to safely travel."

BJ didn't intend to flee. "No. Don'tcha see? This is the time to strike. Our chance to finish this. Havana's blinded by rage, thinks I'm on the run. Gives us the advantage." She'd chosen her words carefully—"our" and "us" gave Tobac ownership. Doses of his own therapeutic medicine.

"This is nonnegotiable," he shot back. "Just as Havana may be blinded by fury, your guilt may cause another lapse of judgment. You're at risk and a liability."

His words stung but BJ countered, "By the time a replacement gets here and up to speed, Havana's recovered her wits."

Tobac sighed. "Not so. Your alternate is at SFO baggage claim as we speak. Been briefed since your first failed attempt to recover O'DAD's hardware."

BJ lurched off the bench. "What? Who?"

"Mai Nguyen."

Seething, BJ said, "Gadget? The lawyer?"

"Gadget? That's uncalled for."

BJ knew Nguyen. Had a thing for undercover accessories. Otherwise, she was cute, gutsy, and all business. But she'd be damned if she'd cut Tobac any slack.

"For crying out loud, everybody calls her Gadget. Her first boss picked up a pen off her desk and got pepper sprayed writin' a note. Thinks she's James Bond. Always ordering stuff from those spy-store websites."

"Her years as Baghdad's legal attaché forged her into an exceptional agent." Tobac met her glare. "Give me the router and phone."

BJ searched Tobac's eyes. He hadn't blinked. But no way she'd give up her leverage to snap Lo's suspension or to keep herself off a plane. "Don't got 'em."

"What?"

"Detective Faeth has 'em," she said, positioning herself to pry off Lo's suspension and buy time for her shot at Havana.

"Why?" he flared, spreading his arms.

"Needs them as a hedge against Havana. At least while he's suspended. The ol' boy's got no backup with me outta the picture and Sandoval hog-tied to a hospital bed. Back on duty, he'll have a fightin' chance. Lift his suspension."

"I haven't received his medical clearance, let alone seen him," Tobac said, his voice hard.

"Rhodes don't know that. See him tomorrow. Put 'em back on duty. Here's his cell number," she said, stuffing a paper in the front pocket of his jeans. He stepped back. BJ swore she felt steam.

"You expect me to expose my cover by asking him for the hardware before or after his evaluation?"

"Neither. I'll ask him when you're done. Save your cover. 'Course, I'll have to stick around till then," BJ said, hoping she'd cornered him.

"This is extortion," he said.

BJ watched Tobac squeeze his fists.

"I'll contact Detective Faeth first thing in the morning. Captain Rhodes will have his clearance in his confidential e-mail shortly after. Immediately after that, I'll expect you, the router, and phone, at my private office. Then I'll personally drive you to SFO. Bring your new ID."

She wasn't finished. She was about to confront Havana alone—the killers would be looking out for her hybrid. "Until I get ya O'DAD's hardware, I can't be spotted in my car. I need another ride."

Tobac looked at his watch. "I'll make the call. Don't get attached to the new car."

"Of course not." BJ grabbed the gym bag. "Thanks for the disguise."

"And BJ. You're off the case. Belongs to Suki MacLeod now."

"Suki MacLeod? Gadget's cover?"

"Yes, yes. Are we clear?"

"As a bell, suh," she said and saluted.

BJ couldn't risk going home. Back in her car she called a reliable contact. Her bank manager. She needed access to her safe-deposit box—tonight. She'd also use the bank's word processor.

After Tobac called and told her where to pick up the car, she dumped her FBI phone. Not that it would buy time, but it would tongue-tie Tobac against spouting orders into her SFPD cell. He knew better than to call her on her O'DAD phone.

Havana's Straitjacket

BJ drove from Lo's motel a second time, now in her window-tinted black Chrysler. She sported Tobac's shoulder-length blond wig, glasses, and a black-and-white baseball cap. She'd dumped the blue contacts. Bad enough she felt like Havana's twin. Didn't need her frigid eyes too.

She'd left the locker key to her and Tobac's drop location in an envelope with a note attached for Lo. But only as backup for him if Havana whacked her. BJ planned to neutralize Havana, and then retrieve the key and note before he came to.

The thumps of potholes as she sped toward her showdown with Havana and Jax didn't distract her from another gnaw at her soul. If she missed her shot at the pair, the stray bullet would nail Lo's reconciliation with Ricky. Another reason not to fail.

She spurred the spirited Chrysler toward the hospital. A site free of O'DAD powder rooms, but not absent of Havana's sympathizers. She'd put Tobac's disguise to good use and blitz the grieving duo at Marilee's bedside. Havana had to know that Marilee witnessed her rogue kill protocol. BJ's fabric for her straitjacket. BJ'd rub Havana's nose into her crappy bind: Confess and surrender, or kill Marilee, prosecution's key witness.

BJ parallel parked the muscle car, slid out, and pulled at the belt loops of Tobac's off-the-rack jeans to squeeze herself back in. She closed her ears to the reaper's rap on Marilee's door. She had to live. Her scheme to force Havana's surrender hinged on the killer ignoring the same knock—that Marilee could die.

She glanced up at a SFPD cruiser passing across the street. Coulda sworn she'd seen the profile of Officer Lakesha Jackson. Her pulse leaped. Havana's forward guard? Or a coincidence? She watched the cruiser's tail-lights fade. BJ recalled that Havana stuck to her own kind, white women with an ax to grind, not African-American ladies. Besides, if Lakesha was after her, she'd be on the lookout for her and her hybrid, not a blonde. Her pulse eased.

Inside, BJ's flashed badge dropped every nurse's palm-up declaration that only family members were allowed to see Dr. Crusher. Seeing no one suspicious traipsing around Marilee's floor, she dumped her hat and glasses. Didn't want the duo guessin' for long who'd barged in.

BJ puffed up and swooped into Marilee's room. Havana sat bent over, her face buried in her arms on Marilee's blanket. Jax paced back and forth.

Jax lurched to a halt. "BJ?" she said, her voice spiked.

BJ kept her eyes on Havana. The killer's head popped up. Her tears vaporized. But Havana's sneering "You've got ovaries coming here" dissolved into white noise as her own gaze tunneled left to Marilee's paralyzed body. She felt the room contract. She couldn't breathe.

Hot breath billowed up BJ's chin. She turned her head into Havana's face, inches from hers. She stumbled back, stammering, "This...this is your fault."

Havana glanced at Marilee. "My fault? What kind of cunt are you? Let your boyfriend beat her into a coma. Left her to die to help him escape."

That Havana hadn't imagined her hitting Marilee and blamed Lo didn't free her lungs. Desperate, BJ gasped a reply: "She...she knows you're a murderer. Helped me shut down your rogue kill protocol." She watched pain crease Havana's face as she turned her gaze on her surrogate mother.

Havana raised an accusatory finger to BJ while she spoke to Marilee: "Traitors like her are the reason I fight fire with fire."

Gulping breath, BJ shook out Havana's straitjacket. "The only way to stop Marilee from turning you in is...is to finish her."

Havana's body flagged but her finger lingered in BJ's face. BJ wrapped her fingers around Havana's hand, gently guiding it down. Havana turned her head away from Marilee. Her misty eyes glanced between their joined hands and BJ's face.

"Havana, surrender," BJ said softly, now with an eye on a petrified Jax.

BJ tried to read the bleed of Havana's sweaty palm. From under whose feet would the floor shift?

Havana listed against the foot of Marilee's bed and slipped her hand out of BJ's. A furtive glance at Jax sent her out of the room. BJ felt the room yaw. Jax split to blow the bugle.

"You're right." Havana cast a longing look at Marilee. "It's what she'd want." Her concession came wrapped in all the sincerity of a pipe bomb. She was stalling.

BJ'd expected Havana's sorrow to distract her from the possibility that Marilee wouldn't awaken. That she'd surrender. It struck BJ that her own grief, not Havana's, denied that Marilee could die. Havana's pain fed on blood. The thread of Havana's straitjacket unraveled at BJ's feet.

"Good," BJ said, looking to escape. "We'll meet at the station tomorrow and negotiate the terms." She spun around to head for the door. Over her shoulder she added, "See ya at nine, then."

Havana grabbed her arm. "Wait. Let's talk about how to keep O'DAD out of it. Then me and Jax will come with you now."

BJ brushed her off. "I won't rob ya of your last night to tend to Marilee." She felt the heat of Havana's glare follow her out.

BJ dumped the wig out of sight of Havana and threaded her way through the hospital corridors. She hoped to confuse Jax's description of her. She didn't see Jax and appeared invisible to the night nurses as long as she headed for the exits. Still, she felt exposed. Tobac's words salted her wounded judgment as she fled: "You're at risk and a liability." Her guilt had caused her to tempt O'DAD's butcher. Her legs became weak. She stumbled, gagging back a wad of puke.

"Hon, why don't you come over here and sit down," said a stout nurse, taking her arm. She'd come out of nowhere. "You're so peaked."

"Bad tummy." BJ allowed herself to be guided to the molded plastic chair.

The nurse bowed eye level to BJ. “You sit here. I’ll be right back with Zofran.”

“Sit here” echoed back as “sitting duck.” BJ bolted as soon as the nurse rounded the corner.

BJ slammed the car door and rammed the key into the ignition. Two headlights crept up on the left and then popped into three. That third a spotlight. BJ didn’t need to see behind the glare to know she’d been corralled by a cop car. Lakesha?

She still had her feet. She scooted over the center console and shoved open the passenger door. As soon as her head pushed out, a gun barrel gouged her temple. “Hands up, bitch,” Jax said.

A Fitting Reward

BJ lay on her side, hooded, her mouth taped shut. Her hands and ankles bound behind her, as if by a bowstring. Had to be past midnight. The odor of stale pee offered no surprise as she lay on the hard tile of a powder room. A fitting reward for her attack on Marilee. Her naive miscalculation that Havana would surrender. Her fold as an agent.

Blind, her eyes turned inward. With the bureau, she'd never before felt like a vulnerable woman. Now, she writhed on a cold floor. A fate no different from a broken man's.

A bleak current sucked her further down. Would she swallow her last breath here? Die, single and childless? Incomplete? Breath spurted out her runny nose. Moments passed before her starved lungs sputtered in another.

"Quit whimpering, bitch," Havana said from across the room. "Your boyfriend's not answering his phone. Guess his beauty sleep is more important than you, huh?"

A flash of rage blanched BJ's pity party. She snorted back her grief. Havana'd been calling Lo from her SFPD phone. Obviously figured Faeth would see her caller ID and answer. If he could. But her cocktail had meant to keep him out of her way until the morning. She hadn't planned on baiting Havana's hook to land him. When Lo came to, he'd answer Havana's invitation and bull his way into her trap. Unless she freed herself.

"As soon as your boyfriend answers his phone, we can get this over with and all go home. Tell us where he is, and we'll bring him to the party," Havana said and snickered.

BJ shook her head no. Braced for a kidney kick.

"Have it your way. For now," Havana said without a step toward her.

Two pairs of footsteps caught BJ's attention. The powder-room door squeaked open and then closed. She heard the latch turn. No more voices. The rank amateurs left her alone. She'd bust up a porcelain toilet-tank lid and cut free against a jagged piece. She squirmed against the bite of the flex-cuffs, certain she'd crawl against a porcelain throne.

A third set of steps clomped toward her and circled. A yank at her ankles dragged her back to what she assumed to be the center of the floor.

The guard stepped away. BJ heard the scoot of chair legs and nothing else but a hiss. But if they were going kill her, why the hood and the silent treatment?

Woman's intuition pulled up alongside the cruiser that had blocked her escape. Suggested that Officer Lakesha Jackson sat nearby. The hood and tape over her mouth made sense only if Lakesha thought she'd survive the kidnapping. Had Havana sold a good cop a load of crap that she guarded a traitor? The kind of lie evil people used to trick good people into doing bad things. Probably fed Lakesha the story that once they recovered their hardware, they'd kick her captive out of O'DAD and let her go. Made the kidney kick that never came also add up. Couldn't strike her in front of Lakesha.

BJ's tongue pierced her lips and rammed the bitter duct tape. She pried it loose enough to squeeze out, "Lakesha, Havana's not gonna let me go. She aims to kill me."

Chair legs scraped the floor, followed by hurried steps. Two knees crammed under her head from behind. The hood drew up but snagged her nose. The tape ripped off.

"Who's Lakesha?" Jax said as her gritty cloth wiped BJ's mouth before she slapped on dry tape. But Jax's coarse rag couldn't erase that she'd counted two sets of footsteps leaving the powder room, or Lakesha's silhouette against the cruiser's glass. If that third pair of feet didn't belong to Lakesha, BJ reckoned they belonged to another dupe.

Though the darkness, silence, and cold floor robbed BJ of an accurate measure of time, a rhythmic rap at the door, a code, followed by the click of tumblers and then a new pair of steps suggested a changing of the guard. She heard only Jax whisper. Presumed Jax told her relief about her callout to Lakesha.

BJ waited until the door opened and then locked again, leaving her with but one pair of feet. Again she prodded the foul tape with her tongue. This time she'd make her plea universal. Keep Lakesha off the spot if was her. Give whomever a chance to loosen her ties, unlock the door, and hightail it without being ID'd.

"Guard. Listen to me. Havana's a killer. Don't care what promise she's made. She's gonna kill me. You'll be an accessory to murder."

Silence. Then the slight scuff of chair legs. Soft steps came around behind her. A gentle hand slipped under her head. Her hood slid up to her nose. "Sh-sh-sh," was all she heard as the damp tape drew slowly back, her lips dried with a soft cloth, and new tape firmly pressed over her mouth.

Once those steps faded in front of her, BJ squeezed and twisted her hand, attempting to dislocate her thumb. Enough of a collapse to slide out of her ties. Pain initially helped her battle fits of sleep. But despite the throb of her gouged wrists, BJ succumbed to a doze. She remained bound.

The clomps of six feet aroused her. She heard Havana bitch to Jax about her unanswered calls to Lo. Then, again, Havana demanded BJ tell her where to find him. Again BJ lay mute but resumed her struggle against the sting of her flex-cuffs. She listened as one set of steps exited, followed by the seal and lock of a door. She knew she'd been left with Havana and Jax.

Rhodes made multiple calls, as did Tobac from behind his business-cover caller ID. Havana's barbs erased any doubt about who'd made those unanswered intrusions. She sneered, "At least your boss is looking for ya." Then gibed without expecting an answer, "Stoccado Business Solutions? Helpin' you with a traitor-bitch start-up?" BJ heard Jax's, "Tah."

BJ strained to collapse her thumb. Finally a painful crack launched a guttural gasp.

"What the—" Havana said. Then she spat, "Jax, check her out."

The screech of circling tennies followed. From behind, Jax cinched her wrists so tight hope for freedom flopped behind finding a sweet spot for circulation. Tingling swallowed up any point of rest. Worse, pigheaded Lo would come to, answer Havana's call, and swallow her hook. Lashed out of her own rescue, would Tobac let Lo parlay her locker key into an alliance with him? Or had her failed plan to sideline Lo and finish Havana only postponed Lo's murder? BJ's hopelessness coagulated into the weight of her capture. Her wrists went numb.

A Shadow-Pocked Mirror

The gritty odor of mildew packed my nose and brought me to. I jerked up on a squeaky box spring. The move spun the room. I grabbed my head, springing the ache in my shoulder. Right, I'd rammed a door. My muscles felt wobbly.

I patted my ribs and relaxed at the confident bulge of my .45. A click of the magazine dropped a load of hollow-point relief. Across the room a shadow-pocked mirror. My scruffy image came into focus. I'd been dumped fully clothed. Tennies on. I recognized the derelict guts of a no-tell motel. Staggering to the window, I spread the kinked miniblinds. A courtyard parking lot. The sun peeked over the roof, but not enough to sizzle the dew off the parked hoopties. Stumbling, I plopped back on the lumpy bed. I'd been drugged and ditched. But where?

I recalled gulping gas, fire alarms, and passing out on a powder room floor. A couple of grainy images floated up, BJ's one of 'em. I'm still breathing. She musta rescued me. When? I squinted at my watch. Down since yesterday.

Fumbling through the pockets of my sweats, past my switchblade and disposable cell, I didn't find my digital recorder. I felt my wallet tucked into my sweatshirt's pouch. BJ's note was gone. "Crap." She'd stolen my proof of what I'd seen.

After a call to my neighbor to make sure Al was okay, I caught sight of my backpack. Despite my muddy brain, I bet BJ took the router and phone.

I yanked the backpack off the cigarette-scorched nightstand. "Ow," I said, reminded again, of my bruised shoulder. Inside lay a sealed envelope addressed to a Stoccado Business Solutions on Van Ness Avenue. Fingering and popping the bubble-lined envelope gave me the distinctive shape of a locker key. Didn't take Einstein to figure the key fit the router and phone's hiding place. But BJ had robbed me of everything else. Why leave this?

BJ had clipped a typed and unsigned note to the envelope. It read, "Bet you hesitated to open an envelope not addressed to you. Either way, wouldn't have done you any good."

That she knew that, ignited my pisstivity at being knocked out of her op. Enough to scorch off a layer of fog. I read on: "If you have this when you wake up and haven't checked your voice mail, do it now. If you're not scheduled today for your psych eval, go to the address on the envelope. My handler is there daily between 1:00 and 2:00 p.m. You'll recognize him, and he won't like that I exposed him. But don't give him the envelope until you're restored to duty. You'll need his help to defend yourself if I'm dead."

Dead? My cell's ring muscled through BJ's "if I'm dead" pounding around my skull. I read the display. "Sandoval," I said out loud, tonguing my dry mouth. My stomach growled for breakfast.

"You're alive," he said and lost his breath. Then he demanded, "Where've you been?"

"Trying to figure that out," I said.

"You got something to tell me?"

"What?" I asked, more loopy than sly.

"You at the Dew Drop Inn last night?" He sounded steamed.

"Me? Why?" I stalled, trying to figure out what gave him such a case of the ass.

"Dr. Crusher's in a coma," he said impatiently. "They found her body in the powder room where you suspected an O'DAD Wi-Fi hot spot."

That other fuzzy image flopping on me dropped into my memory. Had to be Crusher. BJ must've clocked her to save me.

"In a coma?"

"You a parrot? You were there, huh?"

My sluggish brain staggered to catch up. “Am I a suspect?”

“Listen, *pendejo*, your name never came up. BJ called 911 and then went missing. The department suspects she’s a vic too. Not answering her cell. I’m the only one that tied you to BJ. Feared Havana fed you to a wood chipper. So quit making me chase my tail. What happened?”

I latched onto my confirmed hunches to pull my way out of the muck. “BJ kept me from being dead right about those alarms and gas.”

After a pause, he said, “No way.”

“Way,” I said and wadded up his tinfoil beanie.

“Details, gimme details.”

“Don’t have time. All I can say is that I was trapped in the powder room and gassed. BJ and Crusher found me unconscious.”

“How’d Crusher end up knocked out? You hit her?”

“No. BJ musta did it. My guess is she interfered with my rescue.”

“It threw me when she tended to me at the wreck. Thought maybe she wasn’t in on the murders,” Sandoval said.

“Looks like she is,” I said, thinking how betrayed BJ felt. She believed Crusher innocent.

“Glad you’re alive, homey. You find out what O’DAD is hiding?” he asked.

“Got a ringer on that too. They got files on all us dogs.”

“You were right,” he said slowly. “And national security?”

“Think about it. Don’t matter what bullshit a terrorist sucks up to justify murder. He’ll be flapping his jaw about his heroic plans if he thinks it’ll get him laid. That bragging ends up in an O’DAD file hyperlinked, or whatever you nerds call it, to a female FBI agent or CIA officer. The next thing Bozo the would-be bomber knows, he’s sitting at Gitmo in an orange jumpsuit.”

“Suppose that supports BJ’s national security rap.”

“Told you she’s undercover. Gotta be bureau.”

“You may be right.…Laszlo said that an Asian FBI chick hit Forensics this morning, brandishing a national security letter. Demanded to see the video of my wreck. Downloaded it. Warned them against violating the letter's gag order."

"Put the fear of god in you both, didn't it?" I said and snickered. "Good thing Laszlo kept his mouth shut."

"By the way, Rhodes sent officers to BJ's house. Obviously she wasn't there. No signs of struggle. Laszlo went with 'em to process the scene if necessary. Took hair samples from combs and brushes to run her DNA. We'll ID her."

I didn't give a shit now, if BJ used a cover name. But curious, I asked, "Results?"

"Nope. Let you know when, though."

I glanced at BJ's envelope. "Sandoval, BJ left me a locker key. Gotta be where she hid the router and phone. Bet Havana kidnapped her to get her hardware back. We gotta find BJ."

"Why leave it with you?...Don't matter." He charged his voice. "Not having their hardware didn't stop the hit on me. Havana might've decided to give up the hardware and kill us all. Don't be disappointed if it's too late."

The fire in my belly wouldn't have it. "I'm not giving up on her. You gonna help or not?"

"Oh sure, a suspended cop and a Chicano in traction are going after the killers that did this to us. They'd better watch out."

"Listen, we're not alone. That agent waving around a national security letter says the FBI is riled up. Besides, you got Laszlo's and the rest of your crew's eyes and ears out here. Take more than an ICU to box you up." Then light cracked through my skull onto what BJ said about her handler: "And don't give him the envelope until you're restored to duty." Only Dr. Tobac stood between me and my badge. Tobac's her handler.

"I'm getting back my badge," I said.

"How?"

"I'll explain later. Can I call you?"

"Yeah, okay. But if I don't answer or sound cagey, hang up and call me back later. If my crew comes up with anything, I'll call you."

I hung up. But before calling Tobac, I checked my missed calls. BJ and the psych clinic had called. About to punch reply to BJ, my damned phone rang. The display showed BJ's SFPD number. I leaped off the bed, my feet steady. "BJ, you okay?"

"Detective Faeth?" a woman asked.

Havana? I dropped back down on the squawky mattress. "Who's this?"

"You first," came her bitter reply.

"It's me, Faeth." I kept my ears wide open for other sounds. Especially BJ's voice.

"Been trying to reach you."

"Where's BJ?"

"Your girlfriend is right here."

"Put her on." I heard a distant muffle. Couldn't tell if it was BJ or not. "Let her talk to me or I'm hanging up," I sneered.

"Don't think so if you want to see her again," Havana said, singsong. "You have things of ours. You swap 'em for her, and nobody gets hurt."

In the background, I could hear what sounded like a muffled "Uh-uh, uh-uh."

BJ?

I had one bone to toss the killer. "Your things are in a locker. Only BJ knows where. But I got the key."

"Okay, Boy Scout, bring that key to the gas station on the corner of Lincoln and La Playa at Ocean Beach. Call me from their pay phone. If you're alone, you'll get further instructions."

Fuck. That pay phone sat off the Great Highway, and I didn't know where I was. "Don't have a car, need some time," I said.

"You got forty-five minutes." The call went dead. She'd left me dangling by the short hairs and knew it. I stuffed BJ's envelope into my backpack and darted outside through the courtyard onto the sidewalk. Down and across the street sat the Cow Palace. Shit. Geneva Avenue, Daly City. If I had a car, I could make the deadline. I called Yellow Cab, growling that it was an emergency. They said they'd come right away. I paced the driveway. Maybe I'd get lucky and catch a taxi going by.

Still suspended, with less than forty-five minutes to get backup, I knew better than to call Rhodes. I dialed Tobac. "This is Detective Faeth from Homicide. Put me through to Dr. Tobac. Don't even think about dumping me into voice jail, understand?" I said, then stumbled, light-headed. Damn, I needed food.

Tobac answered. "Detective Faeth, I've been trying to get hold of you. Want you to come in today for your evaluation," the shrink said, his voice tense.

He didn't know I'd figured out who he was. Havana's ultimatum left no time for chitchat. "Havana's got BJ. Can you get me backup?"

"Havana? Who's BJ?"

"Weak, man. Listen, I know, all right? I gotta rendezvous with a pay phone in forty minutes. I'm on the wrong side of the peninsula, sweatin' a taxi."

After a tight hiss, the shrink said, "BJ's a hostage."

"Did I stutter?" I said.

"Where is she?"

"Don't know. I'll get further instructions at that phone. You helpin' or not?"

"Yes, of course. But national security demands we keep this as quiet as possible. Understand?"

"Yeah, yeah. Well?"

"Tell me where you are. I'll send the taxi. Suki, my agent, will be driving."

"Suki?" The name struck me as a kid's. And I almost asked if she'd been to Forensics this morning. But that gag order caught my tongue. Keep Laszlo outta trouble.

"That's right, Suki. Disarming, as intended," he stressed. "She's Vietnamese American, petite, but fully capable of dropping a man twice her size."

Fucken civilian didn't have to remind me how tough the Vietnamese could be, male or female.

"I'll get her there in a white Veterans Cab. She'll be wearing a black baseball cap, no logo. Brief her on what you know, then follow her instructions to the letter."

I glared at the phone. The guy who didn't know Havana kidnapped his agent is giving me orders. I spotted a Yellow Cab and jumped into the street, waving and shouting, "Over here!"

I got back on the phone with Tobac. "Got my own cab, but if Suki is at the corner of Sloat and Thirty-fifth when I get there, she can take me the rest of the way." For a pinned-down GI, any help was better than none. But Suki? "By the way, I'm starving. Have her bring me a breakfast burrito."

"No time, but she'll meet you. And give her the router and phone." He hung up before I could tell him I didn't have them. Don't think he liked me.

The cab rolled to a halt. I stuck my badge under the driver's nose. "Sloat and Thirty-fifth." I hopped into the backseat. "Punch it," I told him, then asked, "You bring your lunch?"

The hack did a double take, then shook his head no. My damned phone rang again. "Sandoval, what is it?"

"Listen, something you might need to know," he said, his usually sharp tongue rolled with a drag that didn't sound medicated.

"Might? Spill it."

"Why so touchy? Thought you were on your way to pick up your badge."

I couldn't tell him I was charging Havana with FBI backup without exposing BJ's handler. "That's what I'm doin'. In a hurry, that's all."

"Remember you speculated about O'DAD's vendetta against the VIPS?"

"What about it?"

"Well, if you're right, Vips get no quarter if caught. Right?"

"What's your point?" I said, my impatience ratcheting up.

"There's a good chance BJ's already dead."

"She's not, dammit." But I stopped before yelling that I thought I'd heard her grunt. "What the hell does the VIPS have to do with BJ?" I glanced at the cabbie. So what if he heard. VIPS meant nothing to him. "I'm hanging up," I said. But before I pounded the red button, my pulse took a dive. What's he tryin' to say?

"Wait," he pitched. "Her DNA came back."

I could barely speak. "Yeah?"

"Came back with a Y chromosome. BJ was a boy. She may be gone."

BJ, a Vips? Every sex fantasy BJ's booty ever triggered bubbled up in a nauseating stew. The thought of rolling into an ambush for a tranny knocked me cold against the seat of the cab. But this time Ricky's ghost didn't kick me in the nuts. I felt Father Harlan press into the seat next to me. His sermons browbeating us to serve the innocent had kept me on the right side of my conscience in Nam. I'd flown out of Saigon without innocent blood on my hands. But Harlan turned his back on gays. They hadn't fit his Adam-and-Eve boilerplate.

Joining Harlan had cost me my brother. Now I squirmed in bed with Havana. About to desert BJ.

A knot inside snapped. I slammed my fist into the seat next to me, startling the cabbie and me. My heart pounded at the base of my throat, but I'd broken Harlan's grip.

I caught my breath and raised my hands. "I'm cool. I'm cool," I said to the driver. His bug eyes darted between me and the road. "Really, I'm okay." He finally settled on the oncoming traffic.

Sandoval's tinny voice stretched from my phone. "What was that?" I heard him say.

"Hit a pothole." Then I added, "You or Laszlo tell anybody?"

"No, no. That's BJ's secret to tell."

"Keep it that way," I demanded. "So, how would Ha—" I peeked at the driver again. "How would anyone know?"

"*¿Quien sabe?* But I thought you should know before risking the rescue of...you know, somebody already gone."

His words oozed outta the same pus-packed sore that infected my conscience.

"You mean, why risk my neck for a tranny?" I said, catching the hack's stunned gaze in the rearview mirror.

"*Cabrón*. I didn't say that."

"Whatever. Get a name?"

"No. Not yet. That'll ta—" was all I heard before hanging up.

With my head outta my ass, I realized the taxi sped down Sloat.

"Turn right on Thirty-fifth. Pull over, and pop your hood," I said as an edge against prying eyes catching me change cabs.

The hack whipped onto Thirty-fifth. A white Veterans Cab sat parked on the other side of the street. I slipped my driver an extra tip for opening his hood and scratching his head. Told him to keep it up until I was out of sight.

From across the street, I hardly made out the baseball cap low behind the steering wheel of the taxi. Sweeping past the open driver's window, I saw a woman in a baggy Cal Berkeley sweatshirt and jeans.

"What's your name, hack?" I asked.

"Suki to you," she quipped.

Hopping into the backseat, I said, "Hit it." Then I noticed her the long, thick, silky hair pouring out the back of her cap.

She cranked up the Crown Victoria but then faced me. Her stern glare couldn't stop her raindrop-shaped eyes and gull-wing lips from melting me back into that young, tongue-tied GI facing his first Vietnamese beauty.

She snapped her fingers in front of my nose. "Detective, Detective. Get your head in the game. The hardware in your backpack?"

"What?" I said, and focused on her damned Bluetooth to bring me back. Reminded me of a tropical roach sucking her ear.

"Too hungry to track? Tobac said you asked for breakfast." She tossed me a couple of granola bars, followed by a metallic ball the size of a popcorn kernel. "Swallow that."

"What is it?" I asked, holding it up between us. "And where's my breakfast burrito?"

"Transponder. SWAT's standing by—So?"

Stumped by her strict voice, but still studying the transponder, I said, "So what?"

"Hand over the hardware," she said, spiking her eyebrows.

"Don't got 'em," I said, swallowed the tracker, and pulled out BJ's envelope.

"What's in there?"

"Locker key. My guess it's where BJ stashed the phone and router."

Suki scratched the air. "Give it here."

"No way. Without it, BJ and me are dead meat."

She clucked her tongue. "Didn't the hit on your CSI tell you the worth of that key? I tossed you a tracker. Once its signal goes stationary, we'll assume you're tied up with Agent Reeves. When that happens, your only chance is for SWAT to move in."

My pulse revved from high to redline. The FBI was using me to bait Havana and Jax. Just like in Vietnam, when some fucken general planted my platoon out in the boonies to draw out a hidden enemy division. Me and BJ would be nothing but sacrificial sheep.

Sizzling, I said, "Listen. Havana didn't give a shit about their equipment when Jax nailed Sandoval because she knew if he didn't have it, I did. And his knowledge of it would die with him. She let her money ride on BJ leading her to me and their hardware. You know, like now. But Sandoval's alive and under guard. She can't get to him. As long as he's breathing and she don't have that router and phone, he could get his hands on them again. Expose O'DAD and her rogue kill protocol. You even know about that?"

"Thanks to Agent Reeves," she said.

"Havana gets her hands back on their hardware and knocks off me and BJ, she can take her sweet time killing Sandoval. He won't be under guard forever." I waved the envelope in Suki's face. "I hand her this key, she has to keep us alive long enough to recover and confirm it's their hardware. Buy time for me and BJ to cook up something before your trigger-happy SWAT comes blasting in." I looked at my watch and demanded we go.

After a quick study, she said, "SWAT will start with stun grenades, Detective. And where you end up will dictate how much time it'll take me to secure the area before I release them. Here take these. You're going to be tied up." She handed me a Kennedy half-dollar and a nickel, put the Ford in gear, and tromped on the gas.

"Fifty-five cents?" I said, pinned down by the acceleration.

"The half-dollar pulls apart."

To my amazement, it slid into halves, the right side bearing a half-circle blade. "This'll cut through flex-cuffs?"

She nodded in the rearview mirror.

"What if I'm cuffed with steel bracelets?"

"I gave you two coins, didn't I? Run our thumb along the edge of that nickel."

"I'll be damned," I said as a cuff key pivoted into view.

"I want those back," she said, looking at my reflection in the rearview mirror. "And those were my granola bars. You owe me."

"No souvenirs, huh?" I said, shoving the coins into my sweats pocket.

When Suki turned onto the Great Highway, I pointed over her shoulder. "Just before the Cliff House is Lincoln Way. Turn right."

"I know. Grew up here," she said without a glance back.

I sat back and ripped open a granola-bar wrapper. Craned my neck to drink in her face reflected in the rearview mirror.

A Damned Leash

I heard a weak "James Bond Theme" coming from the front seat. Suki tapped her Bluetooth. I hated personalized ringtones. A damn phone oughta ring.

"Suki," she said with all the charm of a motor-vehicle clerk. She glanced at me in the rearview mirror. "Dropping the package in a sec. Be on my way."

She rocked the cab to a halt in front of the phone at the gas station.

"That Tobac?" I asked.

She glared. Sticking her hand out, she said, "Act like you're paying me. Then go make your call."

I slapped a couple of dollars into her hand. Her face softened. "Careful, Detective," she said, nodding toward the pay phone. "Gotta go," she added. Me with BJ's envelope hit the pavement, and the cab peeled out.

Standing before the phone in a cloud of burned rubber, I pulled my cell to retrieve BJ's number. The crunch of tires behind me interrupted my scroll. I turned in time to note the plate number of the windowless gray van easing up. The sliding door opened, framing a brunette Havana.

"C'mere," she demanded.

"And you are?" I said, playing dumb, before stepping toward the van.

"Your guide to your girlfriend. Hands up. On your knees into the van."

I did as she said, and she slammed the door behind me. Looking around the van, didn't notice bloodstains on the metal floor or empty body bags. I liked that. It occurred to me that I'd flown in transport planes with better accommodations. The only seats in the van were the driver's and passenger's. But Jax leaned over from behind the wheel, her pistol aimed at my chest. Her youth gouged up every GI's nightmare: an armed kid with a bead on you.

"The key in there?" Havana snatched BJ's envelope from over my head. Then she ordered, "Turn around. Sit. Hands behind your back." I'd noted Jax's double-action revolver. She'd left the hammer down. Take a long pull to rotate that cylinder and draw back the hammer. Split seconds might be all that stood between me and a slug. Havana's pat search easily caught my .45 and switchblade. Over my shoulder, I watched her slip them into a gym bag.

Havana zipped tight a flex-cuff around my wrists. She took my phone and along with another threw them out the passenger window.

"Whose phone?" I asked.

"Your girlfriend's. Now that we have you, don't need it anymore. Turn around," she said, and pulled all my stuff out of my pockets and dumped it on the floor.

"Hey, you're tossing everything like I'll never see it again. Thought you're gonna let us go once you got your hardware back." Least she could do was act like she didn't plan to snuff us. "If I got nothing to lose, I'll start kicking and squealing like a pig. Gag me and tie my legs, but then you gotta lug me around. Kill me, you lose your leverage over BJ. You'll need it. At least until you confirm that's the key to your router and phone." I watched Havana suck in her lips, sickened that her face might be the last woman's I'd ever see.

"All we want is our equipment back. Just making sure you're disarmed," she said, apparently realizing she'd let the con slip. She looked around, snatched up my wallet, and stuffed it into my pouch.

I spotted Suki's half-dollar behind the driver's seat the same time she did. "Mind if I save that for a phone call after you release us?"

"Pay phones don't take those."

"It'll get me two quarters," I said and felt my pores go damp.

"Whatever."

I scooted over to pick it up, but she grabbed it and put it in my pants pocket. I didn't see the nickel and hoped she didn't find it and discover its cuff key. But lost, Suki's gonna be pissed. I couldn't win with the gals.

She turned to Jax and said, “Let’s go.” Then Havana slipped a hood over my head. She wouldn’t care what I saw if she planned to kill us. Would she let us go after she recovered O’DAD’s hardware? My granola-filled gut burped back my wishful thinking. The hood was an act. Sucker me into cooperating. Then I heard my switchblade click open. My heart thumped. Gutted by my own blade?

The sound of an envelope slicing open settled me like a shot of Frank’s tequila. I heard Havana rifle the envelope. That sound stopped, but I heard her snort. Bet all she found was the key. Like BJ wrote, opening it wouldn’t help. I guessed that key fit a locker known only to her and maybe Tobac.

The van spurted short distances, then stopped. Sometimes long like at a light, others rolling stops before tilting into multiple right turns. Typical San Francisco stop and go. Jax drove in an expanding circle before a few left turns ended up shooting us down a stretch of highway. I smelled salt air and suspected we’d stayed in San Francisco. My gut said we’d doubled back to the Great Highway. Still, I dumbed up and said, “Where are we?”

“Patience, big boy,” Havana said as the van swayed into a hard left. The front dipped, as if hitting a driveway, followed by the crunch of gravel. The boarded-up Sunset Lounge sat on the lower side of the Great Highway. A title dispute kept its gravel parking lot empty. The engine stopped and Havana slipped what felt like a chain around my neck. I heard a click and felt her tug the fucken choke collar. She’d tied me to a damned leash.

The door slid open. I heard waves crashing and seagulls squawking above. “Get out,” she demanded, followed by the crunch of footsteps. She jerked me to the ground as soon as I’d planted my feet on the gravel. Rocks gouged my knees.

“Get up.”

Gasping for air, I staggered to my feet.

Havana’s footsteps ground to my front. She throttled me forward. Stumbling to slacken the leash, I tried to imagine the back entrance to the Sunset Lounge. My buddy Les brought me and Frank here a few times back in our counseling days. Me and my belly agreed, Havana planned this as my last march. Right into a powder room.

She gagged me to a halt. The rattle of keys made it into my hood, followed by the squeak of hinges. Havana's tug went limp and she said, "Bend forward." One of 'em lifted off the collar. I caught a whiff of Juicy Fruit—Havana.

"Move it," Jax said, shoving me from behind at gunpoint. I stumbled over a doorstep and after the moan of rusty hinges, I heard the slide of a deadbolt. If I'd entered the old Sunset Lounge, the ladies' room lay a few steps to my right down a narrow hallway.

"Straight ahead," Jax said. After a few steps, she ordered, "Hold up." To my right, somebody knocked with measured thumps. A signal. The minor clunks of tumblers and twist of a doorknob followed. I turned to their sounds. "We'll take it from here," Havana said.

I listened for a reply that didn't happen. The gust of a body blew by me, followed by footsteps growing faint. No perfume. Smart. But why the silent treatment? She have a voice I'd recognize? Madge? I'd thought our divorce was friendly until I'd read, "Size 13 = red herring."

Somebody shoved me forward, and I heard a muffled voice. "BJ?" I said.

Havana swiped off my hood. "Told you she was alive," she snapped. "And don't talk to her." Behind us, Jax locked the powder-room door.

Under the glow of track lights, the hooded woman on the checkered tile lay bowed back on her side by a line stretched between her bound ankles and wrists. Havana leaned down and yanked off the gal's hood. Duct tape sealed BJ's mouth. She looked like the life had been sapped out of her. But she glared at me from sunken eyes.

I knew I'd pissed her off by giving Havana her key. And despite our fucked-up situation, I found myself struck by thinking of her as, well, her. Still, I wondered who she was. Ricky's voice cracked outta my conscience, "The partner who saved your bigoted ass." Then I thought, I'm gonna find Ricky—if we survive this.

♦ ♦ ♦

BJ fumed, seeing her envelope dangle from Havana's hand. Lo gave up their trump card. What the hell was that boy thinking, traipsing into Havana's trap defenseless? Shoulda known better than to trust anybody but herself.

She had to leverage that key into getting Havana to untie her. Had to speak.

♦ ♦ ♦

I wanted to tell my partner SWAT was on its way. But if I did, Havana'd move us.

Be damned if I didn't hear the jingle of what sounded like a real phone and watch Havana answer her cell. That cinched it. I hated all ringtones.

Havana froze, didn't say a word. Then she tapped off the ring. It rang again. Her chest heaved a shaky breath as she silenced it again and slid it back into her pants pocket.

"Who was it? You okay?" Jax asked.

Havana blinked away whatever bugged her and said, "Nobody." Then she snapped at Jax, "Don't take your eyes off these two." She turned to me. "You, on the floor."

I sat down between BJ and a line of toilet stalls and faced the killers. Sorry BJ couldn't see my hands behind me. Woulda liked her seeing me cutting my straps. Havana flex-cuffed my ankles.

"Girls Just Want to Have Fun" jingled from Jax's bib pocket. "Don't answer that," Havana spat, but Jax had scooped up her phone. Her eyes locked on the display. The revolver drifted toward the floor.

"But it's Mar—" Jax started to say with a hint of a grin. Havana interrupted her: "Shaddup." The corners of Jax's mouth fell, and her eyelids fluttered. Havana tore into her. "Somebody's going through her numbers. Phishing. Get it?"

I twisted my pants around to reach my pocket and clawed out Suki's half-dollar. The tight cords limited me to short finger strokes.

"What if it is Marilee?" Jax asked, her voice weak.

Havana's face burst red. She grabbed Jax's phone. "Gimme it." Jax let go and looked at her like a kid asking, What'd I do?

Havana clenched Jax's wrist and leveled her pistol at me. Glaring into her eyes, she demanded, "Concentrate."

Jax blinked away her confusion and locked her gaze on me.

♦ ♦ ♦

The bounce of BJ's heart knocked the anvil off her chest. Marilee's alive, conscious.

Havana stomped over to her and ripped off the tape, leaving a welt. She held up the envelope and demanded, "Where's the locker?"

BJ squinted at Lo as if to say, What were you thinking?

"He know where it is?" Havana said, her voice climbing.

BJ shook her head. "He don't know a dang thing," she said, happy to speak. Next, she'd get her hands free.

♦ ♦ ♦

I couldn't blame BJ for her snipe. I pushed Suki's blade hard. Right off the flex-cuff, deep into my wrist. I felt blood. Trickle or squirt? Shit. I focused on my pounding pulse. No geyser but enough to slop up my grip.

♦ ♦ ♦

Havana shoved the address into BJ's face. "The locker here?" Then Havana glared at the envelope. "Stoccado Business Solutions. That's who called you. Who are they?"

"Don't matter who," BJ said. "What matters is where's the locker. And no, it's not there." BJ turned away.

"Tell me where, then, or your boyfriend gets it." Havana nodded at Jax, who aimed at Lo's head.

"You need me to get it." BJ glanced at Lo, adding, "Shoot him, I ain't gonna help ya. May as well shoot me too and get it over with." BJ swept her gaze around the powder room. "Two shot-dead detectives in an abandoned bathroom, hmm? How you gonna spin that into one of your bogus robbery-homicides?"

"Told you, the router and the phone for your freedom. I go get them, come back, test 'em, then me and Jax are off. I'll leave your boyfriend's knife, and you two can cut yourselves free. He's got money for a pay phone."

"You're not paying attention. I said you need me to get it. All you're gonna find in that locker is a safe-deposit-box key. You'll still hafta get to the bank and your hardware. Where they ain't gonna let anybody in but me to open it."

"You're lying," Havana sneered.

"Go on, see for yourself. Lake Merced Golf Club locker room. Waste a trip. Suppose we'll all be here when ya get back," BJ said. "Unless whoever's expectin' that key finds us first."

Havana clucked her tongue. "I disabled your phone's tracker long before I tossed it. I'll go see if you're lying about that other key." She started to hand back Jax's phone but then withdrew her hand. Nose to nose with Jax, she said, "Do not answer any calls except mine. Understand?"

"Uh-huh. Yes," Jax said, nodding her head as she reached for her cell.

♦ ♦ ♦

I couldn't let Havana get away. "Listen. You think I came here alone? SWAT's right behind me." I watched BJ's eyes lock onto mine. She think I was bluffing?

Havana cupped her ear, jutting it toward the door. "Quiet bunch, aren't they?"

"I swallowed a tracker."

"Really? Double oh seven your new BFF?"

"I'm teamed with the FBI."

"Uh-huh, from suspended drunk to FBI agent. Quite a comeback." Havana rolled her eyes, unzipped her gym bag, and pulled out a roll of duct tape. She slapped a patch over each of our mouths, then strutted out the door.

Jax locked it behind her without taking her eyes off me and BJ.

♦ ♦ ♦

BJ stared at Lo. He'd want Havana here if SWAT came. Then her heart spiked. She knew the FBI's SWAT commander, Ashley Kurtz. In Kurtz's single-lane brain, any risk to O'DAD meant a threat to the nation. Shielded by national security, it didn't make Kurtz no never mind how much collateral damage bled in her wake. Even with hostages at stake, she'd need to know they were alive. Otherwise, she and her team would barge in, guns ablazin'.

BJ pounded her tongue against the duct tape's bitter glue.

Girls Just Want to Have Fun

The tie began to give. Almost through? "Girls Just Want to Have Fun" chimed on Jax's phone. Her eyes lingered on her display, but I couldn't break the damned tie. A yank gouged my deepest cut. "Ugh," muffled against the tape before I could stop it.

Jax heard me and raised her pistol to my forehead. The hammer down. Her BB eyes ping-ponged between me and her phone. Crusher calling? The half-dollar slipped outta my bloody fingers and fell. The tie followed.

I lunged. My left hand clamped Jax's wrist, and my bloodied right grabbed the .38's cylinder, bending the gun toward a stall. But my momentum slammed us to the floor, sandwiching the pistol between us before I could break her grip. The cylinder rolled in my bloody palm. The pistol barked. Hot lead ripped my skin.

Jax squirmed beneath me. "Get off me," she grunted as she hammered her fist into my temple.

Blood gushed, soaking our clothes. Had to snatch the gun before my blood and adrenaline petered out. I felt the .38's cylinder rotate again. I slid the skin between my thumb and index finger between the pistol's hammer and firing pin. The hammer struck, tearing my skin, but the gun didn't shoot. Jax's blows grew weak, her breathing shallow. Her grip on the pistol fell limp. I snatched the .38 and stuck it in her face, but her eyes glazed over. I looked down to see that the bullet grazed me but tore a chunk out of her side. We'd wrestled in her blood.

I tossed the pistol, ripped the tape off my mouth, and planted my ear on her chest. Weak heartbeat. I tore off my sweatshirt, pressed it into Jax's wound, and with my other hand grabbed her phone to call 911.

The building shuddered from simultaneous crashes. Battering rams at the front and back doors. Some woman yelled, "FBI! Surrender!"

I dropped Jax's phone and yelled back, "In here! We're o—" Blasts at the entrances cut off my voice. Stun grenades?

♦ ♦ ♦

Shielded from the bursts outside, BJ heard the rush of boot steps stop at their door. Lo shouted, "Don't shoot! We're all right." The door shattered, and she clamped her eyes shut against a shower of splinters. She heard the click and roll of a canister. Grenade. The white flash pierced her eyelids, and the blast blew out her eardrums. Deaf, blind, and dizzy, smoke curled up her nose. Hell's bells, a fire?

♦ ♦ ♦

The shock and blinding burst knocked me dizzy, but I stayed on Jax's wound. Then my hand started to burn and I smelled smoke. Son of a bitch. I didn't know if I thought it or screamed it, but a couple of goons grabbed my arms and dragged me off the kid.

My eyesight began to clear, and though still deaf, I tried to squirm free. But the two grunts pinned me flat on my back. I craned my neck. Didn't see BJ. But another vision poured in. Suki, outta her sweatshirt and in a gray business suit. She stood eye to eye with a bent-over, box-faced woman in a helmet and fatigues holding a carbine. Obviously SWAT.

Suki's hand clamped her hip, her jacket hung behind. She shook my bloodied and burned sweatshirt in her other hand. Her skirt hugged the curve of her thigh and stopped just above her knees. But she'd roped her silky hair into a bun atop her head and speared it in place, along with a headset, with a chopstick. Damn.

The SWAT gal's slack, wandering jaw left no doubt about her ass-chewing. Suki didn't take up much space, but what she did, she packed. But why so mad? Because Havana got away? Or because SWAT charged in and set me on fire? The room spun. The back of my head kissed the tile, and I closed my eyes. Who was I kidding? Suki's pisstivity boiled at Havana's escape. Not over me.

Someone knelt down beside me. I opened my eyes to Suki. Gloved up, she tore open a pack of gauze and poured on antiseptic. She scrubbed my bloody hand and wrists. Stung like hell.

Her outsized voice muscled through my plugged-up ears: "Tear off his T-shirt and cut his ankles free." The guys holding me down turned out to be women in combat gear. They let go of me, and one pulled a bowie knife. Gave me a rush, but not a good one. She sliced and tore around my shoulder holster, leaving only the shirt collar. Luckily, no nicks.

Suki cracked a weak smile. I couldn't tell what lit up more—me or her face?

"Nice outfit, but I could've done without seeing you half naked."

She started wiping my gunshot. The bullet's gully burned but wasn't deep.

"Where'd you get that nasty bruise?"

I propped up on my elbows, but listed, partial to my sore shoulder. "Lost a fight with a door." My voice sounded miles away.

"No need to shout. I can hear you. Your hearing will recover soon," Suki said.

I glanced around the powder room. Looked for BJ. Jax lay on the floor by a toppled chair. Whoever tended to her had her back to me. That frizzy, tied-back hair looked like Crusher's.

"Who's that with Jax? And where's BJ?"

"BJ's out in an ambulance. Dr. Crusher's treating Jax." Suki stuck her face in mine. "Like you and Detective Reeves," she said, widening her eyelids, "Dr. Crusher has joined my covert operation." Her clean breath patted my nose, as if to drive home her shorthand to shut up about BJ's FBI credentials and to keep quiet about Tobac too.

Fine about their op, but Crusher needed to be locked up. I grabbed for my .45 but slapped my empty holster. I shouted on purpose, "Ya dumb shits, Crusher's a killer. Arrest her." More of the cotton in my ears evaporated. I jerked forward and sat up.

Suki pressed firmly on my chest. I wished her hand naked but her touch still cracked through my temper. "You're wrong. Relax." Suki patted me like a good mutt. I lay back down.

"I can't blame you, Detective Faeth," Crusher said, now staring over at me, "but you must believe—"

"She's innocent, Lo," I heard BJ say and saw her appear in the doorway.

"Detective Reeves, get to the hospital," Crusher said.

♦ ♦ ♦

BJ felt the thump of Marilee addressing her as Detective Reeves. Her words struck and then fell like bricks, constructing a wall between them. Marilee's demand to get to the hospital bore out of her Hippocratic oath, not maternal worry. Marilee'd never forgive her for damn near killing her. Neither would she.

"The paramedic just had to pop my thumb back into place," BJ said and then talked to the floor. "I don't need to go to the hospital. A choice I didn't give you." Guilt wrung moisture out of her eyes. She wiped it away.

BJ raised her head to look at Marilee, who tilted her face and said with a puzzled look, "What on earth do you mean?"

Made BJ wonder if she'd smacked away Marilee's memory. A foul but logical reach followed: Marilee didn't remember Havana's rogue kill protocol. But if not, what's she doing here? Looking for evidence to exonerate Havana? If that's what she intended, Suki wouldn't have brought her. Would she?

"Excuse us, please," said one of the paramedics behind BJ as she and her partner rolled in a gurney. BJ stepped aside. Marilee whipped her stethoscope behind her neck and briefed them on Jax's condition as they lifted the unconscious teen onto the gurney. "Vitals weak but stable," BJ heard her say.

BJ squatted on her heels next to the overturned chair by the door. She wrung her face in her hand. Out of the corner of her eye, she watched Marilee step toward Lo and kneel down next to Suki. I hafta confess I hit her, BJ told herself.

♦ ♦ ♦

Crusher looked at me, then over to BJ. "I bear responsibility for you two detectives' injuries. Even after my coma broke and Agent Suki arrived to show me the video of Jax fleeing Dr. Sandoval's wreck, I still didn't want to believe that Havana was guilty. But I agreed to come and allow Suki her chance to prove BJ's suspicions." Crusher's voice cracked and her eyes wandered. "I can't deny the dreadful truth now."

Sounded like BJ was right about Crusher's innocence. And she didn't remember BJ socked her. I shot a look at BJ, all balled up in grief. Crusher's memory lapse wouldn't stop guilt's hard grind. Something I knew about.

Crusher looked at Suki. "Nice job cleaning his wounds." She turned to me and asked, "May I take a look?"

"Yeah, sure. Go ahead," I said, not caring if I sounded like a convert. Hell, she'd made BJ smack her. BJ wouldn't of done it otherwise.

"That grenade exploded next to you. Thank god only your sweatshirt caught fire. Were you burned?" Crusher took my hand. "Looks a little red around the knuckles."

I squeezed my fist. Only a minor sting bit back. "It's fine."

"Your wrists are crisscrossed with cuts, and what on earth bit you between your thumb and index finger?"

"Jax's pistol," I said and watched Crusher's eyes cloud up.

"You saved her life. Let me dress your wounds." Crusher looked back at BJ as she went to work. "I ignored the obvious at the Dew Drop Inn, blinded by my love for Havana." She stopped, stared at the floor, then said, "I delivered her. Her mother, Delphia, and I were best friends." She glanced at me through a thousand-yard stare. "Delphia's dead, you know." Then she nodded, sent an upside-down smile back toward BJ, and went on. "My fall in the powder room didn't knock any sense into me."

I looked back at BJ on her haunches. Her hand covered her mouth. It didn't matter that the doc thought she fell. Her shot to Crusher cost BJ a chunk of her soul.

I caught myself staring at BJ's hands. Those long fingers and narrow palms had distracted me from their size. I saw the bulk of a man for the first time. Licking the inside of my mouth couldn't tongue away the sour taste. My petty reflex cost me a step ahead of Father Harlan.

The vise-jawed gal in fatigues stomped over. "He know where Havana is?"

"Detective Faeth, meet Special Agent Kurtz, FBI SWAT team leader," Suki said, glaring at Kurtz as if to say, Where's your manners?

"Lake Merced Golf Club."

Kurtz pointed to the sky, whipped her finger in a circle like a butter-bar second louie fresh outta OCS, and shouted, "Saddle up. We're goin' golfin'."

The two grunts that had held me followed Kurtz toward the door.

Suki jumped to her feet. "Hold on," she hollered.

Kurtz and her team rocked to a halt.

"Too many civilians there. We stay put. Havana's coming back with O'DAD's hardware."

"The hardware's not at the golf course," BJ piped up. "But she'll be back for me."

Suki did a double take at BJ. Then she put her finger up in Kurtz's face to quiet her. "What?"

"All she'll find at the golf course is my safe deposit key. The router and phone are at my bank," BJ said.

Suki tilted her head, nodding admiringly at BJ. "Where?"

"Around the corner from my precinct. But we gotta stop Havana here. Just up against me, Faeth, and Sandoval, all she has to do to save herself and her protocol is to recover the hardware and knock off the three of us. The second she knows that Dr. Crusher is well, on to her, and sees y'all, that hardware is worthless."

Suki leveled her gaze at Kurtz. "You bashed in the front door instead of covering it like I told you. Why bother hiding our vehicles, then? Better hope Havana doesn't notice the debris and disappear before she's trapped inside our perimeter."

"If we don't go get her, you're gonna let her escape," Kurtz said.

"That's up to your spotters outside, isn't it?" Suki countered.

"Only if she does come back," Kurtz snapped, glancing at BJ.

Watching their pissing contest, I had to remind myself they were women.

♦ ♦ ♦

The jingle of "Girls Just Want to Have Fun" spilled from Jax's phone. BJ had scooped it up when SWAT cut her ties. She read the display out loud, "It's Havana."

Marilee shot up. "I'll answer." BJ rose and handed her the phone.

"Havana. Surrender this minute.…Havana? Havana?"

Suki pressed her finger to her lips. "Put her on speaker," Suki whispered as she met BJ and Marilee. Kurtz snuck into their huddle.

Marilee thumbed the phone. "Is…is it really you?" Havana asked over speaker. Her childish timbre touched BJ. She imagined hearing her own mother's voice after being told she'd died. Her contempt for the other orphan stumbled like a drunk in a windstorm.

"It is, hon."

"Are you really okay?" she asked, her tone weak, as if bracing for the worst.

"I am." Marilee's voice crackled. "Where are you?"

"You answered Jax's phone. Did she tell you where to find us?" Havana sputtered.

"No, hon. She didn't. I'm here with—"

BJ bumped shoulders with Suki as they both frantically waved their palms in Marilee's face and shook their heads no.

"The FBI," Havana spat. "Beer belly wasn't bluffing about his transponder. Gimme Jax."

BJ heard the clap of their empty trap. Havana'd disappear. But that spite in Havana's voice fired up BJ's goad to get her.

"Hon, Jax has been shot. She's on her way to the hospital." Tears spilled down Marilee's cheeks.

BJ felt Marilee's maternal grief stir a sour mash of envy and self-doubt. Would her own mom have embraced her with the same passion?

"Who shot her?" Havana said in her subzero chill.

"She shot herself," Marilee sputtered.

"I don't believe you," Havana spat back.

"My god, Havana, you left a child with a gun. What were you thinking?"

Marilee stumbled and wiped her brow with the back of her hand. BJ lurched to steady her, unable to tame her dart to help Mommy. Marilee blanched and then fluttered her eyelids as if she'd startled herself.

BJ read Marilee's flinch. She'd lied about falling. Knew she'd hit her. BJ grabbed her chest. Brought her hands over her heart, as if to smother the fires of loss. She told herself to muster her wits. Clean up her mess before anybody else got hurt. Why Marilee lied would have to wait.

"Who else?" Havana demanded.

"Who...who else what?" Marilee stammered.

"Went to the hospital."

"No one yet." Marilee looked over at Lo and then back at BJ. She added, "But I have injured here waiting to go."

"Then BJ and her boyfriend are still alive." Havana's voice drifted, as if carried by the smoke of snuffed hope.

BJ watched Marilee's face paste over as she braced herself against the counter behind her. Doddering from her child's murderous dejection.

"Why is the front door dangling from its hinges?" Havana sneered.

♦ ♦ ♦

Suki mouthed, "Off speaker," as her hand chopped the air under her chin. Crusher complied and put the phone to her ear. I watched Suki glare at Kurtz, who shrugged. Then Suki, Kurtz, and her battle-ready girls stepped over to my end of the powder room. Kurtz pinched the mic of her headset toward her mouth and whispered, "Havana's outside. Got a visual?" She looked back at Suki and shook her head no.

I staggered to my feet. "Look for a gray van," I said under my breath and gave them the license number.

While Kurtz quietly spoke into her mic, Suki glanced at me and in an exasperated whisper told one of Kurtz's grunts, "Get him a shirt. Please."

By the time I took off my shoulder holster, the gal in cammies had handed me a fatigue shirt. I had a helluva time with the buttons over my belly. "Nothing bigger?" I asked, looking at the skin showing between the buttons.

"Women's sizes only. Get over it." Suki handed me a Glock.

From across the room, we heard Crusher, her voice bubbling through emotional muck: "Havana, you kidnapped police officers, left them to be murdered by a child. In the name of your mother, come to your senses."

"Parked gray van to the south," Kurtz muttered to Suki. "No visual on the driver. But my sniper can take out the tires."

"Wait, she's been to the golf course," Suki said. She turned to Crusher. "Ask her if she's alone."

Crusher caught her breath and said, "She has a hostage. Said she'd exchange him for BJ and Detective Faeth."

"Let my sniper take the shot," Kurtz demanded.

"Unleash bullets on a blind box with a hostage? No way," Suki said, impressing me with her restraint.

"Hon, please surrender," Crusher begged. "I witnessed your rogue kill protocol. It betrays everything O'DAD stands for."

"Order BJ to get back here," Kurtz shouted into her headset.

I looked around. BJ was gone. All eyes landed on Kurtz. "Detective Reeves is charging toward the van," she said.

We ran toward the front door, stumbling over debris. Clogging the doorway, we choked on chalky dust. The butt of the van sat facing us, down the street. We watched BJ disappear around the passenger side. I started to shoulder my way through the bottleneck, but Suki pushed me back out of sight. "I'm not giving her another hostage."

I couldn't leave BJ to Havana. My thumping heart said go, but Suki was right. Then it struck me. I could be BJ's tracker.

Slick Willy

"Havana. Here I am," BJ said with her hands up as she eased into Havana's view on the van's passenger side. She peeked in. A chill radiated out of her chest. Havana's trembling hostage sat at the wheel. Behind him crouched the killer, one hand on the phone. The other pressing a .45 into the back of the ol' golfer's skull, its hammer cocked. He sat a hair trigger away from the pink cloud of eternity and knew it.

"Get in," Havana said and then nodded at the guy. "His future depends on you." Havana ordered her sweaty bag of bones, "Search her and don't be shy."

The balding white guy avoided eye contact as his palms groped BJ. Fear seemed to have sucked his eyes, nose, and mouth toward the center of his orbital face. He didn't find a thing.

"Slick Willy told me I could call him Bill when I winked at his putter. Thought he'd sink a hole in one before returning home to the missus," Havana said, her contempt palpable.

The man glanced up at BJ and in a quavering voice pleaded, "Please don't tell my wife, but get me out of this."

"Where's BJ's boyfriend, Mom?" Havana mocked into her phone.

♦ ♦ ♦

"My god, why didn't I listen to BJ?" we heard Crusher say, then watched her drop the phone. She wept into her palms.

Suki snatched it up. Musta hit speaker again, 'cause we heard BJ: "Marilee. It's nobody's fault but mine. Can't let nobody else pay for my mess."

Then Havana chimed in. "The bitch is right, and I'm the only one with ovaries enough to collect. Now, where's fatso?"

Suki stuck her finger toward my nose. Just like Lily did to Les. That how Vietnamese women whip their boys into shape?

"Jax shot him," BJ said.

I traded glances with Suki before she slapped the phone into Crusher's hand and cocked her head toward it.

Crusher sucked back her tears. "BJ's right, he's lost too much blood," she said, staring at me.

"Don't have time to tell if you're lying. So I'm keeping these two. Follow us and their blood is on your hands."

Crusher raised her soggy eyes toward us and said, "She hung up."

"Our shot, before they get away," Kurtz demanded.

"No," Suki countered. "Detective Faeth and I will shadow them in the cab. Get your chopper and follow his tracker."

♦ ♦ ♦

"You have me. Let him go," BJ said, knowing without Bill to drive, she'd have to.

"Uh-uh. He's gonna keep your friends from following us, and keep you in line."

BJ knew she and Bill would live only long enough to guarantee Havana's escape. And she'd had enough of her mopey self. Wasn't going to let herself be hog-tied again.

Havana handed Bill a flex-cuff. "Better be tight. I'm gonna check," she said. Then told BJ, "Turn around. Hands behind you."

BJ looked at Bill, sweat glistening off his furrowed brow. She needed to jangle him into a puddle of nerves. Get him outta the driver's seat. She turned but kept moving her wrists while Bill's slippery hands fumbled with the cuff. He dropped the first one. Then the second.

"Cross your wrists," Havana said to BJ. "Quit stalling." Havana handed Bill a third flex-cuff and gouged the muzzle of the pistol into his temple.

Bill's tremors erupted into spasms. A throaty sputter outta Bill's bottom cut loose the stench of a ruptured sewer.

BJ twisted back to meet Havana's pinched face with her own. Havana's left hand shot for the driver's side door handle while she waved the .45 toward the door. "Out, out," she sneered at Bill and shoved him to the street. "Drive," she told BJ. "And keep the windows down."

BJ peered at the driver's seat and said, "That dry?"

"Move," Havana demanded.

BJ slid into the driver's seat and felt no moisture. "Thank ya, Jesus," she said to herself and watched Bill scurry away from the van on his hands and knees. She started the van and tromped the gas.

She heard Havana get back on her phone. "Delete protocol."

BJ added Havana's phone to her must-have evidence list.

♦ ♦ ♦

Suki insisted on driving. Felt responsible for the cab. I yanked open the passenger door.

"I'm telling ya, BJ's chances are better if Havana knows we're on her tail."

"You heard Havana. If she sees us follow them, she kills BJ and the hostage," Suki said.

My throat shriveled up over BJ's iffy future.

"Havana did what?" Suki said into her mic. She turned to me and added, "Havana dumped her hostage."

I coughed, then rasped, "If we lag behind, BJ will be gutter meat by the time we catch up to 'em."

Suki hesitated, then slid behind the wheel. "I'll alert Tobac and Kurtz," she said and spoke into her mic. Advised Tobac we'd be in pursuit and needed SFPD and CHP backup to clear the roads. Reminded him to give them the cab's ID. Then she told Kurtz, "This is no longer a tail. It's a pursuit. Swoop them in your bird. And Kurtz, I don't wanna hear 'Ride of the Valkyries.'" Then she squeezed her voice through clenched teeth, "It is not the same as a James Bond ringtone."

Valkyries? What are they arguing about, now? I wondered. But when Suki grabbed her baseball cap off the bench seat and yanked the chopstick outta her hair, I forgot about the Valkyries. Wanted to see those silky locks splash down all over her shoulders. Instead, she slapped her hat over her bun and stabbed it in place with that damned spear. She cranked up the cab and did a doughnut toward the driveway. Gravel rooster tailed behind the cab and peppered the wheel wells.

Ahead of us sped the van. It careened right on Sloat toward the upper highway. To our left, a red-faced man flanked by two of Kurtz's team walked bowlegged toward an approaching ambulance. The grunts waved their hands in front of their noses. What the hell?

Ride of the Valkyries

Suki swerved through traffic, trying to gain on Havana. I twisted my body and craned my neck to search the sky. I didn't see Kurtz's chopper.

"Where's Kurtz?" I said. "Gotta clear this traffic, too. Where the hell's the cops?"

"Chill, Detective. The cavalry's coming," Suki said, throttling the cab nearly up the trunk of a sedan and then careening around it to pass. "I get that Agent Reeves is your partner."

"You don't know the half of it." I braced my hands against the dash. Couldn't shove back images of BJ's twin-teardrop booty. Its sweet sway soured by Sandoval's XY news.

Suki cast me a sideways look. "Understand you have the dubious distinction of being the only survivor of Havana's rogue kill protocol."

"Thanks to BJ," I said, stoking a fever to burn away the bigoted brakes on my conscience. Then I heard music mixed up with the thump of chopper blades.

"What the—" I said, peering out the back window at the rushing black chopper.

"'Ride of the Valkyries,'" Suki said through clenched teeth.

"Huh?"

"Thought you were a vet. You see *Apocalypse Now*?"

"Don't watch fucken war movies," I snapped, pissed at anybody who made a buck off smut.

♦ ♦ ♦

BJ met Havana's glance in the rearview mirror when music whipped in on churning props. Both wrinkled their brows and mouthed "'Ride of the

Valkyries'?" Then Havana scurried to the back of the van and peered out the rear window.

"I'm collateral damage," BJ said. "Nothin' but the cost of taking their objective. *You*. You're done, Havana. I'm pulling over." BJ checked her side-view mirrors.

The boom of the .45 jolted BJ and hurled a slug past her ear through the front window. "Hell's bells Havana, ya coulda hit a civilian," she hollered.

"Then you get my point if you don't lose your friends," Havana said, now inches behind her as the copter buzzed them. A siren's scream grew louder and then dashed by. The cop car's lights ablaze.

♦ ♦ ♦

Me and Suki watched Kurtz swoop the speeding van and start to circle back, then a CHP cruiser shot past 'em.

"Bet they heard those raps at their door," I said.

Suki pinched her mic. "Jettison the music, Kurtz....Say again." She turned to me. Her jaw slid to one side. "Kurtz says there's a bullet hole in the windshield."

My gut cramped. "Who's driving?" I gulped back the spiked clump at my throat.

"BJ."

My belly backed off. "Catch 'em."

Suki punched it.

♦ ♦ ♦

"I'm calling Marilee," Havana said. "You tell that other traitor, to get your friends to disappear, or I'll litter the highway with their victims."

BJ cringed at Havana's swat at Marilee. Traitor put Marilee downrange. Right next to the VIPS.

"Doctor. BJ has a warning for you," Havana said and pushed the phone under BJ's chin. "She's on speaker."

At the hospital, BJ'd seen Havana's body flag when she told her Marilee knew she was a murderer. And minutes ago Havana's voice shrank to that of a child when she heard Marilee's voice over the phone. BJ grasped for a survivable straw. "Marilee, let Havana know she'll lose the only mom she's got if she hurts anyone else."

The killer yanked away the phone and spat, "I'm gonna start shooting"—she glanced at BJ—"'civilians,' unless you call off the pursuit."

"My god, Havana, not even your mother could forgive you for what you're doing," Marilee sputtered, her voice drowned out by more sirens rushing to clear the highway.

Havana took aim out the passenger window at a slowing convertible. Its top down.

BJ swerved into the next lane, pinning Havana to the wall of the van, ruining her aim. Screeching tires and horn blasts trailed behind.

Havana slid back behind BJ and crammed the muzzle of the .45 against the back of her head. "Put in a position where I've got nothing to lose, we're both dead. But you'll be first. Then I'll step on the gas. How many of your precious civilians will get hurt when this thing spins outta control?"

"All right, all right. I'll tell 'em to stop chasing us," BJ said as she glanced over her shoulder at Havana, imagining her wearing a bull's-eye for Kurtz's sniper. "Why don't you sit down and buckle up?"

"Give your friends a target? Don't think so."

BJ saw her survivable options blow out the window. Leaving her with nothing but a doomsday choice. A head-on with a pylon would do. BJ hit the gas and scanned the road ahead. Her soul sank into a final muse. Sought comfort in the irony of her death. Nobody but bigots be grievin' Havana. As for herself? She'd corrected the error of her birth long ago. The identity of the boy she'd been, known only to herself. Dead, there'd be no hateful Havanas to spit on her grave. She'd achieve in death the aspiration of all women like her. To be judged by her deeds. The only things pried from the wreckage would be a dead murderer and a hero's sacrifice.

"Watch out!" Havana shot her finger toward the window.

A texting kid drifted into their lane. Too late to hit the brakes. BJ yanked the wheel to the left. The van teetered on two wheels. BJ compensated to the right. Hard. The van slammed to the ground, its left-front wheel folded into itself. The rear end swung around, lifted, and flipped the van onto its left side. Sparks spit into the screeching hulk, spraying BJ like a hateful sparkler. Air bags punched her nose and temple.

♦ ♦ ♦

Suki slammed on the brakes, brought the cab a broadside twenty feet from the van. Facing the undercarriage, she yelled into her headset, "Kurtz, get your people in here to secure the van and establish a perimeter. We need medics. And get the citizens outta range. No pics. Confiscate all phones and any cameras."

I leaped outta the cab and ran toward the van, hoping to hell that BJ survived. Glancing over my shoulder I saw Suki charging up, both hands on her Glock.

A puddle of gas grew from the back of the van. Flames burst up.

"BJ! BJ!" I shouted through the billowing smoke. I climbed onto the front of the van. Couldn't see a damned thing 'cept an air bag. But sure as hell felt the heat. Smelled mean, like napalm. My head spun back to Nam.

"*Beaucoup dinky dau*," a kid hollered behind me.

"Get outta here!" I yelled at the Vietnamese girl hopping on my burning APC. "You're the crazy one."

"Not without you!" Suki shouted back.

Suki's mettle pierced my flashback. I gave my head a violent shake to scatter the war.

The sliding door popped open and slid back. BJ stood, scraped-up nose and all, cradling a bloody and bruised Havana.

"Help me with her. She's alive."

"This is gonna blow!" Suki yelled as flames swallowed the back of the van.

BJ glanced at the fire, but started to hand Havana to me. "Take her. Gotta find her phone."

Havana's eyes popped open. In her hand clicked my switchblade. "Drop her, BJ!" I shouted.

"No, she'll die," BJ hollered back, lips snarled, as if asking, What's wrong with you?

I caught Havana's thrust and twisted the blade out of her hand. My old switchblade dropped into the smoky van. Never see it or my .45 again, goddammit.

I took Havana. Suki reached over and cuffed her. The killer's eyes rolled under their lids, and her body fell limp.

"We gotta move," Suki said.

"One a ya got a flashlight?" BJ yelled and then ducked into the van, arm raised for a light we didn't have.

"Don't got one. And we're outta time," Suki hollered.

Heat and rubber's stink sucked up breathable air.

"BJ, we gotta split!" I yelled. Her arm disappeared. "BJ? BJ?" I couldn't see her.

"Take Havana," I told Suki, but BJ's head popped up, coughing.

"Hell's bells, nothin'," BJ said, face down in the smoke. Then she looked at us. "Y'all still here? Let's skedaddle."

We slid off the van and bolted toward an arriving ambulance. Skinny Havana bounced in my arms. But BJ's stride lagged as she gasped for breath and squeezed her ribs. I tossed Havana over my shoulder and joined Suki, who'd hooked her arm around BJ's waist. Tiny Suki had to be all muscle. We ran with BJ in between us.

Ahead of us, at the back of the ambulance, Crusher frantically waved and shouted, "Hurry, hurry!"

I laid an unconscious—maybe dead—Havana on a waiting gurney. Crusher whipped out her stethoscope. "Leave her to the paramedics.

BJ's hurt," I spat at Crusher. She glanced at me with a pinched face, then ignored me as she checked out the killer.

Suki and I helped ease BJ onto the bumper of the rig.

"BJ, you all right?" I asked as I let the paramedic butt in.

"Fine," she gasped before turning to the medic. I stepped back and asked Suki how she was doing. She nodded okay, then strode off, talking into her mic.

I watched the paramedic tend to BJ, proud that I'd stopped Havana from stabbing her. I'd recovered my step ahead of Father Harlan—but that pride didn't mean I was gay, right? I coughed up the smell of the gas fire that had yanked me back to Nam. Couldn't believe Nam made more sense than the confusion swirling between me, BJ, and my manhood. I heard my belly grumble. I'd burned up Suki's granola. Gotta eat.

A local news chopper tried to position itself above the scene. I snickered as Kurtz's black Loach swooped in and faced off with 'em so close I expected their blades to clap. The news pimps backed off and hovered out over the Pacific.

"She's got a beat," Crusher said. "It sounds like a punctured lung. We've got to go." She turned to BJ. "You too, hon. No argument this time." A brief smile lit up BJ's welted mouth.

BJ nodded me over as she carefully reached behind herself and pulled out my .45. Her left cheek streaked with what looked like powder bursts. "This yours?"

"How'd you know?" I asked.

"Saw it when I searched your condo." Then she pursed her lips. "Your tummy's showin'."

I took my old friend as BJ poked and tickled my exposed skin. Left me thankful that a woman who used to have a pecker tickled me. But that gratitude took a stumble. Did my step ahead of Harlan cost me a testicle?

Behind us, the van blew, spewing burning debris. A wall of heat smacked us. Hunched up, I said to BJ, "Get to the hospital. I'll be right behind you."

"You too, Detective Faeth," Crusher said as BJ stepped into the rig behind Havana's gurney.

"After lunch," I said and reached to help Crusher into the rig.

"I've a powder-room stop to make before going to the hospital," she said, more to BJ than me, as she closed the ambulance doors. The look they'd traded told me I'd witnessed a coded O'DAD communication.

Suki stomped over to me. "All right, hero, we're wanted at your mayor's office for a photo op." Behind her, Chief Ferrus's fire engine sped toward the burning hulk.

"Hero? Mayor's office? No way," I said, not giving a crap about feeding the mayor's image. I had more important things to do. Like stumbling over my quaking manhood and making sure BJ was okay. "I'm following BJ to the hospital, then I'm gonna go scarf up a plate of huevos rancheros."

Suki shook her head, glanced at my belly, and muttered, "I don't deserve this." Then she pointed her finger at my nose. "Get in the car."

A Slight Wrinkle

BJ peered out the back window of the ambulance. The rig bulled around stalled cars, police cruisers, and stunned drivers handing their phones and cameras to FBI agents. Its siren and horn squawked in turns. At every dip and sway, her fractured ribs chafed like broken glass.

She knew Marilee detoured to an O'DAD website to dismiss Havana's BOLO against her and Lo. Marilee would cash in on her lie about falling to take them off Havana's hook. But it'd taken Marilee's finding Jax shot and witnessing a kidnapping before the scales fell from her eyes. Of course, she'd continue to ignore the bile that fueled murder.

BJ felt her body throb to the steady beeps of Havana's heart monitor. The pain aroused the devil in her. She shifted her eyes to the unconscious killer. She coulda let her burn.

The smell of disinfectant pierced the burned sludge that caked BJ's nose. She watched the medic staunch a bleed to Havana's head and then toss the bloody gauze into a biohazard container.

Saving Havana had saved her from being Havana, BJ decided.

♦ ♦ ♦

I watched BJ's rig nose through the cordoned-off perimeter, guided by an SFPD cruiser. Then they both shot off toward San Francisco General, sirens wailing.

"Follow them," I said as I buckled up in Suki's cab.

"Like I said, no time. You'll hafta visit BJ after the press conference," Suki growled as she steered the cab away from the crackling heap of a van. "We can't stand up your mayor or the other actors prepped to cook this show into something it's not."

What kind of bullshit had they drawn up for the news pimps? And no sugar coating from Suki. I respected that but looked at her smooth, innocent profile. The kid's political savvy left a slight wrinkle that'd get uglier over time. I hated seein' it. But keeping me from BJ to serve up that lie riled me.

"Dammit, Suki, leave me outta your sideshow," I sneered.

She hit the brakes, jammed the shift into park, popped outta her seat belt, and perched at the edge of her seat. "This is not only about keeping O'DAD as an intel asset. It's also about protecting you and Dr. Sandoval. You both know too much."

My turn to perch. I clicked off my seat belt, hackles up. "Sounds like a threat," I barked, now thankful that her hair stood wadded up under her cap. I'd've choked otherwise. Feeling my futile attraction to Suki, helped steady the macho shaken by BJ's tickle.

Suki opened her mouth, but Kurtz's chopper buzzed by. Her eyes followed the bird as she pounded her fist against the wheel. "You two are the only nonvetted men who know O'DAD exists. Tobac is one of less than a handful."

I remembered BJ's earlier rant: "No man denies his pecker, low-watt fanatic or not." Sure, they had reason not to trust most men. But hell, I wasn't most men. And without concrete evidence, Sandoval's digital brain stayed locked up tighter than Fort Knox.

"I get it," I said. "But hell, loyalty to BJ and respect for national security are enough to keep my trap shut. And if your highfalutin bureau knew anything about Sandoval, you'd understand that without O'DAD's router and phone, he's got nothing to say. I'd rather stay a suspended juicer than be photo opted with a bunch of lying politicians. I belong with BJ." Then a shot of myself coming to at the inn, wondering who'd kissed me, brought BJ's lips to mind. Revulsion shriveled me up inside. I slid back in my seat and buckled up again. Okay, so I'm not gay. But I still felt smaller than I did a second ago.

Suki rocked her head. "Your word and your faith in Dr. Sandoval may be good enough for me, but if you refuse to participate in their dog-and-pony show, you exclude yourself from the lie. You could come back without reversing yourself and say, That's not what happened. The way they see it, if you're wrapped in their dirty sheets with them, it'll counter whatever Dr. Sandoval might say."

Her harsh grip on the con said this wasn't the first time she'd flat-backed for 'em. Disgusted, I spoke as if trying to spit out the taste. "What's it gonna take for you to realize that politicos take a pound of your soul to give up an ounce of what's right?"

Suki blinked and turned her head away. I'd ground her nose into the shit. Her guilt thumped mine. Hell, it'd just hit me today that the priest whose sermons kept me from shooting innocent Vietnamese also spewed crap that cost me my brother.

"Never mind," I said and stared out at the piles of smoldering debris. "Can we stop and get me a change of clothes? Wanna look right for the mayor....How about you? Your outfit's pretty scuffed up too."

Suki drew in a long breath, as if relieved. Avoiding eye contact, she said in a dull voice, "These scorched clothes speak to the risks taken by the bureau. Showing up like this demonstrates the FBI's heroism."

I ignored the scripted rap. About as sincere as, "How may I provide you with excellent service today?"

"So I don't have to change, then?" I said, glancing at my patches of exposed belly.

Suki buckled up, put the taxi in gear, and said, "Crude doesn't sell. Have to change your sooty bandages too."

"You gonna tell me what disaster we averted?"

"Part of my job, isn't it. Be glad you won't have to speak. All you'll have to do is stand there and..." She glanced at me sideways. Swore I saw the opening pull of a smile as she added, "look pretty."

I stumbled over that crack in Suki's bureaucratic armor. Shamelessly wished I had the youth and good looks to complete her smile. Wished to hell my feelings were as clear when it came to BJ. I gave Suki directions to my condo.

The Lowest Common Denominator

"Let me get this straight," I said, sitting sideways, straining against my seat belt. "You're gonna feed the public crap about a white supremacist plan to blow up the Golden Gate Bridge and then blame it on Muslims posing as Mexicans in order to stir up lynch mobs. How's that pardon us for forgetting the real vics? Letting their killers off the hook?

"Tell 'em about Havana. Who she killed. Don't hafta say shit about O'DAD. Keep your damned asset."

"Detective," she slapped back, disappointing me that I didn't hear my name glide off her tongue. "Our Burning Man spectacle forced us to involve local and state authorities. Fiefdoms blindsided by invading feds lit up the phone lines to your governor and mayor." Suki rocked the cab to a halt at a light. "Tobac had a nanosecond to draft a palatable cover story."

"Christ, the mayor supports gay marriage. Won't be embarrassed by his cops stopping tranny murders." But as soon as I said it, I knew that point fell blunt at the governator's feet.

"Yeah, and your governor said that gay marriage should be between a man and a woman," Suki said, glancing between me and the light. "Tobac's sop has to appeal to the lowest common denominator."

Years of missing Ricky, swollen by guilt's compound interest, had cracked open the door to accepting BJ. But a lifetime of knee-jerk stupidity doesn't vanish with a single punch to a car seat. Most of my life, I'd shit and fell back in it, right there with the governator.

The light turned green. Suki shot us through the intersection. "What kinda glory pie you feedin' the press?" I asked.

Suki drew in a deep breath. "The governor and mayor are taking credit for their leadership in stopping the attack on the Golden Gate Bridge. For apprehending the ringleader."

I melted into the seat, disgusted at my part in the sham. For letting BJ down, like I did my brother.

I unlocked the door to my condo, motioned for Suki to go ahead of me, but warned her, "Don't let out my cat."

"You have a pet?" Suki asked over her shoulder.

"Name's Al," I said and cracked open the door. Al lay on the back of the sofa, facing us.

"Anh," Al said. Then he yawned, stretching his front paws as if to crawl. He lost his balance, tipped, then fell. One paw caught the back of the couch, swinging his ass toward the floor. He let go and, without a glance back, padded his way toward the dining room.

"Sounds more like a game-show dunce buzzer than a cat," Suki said.

"Vet says that's because he's deaf. Thinks he's hearing it if he feels the vibration."

I followed Al to his empty bowls. From under the sink, I grabbed a can of cat food, stood, and started to pull it open.

Suki stomped in, glanced between Al and the can, then her watch, and said, "Cat needs to be on a diet. Feed him when you get back. We gotta go."

"Anh," Al said, springing up on his hind legs, front paws on my shin.

"He don't eat. I quit the circus," I said to Suki.

"I'll feed him. You go change." She grabbed the can. "Low-mercury, wild-caught albacore tuna?"

I pointed to the fridge. "Don't forget to freshen up his water bowl. Use the spring water in the glass bottle."

"Go get dressed," she said as she popped open Al's lunch.

I strode into my bedroom and called the hospital. Nobody would tell me a thing over the phone. Security was tight. I couldn't tell what I was sorrier for: that I couldn't talk to BJ or for being window dressing for the mayor.

Carrying my clean slacks, a button-down shirt, and corduroy jacket, I headed into my bathroom for a shower.

With the soot scrubbed away, I glanced in the mirror at my gravel chafed knees, gunshot, cuts, and bruise. Helluva lot luckier than BJ. I patched the bleeds with fresh gauze.

♦ ♦ ♦

BJ's coffee-colored attendant, Victor, had wheeled her in her hospital bed to X-ray to avoid painful transfers to a gurney and back. Not that the muscular hunk couldn't handle the weight. He'd done it out of tenderness. Along with them swaggered an alert, young, uniformed SFPD guard in case Havana's cutthroats came after her. He carried a clipboard with the names of authorized medical staff and police personnel allowed contact. All security screened and committed to her anonymity. She'd made sure Lo was on that list.

♦ ♦ ♦

I came out of the bathroom dressed up, saw that fur pig was eating, and stepped into my kitchen. Took two frozen burritos out of my freezer, threw 'em into my greasy microwave, and offered one to Suki.

She clucked her tongue, said she'd stick to granola. Looked at her watch again and told me I'd have to eat them on the way.

"How long is that gonna take?" she asked and started pacing around the living room, her hair stuck up under that damned baseball cap.

"A couple of minutes is all," I said, punching thaw. At least I'd stopped irritating one gal, BJ. It shouldn't matter she'd started off as a guy. I owed her my life, for Christ's sake. After the *Muppet Show*, I'd head straight to BJ's side. Told myself I'd gotten cleaned up for her, not the paparazzi.

Suki's "James Bond Theme" ringtone stopped her pacing. She spoke into her headset.

"Please tell me I'm kicked off *The Howdy Doody Show*," I griped as I timed cook on my microwave.

Suki hung up. "The news conference is outside on the steps of city hall. Sorry, Faeth."

She'd called me Faeth. Teased that she hadn't said my first name, I said, "Lo. Call me Lo. My nickname."

♦ ♦ ♦

"Hairline fractures, but no frayed bones to puncture your lungs, hon," Marilee said, passing BJ an open smile. Marilee had read her X-ray results in the absence of her tardy attending.

A signpost of forgiveness? That question lay silent in front of the X-ray tech. Still, that Marilee had left Havana's treatment to a stranger in ER pumped guilt's antidote through BJ like a rippling balm.

Marilee turned to the tech. "May we have a moment?"

She took BJ's hand, her eyes sloppy troughs. "Hon, I watched you in that tinderbox hand Havana to Detective Faeth. No one would've faulted you if you'd left her to save yourself." She stroked BJ's left cheek, the one without spark trails. She added, "Thanks to you, she may survive."

"We're both orphans," BJ said, swooning over Marilee's touch. Awed at the power of her caress to mute the bite of her injuries.

Marilee drew her head back. "But the circumstances have nothing in common."

"Don't matter," BJ said softly. "We're abandoned kids. Both left knee-deep in self-doubt and resentment. Havana swallowed those pills sideways. Let 'em dissolve into murderous rage. If I'd let her die, I'd be no better."

Marilee started to speak, but a knock at the door interrupted. BJ's guard, holding his mic, stuck his head in. "Dr. Tobac is waiting for Detective Reeves in her room. Says it's important."

"Tell him she's on her way," Marilee said and turned to BJ. Creasing her forehead, she added, "Fitness for duty evaluation, now? Couldn't he wait?"

"Guess not," BJ said, peaking her eyebrows to distract Marilee from her and Tobac's FBI credentials. She figured he'd hand her a one-way ticket to DC.

Marilee squeezed her hand and excused herself to go check on Havana. BJ's curiosity over what Marilee had said to counter Havana's BOLO melted under the grande dame's warmth. She felt on the mend.

Slow to Cool

Rolling down the hall from X-ray, BJ took in Victor's upside-down face with his perpetual grin. The sparkle in his brown eyes didn't falter as they passed under the ceiling lamps alternating light and shadow. Cute as a bug's ear, she thought as his words of support gently fluttered on his sweet Nigerian accent. She curled her smile all the way around her ears. Then she remembered her scraped-up nose, spark-streaked cheek, and welted lips. Left her lookin' like Bozo with a side of cat whiskers. She clucked her tongue and shot her hand over her face. Hot spikes stomped up her side. "Ah," she gasped and then slowly lowered her arm."

"No, no. No sudden moves, Detective," Victor said. "Please be careful."

Razor-sharp points jabbed from within. Slow to cool.

"Yes, suh," she said, her lighthearted lilt betrayed by a grimace. As her frown faded, her attention spilled from her battered appearance into that tingle between her legs. She'd wanted to jump Victor's bones. Her typical slam dunk, thank you sir. An intimacy ending at orgasm. Empty of possibility.

Her memory lapsed back onto the powder-room floor, where her thoughts had wilted on achievements no better than a man's. The woman behind the badge never ventured beyond a one-night stand. Fled tests of a relationship beyond a fuck. BJ muffled her ironic chuckle. She'd faced down a killer and defied fire but spent her life fearing rejection.

"Hold up," her guard said and entered her room first. She couldn't make out what the voices said until her guard demanded ID. He came out and asked if she felt up to seeing Dr. Tobac.

"You didn't recognize him?" she asked, fearing an imposter.

"Never met him. Just heard of him," her guard said, adding, "He and his ID match."

"What's he look like?"

After the officer's description, BJ said, "Good job. I'll see him."

Victor rolled her in, and she caught Tobac's wilted stance against the windowsill blanched by the sun. Behind her, she heard the door open again, and Tobac snapped to. Looking past her, he said, "Dr. Galen, how are you?"

"Well, thanks," Galen said. She caught his spotless, flowing white coat as he came around to shake hands with Tobac. A rotund nurse waddled behind in her baggy blue scrubs. BJ made a note of her name badge: Sheila.

"Checking on your detective?" Galen said to Tobac. "Don't worry. I'm taking good care of her."

"Wouldn't expect anything less," Tobac said without a glance at BJ.

Victor moved to the foot of her bed, backed it in, aligning it with the head panel. BJ spoke out against his invisibility as he tiptoed out. "Thank ya, Victor, for everything." Then she announced her and her nurse's presence, "Hi, Sheila. I'm BJ."

Sheila grinned, shuffled over to BJ's bedside, and whispered, "My pleasure."

Tobac stepped aside so Galen could slide in between the window and BJ's bed, opposite Sheila. "You're dry as a bone, Detective Reeves. I've ordered your nurse to set up an IV drip to hydrate you. X-rays reveal multiple but minor linear fractures. Nary a threat to your lungs."

Nothing she didn't already know, BJ thought, shooting her gaze to her nurse. "I'm sure Sheila will get me up and runnin' in no time. Won'tcha, dahlin'?"

Sheila patted BJ's arm. "Bet on it." They traded glances as they eyed Tobac walking Galen to the door. Both docs blind to their treatment of everyone else as no more than a parking valet, handmaiden, and cracked vase.

"Little sting, BJ," Sheila said, aiming the IV needle.

"Ready when you are, dahlin'," she said, but her words were followed by an ancient ache that muted the prick. BJ doubted Sheila'd be so kind if she knew her patient had started out with a penis.

Tobac meandered over and leaned on BJ's bed rail. "Finished, nurse? I need a private word with Detective Reeves."

Sheila looked at Tobac but spoke to BJ. "You got an order for serious pain meds. I could give ya one before I'm dismissed."

"Tempting, but not now." BJ needed a clear head to deal with her handler.

Sheila ambled to the door, adding over her shoulder, "When ya get a chance, turn on your TV. That chase is all over the news. I know you're one of those heroes."

"Close the door behind you," Tobac commanded.

"Thank ya, dahlin'," BJ hollered, glaring at Tobac. Her interest in the chase fell laps behind how to dodge Tobac's boot.

A Wet One from Bozo

Suki parked the cab in city hall's underground garage and slid the chopstick out of her baseball cap. Her hair uncoiled after she pulled off the hat and headset. She swayed her head as her slender fingers flared those silky locks over her shoulders. Even in the garage's low light, that hair sparkled.

"What?" she snapped. Her glare scorched my trance.

"Wha…what?" I stammered, busted.

♦ ♦ ♦

"Gotcha Havana. Gonna keep me on the case?" BJ asked, her voice stoked.

Tobac puffed his chest. "You disobeyed orders."

"This about you? Or stoppin' Havana?" she snapped, her sides left stinging. "Hell's bells, I'm lying here banged up, but you're riled 'cause when you said, Jump, I didn't ask, How high?" She watched his eyes wander. She'd nicked a cord.

"You could've been killed. You're still at risk," he said, jutting his chin toward her door, reminding her of the guard.

"Not buyin' your cock-and-bull concern," BJ said, on the offensive, despite each breath scraping a wall of nails. But she shifted her attack from the personal to their op. "I still have my cop cover."

Tobac straightened his back. "Not to your partner. Who no doubt revealed it to Dr. Sandoval."

"After what's happened, those boys play for our team. Besides, what's more important? My cover or stopping the murders? Havana's butchers now know Marilee and me are on the same page—and that we're onto them. They'd be less likely to carry on killin' with me around. Until we round 'em up, I'm a deterrent." BJ clenched her teeth against crackling bones and leered at Tobac.

The doc cupped an elbow with one hand, and with the other he scratched his cheek. "What makes you think Dr. Crusher's indictment of Havana isn't enough to frighten them off?"

"God love Dr. Crusher, but Havana's thugs gotta have something more to fear than her judgment. She ain't a cop. Can't enforce nada. I'd be so far up their skirts, all they'd be doin' is trying to skedaddle. No time for killin'."

BJ watched Tobac stroke his lips with his fingers.

♦ ♦ ♦

That ham Rhodes tripped over me getting down front between our chief of police and the CHP Commissioner on city hall's steps. Suki had said our chief told Rhodes that my suspension was a ruse to get Havana to underestimate me. That the chief invited him to cheese it in the photo op as a booby prize for being cut outta the loop. Suki wouldn't cop to it, but our lady chief had to be an O'DAD big shot.

The chief shooed Rhodes back, where he shook my hand, pulled me in, and griped that I'd better tell him the next time she put me and BJ undercover behind his back.

"Sure, sure," I said. His smile never broke.

Chief Ferrus slid in next to Suki, protective gear and all. He looked over at me and said, "At least they let you clean up." The mayor coaxed him down to his podium to stand next to our chief. Ferrus's face knotted up as tight as my gut as he stepped forward.

♦ ♦ ♦

Tobac grasped BJ's bed rail. "Suki—" he started to say, but BJ interrupted.

"Who's Suki? That's right. They're askin'. Who's Suki? You want one of Havana's cutthroats to kill a Vips to test her? See what she's made of?

You can't give 'em that slack. I'm the bitch who put Havana in traction, not Suki."

Her volley left her throbbing. BJ stifled a groan and watched the shrink step away, arms akimbo. Had she knocked him to the ropes? Or boosted her booty toward DC? She coulda used Sheila's pill.

♦ ♦ ♦

After the mayor bragged that he and the governor had co-led a joint investigation that thwarted a racist attack on the Golden Gate Bridge, he handed the mic to our chief. She explained that our "highly coordinated operation" had resulted in injuries but no deaths. That an officer and two suspects were at undisclosed hospitals and were expected to recover. But BJ wasn't the only torn-up cop. What about Sandoval? I thought, fuming.

A hippie-looking male reporter shouted, "Why the all-girl FBI team?"

The chief didn't blink, nodded to me, swerved her broad smile back into the crowd, and said, "Detective Faeth, as part of that team, may take issue with you on that." She'd made me one of the gals, then busted a giggle. The crowd followed with a roar of laughter. Especially the female newshounds. O'DAD owed me.

Our chief passed the mic back to the mayor, who pointed to the big screen mounted behind us and introduced "Our busy governor tied up in Sacramento." After the governator's "fantastic" speech, I needed another shower. But I'd hold my nose until after I saw BJ.

After the backslapping, I unloaded on Suki about the chief's ignoring Sandoval. She huffed and reminded me that he'd made up his own cover story with his gangland hit. Then she offered me a ride to the hospital. I hadn't asked. Thought she'd want to get into clean clothes while I cabbed it and said so.

"Come on, one last taxi ride," she smirked. The flinty kid crawled deeper under my skin.

♦ ♦ ♦

Tobac had circled back to BJ's bedside and cast his gaze from her head to her toes. "I told you at the park that you're at risk and a liability. These injuries suggest I was half right."

"Half right?" she said, her face pinched.

"Perhaps your commitment to the case is less a liability than an asset," he said, stroking his chin. He looked up and added, "And Dr. Crusher's message countering Havana's made a certain Detective Reeves pivotal to stopping the carnage."

"Then I'm stayin'?" BJ asked, jerking her head up but then grunting over the pepper shot cascading down her torso.

"There's a condition." Tobac wrapped both hands around her bed rail. "Suki stays and assists. We"—he nodded for emphasis—"owe her that. And if I'm wrong about you, then you and I are both on a plane to headquarters."

Stunned, BJ said, "You stuck your neck out for me?" Now she wanted to hug him. Memories of her daddy flared.

Tobac leveled his gaze to hers. "Not just you, but Detective Faeth and his CSI friend. Their ice is under my feet too."

BJ didn't feel a chill. Knew she could count on Lo and Sandoval. Her tension collapsed and her spirit rose with the revived opportunity to reconcile Lo with his brother. Relieved, she said, "Now ya make me wanna kiss ya." She glanced away and then back again. "Not that you'd want a wet one from Bozo."

Tobac grinned.

"A smile? Another first," BJ said. Then she recalled her 911 call about Marilee. "Ah, listen here. That anonymous tip about Dr. Crusher—"

Tobac waved her off. "Traced to your SFPD cell. Your chief took care of it. As far as the SFPD are concerned, you'd reported it lost. Dr. Crusher'd found it. A Good Samaritan found Dr. Crusher and your phone on the powder-room floor. Used it to call 911. End of story."

"Dang, you manage your assets well, don't ya? Hey, they still sifting through the van's wreckage?"

"As we speak," he said. "So far, they've found a switchblade and a nickel with a hidden handcuff key."

Their eyes met.

"Gadget," BJ said.

"Suki," Tobac scolded.

"Gotta find Havana's phone. In the van she called one of her flunkies to delete their protocol."

Tobac pursed his lips. "I'll remind Forensics to treat every stack of debris like an archaeological dig."

"Gonna be burned and busted up, but if ya find it, you oughta let Dr. Sandoval take a look. That boy's a scalpel."

Tobac glared and shook his head. "Don't press your luck, Agent Reeves. This remains in-house. Understood?"

"I suppose."

"Suppose?" Tobac sneered.

"In-house, suh. We'll keep it thataway," she said. Then they both heard a knock and turned to the door. "Yes'm?" BJ hollered.

Sheila stuck her head in. "Did ya catch the mayor's press conference?" She pointed to the blank TV.

"Not yet," BJ said. Sheila lingered, and BJ figured she'd seen it. "Dahlin', give us a sec, and then you and I can catch its rerun."

Sheila closed the door, leaving BJ alone with Tobac. Under her breath she asked him, "What kinda bullpucky you offer the locals?"

"Take the spin, no questions asked. And they get all the credit for saving the Golden Gate."

"They? How far up the food chain you have toss the grub?" BJ asked.

"Governor and mayor." Tobac punched the remote. "Have a look."

After a few minutes, BJ turned it off and said, "Defending the bridge gets 'em votes. Protecting trannies dashes reelection. Humph."

Tobac shrugged, "Politics. A tacky business."

Hell, without bells this time, BJ simmered. What more could she expect? Her last family member had turned on her when he'd found out. Couldn't expect more from the petty bigots people elect.

Expecting no more from Marilee, she asked, "And Dr. Crusher's message?"

"I was briefed that she did a video. Reported that you and Detective Faeth had discovered that Havana is the mastermind behind a series of Vips murders. That Havana'd exploited her coma to destroy yours and Faeth's credibility."

"She actually cited the VIPS?" BJ asked.

"I'm told she tearfully speculated that Havana wished her to die. Planned to use her as an anti-VIPS martyr."

Marilee had opened her eyes wide and broken her silence on the divide. But how far did she go? BJ caught her breath. "She say anything else?"

"That in order to restore O'DAD's moral authority, O'DAD must open membership to all women, regardless of any error of birth."

"She said, 'error of birth'?" BJ relished her shock.

Tobac's chin bobbed in the affirmative. "Verbatim, I'm told."

"Damn," BJ said in pleased disbelief. But if Marilee broadcast that Havana'd been caught in their fiery crash, it'd fly in the face of Tobac's spin. "Marilee mention our chase?"

"Not a word. Left Havana's arrest and the terrorist plot open to treatment as separate events."

"But did Kurtz scare off the news copter before they got a shot of Havana?"

"Appears so. Also understand that the reporter is an O'DAD member interested in protecting the sisterhood."

"And drivers on the ground with their camera phones?"

Tobac flipped his hand in the air. "Officers were ordered to confiscate everyone's phones or cameras as evidence. They'll get them back after Forensics scours them. Without photos, Detective Faeth could've been carrying anyone. Besides, Kurtz's team established a broad perimeter, you were surrounded by smoke, and your partner threw Havana over his shoulder like a sack of potatoes, face down. Even if a few shots get through, they'll be too far away for a positive ID of Havana. Deniability should be sufficiently preserved."

BJ relaxed but said, "Havana's minions won't be fooled. But they ain't gonna expose themselves by saying anything."

“Even if one should, we’ll dismiss her as a conspiracy nut. I’ll check in with you after I brief Suki. Your new silent partner.” Tobac stepped toward the door. “I’ll let your nurse in.”

Sheila hurried to BJ’s bedside. “Have you seen it?” She grabbed and pointed the remote toward the TV.

“Just a smidgen,” BJ said. A replay of the chase filled the screen as the ’caster’s squawk crammed the room. “Turn it down a bit, will ya, dahlin’?”

Lo’s grimaced smile caught BJ’s attention when the mayor’s news conference came on. She recognized his subtle squirm. Knew he hated the spotlight. The lie worse. But when she saw Suki, she figured she’d struck the match that lit Lo’s hop through the hoops. Lonely ol’ boy hadn’t a chance against that fetching firecracker. BJ chuckled under her breath. Stung just a tad.

Sheila musta seen Marilee’s O’DAD message. Told BJ, “Got your hands full, don’tcha?” BJ knew the crack between Tobac’s spin and Marilee’s video left Sheila thinking her patient stood knee-deep in two investigations. As intended. “You know I can’t say, dahlin’.”

The dutiful nurse winked and said, “Gotcha. Top secret.”

BJ watched the chief spin Lo into a punch line to garrote the question about the female FBI team. But Lo’s cringed glance away from the camera’s zoom showed he didn’t like being forced into something he’s not. His dodge stumbled into her own bitter scab. Would he have jumped on that van to save her if he’d known she’d exited the womb with a penis?

“That reporter wouldn’t’ve questioned it if they were all men, huh, BJ?” Sheila spouted over the TV’s receding wave of laughter.

“S’pose not,” BJ said, thinking Lo would’ve let her burn if he’d known.

Best of Three Takes All

BJ's guard stood up and said, "You're Detective Faeth. Saw the news conference on TV." He stuck out his hand. "It's an honor."

His shake was firm, didn't linger. Not like the limp-dick pulls I'd gotten at city hall. But I looked up and down the hallway. Didn't see a TV. How'd he recognize me? "How long you been guarding Detective Reeves?"

"Since her arrival, sir."

"You leave your post to catch the show?" I said, riding my clutch.

"No…no, sir." The kid fumbled out his iPhone.

"Never mind," I said and saw his clipboard's list of authorized visitors. I pulled out my ID, then pointed, "My name on there?"

"Must be. But let me check." He took my ID and scanned his list.

"Right here, Detective Faeth." He ran his finger under my name.

♦ ♦ ♦

Sheila looked up. "BJ, it's Detective Faeth."

"Detective Faeth, meet Sheila. My sweetie nurse," BJ said, trying to climb outta her doubts about him.

She felt a minor sway and noticed that Sheila had grasped her bed rail and was pushing it back and forth. Sheila gaped at Lo. He glanced over his shoulder. Musta thought somebody important followed him in.

Sheila scurried around the bed to greet him, and he shook her outstretched hand. "Th-thanks for taking care of my partner," he said.

Sheila curtsied. "My pleasure." Then she looked back at BJ, winked, and added, "I'll leave you two alone. Hit your call light if you need anything."

Lo watched her leave and shut the door. "What the hell?"

"You're a hero," she said, snickering but still heated by whether or not he would've rescued her if he'd known.

"Maybe you. You stopped Havana. I'm just another jackass kickin' the teeth outta the truth." Lo stepped to her bedside, his hands in his pockets. His eyes evaded hers.

BJ decided the lie pained him. Not the murdered women no one alive risked speaking up for. Raw, she blurted, "Watta ya mopin' about? Nobody'll accuse you of savin' trannies."

♦ ♦ ♦

I flung my hands outta my pockets. "That's what you think of me? That I don't care because they're VIPS? Dammit, BJ, I played along to keep your precious O'DAD outta sight." I glared, but she'd turned away.

Ricky kicked outta his closet, waving BJ's secret. She'd been a boy. Yeah, she's sore that Vips' lives been kicked under the rug. Certainly was smacked around before any trace of that boy disappeared under her skirt. By people like me. That bigoted whip snapped back to knock me off balance. I grabbed a nearby plastic chair and plopped down.

♦ ♦ ♦

BJ heard Lo say, "VIPS." Of course the old hound had sniffed 'em out. Then the scrape of chair legs followed by the thump of a rump snatched her attention. She turned back toward him, careful to avoid sudden moves. There he sat. Hunched over. Hands massaging his knees. What felled him? Guilty conscience?

♦ ♦ ♦

The door cracked open and slammed shut. I snapped to my feet and yanked out my Colt. Heard the muffled voice of the guard, "You're not on the list."

Lakesha Jackson's voice followed. "I'm a cop, here to see BJ."

I glanced at BJ and back at the door. "Sounds like Jackson. Want me to let her in if it is?" I asked, holstering my piece.

♦ ♦ ♦

Lakesha had knocked Lo off BJ's anvil—for the moment.

"Uh-huh. But Lo, didn't ya wonder why Havana hooded us when she meant to kill us anyway?"

"Yeah. Why?" he said, focusing on the door.

"There was a third gal with Havana and Jax."

"Right. Blew by me in the hallway before they shoved me through the door. Never said a word."

"I think it was Lakesha," BJ said.

Lo reached for his .45 again and headed toward the voices outside.

"No, dahlin'. She's not here to finish me. Hiding who she was made no sense if she was in on the murders. She's a good cop. I think Havana duped her. Fed her some cock-and-bull about me betraying O'DAD. Likely in cahoots with Havana for awhile. Suspect Havana took advantage of her eyes and ears on me at the precinct. Used the hoods to fool Lakesha into believing we'd be let go once she recovered O'DAD's hardware. Lakesha expected to see us again."

"Then why is she here?" Lo asked, gripping his Colt, one ear cocked toward Jackson's tiff with the guard.

"To apologize," BJ said.

Lo glanced at BJ. "Get outta town."

BJ rolled her eyes. "Dr. Crusher exposed Havana on O'DAD's website. Trust me, the girl is here to shed her guilt at bein' buffaloed. Let her in."

Lo blinked and then insisted, "Mr. Forty-five stays handy. Otherwise, no dice."

"Have it your way, dahlin'. Now go on, get her." BJ had fishing to do. Establish Lakesha as the third guard, a dupe, and start to rule her out as an accomplice to murder. And if she'd lost hold of her judgment again, Lo stood by with his hammer back.

♦ ♦ ♦

I went to the door and opened it, Mr. Colt held behind me. Jackson stood there in her pressed blues. Holstered sidearm.

"Detective Faeth," Lakesha said. She looked me up and down. "Saw you at the press conference. I'm so glad you're all right." She glanced back at the guard. "Tell him I can see BJ, will you?"

"She, is, not, on, the, list," the officer said, each word pumped with equal rank.

"It's okay," I said, then glared at Jackson. "Detective Reeves vouches for her."

The officer stepped aside, heaving his chest. "All right, Detective, I'll add her name to the list."

"I didn't say that, did I? She can come in this time." I watched Lakesha glance away, cluck her tongue. "Don't want you to get in any trouble adding names by yourself," I said without taking my eyes off Jackson.

"Yes, sir. Thank you," he said.

"Thanks," Lakesha said, her tone flat.

I stepped back, pushing the door with me. Let her pass in front of me and closed the door.

"You can holster your gun, Detective," Jackson said, keeping her eyes on me.

"Gimme yours first," I said, not sharing BJ's confidence.

"Play nice, kids," BJ said. "Officer Jackson's here to support my recovery. Ain'tcha, dahlin'?"

"It's fine, BJ," Jackson said, turning her head toward her and back. "Can't blame him." Her voice dipped.

"That a confession?" I snapped, convinced she'd guarded BJ.

"Lo," BJ fired back. "Go lie down outside. Let us girls have a moment."

"Not without her sidearm." I glanced at BJ. She rolled her eyes.

BJ said, "Lo—"

But Jackson interrupted and spoke to me: "Thumb and index finger only. Then on the floor. All right?" Her eyes glued to mine.

"Go ahead," I said as she raised one hand and unstrapped her holster with the other. She lifted her piece—pinched between her fingers—squatted and placed it on the floor. She kicked it over to me. I put it in my belt. "And your throwaway?"

"Don't pack a throwaway. Not that kind of cop." Then she laced her fingers behind her head, turned her back to me, and spread her legs. "See for yourself."

Not that kind of cop? How hoity-toity, I thought as I patted her down. She didn't flinch. "She's clean," I said.

"Now can we have that moment?" BJ said.

"I'll be right outside. Ear to the door."

♦ ♦ ♦

BJ waited for Lo to close the door behind him. "The boy's protective. Thanks for indulging him," BJ said, and watched Lakesha's eyelids flutter.

"I am so glad I didn't find you in intensive care. How are you feeling?" she asked, standing feet away from the bed. One hand fondled a gold cross dangling from her neck.

"I'm gonna be just fine." BJ studied her fellow officer.

"I can't tell you what a relief that is after watching that awful wreck on TV." Her eyes wandered as she patted her chest below her neck. Her gaze fell to the floor. "I knew that was you in that van."

BJ recognized her confession. As her third guard, she knew who crashed in that van. BJ also heard relief in Jackson's tone and read guilt in her body's flap. BJ pursed her lips. Which bait did the Aryan mistress use to snare the African American cop? BJ lowered her voice to a whisper. "What'd you think of Havana's BOLO against me?"

Lakesha cleared her throat. Pulled and dragged her cross back and forth against its chain. "Could see how it'd turn women against you."

"And Marilee's announcement?" BJ asked, stomping her shovel.

"Like a slap in the face," she said. Lakesha glanced up and then returned her stare to the floor. "Ah, I mean for the women, ah...who got fooled into helping Havana."

BJ heard shame in Lakesha's fitful stammer. Didn't believe she'd participate in murder. "Whatcha think about Marilee opening membership to the VIPS?" Lakesha's reply would hock up Havana's hook. O'DAD security? Or malice toward women like her?

"Shocked," Jackson huffed, squinting at BJ. "She went too far. Vips aren't women, they're sick." She put her hands on her hips. "Should be treated by a doctor."

A gush of disappointment about swamped BJ's spite. Still, she shot back, "Think they oughta ride in the back of the bus too?" BJ didn't flinch at the heat of Lakesha's glare. Watched her hands slip off her hips and ball into fists.

Jackson gulped a breath and snapped, "Not the same."

"Really? How?"

Lakesha's eyes darted about the room as if itchin' for an exit. "Something wrong with you if you can't see it."

"I'm not the one who needs glasses," BJ spat.

Lakesha's gaze returned to BJ and lingered. She opened her mouth as if to speak. Instead she opened her fists and then said, "Well. I'm glad you're all right. See you at the precinct when you're well."

"Till then." BJ watched Lakesha saunter out the door. Knew in a gunfight Jackson would think twice before sticking her neck out for a Vips booster. Then she thought, God help Lakesha find the strength to pull that trigger if she knew my birthday suit came with male junk.

Lo popped his head in. "How'd it go?" He glanced over his shoulder at Jackson and then shut the door behind him. At her bedside, he moved his face close and whispered, "She admit guarding you?"

"Not directly. But it was her." BJ trained her sights back on what had made her earlier snipe knock Lo to his chair. This time she'd ride Marilee's and Lakesha's coattails for his stand on VIPS.

"What'd Jackson say?" Lo asked.

BJ leveled her gaze at him. "She'd seen Dr. Crusher's O'DAD announcement about murder evidence against Havana. Her reaction convinced me she's not likely a party to killin'." BJ paused and then took her shot. "What I didn't tell ya was Dr. Crusher opened O'DAD membership to the VIPS. That did turn Lakesha foul. Said they're not women, that they're sick. Reminded me of you."

♦ ♦ ♦

BJ thought I woulda left her in that van if I'd known she'd started as a boy. But this time I stayed on my feet. "Didn't keep me from you," I said in my soft voice reserved for crime victims.

♦ ♦ ♦

BJ'd braced for the worst, but Lo's words rippled through her soul, seizing vacancies she'd only prayed he could fill. His face blurred behind her disbelief. The boy knew. Saved her anyway. She lost her breath.

♦ ♦ ♦

The color dropped outta BJ's face. She stopped breathing.

"Where's your panic button?" I said, hopping around, patting her covers. "Gotta get a doc."

She grabbed my wrist, tight. "No. I…I'm all right. You knew…know?"

The color returned to BJ's cheeks. Her eyes studied my face. I freed my wrist to cup her hand in mine. Made myself think of it as a girl's.

"I know, BJ. And I'll always have your back."

She laced her fingers through mine. Her face relaxed into a smile.

♦ ♦ ♦

BJ savored the warmth of Lo's touch. Didn't want to lose it. But Lakesha's chill splashed her spine. Who else knew?

"Who told you? How'd they find out?" she asked, clenching his hand.

"Rhodes ordered an officer to your house when you went missing. Laszlo Singh tagged along. Took hair samples from brushes and combs."

"Who else besides Laszlo knows?" she demanded, feeling vulnerability dampen her grip.

"Nobody 'cept me and Sandoval. But BJ, Laszlo and Sandoval are good cops. Your...your Vips bravery will pry their heads outta their asses." His gaze dropped to the floor. "You know, like it did mine."

"Vips?" BJ yanked her hand away. "Never needed a sorority to vouch for my vagina. But if my 'bravery' don't cause them to see me as anything more than a freak, I'm left outted while they pat you on the head for saving your twisted tranny partner. That's about your guilty conscience, not me."

♦ ♦ ♦

Left staring at my empty hand, I thought, Is she right? But with me beside her, we'd face the devil that drove me from my brother and her underground.

"Don't be afraid to let 'em know who you really are, BJ."

♦ ♦ ♦

"Who I really am? You don't know and don't get it. You're looking at who I really am. But you stand there, safely wrapped up in the right skin, never having to use your fists to defend it. You don't have a clue what it took to correct the mistake of my birth. To keep that mean contradiction from a cruel public." The sparks out of her mouth matched those scorching her rib cage. She slowed her breathing to cool.

BJ focused back on a flat-footed Lo, his empty hand where she'd left it. "You tell Sandoval and Singh that those were my boyfriend's hairs, ya hear?"

♦ ♦ ♦

I stepped back from her bed. "BJ, I'm sorry. You're right. I don't get what, you know, gals like you"—I cringed, clumsily looking for the right words—"with the wrong start go through."

♦ ♦ ♦

"Can't find the words, can ya?" BJ spat. "Gals like me can't even agree on how to describe ourselves. But the message the rest of ya'll give us is hella clear. Hide in the dark if you don't wanna get punched around or killed. Hell's bells, how much light did it take to get your brother locked in a closet after you caught him trying on the right clothes?" BJ gasped. Too late to halt Ricky's escape. Her face burned as she watched Lo flag.

♦ ♦ ♦

What the hell? How'd she know about Ricky? O'DAD, of course. Guilt clamped my chest, froze my lungs. The floor rocked.

♦ ♦ ♦

BJ watched Lo flop onto the chair, relieved he'd caught the seat.

"Lo…Lo, you all right?" Her temperature cooled by his collapse.

"You read my O'DAD file."

Though not the ceremonious fantasy she'd embraced in telling him about his brother, she couldn't cork that genie now. "More than that. I knew Ricky," BJ said softly.

"Knew? Ricky's dead," he choked. His hands covered his face.

Lo's grief erased any lingering doubt about his readiness to meet his lost sibling. "Lo. Bad choice of words. Apologize," she said, wishing she could enfold him in her arms.

"My brother's alive?" Lo's hands slid from his face.

She cleared her throat. "Yes. She's alive. She'd like you to meet her." BJ watched to see if the narrow legs of Lo's chair would collapse under the weight of Ricky's gender.

"She? Of course. Yeah, when? Tell him...her, I'm sorry. That I miss him...her. I didn't know him as a she. Wouldn't stand for it. My fault I lost... my sister."

She'd never witnessed Lo unravel without getting mad. Touched, BJ lifted her hand. "Come on, take it," she said.

♦ ♦ ♦

I gripped BJ's hand to steady myself. Recalled Sandoval's vic's transformation from male to female. My flooded eyes blurred more by foggy images of what my brother—no, sister—might look like.

BJ again wove her fingers through mine, squeezed, then, without a hint of twang, said, "Wanna wrestle? Best of three takes all?"

Little Ricky's words slammed into my gut. Knocked the wind outta me. My ears cracked with static, and the room tilted as the world disintegrated into fuzzy dots. Only BJ's hand kept me on the chair instead of the floor. Despite her face's distance from Ricky's, her assault on Crusher to save me and her tight fit as my partner pinched out of the ruckus to make sense. I tried to speak between broken gulps. "Ri...Ricky?"

"BJ. Your sister," she corrected.

My brain shuddered, but my ticker ate up the shock. Relieved that Ricky—no, my sister—lived.

"Lo. You okay?"

"Yeah. I think so." The buzz in my head faded. My taste for her curves, my wish for that peck on my cheek she'd mentioned at Yerba Buena Gardens, and now knowing we're related curdled into nausea. I squeezed against my mean urge to fling away her hand.

"Ow," BJ said. "Easy on my fingers."

"Oh, sorry," I said, loosening my grip.

"Lo, you don't look okay."

"You...you saved my life," I managed to mumble.

"Sounds like you're trying to convince yourself of something." BJ slipped her fingers from mine. Her eyes searched my face. I recognized fear tugging at the corners of her mouth.

I stood up to convince us both I could stand on solid ground. "No. No, BJ. You don't know how I've worried about you. The shame I feel for rejecting you. I...I thought I'd be better prepared for this day."

BJ sighed with a slight grimace. "No Emily Post to tell ya how to greet your long-lost 'tranny' sister, is there?"

"Look, I'm not gonna lie. I clamped your hand to keep from letting go....I guess just because I quit marching for the wrong side, it doesn't mean I cleared their minefield."

"Nothing blew you off course when you charged that burning van."

I brought my hands up to scrape the moisture from my cheeks. "What I'm saying is that I got a shitload of knee jerks buried to pop up and kick both our asses."

"Got a few of my own. The bitch in me will kick right back. Bottom line is that our family closet is open. Together we'll clean out the debris."

BJ's confidence melted a smile into my mug. "Yeah. Together."

She tilted her head and rested her hand on mine. "Lo, you think Mom and Pops would still love me?"

I thought that was the easiest hard question I ever got. "How could Mom resist? She saw way below people's skin. Recognized character. Hell, she saw the man in my father when all most people saw was a gimp.

"As for your dad? No-brainer." I took in a heavy breath. "I let his lefty politics get between us. But his free thinking woulda never put the brakes on his love for you." My words bumped my regret that I'd rejected him too. Bet I did name Al after him.

♦ ♦ ♦

BJ let her smile take over her face. "I do appreciate what it means to you to prove to me your acceptance by going public." Then she loaded her throat with twang, and said, "But we're the only ones who can know the outcome of this come-to-Jesus meetin'. Ya gotta understand the same elixir that doused the fires of hatred in you will inflame them in others. One thing laughing at a tranny singin' and dancin' for ducats, but quite another having one locked and loaded, capable of defendin' herself. I don't need an arms race with haters distracting me from rounding up Havana's flunkies. I ain't sayin' Sandoval and Singh are hateful, but all it takes is one slip of the tongue to someone who is. Understand?" BJ watched Lo deflate.

"I get it. I do." The warmth in his voice matched the glow in his eyes. "I'm just glad you're home."

BJ felt a soothing tingle sparkle through her body but said, "How you gonna convince Sandoval and Singh that hair recovered from my place belonged to a boyfriend?"

♦ ♦ ♦

"Both thorough bastards," I said and sat back down. "Singh woulda snatched hair samples from multiple sources. Sandoval would've demanded 100 percent consistent results before telling me they were yours."

I patted my knees. "BJ, you haven't been home much. But that boyfriend of yours? Bet he's there, waiting for you like a loyal pup. Shedding his hair all over the damned place."

BJ tapped her fingers against the bed rail. “Suppose it’s less important that they believe you than fail to prove otherwise. With me gone and my ‘boyfriend’ there alone, it raises plausible doubt.” BJ grinned.

“That’s what I’m talking about,” I said.

Looks Good on You

The stern, fiftyish nurse stood up in the middle of the nurses' station. Put her hands on her wide hips.

"Detective, keep your visit brief."

"Yes, ma'am," I said out of a mix of respect and intimidation.

The young cop at Sandoval's door jumped out of his seat. "You're that detective on TV. Go on in, sir."

"My name on your authorized visitor list?" I said, and watched him reach behind for the clipboard on his chair.

"I-I just presumed, sir," he stammered as he scanned the list. "Detective Faeth, right?"

"Dunno. You better check my ID." Then I stepped into his face. The poor kid stumbled back. "And that goes double for every other joker wanting in, especially docs and nurses." I poked his chest hard, dropping him to his chair, and then bent down, nose to nose. "Anything happens to my pal, this'll get butt-ugly personal."

He gulped, then asked for my ID. After a careful study and a check against the visitors list, he said, "You're on the list, sir."

"Gimme my ID." I snatched it from between his fingers. Didn't release him from my glare until past Sandoval's doorway.

Sandoval slept with his Bluetooth stuck in his ear. With his multiple IVs and wire leads strung to beeping monitors, he reminded me of an extra in a cheap sci-fi movie. While I tilted my head, trying to decide which part of his body to nudge without hurting him, his eyes blinked open, and he glanced at my bandaged hand. After sucking air, he said, "Homeboy, how are you?"

"Better off than you. Lay still. I'll slap that blue roach outta your ear."

Sandoval spurted a laugh that torqued his lips in pain.

"Sorry," I said.

"*No hay problema.*" He thumbed his morphine pump. "I'm in doper paradise. Saw the chase on TV. Couldn't see much through all that smoke, but even before the news conference, I knew it was you and BJ running away from that burning van. Was that *chica* with you the agent who brought the national security letter to Forensics?"

"Yeah. Real spark plug," I said, flashing on the sheen of Suki's hair falling down around her shoulders.

"You got Havana. Liked the spin too. O'DAD stays a secret. Gotta hand it to that *panza* of yours. Knew all along that BJ was righteous."

"Yeah. She deserves the collar," I said absentmindedly, thinking of how to protect BJ's secret.

"How is she?"

"She's gonna be fine." I moved in and grabbed a rail. "You said 'she,'" I said, bumbling for an opening.

"So did you. You're the one who chokes on callin' Vips shes," he answered, his face scrunched, puzzled.

"BJ's not in the VIPS, and she got pissed off when I told her that you said she started as a boy." I hadn't lied, but I stood needled at how easily I'd twisted the truth in service of a lie.

Sandoval glared and said, "Of course she did. We busted her."

I forced myself back onto the steps of city hall. "Dammit, Sandoval, Laszlo tested her boyfriend's hair. The dangers of the case kept BJ away from home. Her boyfriend house-sat."

Sandoval's lips knotted up toward his diving forehead. "Boyfriend? No way. Laszlo's OCD is stuck faster than a one-trick pony's. If anyone else lived there, he would've found another hair sample. Woulda factored that in before drawing his conclusion. Besides, you never mentioned a boyfriend." He raised his eyebrows. "You ever meet one?"

He knew I would've told him if I did. I had to level with him, at least a little.

"Listen," I said, looking around for a chair. Spotting one in the corner, I dragged it to his bedside, sat, and looked him in the eye. "'She' saved my life."

"'She' did, didn't she," he said, his voice empty of challenge. "Looks like she knocked you past your LGBT phobias too. Looks good on you." This time, an upside-down grin creased his chin. "You know what? I'll let Laszlo know that he tested BJ's boyfriend's hair."

"How you going to convince him?" I asked, worried about questioning Laszlo. The skittish CSI took well-deserved pride in his work.

"He knows BJ disappeared before the highway showdown. Laszlo's gonna find out that when she split from her casa, her boyfriend stayed behind to keep an eye on things. Musta been out when he stopped by. Can't rule out that it wasn't his hair."

"What if he doesn't buy it?" I said.

"If he balks, I'll remind him of my homey at Immigration, who could speed up or lose his brother-in-law's green-card application."

"You know somebody at ICE?"

"Nah, but Laszlo doesn't know that." Sandoval raised his right hand for a shake.

I stood and shook his hand. "I owe you."

"Nah, homey. We both owe BJ."

One Too Many Surprises

BJ scurried up the stairs to Lo's condo. The clear Indian-summer night's warmth agreed with her. But nothing like her heart's glow toward her brother. In his hunger for details about her absence, his grief over her pain, she recognized his spoil to shed the blight that had driven her away.

Before knocking on Lo's door, she cupped a giggle, recalling Lupe's threat: "Faeth, I know where you live. Either bring BJ to Mac's, or I'll drag her over to your casa with Frank, pick your lock, and party there." Without that threat, Lo wouldn't have taken up Lupe and Frank's invitation for drinks in honor of "saving the Golden Gate." She figured he suspected that she and Lupe were in cahoots. Especially after Lupe's threat to pick his lock.

BJ slammed her fist on Lo's door twice before hollering, "Come on, Lo. Time to go."

"Almost ready. Come in," she heard from the other side. She swung the door open. All she saw was Lo's bent-over butt, and she heard Al's "Anh."

"Dammit, Al, go eat. Be back later," Lo said, blocking Al's lunges toward the door like a harried goalie. He finally got Al turned around. Stepping outside, Lo spread his arms. "Please tell me I don't look like a pimp."

"Shush, or I ain't buying you no more new clothes." BJ reached over and tucked the collar of his crisp beige dress shirt back inside his new suede sport coat. She stepped back and said, "It all goes nicely with your pleated slacks and those shiny wingtips."

"Don't know why I have to get dressed up for Mac's," Lo grumbled.

BJ recognized his suspicious leer. But too late. He couldn't back out now.

"Told ya. It's the least we could do to show our appreciation for their hospitality."

Lo looked her up and down. "Not used to seeing you in a dress. Hafta admit you're never trashy," he said and led the way down the stairs.

"What about my gladiator sandals? Don'tcha like 'em?" BJ asked as she chased him, smoothing down her black-linen sheath.

◆ ◆ ◆

I slid into the passenger seat of BJ's black Chrysler. "Don't you miss your tree-hugger ride?"

"Buckle up," she said and kicked over the now-rumbling Hemi. "Hang on to your britches."

Tires squealed, and the back of my neck hit the headrest. "I guess not," I said, catching her smirk.

I knew she and Lupe were thick as thieves the moment Lupe called and threatened to pick my lock. BJ making me dress up told me we were in for more than Lupe's "free shots" at Mac's.

I eyed my sister, grinning as she punched the Chrysler through a yellow light. The Hemi roared. Startled pedestrians glanced up from their phones, and scattered toward the curbs.

Since BJ's revelation at the hospital, I'd suffered moments of brutal recollection between us. Stubbed my toes against BJ's feelings more than once. Hard to kick away a lifetime of ugly habits. But most of the time, I just enjoyed the lightness in my chest being around her. Made hanging out with other people enjoyable too. Figured tonight we'd have drinks with Frank and Lupe and might get surprise visits from Les and Max. I'd like that. Too bad Sandoval could still barely walk. Doc ordered him to take it easy at home. He hadn't gotten out of the hospital until this week, the same day BJ's doc cleared her for duty.

I slowed at Mac's door to let BJ go in first. She opened it. The place was black and dead silent. I gulped.

"Come on," she said, reaching back to grab my hand and tow me in.

"Surprise, Golden Gate heroes, surprise," a chorus hollered as Mac's dim lights sparkled on, followed by the opening riffs of "Susie-Q." I tried to make out the faces gathering in front of us as my eyes adjusted, but had no problem lapping up Lupe's spicy scent as she swooped up, pecked me on the cheek, and said, "Excuse me for a sec, gotta hang this on the door." She waved her sign: Closed for Private Party. I shoulda known.

Frank gave me a hug—what he'd call an *abrazo*—and said, "Sorry, these girls ganged up on me. No stoppin' 'em."

"Tell me about it. See how I'm dressed?"

Frank stepped back for a look. Then I noticed they'd cleared the tables from the middle of the floor. No way I'd be dancing.

"BJ cleaned you up pretty good," Frank said as BJ's friend from the hospital, Victor, stepped up in a slick suit and tie to give her a loose hug. Knew it wasn't his idea, because BJ'd told me she'd keep her distance unless he proved worthy of her secret. Damn, I knew what a snarled-up heart felt like, but could only imagine the knots in hers.

"How ya doin', Vic?" I said. We shook hands. He started to get out of the way of the gang edging up to greet us, but BJ told him to stay so she could introduce him. His face lit up. Musta took it as encouragement.

Damned if that frog-shaped Roscoe from the Tenderloin Station and his still-slim wife, Daphne, didn't pull up. I flashed on our academy days, when we were both trim, and Roscoe landed his first date with Daphne. Still a looker, with her graying blond hair parted in the middle, draping her bright baby blues.

Roscoe's gravelly voice poured in, widening my grin until it hit me that he could mouth off about "fags" at any time. I wanted him away from BJ.

"Know ya hate surprises, but I'm retiring next month. So when news of a bash in your honor hit the grapevine, I called your partner"—he tipped his head toward BJ—"and invited myself. Fuck ya if ya can't take a joke." Daphne giggled and covered her mouth.

"Glad you called," BJ said and then introduced Victor.

"Good to see you two," I said—not a complete lie. I gave him and Daphne *abrazos*, then looked around and pointed to an empty booth. "Hey, why don't you grab that table, and I'll join ya for a beer later?"

"But we got catching up to do," Roscoe said, wrinkling his billboard brow.

"Later," Daphne said, threading her arm through Roscoe's. "Can't bogart the guests of honor." She pulled him toward the booth.

I turned to BJ. Wanted to warn her about Roscoe. But stood tongue-tied.

BJ grabbed my sleeve and whispered in my ear, "I remembered Roscoe and Daphne from when I was a kid. Figured you'd like to see them. A mistake?" BJ's eyes crowded my face.

I whispered back, "Nah. Just afraid of what that redneck Roscoe's liable to say."

The question mark twisting her face melted into a warm grin. Then a glint in her eye sparked devious. "Sorry your pals from the clinic, Tsige and Dr. Snyder, couldn't come."

Tickled, I said, "Tsige, yeah. But Snyder?"

Her giggling bent her forward. "Tsige told me to tease you about him and apologized. She's visiting family out of the country."

I shook my head. Sure, she knew about Tsige. Friggin' O'DAD.

I turned back to the sound of Jack's voice. Never seen him outta jeans, and he'd added a sport coat. Grinning, I said, "Where'd you get the blazer?"

Jack's head dropped for a sec, then came up. He glanced toward the bar at a nicely dressed guy I didn't recognize. He looked at BJ, who nodded. "From my boyfriend," he said.

It took all my mettle to keep from stumbling back at the shock that he was gay. I forced open my windpipe and said, "Wave him over. Like to meet him."

After I met Jack's partner, I asked BJ how I'd done. She told me she wouldn't've invited them if she'd any doubts. Then I asked how she knew about Jack.

She punched my arm and added with her roller-coaster tease: "Sandoval."

Did Sandoval know Jack was gay?

Max strolled up in his crisp Dockers and introduced us to his hybrid girlfriend. Hadn't seen such an indefinable mix since R&R in Hawaii. Gorgeous.

"Look at you," he said clamping me in another *abrazo.* Then he stepped back and glanced around my ankles. "Where's fat Albert?"

"Auditioning for *The Biggest Loser*," I said with a chuckle.

Les followed and introduced us to Lily. Happy to see them, I caught myself before blurting, We met. Les musta caught my flinch, because he ran his fingers inside his turtleneck as if to free his choked-up relief. Supposed I'd just saved him from a slap in the chest and her finger to his nose.

I assumed Frank invited them, but when I started to introduce them to BJ, she winked and said, "Already met."

BJ hugged them both, introduced Victor, and thanked them for coming. Complimented Lily's "shawl-collar jacket." Whatever the hell that meant.

"Have a drink with ya later. Gonna join your buddy Roscoe. Lily has taken to Daphne," Les said, passing a smile to Lily.

"Nice person," Lily said as she led him toward Roscoe and Daphne's booth.

"You're on," I said, sure that Lily and Daphne had teamed up to check O'DAD's notes on me, their old men's single dog.

BJ and I turned to a knock at the door. Frank rushed to open it, and in came Chief Ferrus and his wife, Poppy. After introductions, damned if Sandoval didn't squirrel out of the back hallway, riding a wheelchair pushed by Chata.

"Couldn't keep him away," BJ said through a toothy grin.

"You disobeying doctor's orders?" I asked, tossing a smile to Chata as they rolled up. Shapely Chata set the chair's brakes and said, "Can't keep him still."

I started to stoop forward, but skinnier than ever, Sandoval pushed himself up to stand, looked around, spread his arms, and said, "I'm here for the rec therapy, homeboy."

We both laughed while Chata came around and hugged me. Don't think I ever saw her in anything but tight blouses and dresses. And tonight she'd spiked her saucy strut with killer heels.

♦ ♦ ♦

"Glad ya made it outta the house," BJ said without a blink, but she still worried that Sandoval hadn't bought Lo's story that Laszlo's hair sample wasn't hers. She always watched him for a telltale study of her hands, feet, or Adam's apple. But, as usual, Sandoval warmly greeted her without a hint of suspicion.

BJ hugged Chata and decided to convince herself that plausible doubt had locked her secret in Sandoval's binary vault. She let out a sigh of relief but her eyes fell on Victor's smiling face chatting it up with Chata and Sandoval. Her secret blocked their progress. Had to be freed if she wanted to live beyond one-night stands.

Sandoval had sat back down, and Victor was leaning forward talking to him. BJ stepped next to him and stroked his back. He gave her a warm grin and continued his conversation with Sandoval.

Could Victor accept her history? Tonight she'd expose him to his first acid test.

♦ ♦ ♦

The smell of onions and peppers perked up my nostrils.

"Anyone else smell salsa?" I asked.

Sandoval craned his neck over his shoulder. Sniffed the air. "Smells fresh. Aah."

Out of the hallway, I caught Dr. Crusher and Suki lugging trays of Mexican food to the bar.

The sight of Suki kicked up my already tall mood. Then my eyeballs flopped onto an older version of the kid, dressed in an elegant silk blue-and-white *áo dài.* Its name plucked from the war without a prick. Had to be Suki's mom gliding out of that hall. Her slender arms balanced a tray of refried beans. Suki had told BJ and me that her father died of cancer in the early 1990s. That her widowed mom kept the books for several of Little Saigon's businesses.

I dug for the courage to go and offer to carry those beans, but before I mustered a step, BJ hooked her arm into mine, and Lupe came up from behind to snag the other. "Excuse us," Lupe said to Chata and Sandoval. "But we're taking him to a guest-of-honor seat."

"What?" I said, but with Victor in tow, they sat me in the middle of the bar's center booth. They'd saved me from making a fool out of myself.

"Best seats in the house for you, BJ, and Suki," Lupe said before jutting her chin toward the bar. "Now, I gotta go and kick Suki off KP. Get her over here." BJ slid in on one side, and next to her scooted Victor.

Not hearing Sandoval named to our table rubbed like a blister in a hair shirt. Fucken city hall had spun him out. I focused on Lupe's tight white jeans for relief. But that Vietnamese beauty at the bar lighting Sterno cans under the food stole my attention.

Suki came out from under the bar's drawbridge and loped over to our booth.

"Surprised you, didn't we?" she said, sliding in on my opposite side, her thigh slightly brushing mine. My ticker spiked despite her baggy jeans, loose blouse, and hair speared atop her head in that awful bun.

"Yep," was the best I could do.

Suki pointed toward her older look-alike. "That's my mother, Ly."

The gal's soft features had fared well over time. Her long salt-and-pepper hair, clipped halfway down her back, sparked coals I'd only felt from huge distances.

Suki snapped her fingers in front of my nose and said, "Okay, quit staring. But if you ask nicely, I'll invite her to sit next to me. I told her that this booth is reserved for the arresting officers and our guests. The rest is up to you. Make me regret it, and they'll never recover your body."

Possibility slammed head-on into panic. "Ah? Don't know what to say?" I stammered.

BJ's elbow shot into my ribs. I flinched and turned into her glare, but the dart of her eyes told me to attend to Suki.

"Be back with Mom. If she agrees," Suki said.

One serious look at this mug, and Ly would stick with the Sterno. Tunnel vision sorted out everything except Suki's stride toward her mom. No sound but the squish of Suki's tennies made it to my brain. But then the two women's Vietnamese danced into my ears. Ly looked toward our booth. After what looked like some hesitation, she came with her daughter to our table. Terror burst out of my chest and pricked my limbs.

Though pinned in, I shot up as far as I could to extend my hand to Ly as Suki's introductions came around to me. She allowed me to gently squeeze her graceful hand but dodged eye contact. "A p-pleasure, ma'am."

"Please call me Ly," she said in perfect English.

If she never spoke to me again, I'd touched heaven at least once.

♦ ♦ ♦

BJ nudged Victor as Lo lifted the table, trying to stand for Suki's mom. She hoped Ly would give her bumbling brother a chance. After the introductions and Lo sat, leveling the table again, BJ said, "Ly, you must be proud of your daughter. You know, if it weren't for her and this big guy"—she stopped to hook an arm around Lo's shoulder and hugged him—"I wouldn't be here."

Lo, palms up, blocked her compliment, and Suki shook her head. But BJ watched Ly's tender stare at her daughter as she replied, "Yes, I've got a brave daughter." Ly fixed her gaze on BJ before adding, "I'm comforted that she is surrounded by others of equal courage." Then she cast a curious glance at Lo. BJ hoped he'd caught it, but he sat there slack-jawed. Her brother needed help to keep from fumbling tonight's ball.

♦ ♦ ♦

Ly's amber eyes twinkled despite landing on my sagging mug. But who was I kidding? Not even my puss could dull those peepers.

"Enchiladas, rice, and beans up," Lupe hollered from behind the bar. Frank added, "Got salad and flan too. Come grab your plates."

Frank and Lupe had snatched my belly's attention. An organ not as risky to feed as my heart. Victor and Ly started to slide out, but Frank waved his hands and shouted, "Not the guests of honor. Table service for you."

Dr. Crusher came from behind the bar with her hair tied back. Looked like a seasoned waitress in her black pants, starched white blouse, and padded shoes. She filled a huge serving tray with plates and drinks, hooked her arm through a folding tray stand, and hauled our dinners to our booth. She set the huge tray on her stand without tipping any of our long-neck beers.

The spicy salsa smell curled up my nose as the opening refrain of "I Left My Heart in San Francisco" filled Mac's.

"Thank you, Doctor," I said when Crusher set my plate in front of me, in shock she'd wait our table.

"Marilee. Please call me Marilee," she said as she set down our drinks, naming them in turn. "Buds for Vic and BJ. Dos Equis for you, Detective. And for Suki and Ly, Arnold Palmers." She added, "I made the enchiladas. Hope you like them."

Damn, she'd cooked for us.

"Call me Lo," I said, noticing BJ's surprised look while I took in Marilee's smile. I did it as much for BJ as I did for Crusher. The doc meant a lot to BJ.

"Lo it is," she said, dipping her head. Then she asked if she could bring us anything else.

"More salsa?" Victor piped up.

"I'll get it." BJ swung her hip against Victor, who began to slide out.

"No, no, hon. That's my job." Marilee shook her head. "Let me honor you tonight." She landed glances on BJ, me, then Suki. Ly took in a deep breath, her pride in her daughter lifting her perfectly tapered breasts.

I followed BJ's gaze on Marilee traipsing back to the bar with her empty serving tray and stand. I knew BJ felt she owed the doc for hitting her, but my belly said Marilee was paying toward her own outstanding debt.

"Mexican food has become a favorite of mine," Ly said to everyone at the table. Joining everybody else, I nodded in agreement.

♦ ♦ ♦

"Lo loves Mexican food," BJ said, hoping to hook her brother into the conversation. Maybe get him to invite Ly to call him Lo, like he did Marilee.

But Ly surprised BJ and spoke to Lo. "Do you like spicy food, Detective?" she asked with a quick glance.

BJ's eyes met Suki's. Both peaked their eyebrows. Maybe they wouldn't have to whip out their ace in the hole.

"Yeah, yes, I d-do," Lo stammered.

"Including Vietnamese food?" Ly said, her eyes lingering on him.

BJ watched Lo straighten up and heard him clear his throat. "Like my pho real spicy," he said.

Good boy. Now invite her to call ya Lo, BJ thought. This time Lo didn't retreat from Ly's gaze.

Ly swallowed hard and looked away. "Please excuse me," she said and headed for the powder room.

"I gotta go too, Mom," Suki said and scurried after her.

BJ shoved her shoulder into Lo's. "She's as shy as you. But I think she's smitten with ya."

"Nah, scared her off." Lo flagged in his seat. He spiked a fork full of enchilada and crammed it into his mouth.

"Suki's mom head for the hills? Or was she overcome by her attraction to my partner?" BJ asked Victor without her eyes budging from her brother.

"She likes you, Detective," Victor said.

"Snowball in hell," he mumbled.

BJ decided those two were gonna need extra innings to hit it off.

Suki returned with her mom. Lo and Ly dodged each other's furtive glances.

"Suki, ya having Vietnamese coffee Monday mornin' at that Larkin Street bistro?" BJ asked, whipping out her and Suki's high card.

"Plan to," Suki said. "Let's all meet to compare case notes." She looked at Lo. "Be there at eight."

♦ ♦ ♦

"Huh?" I said, with hope for no more than another enchilada. BJ's sandal slammed into my shin. "Ow." I reached down to massage my leg.

"Quit cryin', dahlin'. Comin' or not?" BJ insisted.

Embarrassed, I looked around the table. Everybody was laughing through their noses. Obviously they knew something I didn't. But if BJ wanted me there, why not?

"Sure. Monday, eight o'clock. Where?"

"Little Saigon," Suki said as she wrote the address on a napkin. She shoved it into my shirt pocket just as Marilee came by to clear some plates. Ly insisted on helping and disappeared with Marilee into the hallway. Suki joined them. She probably detoured her mom into the powder room and to my O'DAD file to delete all comments except "Loser."

♦ ♦ ♦

BJ wasn't about to tell Lo that Ly would be sipping coffee with them on Monday. He might chicken out. She gave him a jarring hug and said, "I ain't lettin' you give up so easy, but right now we're goin' dancin'." She turned to Victor. "Come on. Help me pick a tune."

The beat brought the ladies to life as they dragged their fellas out to dance. Chata rolled a protesting Sandoval into the middle of the floor, locked his wheels, and then twirled her hips better than any lap dancer BJ'd ever seen. She watched Sandoval fold his arms, hypnotized by Chata's dangerously rising skirt. The rocking crowd burst into laughter.

♦ ♦ ♦

Through the laughing, I thought, Could BJ be right? Do I have a chance with Suki's mom? Should I ask Ly to dance if she comes back? Right, and risk hopping around like a jackass to cancel all bets. Shoot-outs been less paralyzing.

♦ ♦ ♦

BJ, following Victor's smooth lead, twirled away, tethered by his gentle grip. His eyes, which never left her face, titillated her. She wound back into his open arms and bent back. Yes, she'd risk holding on for more than a one-night stand. But before any kiss, he'd have to know. Tonight she'd crack open the door ever so slightly. Introduce him to her pet cold case, the disappearance of Syklona Haez. One smack of his lips in revulsion toward her transgender vic would make this their last party together.

♦ ♦ ♦

Les and Lily strolled up. "Can I scoot in?" Les asked as Lily excused herself.

"Sure." I watched Lily walk up to Suki and her mom, chatting at the bar. Then the three gals headed to the floor to dance together.

"Nice party," Les said.

"Swell." I sat balled up about Ly.

Jack showed up with a couple of long necks. "Had to take over the bar," he said, nodding over his shoulder at the dancers.

"Join us," I said, but he pulled a scratch sheet out of his back pocket and said, "Later. My partner's gonna serve while I make a call."

Roscoe and Daphne left the dance floor and ambled over holding hands. After a long look over his shoulder at Ly, Roscoe said, "Blew it, didn't ya, Faeth?" Then he winked at his wife. "We'll see if we can help ya out. Come on, doll, let's find a slow one on the jukebox for Mr. Two Left Feet."

"No, no, that's okay," I said, but it didn't stop them.

"Faeth, Faeth," Les cut in. "Don't worry about it. Ly's Vietnamese. Proper Vietnamese women aren't gonna see you without a chaperone on the first few dates. Even a dance may be too intimate right now. Patience and persistence are what will pay off."

"Yeah, but I'll never see her again after tonight."

Les cocked his head. "Lily told me you and BJ were meeting Suki and her mom for coffee Monday morning."

"What?" I said, suddenly weightless. "I never had a chance, did I?"

"Huh?" Les jerked back his head.

"Suki left out that her mom would be there," I said, feeling the tickle of Suki's note in my pocket.

Les chuckled. "You're right. Not a chance."

Out on the floor, Ly danced to the music along with her daughter and Lily. Her silk *áo dài* sparkled in the bar's meager light.

"But why go for a guy with this mug?" I said, rubbing my face.

"Don't kid yourself. You're fine. You should understand that a woman like that is more interested in the quality of a man's character."

Eased by Les's generous words, I feasted on Ly's rhythmic sway. Hardly noticed the music fade until it came up again as a 1950s dirty-grind standard. I looked over at Roscoe and Daphne by the jukebox. Daphne darted her eyes between me and Ly. But Frank shouted a reprieve, "Toasts to the guests of honor. Everybody grab a glass."

Ferrus blurted out, "Hear, hear," as the dancers diverted their steps toward the bar.

"BJ, Suki, back to your thrones. I'm bringin' yours," Lupe said, loading a tray with three shots. I understood tequila for me and even, on occasion, BJ. But Suki?

Les excused himself against my protest, explaining, "Hey, I'm part of the honor guard." He took up a position with Frank and the rest of the fellas in front of the bar.

Suki scooted in on one side, followed by BJ on the other, as Lupe stepped into the middle of the floor after unloading our shots. Frank handed her champagne. She raised her glass, rang it with a fork, and said, "Ladies and gentlemen, a toast to the Golden Gate saviors."

I swore Lupe looked right at me, her big browns flashing a knowing twinkle. A glimpse of the spin? She knew the truth, didn't she? The crowd raised their glasses and in unison bellowed, "Our heroes."

I joined my tablemates in slamming back the Porfidio. From the corner of my eye, I noticed Suki hadn't flinched. "You're just full of surprises, aren't you."

"Don't you forget it, either," she said and glanced between me and her mom out on the dance floor.

I peered over at Ly, then paused my gaze on BJ before looking back at Suki.

"Don't worry. I got a new nose for the priceless." Be damned if the glow behind my words didn't come from me, not the Porfidio. But Sandoval's image, raising a glass from his wheelchair, backhanded me.

"Dammit, everybody." I pointed at Sandoval. "That man right there should be sitting here too." I held up my glass. "To Dr. Murrieta Sandoval. The brains of the SFPD."

"Wait, wait!" Lupe shouted, grabbing the Porfidio. She ran over and filled our shot glasses.

"To Dr. Sandoval," I said, then gulped it back to a round of applause.

"Speech, speech!" Roscoe blared, followed by louder clapping.

"Don't look at me," I said, darting my eyes between BJ and Suki.

After her knowing glance at Suki, the two shoveled their hands toward me, and BJ addressed the crowd. "All those in favor of our senior detective speaking for us, say aye."

The mob's "Aye!" rattled my fillings.

"Sorry, gotta hit the head," I said, but bookended by Suki and BJ, I sat trapped.

BJ elbowed my ribs and said, "Go on, say something nice." Then she squinted, adding, "Don't spill any beans."

She'd reminded me to stay on city hall's steps. My eyes blurred, and the crowd turned into a fuzzy glob. I froze.

"Need another shot?" Max hollered. Giggles bubbled through the crowd.

Les chimed in. "You can do it."

BJ stroked my knee. "Come on. Make us proud."

"Ah, what can I say?" I didn't want to lie but couldn't betray the spin. I cleared my throat. "Cases come and go, and maybe we learn a thing or two and get better at our jobs."

The crowd stared back, some with their heads tilted in polite attention. The Porfidio helped this time, because I latched onto a truth I could talk about. "Don't imagine myself a hero. Doubt these brave ladies do, either. We do our jobs and hope like hell that they don't harden us too much. And if you're lucky, once in a while a case comes along to rip the calluses off why we became cops in the first place. To protect the innocent." Ice cubes tinkled as people raised their glasses to that.

"Speaking for myself, I gotta say that this case cracked open my head and soul to teach me things about myself and others that I didn't think I needed to know. Be damned if I didn't pinch out better for it. For that, I'm grateful." I paused. "So, uh, thanks for listening."

BJ began a slow clap to my right. I looked at her misty eyes. Suki followed. Then from the floor came another gradual clap, this time from Marilee. Glances among the crowd preceded their splattering applause.

Roscoe didn't clap. "Give us the dirt!" he shouted. "Details, details!"

Suki's palms shot up. "Can't. National security," she said pulling me off the hook. Made me want to adopt her.

Roscoe slapped the air as he growled, "That's BS."

"Give 'em a break," Lupe said from over by the jukebox. She followed with: "Any requests?"

"'Theme from A Summer Place,'" Marilee chimed in.

BJ spouted off, "Marilee, this is a celebration, not a slumber party," triggering laughter.

I watched Marilee deflate as she said, "Oh, right."

"Now go pee," BJ said and slid off toward Lupe.

"How about 'Like a Virgin'?" Lupe said, and the women yelped in agreement.

Roscoe looked around and, without a word, shook his head and wagged his finger at me.

On my way to the head, I patted his shoulder as I passed.

"Those broads rescued ya, didn't they? Never took ya for such a ladies' man," he said.

"I'm a regular Rudolph Valentino." He had no idea O'DAD had just gagged him.

I came outta the head and leaned against the mouth of the hallway. Seemed everybody had spilled onto the dance floor. I watched that lucky bastard Les prance around with Lily, Suki, and Ly. Wrapping myself in BJ's and Les's encouragement, I promised myself that on Monday, I'd invite Ly out for a Mexican dinner, along with Suki as chaperone. Hadn't felt this fluttery since Madge.

Sandoval rolled up and parked next to me. "Thanks for the toast," he said. Then he looked around to make sure nobody listened and added with a chuckle, "The ladies distracted your buddy Roscoe before he could wring out any details, eh?"

"I wouldn't have let him. Too much at stake, I guess." I slid my dirty hands into my pockets. I'd helped bury the real victims under the spin.

"You don't sound convinced." Sandoval's eyes lingered until he patted his pocket. "Phone's on vibrate. Hold up a sec....Sandoval," he answered...."Laszlo. Told you to drop it and come to the party. BJ's boyfriend's name don't matter anymore. Besides, she's got a new one....All right, tell me....Traced to UC Berkeley, eh. Thanks....Uh-huh, good work. Now let it go."

Laszlo discovered my brother's name. I choked back my thumping heart.

"What's wrong with you, homeboy?" I heard Sandoval say through my crackling brain.

I flung my sweaty palms outta my pockets. "Nothing. Why?"

"Your face blew up. It's all red." He started to pocket his phone but hesitated. He glanced between me and his cell.

I tried to settle my voice. "I'm fine," I said. "I'm fine." Despite never mentioning my brother to Sandoval and that Ricky and I had different last names, my scrambling pulse threatened to rupture my cringing veins. Especially when Roscoe and Daphne headed our way. They'd met Ricky when he was a kid. What if they asked about him—by name?

Sandoval turned to Roscoe and Daphne as they greeted us. Put his phone away.

Roscoe slapped my shoulder but glanced at Daphne before winking at Sandoval. "Babe, think this hero detective and fancy doc will speak to us?"

I froze like a buck caught in a spotlight. Reminding myself that Roscoe had given up asking about Ricky years ago didn't help. If he blabbed about Ricky now, Sandoval would add it up.

Sandoval chuckled at Roscoe. Spread his hands as he looked down at his seated self and said, "I need to gain weight, but fattening my ego won't add pounds."

"Heard about the hit. Glad ya made it, kid." Roscoe glanced at me but spoke to Sandoval. "Faeth says you're the sharpest tack at Forensics."

"Lotta sharp tacks there." Sandoval flapped the air with one hand.

"Not like you, according to Faeth. And he's never lied to me."

I'd lied to everybody. Now those tales tied me to the firing squad's post, without a blindfold for anybody.

"That's his gut talking," Sandoval said and laughed.

Roscoe chuckled too. "He is the hunchster, isn't he?"

"He is," Sandoval said. He started to say something else, but we were interrupted by Frank. I'd never told him that the subject of my brother was not up for public discussion. I'd counted on my old rap-group partner to recognize when I shut my emotional doors. How could I signal him now, trapped in this liquor-lubed corner?

"Police business only, or can I join this crowd?" Frank asked.

"This meetin' is for members and nonmembers only," Roscoe kidded.

"Count me in, then," Frank said. "So, what's up?"

I felt the ropes tighten. My lies pressed Frank's finger against a trigger too.

"Just yakking," Daphne said.

"Frank—" I said. But before I could think of an excuse to tear him and me away from the gang, Daphne interrupted.

"Say, Faeth, you're gonna be the last of the old-timers when Roscoe retires. When you thinkin' of givin' it up to the youngsters?"

"Yeah. Remember you talked about finding your brother," Frank said.

I heard Sandoval whisper, "Brother?" I caught his eyes turning inward. My back hit the corner of the wall. Propped me upright.

"You all right?" Frank asked, tilting his head.

"Tipsy is all," I managed to say. "I'll be fine." I'd lied.

Then Roscoe opened up while staring off. "Yeah, your half brother's name was Rich? No...Ricky...Richard Devlin. Yeah, that's it, Richard 'Ricky' Devlin." Roscoe turned to me. "Right, Faeth?"

I puked in my mouth, swallowed, and could only nod. Then I watched Sandoval's brow shrivel against the burst of Ricky's name. I imagined his digital brain barreling through the static to nail the obvious. I'd tied BJ to the target post with me. I braced for the shot. Then I heard Sandoval's voice like an echo.

"He didn't tell you? This guy. You always got a pry the good news outta him."

"Ain't that the truth," Roscoe said, trading nods with Daphne.

My head reeled. What'd he mean?

"His partner, BJ, knew Ricky at Berkeley," Sandoval said. "Took 'em both a couple of years to put it together." Sandoval snickered and added, "Great detectives, eh?"

Everybody except me chuckled.

"Once they figured it out, BJ got 'em together." Sandoval squinted into my gaping stare and added, "Small world, huh?"

Blood rushed in to boost me up. I shoved off the wall and cleared my throat. "Yeah, was gonna tell you guys. Hadn't got around to it yet."

"*Hermano*, that's great news," Frank said, stepping up and spreading his arms for an *abrazo*. With strength back in my legs, I met him with open arms. Gave him a hug that belonged to Sandoval.

"Great news. C'mere," Daphne said, flapping her hands for me to step over and hug her too. "I remember when Ricky was a teenager. Handsome boy." After Daphne's embrace, Roscoe patted my back. "Woulda liked to have been at that reunion."

"Yeah, it was somethin'," I said, nodding more toward Sandoval. Grateful to him for the air in my lungs.

Then Frank said, "Gotta bring him by. Wanna meet him. Know Lupe will too."

"Love to see him all grown up," Daphne said, clasping her hands.

Freed from the executioner's post hadn't saved me from my oily spin. I gulped back another jagged breath. "Will do, when he's free," I said, hardly conscious of what I meant.

"When he's free?" Frank asked.

"Yeah," I said, stalling to think of a plausible excuse.

"Deep undercover for the feds right now," Sandoval said. Then looked at me and added, "Probably shouldn't've told them, eh?... Sorry."

I cocked my head at him like he'd said too much. "No harm done. But can't say any more."

"He ended up in law enforcement, after all," Frank said.

"CIA, I'll bet," Roscoe added. "But mum's the word, right?"

Everybody nodded in agreement. Sandoval and me couldn't have done better if we'd rehearsed.

"So, when ya retiring?" Daphne asked.

I latched on to her question like a reprieve. "Don't know," I said and looked toward BJ out on the dance floor. "Me and my partner got a lot work to do." I watched BJ curtsy to Victor at the end of a song. Finding her had spun back my odometer. Didn't intend to leave her to fight the likes of Havana alone for a long time. I jutted my chin toward Roscoe but said to Daphne, "Besides, I don't got a girl like you to come home to every night."

Daphne glanced over her shoulder at Suki and her mom. They began heading our way. "Maybe you will," she said with a sideways grin.

I watched Ly and Suki glide up to us. I racked my brain for something clever to say.

Suki saved me before I spit up something stupid. "Mom and I have to leave, but we wanted to say good night." She and her mom shook everybody's hands, saying how pleased they were to have met them.

Roscoe said, "I was in Saigon in '69. Where you from?"

Daphne yanked him away. "Quit yakking and get me a drink. Jeez."

Roscoe sidestepped to keep on his feet, saying, "Oh, yeah, right. Sure thing, doll."

"Let me pour 'em for you," Frank said with a big grin, glancing between me and Ly.

"Need a hand?" Sandoval said, releasing his brakes.

Alone with Suki and her mom, I felt a thousand sparks tickle my skin. Ly extended her hand to me and said, "It has been a pleasure to meet you."

My fingers soaked up her touch. "The pleasure's mine, ma'am."

"Please, it is Ly," she said and squeezed my fingers for emphasis.

Suki glanced at her mom, then said, "Her name means lion, by the way."

Her mom slapped Suki's shoulder and evaded my grin. Of course, I thought. She's tough Suki's mom. I liked a woman who'd keep me on my toes.

"See you Monday, right?" Suki asked.

"Bet on it," I said. Then thought, What a bonehead reply, but I ate up the subtle rock of Ly's hips all the way out the door. Don't know how long I stared after they disappeared but somebody punched up "Oh, Pretty Woman." Over to my left at the jukebox, Lupe smirked. Busted, I shook my head.

I started to head toward the bar, where most of the folks had bellied up. But BJ and Victor intercepted me. She held Victor's hand. The guy beamed.

"Having a good time?" BJ said.

"Feels like I just got my legs back after a monster roller-coaster ride," I said, but changed the subject. "So Victor. How you doing around all these flatfoots?"

Victor tilted his head and mumbled, "Flatfoots?"

"Lo. This is the twenty-first century," BJ scolded, then turned to Vic. "He means cops."

"Oh," he said. "Flatfoots. I'll remember that." Then he continued: "Incredible. BJ told me about her troubling cold case." He glanced at her. "A woman was murdered by her lover's daughter. The man had left his wife for her even though she'd been born a man. Can you imagine?"

I watched BJ study Victor. She watched for a blink. So did I. "What do you mean?" I said.

Victor darted his eyes and sucked in his lips, as if searching for words. "It didn't matter to her that he was married. And it didn't matter to him that she'd had her sex changed. The power of love, Detective, knows no limits." Then Victor cast BJ a longing look. She glowed.

Victor hadn't flinched. I believed he'd made it to first base with BJ.

"Theme from a Summer Place" floated in. The three of us turned our heads toward the jukebox. Marilee and Lupe caught our glances. Marilee shrugged, palms up, and said, "Thought everybody could use a break from all that bebop. Lupe said okay."

Lupe nodded, her delicious lower lip poking out.

"Homeboy, BJ, bring Victor over here for a toast," Sandoval hollered from the bar.

BJ and Victor sped off, but I took in the scene before clomping over. Looked like the friggin' Rainbow Coalition took over Mac's. Sure wasn't the gang I'd mingled with growing up. But I'd be damned if it wasn't the crowd I'd grown up in. Drawing in a deep breath, I tasted the clean air of a less hateful place. Felt warm. Like I'd been welcomed into a world where we all belong.

www.ingramcontent.com/pod-product-compliance
Lightning Source LLC
Chambersburg PA
CBHW051419170626
46809CB00006B/2231

9780692824696